Tagged

Amanda Heit

This is a work of fiction. All similarities to real life are coincidental and unintentional. Names, characters, places, and incidents are products of the author's imagination and used fictitiously. Enjoy the story!

Teen/Young Adult

Heit, Amanda.
Tagged / by Amanda Heit.
1st edition.
ISBN-13: 978-1-949858-00-6
ISBN-10: 1-949858-00-6

Printed in the United States of America
October 2018
10 9 8 7 6 5 4 3 2 1
First Edition

Contents

Chapter 1

Millie

I was still alive, still breathing. I was going onward. Picking up the pace, I stepped out into the hot sun from the safety that the small tree had provided. The tarp I had draped across the branches to block out the wind was a meager, laughable shelter, but it had been all mine last night. It had done little to help, and I'd had to tug it down and wrap the entire thing around me instead.

Then I blinked.

Sleeping, like I was right now, had been a real drag lately. It was easier to be awake when I didn't feel like I was shifting through multiple lives all the time. Last night hadn't been too bad. I'd had worse. Like the time where I'd jumped onto a charging rhino to rip a shirt off its horn. There had been a man stuck inside of the shirt stuck on the horn, and well, frankly, I was dreaming. I'd known I was dreaming, and what would it hurt if I jumped out of the tree and

1

ripped a shirt?

I shook my head at it all now. The man had tumbled free, and I had glanced behind me to see if he had managed to live after the fall. He'd sat up and looked alright. Then the rhino shook his head and had stepped on me. Yup. The shock of dying had mentally hurt.

Where was this next dream going? At least my dreams took me away from the dirt floor that was currently my bed. I didn't want to think about what was really around me. I blocked images of packing my things to move only to leave everything behind. I blocked my parents' voices talking about a happier future. At nearly eighteen I often thought of cheerful futures, and since my reality was anything but pleasant, I blocked it from my mind again.

In my sleep I was standing in the middle of a relaxed street. I walked to the edge of the road, looking at my surroundings and down at whomever I was. These dreams always placed me inside of random avatars. I was wearing an ugly brown dress with no shoes like a street urchin. I felt my hair—matted, a mess. I ran my fingers through it until I heard a laugh behind me. There was an equally shattered-looking person, tired, rugged, but with shoes. He may have slept on the ground right there last night. My avatar may have too.

"Hon, fixing your hair won't get his attention."

Whose? I looked back to the street and scanned it

again. All the narrow compact buildings had red roofs, and there were more walkers than drivers on the cobblestone road. Was I in a touristy part of town? I scanned around, trying to make the connection.

"Whose attention?" I asked and found my voice hoarse, thirsty.

The ragged man behind me pointed. That's when I saw him. Mr. Rhino Man. He was not looking as bad as I was at all. In fact, he was wearing comfortable shoes, and did not have a hole in his shirt. The build of his body was different this time around. He was wider, for one thing, but his face was the same. He had a clean, classic look with slightly large eyebrows and stunning green eyes. It was the kind of chiseled face that tempted me to stare. I smiled despite myself and went back to trying to untangle the knots in my hair. How curious it was that we should meet again. Mr. Rhino was standing on the other side of the street looking at a lean-faced man. I glanced between the two, already sensing the tension there. I gave up on my hair and started to inch closer.

The stranger, although they were all strangers, started to walk toward Rhino Man as well. He had his hands in his pockets, and I didn't like it. I slipped across the road, placing myself strategically close. My street urchin cohort had been right—no one glanced at me.

"I told you to get lost," the stranger told Mr. Rhino.

"And I told you that I'm here for the long haul," Mr. Rhino answered. "Let's work this out."

"Done," the stranger said.

He jumped toward Mr. Rhino, and I didn't know why but I jumped in front of him. The stranger plunged a knife upwards into my avatar's chest. My cohort screamed something ugly as he ran up behind the man with a knife of his own and shoved it between the stranger's shoulder blades. Mr. Rhino stood there, shocked. I slumped to the ground and found myself fading again.

"Are either of you two real?" Mr. Rhino asked.

"Only dreaming, Rhino Man," I told him as the world grew dark.

Blink.

A desert temple? It was a new dream, in any case. I was hot and thirsty again. There was a well in front of me, but the bucket to draw water was being used, and I found I had no cup. I had shoes this time and traveling gear. The man with the bucket had a crossbow resting at his feet. He was dressed all in tan, trying to hide.

"May I have some?" I asked.

The man with the water held out his cup for me. Then he picked up his crossbow while I drank and gazed at the front of the desert temple. My eyes instantly rested on the smooth face of Mr. Rhino. I almost choked on the water.

What was it to be this time? How was he going to be in danger?

I scanned the area again. It looked like most of the people heading into the temple were going for a pilgrimage—they had no weapons of any kind. I looked down at Mr. Crossbow's feet and found his gear. It wasn't hard. I already knew what to do. I picked up his stuff.

"Here." I handed him an arrow. He took it and, as predicted, started to aim at Mr. Rhino. My Rhino friend was a bad omen. I hefted the rest of the gear onto the edge of the well, and then shoved it in.

"Hey!" Mr. Crossbow screamed. He tried to grab at his stuff, then turned to me angrily. "Now I've only got one shot!"

"Sorry, it just..." That was as far as I got. Mr. Crossbow picked up a sword by his feet and severed me in half. Somehow I remembered to scream for Mr. Rhino to run...

Chapter 2

Sebastian

"Seb, you alright? Seb! Seb!" I heard Leer shout.

I jerked upwards from the terminal bed, nearly bonking heads with Leer. Someone had named me Mr. Rhino. I wasn't sure I liked the name. I was sweating. It came as a bit of a shock, but I should have expected the sweat, considering what I had just experienced. What was I going to do? I was being followed.

I yanked up on my armband, the one topically feeding me a drug that kept me in the game world, looking at the screen to check my number.

"What is it?" Leer asked. "You're secure."

Leer was such a strong man that I bet Leer worked out in a gym every night. His muscles bulged. He had a head full of black hair like a shaggy surfer.

7

Should I tell him? I was tagged. Somehow all of my avatars were being followed. That usually meant my real life was in danger instead of my sleeping one, but I couldn't bring myself to say anything to Leer. He'd panic. Maybe I would bring this up with Nick. He was more level-headed and wouldn't fire me for getting tagged so early in my career. Maybe.

The thing with the tag was that I hadn't expected to see the girl in any of the missions, and it wasn't like the girl was trying to kill me. Quite the opposite. She had just sacrificed herself to save me several times. My missions were supposed to be safe.

"Go get Nick," I told Leer.

He looked at me worried, and I wondered why he had pulled my cord early. Had I been straining? My time wasn't up yet. I still had more work to do. While Leer raced from the room, I went back to the screen and checked the numbers myself. They reflected what I already knew: I would have failed each mission if it wasn't for that girl. I would have felt the stab of death. My job was to collect illegal items from games and destroy them. I was a spy sneaking into virtual worlds to take apart hackers. Our company had several game creators that employed us for multiple games. I'd barely had time to dispose of the illegally planted items before death reached me. Why was this girl taking my place? Who was she? What kind of strange tagger was following my avatars?

Nick came in chewing a beef stick as long as his arm. He always spiked up his blond hair with gel. He was dressed the same as me with black shirt, black pants, and gray shoes. Our work uniform showed no logos. I was going to be scared to leave work today.

"Sup?"

"These are not safe contacts," I told Nick. "I've been almost killed in all of them."

"What?" Nick asked. He rushed to the screen, already jumping to the conclusion that I was still hesitant to voice.

"Are you tagged?"

"It wasn't the same person trying to kill me in each one. It's been different people."

"Are you sure?" Nick asked.

I nodded. He exchanged a look with Leer. I had seen my attempted killer each time. I'd had the chance to get a good look at each of them, thanks to the girl who kept jumping in the way of my final blow. Maybe I should be grateful that I was tagged? Or was this girl playing with me? Would she show up again, in my real life, and take me out painfully for all the times she had just died for me?

"Nick!" I heard Justin scream.

Nick turned away from my screen with a shrug as he looked at Justin. Justin slid into the room at a full run his heart pounding from the look of his flushed face. "Dean is out. They got him and I can't wake him up."

"Dean?" Leer asked, turning white as a sheet. I swallowed. If he had just seen what I may have, I wasn't surprised that he was taken out.

Nick looked over at me, and then held up my armband. "Strap in. You're going in after Dean."

"But I…" Fine. If I was tagged, it was already too late and I would be next either way. I could only hope that whoever had tagged me wasn't trying to get me killed in real life. "Right."

"I'm watching the feed," Nick said.

"You're not allowed…" Nick wasn't actually my boss. He just worked closely with Leer regardless. I shrugged it off. "Okay."

I could handle that. I could handle Nick staring over my shoulder at my work. I lay down on the bed and connected the armband again. Then I closed my eyes, trying not to picture my demise. What could go wrong this time? With Dean already knocked out of his world, maybe no one would suspect *me* being there. Of course, if I was tagged it wouldn't matter. I guess this would prove if it was the system that was tagged or the people.

The drug worked into my arm, pulling me to sleep. I saw the mission criteria flash before me, modified by Nick, no doubt, as he scanned my visuals with me.

Find Dean and wake him up. He was supposed to be buying a silver bow from the blacksmith. There was a map of the area with the blacksmith shop highlighted.

I stepped cautiously into the world of the Wild West, looking around this time for the girl right away. I hadn't noticed her in any of the other areas until it was too late, but I was on edge this time. Things looked normal. I was dressed for the part, wearing a white shirt and cowboy boots. Slowly I walked my way to the blacksmith shop. Hopefully, whoever had tagged Dean was already long gone after completing the mission to destroy him. That was my best guess. My worst guess was that all of our contacts for today had been leaked—and the longer we worked today the worse it would be. We would have to shut down and lose revenue. Actually, from a personal perspective I liked that idea better. That way I would be able to sleep tonight without fear of being suffocated.

"Doc!" A woman rushed from a shop, not the blacksmith's. "There's a..." The woman pointed.

I looked behind me before I got another message flashing across my eyes in big bold letters that no one else could see. This was why I didn't want Nick monitoring my visuals. It was distracting. He wrote that I was playing the

11

part of the doctor. It was helpful, but like I said, distracting. I had to act like I wasn't reading messages in the air.

"A what?" I asked, heading in the direction the woman was pointing. I hoped she would tell me that there was a fallen man over there. I heard a gunshot, and then a faint thud. When I turned around and noticed my dying angel on the ground, the smoke rising from the strange woman's gun, I swore. Then I ran for it. I rushed for a building to take cover.

I was tagged. There was no way to explain it, but if I told Nick about it, my career was over. I might as well start packing my things—upturn my family's life again by leaving them with no financial support.... I couldn't do that. Maybe I could stick it out? Yeah there were rules against it, but if this was taken as a system problem instead of a tag, I could get away with having a guardian angel, right? She wasn't actually out to get me...

My chosen shelter was a tanner's shop with skins drying on the walls and scary tools hanging there too. There was no back door, but there was a window. I crossed the room carefully and hefted up the heavy window. The glass was thick and not very clear, but it let in the light—barely. I slid out the window (more carefully than the last time), and crept around the edge of the building.

Where was everyone? Who had taken the normal people out of this program and only left the real people? No wonder Dean had trouble here. There was no way to blend in. I could see the blacksmith shop, but if I was going to make a run for it, I would have to cross the path of the crazy lady again. She had ducked out of sight. I felt like she might jump out of the same building she had before and try to get me.

We had little training for dying when asleep. People playing in game modes would be put back at a loading screen, so they realized they were fine, but spies like us didn't get loading screens. We got darkness. The shock of it could render a person a vegetable. Dean probably thought he was really dead. He would be if I couldn't find him and wake him up. I looked for the scary lady again, and then realized that she was probably behind me.

I made a mad run for the blacksmith shop, glancing at the dirt where my tagger had died. She wasn't there, which was nice. She must have been able to wake up. As if I cared or something. Why was I caring if my tagger was alright? The person could put my real life in danger.

Before I made it inside the shop, the door burst open. I was dragged inside and the door slammed shut behind me before I could bring my feet to a stop. I pulled a punch on whoever it was that had got me, but was hit first. I wheezed.

"Shh! Fools! She's still out there," a man in the back of the room hissed.

I had found the town's people. When my eyes

adjusted, I could see that everyone was huddled inside the blacksmith's shop. Placed in the corner was Dean, not bleeding, but shot clean through. I crossed the room to him, glad that the simulated people let me through easily.

"He's already gone," the man in the back told me.

I put my hand on Dean's head anyway. Then I looked around for anything that would help me wake him up. If I was asleep, the thing that woke me up would be my armband being messed with. I could use that to my advantage, right? My eyes settled on a scrap piece of sandpaper on the floor. I rushed to it, ignoring the other people telling me to keep quiet. Then I used the paper against Dean's arm, harshly vibrating it across his skin to resemble his band being tampered with. It worked. Dean's eyes flew open. He registered surprise before he woke up in real life.

I gave myself a smile—another mission complete. I expected the simulation to end and Nick to tell me that I still had a job. That didn't happen. I looked around at the fake people, wondering if all of them were fake. None had registered surprise that Dean had vanished into thin air when I woke him up. None, that is, except for the girl whose eyes met mine. She gave me a shake of her head as she looked around. I felt my insides flinch. I was probably thrashing in real life, trying to wake myself up.

"We're still here. That's not a good sign," the tagger

girl told me.

I knew it was her, just by looking at her, even if she had adopted the face of the character she inhabited. She wasn't calling me Mr. Rhino or dying for me right then, but I was dead certain that it was the same tagger even when she looked different each time. No one else was looking at me. This tagger was dangerous. She was probably a sniper— even more reason for me to run now while I had the chance. Snipers used facial recognition as one of their main methods to hunt down players that kept getting in their way. They were hired by hackers to scare, bribe, or kill security guards before the guards ruined the hackers enterprises. Hackers could make a lot of money off of selling in-game items and avatars that they either created or stole from the games. She had seen my face several times. I agreed that being here was not a good thing, but I couldn't talk.

"Well? Who's got a gun? Hand it over," the girl insisted.

One of the simulations handed her one, and I watched with my eyes wide as she took it in her hand. She had it aimed at the ground, but she could flick it up at any moment and shoot me. Would I wake up or just feel dead like Dean had? Who would come in and find me? Maybe no one, if the system was being shut down. Perhaps Nick had rushed off to do that, thinking the problem was someone hacking into our workload instead of tagging our players.

15

Against the better judgement of everyone, the girl opened the blacksmith door and went outside. Several avatars covered their ears when gunshots sounded off. However, one simulation that was braver than the rest of us looked out the door and told us that my tagger had shot the sniper. Before I could look out and see for myself, I found myself waking from the same trick I had used on Dean—my armband was pulled off.

"Seb?" I heard a shaky voice. I kept my eyes closed for just a little while. It felt so real, like an alternate reality gone horribly, horribly wrong where the stakes could cost my life.

"Seb?" It was Dean. I opened my eyes and gave him a smile. "Thanks. You saved me," Dean said.

When I sat up, I had quite the crowd in my room. Half the people who worked for Leer and Nick crowded inside my small work space. They even spilled out the door.

"Well?" I asked. "Different people each time?" I could pull this off. Dean and I could keep our jobs. We'd both made it this far.

"Looks that way. We had several other attacks," Nick confirmed, looking at some of the other guys who trembled thinking about their own attacks.

"So we're good, right?" I couldn't help but prod. "We'll have to shut down for today, but tomorrow we'll be good?"

"I don't know, Sebastian," Nick told me. "Grant is coming to take a look. If he doesn't find anything right away, it might take a week."

"I need work, Nick," I insisted.

I knew I shouldn't push it, but I really did need the work. Would anyone else who was tagged insist on working when they should be moving to a different place and possibly running for the rest of their life? I couldn't. I could see my mother's terror if I ever told her where I had picked up a job and why I was asking her to run with me. I could see my little brother's tears.

"You got lucky that time," Nick told me. "If that NPC hadn't still been running to the blacksmith's, you could have been shot."

"Yup," was all I had for him. I would have been trampled by a rhino, stabbed with a knife, shot with a crossbow, and filled with lead today if it wasn't for my face-changing angel.

"Maybe... forget it."

I gave Nick a smile, not wanting to voice that thought. She really could be a guardian angel. What if she was trying to stop the people who were sabotaging our system? She could be one of our own people down in security. But if I was wrong about that and said anything, I was busted.

"I can't give you another guy's work," Nick said as if I was going to ask for it. It wasn't a bad idea. "You'll have to make do until we get it sorted. You guys go home. I'll call you if I need any of you back today."

Dean looked ready to leave. He pushed past the other guys to get out first. I lingered, watching as Leer shut down my screen. He was polite and didn't make a note on my record for the times my heart had spiked... or when it looked like I had stopped breathing. Is that why Leer had pulled the cord on me?

"Leer, I can still do this," I told him, scared that he was going to report me and pull me from the team for my physical inability.

"You did fine." Leer patted my shoulder. "There's this little old lady on Sumac Street who collects marbles."

"That's nice?" I scratched my head.

"If you bring her one she'll give you dusting, or cleaning, or yard work to do. It doesn't pay much, but it's handy in a pinch."

"Oh." Maybe I had underestimated Leer. "Thanks."

Sumac Street wasn't too far from here. I could make use of that information and get some extra work in. I wasn't getting anything here today even if I had pulled off a rescue mission. I headed away toward my private changing room where I would put on my best clothes before disappearing into the crowds in the real world. No one knew that I wore the same thing to work for the past two weeks thanks to the uniform. I checked my pulse as I walked, making sure that my heart was cooperating at normal levels. It would be really bad if I had a heart attack at work. No one would know where to put my dead body. I had lied about my address. I collected my pay at the end of each day, instead of having it sent home. Lots of people did that, but they did it for added security reasons, not because they were lying about their eligibility to work here.

"Seb," Nick caught me before I made it too far. Hoping he didn't know about the girl, I gave him my game face. I could conceal this and not get fired.

"I could use you. When Grant finds the placement, we'll need someone to go in and destroy it."

"I'm all in," I answered before I could stop myself. Wasn't that security's job? Was security shut down too? I didn't want to ask the question. I could still run around in my sleep, passing over encoded information that looked like solid objects in a gaming world. I would just need to keep my heart rate in check. After all, being a spy was all about lying, wasn't it?

Chapter 3

Millie

This was nice. It was night again and there were no other people around. No possible way to run into Mr. Rhino. I was dressed in a white nightgown that came to my ankles, and I was sitting in a chair in a Victorian-style room. I had a four-poster bed and vanity set. My chair was a rocker with a cushion. I closed my eyes, letting the calmness take me. I could get used to this. It was much better than the real place I had lain down to sleep tonight.

Knock. Knock. I wished the quiet of the night lasted longer. I looked to the door as it opened. There stood a man with a potbelly dressed in an impressive black jacket with tails and a cravat at his neck. He poked his balding head in and gave me a smile.

"It's late. You should get in bed."

"I will soon," I told him.

21

The man stepped into the room, carrying a black box that he pushed into one of the drawers of my vanity set. His movements were shaky and fearful, and his belly heaved as he carried out his actions.

"Is everything alright?" I asked him.

"Popping good!" he said with a chuckle, as if this was an inside joke. Not knowing what else to do, I gave him a short laugh. "Goodnight, Dove." He kissed the top of my head and walked out.

Great. I made myself comfortable in the chair and picked up a book beside me. It was a prop. The pages inside were blank. The cover said "Constructive Poetry." I was just about to put the book down when the window creaked open and in jumped a man dressed all in black. Despite the black eye mask, I didn't need to be told who he was. He took one look at me and pressed his finger to his lips.

Why would I squeal, Mr. Rhino? Really? Was I hoping to save you again right now? Nope, I thought. I opened the book again and went back to my enjoyable blank reading.

"I need you to stay quiet," Mr. Rhino directed. I looked at him and smiled. That I could do just as long as *he* was quiet and didn't send anyone charging into the room to kick him out for breaking in.

"Are you going to stay quiet?" he asked, inching farther in.

He looked back at the window, and then at me. I raised my eyebrows. I *was* being quiet. He took another step closer. Then he crossed to the bed and started to search it. He rifled through the whole thing looking up at me as he went.

"Are you a ghost?" he asked as if he couldn't stay quiet for the life of him. He crossed to the other side of the room and opened a chest. He slowly started taking things out. His arms shook a little as if he was scared. Of me? Hello, I had been saving him.

"I thought I was a girl wearing pajamas," I whispered. "That's better than a man stuck on a rhinoceros. How does one end up on top of a rhino?"

Mr. Rhino paused, staring at me before he took up the task of searching again, this time with a sarcastic smile on his face.

"What are you going to do when you find the black box?" I asked. "Do tell me it's not a bomb."

He had to be here for the box that Mr. Potbelly had just put down. What else was suspicious about this room? Mr. Rhino reached the bottom of the chest and started to load the things back inside before he spoke to me again. He kept glancing at me every few seconds like I was going to scream.

"I'm robbing you of a necklace," Mr. Rhino informed

23

me.

"Fantastic. Is that all you came for?"

I held the book up to look busy while he continued to rob me of a necklace. He looked under the bed next and started checking floorboards.

"You're not remotely scared?" Mr. Rhino questioned.

"Scared? Of a man dressed all in black searching everywhere but the vanity? Nope. I think I'm more scared of the people who are downstairs."

"Do they mistreat you?"

He stood up from his search, only to search my face again. I shrugged and he came over to steal the book from my hands. Then he told me to stand up so he could examine the chair. He was really slow at reaching the vanity. Why wasn't he going there? Maybe it was a bomb. I rolled my eyes and went to the suspicious drawer, wondering if it would blow up in my hands, thereby forcing me to save his life again. He watched me.

"I can't decide if I should thank you or run in terror when I see your face," Mr. Rhino admitted. He was still holding the book, and I wondered if he suspected that I had hidden the necklace inside of it.

"Run from me? Shouldn't it be the other way around? You'll turn out perfectly fine."

24

"So I should thank you? You have no nefarious intentions?"

Nefarious? Was he trying to match the style of the age around us by using a word like nefarious? I smiled at him, and then opened the drawer in the vanity.

Both of us jumped when another man in black leapt through the window. I wasn't in a spot where I could block Mr. Rhino from anything. Maybe I would have enough time to move?

"You're caught," the other man in black stated, looking at me with caution.

"She's alright. I promise," Mr. Rhino told him.

"That's the—"

"I've never seen her before," Mr. Rhino insisted. He flipped through the pages of the book, finding them blank, before he tossed it onto the vacant chair.

"The daughter of your sworn enemy is alright?" the other thief asked.

"She is right now. We've got a pact."

"A pact? How did the great Flying Falcon make a pact with the grease monkey's daughter?"

I got it. I was the person who would have killed Mr. Rhino tonight. I would have screamed or run for some hidden weapon in the room if I hadn't taken over the

25

presence of this particular avatar in this dream story.

I pulled out the black box, which I passed over to Mr. Rhino. He made a point of touching my hand when he took it, staring directly into my eyes as if he couldn't believe I wasn't a ghost. What was he, then? He kept popping up in my dreams. He had been there all night long needing rescuing. If I was lucky, this dream wouldn't end in death. I was pretty sure that I was going to get lucky in this one.

"Is this it?"

"No idea." I shrugged.

"Veronica, are you in bed yet, Dove?" came the potbelly man's voice from down the hall. That would be my father and I doubted his real name was "grease monkey." I jumped to the door to block it in case this was the moment it would open and cause my newest version of death. What would it be this time? Bludgeoned with a candlestick?

"The book is too interesting," I claimed while shooing the thieves out the window. Mr. Rhino opened the black box, causing me to nearly scream. What if it blew up on him?! But it didn't. He nodded his thanks and made his way to the window.

"Read me a passage," the voice lingered in the hallway just on the other side of the door. I made up what I hoped was a fitting rendition of poetry.

"Very good—now go to sleep. Your mother will be

upset if you don't."

"I will. Goodnight, Papa," I told him.

Then I waited impatiently. I pressed my ear to the door, and when I heard nothing, I ran to the window to check out the thieves. I couldn't see them anywhere, but I did see a large field and a fence and sheep. I climbed into the bed as the door opened again and pretended to be asleep. The door closed and I let out the breath I had been holding. Not too bad. That dream hadn't hurt anything.

Blink.

The sun rose into the sky so suddenly, that I marveled at the pink glow that swept into my window for only a moment before the sunrise was replaced with a yellow shine. I was still being the grease monkey's daughter. I guess the position felt too comfortable to give up. My mind didn't want to leave the dream. It was a lovely thought to be part of a home where everyone was still there and alive. I had no idea what had happened to my real family, and my current living circumstances were dreadful.

"Veronica!" I heard Mr. Potbelly holler. That was me. I sat up in the bed and yawned. The real Veronica may have screamed. Everything around me was a mess, as if the thieves who had come through hadn't replaced anything stealthily. I looked at the vanity where the drawer that held the black box was hanging open.

"Are you still there?!" I heard my dream father shout.

"Yes, but my room is a mess," I told him.

Mr. Potbelly pushed the door open and strode inside. Behind him came two other men—servants I guessed—who surveyed the room with him. Both of the servants were dressed the same in white shirts with blue vests and blue slacks. One had a mole on his nose as his defining feature, and the other was missing an ear.

"No."

My father started to tear apart the room, asking me why I hadn't woken up when the thieves came in. Only he didn't call them thieves. He called them corporate saboteurs and correctly named the Flying Falcon.

"Your mother has been taken. You will have to tell us where the Bird Hunters have moved the probe."

"I need to do what?" I asked without a clue as to what he was talking about.

"The black box, Veronica. Make a map on your hand of where the black box has gone."

"Shouldn't we be trying to find your wife?" the servant with the mole asked him. "Veronica's powers only extend through—"

"Find the black box!" Mr. Potbelly screamed at me,

cutting off the servant.

My dream father gave me an angry stare with his temples pulsing. He had lost a probe. What did it probe? Was it a good thing or a bad thing that it was lost? Did it really matter? It was all a dream, but apparently my hand had magic map making powers. I looked at my hands, both of which appeared normal. I traced a few of my lines, following them across my hand before looking back at my father with a shrug.

"Veronica's powers only work if your wife—"

"Fine."

My father stormed from the room. That left me with the two male servants. I looked around the room, and my eyes fell on a dress that I could put on. Even with an angry father, the thought of a real breakfast in a dream was still keeping me here. That's what I was thinking about more than mysterious maps.

"He's in a mood," the man with the missing ear told me.

I tried to not look at the gap in the side of his head, but I was confused. Maybe it was because I was thinking of family relationships, but this guy kind of sounded like my dad.

"Let me see your feet. He doesn't need to know where your power lies—he would use it for the most trivial things. I think he's broken. We need to find your mother."

My feet? Well this dream kept getting stranger and stranger. I pulled my feet out from under the blankets and tugged off the long stockings. Would you look at that? On the bottom of my left foot was a mark that resembled the letter "A" with a "W" sitting underneath the inside cross bar. Maybe it was supposed to look like a funny arrowhead.

"Now tap your foot five times and show us what happened to your mother."

When I followed the instructions, I quizzically watched as a 3D display of a woman being shoved inside a black carriage in the woods appeared. It was like watching a movie scene.

"The Bird Hunters don't have your mother," the earless man told me, still reminding me of my dad and the fact that I was dreaming. "She was taken by the Veterans. I wonder why they want her. What if they discovered that she can predict the future and you show the past? At least the Bird Hunters don't know about you, yes? They left you right here. Now where did that black box go?"

I shrugged, but even as I did so an image of Mr. Rhino dressed as the Flying Falcon appeared. He was holding the box and jumping out the window. He spread his arms and wings appeared on him. With little effort he was flying through the air and away from the house. I was glad it did not show me handing him the box.

"He came in person." The other servant with the mole frowned. "I wish they had not written such a scoundrel into this program. Where is the box now?"

Nothing showed up, and I shrugged. "Maybe it's not anywhere yet. It could still be in the air or you may need to change your question. *Now* does not apply to the past." I tugged my socks back on and walked over to the dress I had spotted. "Breakfast?" I asked.

It was strange that this servant knew more about Veronica's weird foot powers than her father did, but I was really looking forward to having breakfast before I actually woke up. I wanted to get this thing started. I pulled on the dress, but I couldn't close it up on my own. The back was all buttons. Who designed dresses like that? Undeterred, I started out my bedroom door, only to be stopped by the earless servant, who pulled me backwards by the open back of my dress.

"Are you okay?" he asked as he started in on the buttons. I wished he really was my dad, but his familiar voice wouldn't stop me. I could smell breakfast. It was going to be so delightful. And then all I could smell was dirt.

"Get up!"

There it was. I was back in the real world—awake. I would take my strange past-revealing powers over this any time. I got up because if I didn't I was dead. That didn't need explaining. I heard a few quiet groans around me. It

31

was harder to stay awake when I was really awake than it was when I was asleep. The dark interior of my surroundings was enough to make anyone groggy all the time. The sunshine in my dreams was something I craved. It was little wonder that I dreamt it up alongside scenarios of dying a heroic death. There was nothing heroic down here.

I was working in a mine along with about fifty other people who had been tricked at the border. We had all been crossing together, and the guy who said he would help us across lied. I had no idea what had happened to anyone that I knew. The raiders did that on purpose. They split up anyone that clung to each other and looked the same. Anyone who tried to make a run for the exit was struck down. Anyone who didn't wake up disappeared. I was missing my parents. We weren't illegal crossers, but we had been sneaking in like we were. We had citizenship and we could prove it. I had been born across the border, but we'd never made it there. When we reached the old shanty town that was supposed to provide a break from the hot desert sands, we had been shoved into cars and taken away amidst fights and screaming.

I glanced at the weary man beside me. His hands were bleeding and we hadn't even started to work again yet. I felt sorry for him, but there wasn't anything I could do. If there was, I would have wrapped his hands for him, cleaned his wounds, and given him a hug. He didn't look back at me. Already the surrounding people kept their heads down, as if the fight in them had left. Maybe they had not dreamed of sunshine and scenarios that forced them to be brave. I kept remembering the fighting at the shanty. I hadn't joined in at the time, but a part of me wished I had.

Hey, I was still awake and still alive, and I was going to keep going. I wiped at my nose as it started running. Never mind. It was bleeding. The dry dust was getting into every part of me, making me crack. I sniffled a bit and followed the others toward our breakfast. We were not starved, but it wasn't exactly a home-cooked meal like my dream had been about to give me.

I received bread and cold soup. The soup was in a can and the bread was in a plastic wrapper. I ate both, drinking the soup first and then eating the bread. I glanced at the walls around me. It was all dirt and rocks. I had a plan to blast a big enough hole today that I would reach the sky above me and let some light trickle in—a cave-in, perhaps. Then I looked at the people making us work. Not many of us captured border crossers looked up anymore. Where had the spark gone? Where was the desire to dig in and get out of here?

I was not given any gunpowder to hold. Today I received nails and was positioned next to a man who was fortifying the dirt walls with wood. I got to hammer in the nails. Nice. Maybe I would get a blister, but for the most part I wouldn't be too bad. It paid off to look like a young girl.

Chapter 4

Sebastian

"You're working overtime." The words flashed across the screen as I landed in the bandit camp. It was already overtime? I had been lost in thoughts about Veronica, the sworn enemy's daughter. Funny how my angel had happened to appear in her role. Angel had a habit of showing up where I would never expect.

"Overtime," I said out loud, still carrying the box cradled in my arm.

I didn't mind. This role was fun. I was a mysterious bandit who got to fly. I had a group of men that did anything I asked of them. I got to dress as a rogue. I wore all black and, get this—I had a chest of masks. When I had read that, I couldn't help but grin. A chest of masks. Perfect! Nothing was better than that to a guy who was tagged. I could disappear –or fly away—whenever I felt like it and no one would see my real face.

I wondered if Nick really did suspect my predicament and that was why he was pushing me to work longer. Then again, it could be because I was still holding this black box, the probe that was somehow linking into our company system through this game. The necklace was stealing the gaming locations we were using for the day so the Vikings could disrupt our operations. There was also the issue that Nick had sent home over half his other workers. I knew that Nick was still watching my screen if he was telling me it was overtime. What if he had understood the exchange between me and my guardian angel? I was trying to keep it simple, but golly if she was standing right there I wanted to know if she had it out for me. Somehow she had managed to infiltrate the game system and get into the real characters. She was without a doubt a better spy than I was, but for which side? Did Veronica work for the evil Vikings or for us? Was she toying with me?

"Over time, sir?" William, a bandit I had known for five years who had saved my life during a rock slide, asked me as I talked. His information appeared in front of me in large letters so I knew who I was speaking to. He had a black cowl with the hood pulled up. I laughed. I *did* want to work overtime. I was just getting started with the fun. This was the part I had signed up for: playing games.

"Yes, William," I replied. "Over time, your hair

grows longer. Remember that." I flicked him on the shoulder as I walked the box away and laughed at his partly concealed confused face.

"And what is that?" Steph, a man whom I had known for two years, who I fenced with—oh that sounded fun—pointed to the box I was holding.

"Beauty with a bite," I told him.

"Where did you get it?" William asked me. "You took off without any reasons and came back with a biting beauty. Is it a snake?"

"It coils, gentlemen," I nodded. I had been told the general location of the necklace I was looking for, no doubt devised through Grant's efforts. He was our company problem solver that Nick and Leer used all the time. I had, in fact, taken off without a word to anyone.

I was now being surrounded by the other bandits whose information flashed across my vision if I looked at them. "I would like a mallet, a sword, a hammer, maybe a hot fire," I told them with a grin. No. I wanted to have more fun with this. "Actually, we shall hold a contest." I looked around and spotted a basket of apples and arrows. Perfect! No need to be boring when I could play to pulverize this device.

"We are going to destroy this."

I took out the jeweled necklace and flashed it

through the air. There were murmurs that I was crazy, and I only laughed. That fit my character description. It was good to see that I was holding up to it.

"Every time we shoot an apple we can smash the necklace. Steph," I looked at him, "fifty yards for those apples to start with I should think, and fetch my bow."

"Very good, sir," Steph said without moving, "but why are we destroying that?"

"Ah! It belongs to my archenemy the belly-filled belfry of bagpipes!"

"The Earl of Key Hill?" Samson, a very good thief I was told, asked me.

"Very good, Samson," I winked back at him. "You've won a promotion. You can go first while I remember how to shoot my bow."

"Seventy yards." Steph grinned. "And may I have the second turn at smashing the bagpipe's jewels?"

"Of course. It shall be jolly good fun."

The men gave out a rallying cry and ran off to get their gear. From my screen, I read a crash course on how to shoot a bow. All I had to do was stand correctly and hold the weapon that was already set up for my character to aim it perfectly. The rest I didn't think was going to be too hard.

It was fun to watch the men scramble together their

things. My bow was amazing. I had been expecting a curved wooden stick with a string attached. Instead, I got a fantastic contraption painted black with a dragon-face clip on the top. It had wheels that my cables, not weak string, ran through. The grip fit my hand perfectly, and to make it even more fascinating, I had a laser that showed me where my shot was going to hit. That was called my sight. The parts of the bow flashed across my screen as I giggled like a lovesick teen. I could find the idler wheel, limb dampener, sight, arrow shelf, grip, string suppression system, and cam. This thing was awesome!

I let Samson and William get the first shots, but everyone was a fool if they thought I was going to wait any longer than that. I followed the instructions and got my feet lined up. Good line habits and posture were essential to a good shot. I put my feet hip width apart, then I angled my less dominant foot—my left—out toward the target a half turn as well as slid it back a half step. The action felt natural.

I ran through the checklist. I had my stance. I pulled my arrow and clicked it against my cable, propped it on the arrow rest. That was only the start of the list. There was more to it than just lining up. The rest of the stuff at the line mattered. I had to keep the hand on my bow loose so I didn't strangle the thing and wobble my shot. I put three fingers on the cable to pull it back. I anchored my pulling hand at the corner of my mouth—aimed. I squeezed my shoulder muscles together on my back. It had to be important. Then I released.

The arrow flew through the air, striking the apple dead center. Shoot, I had this down!

"It's applesauce tonight, baby!" I shouted.

I twirled my bow above my head, easy after all my table waiting and dancing, while I pulled off a few hip-hop dance moves. I had passed my teens two years ago, but I could still boogie.

"You guys better watch out. I'm gearing to go again!"

I handed my bow to Phil, a nice thief who I had a habit of teasing, before I took up the large hammer and smashed down on the necklace that was tied over a large rock. A jewel ricocheted off.

"I love it when he's in a good mood," Steph told Phil. "Maybe he'll break open the rum."

"No rum," I told Steph, putting down the hammer. I was at legal drinking age, but I wasn't about to get my team drunk, even virtually, when I needed them. "See, Mr. Jewel Hog is going to be mad. He might decide to lead a team out against us. This thing is important. At least it was." I grinned. "We need to be alert in case he shows up, savvy?"

"No one can find our hideout," Phil told me. We were in a hidden valley and there were rocks and trees everywhere around us, but I wasn't about to get careless in a game. Games had the habit of surprising you.

"Tell that to my baby sister," I told Phil.

I retrieved my bow back from his fingers and moonwalked backwards away from him.

"Falcon, you don't have a baby sister," Phil pointed out.

"Who are you going to tell that to, then?" I questioned. Phil scratched his head. Steph was looking at me, trying to figure out my feet. I laughed and got in line to go again.

Nick was being nice to me. He let me have my run with the lads. I shot away eight apples, riled the lads, and made some plans for attacking the Earl of Key Hill when he carted some stolen goods across the forest path tomorrow. That was also known as interrupting his transmission to his boss that we had messed up his probe. Then I found my mask collection, picked out a mask that looked like a yeti, and had fun teasing Phil.

Nick was smiling at me when I came out of the simulation, although I didn't think he had as much fun as me. He asked me if I had enjoyed overtime and he got an enthusiastic response. Then Nick said magical words. He'd let me go with the team to interrupt the transmission tomorrow. He wasn't going to put anyone else into Mr. Flying Falcon's shoes. I could have hugged him.

Chapter 5

Millie

I was packed up and ready to move. My father, also known as the Earl of Key Hill, had finally taken the advice of the squat servant and decided that we needed to go rescue my kidnapped mother. Since I had this strange ability with my left foot to tell the past, he didn't want to leave me behind. Plus, he couldn't get me to use my powers if I wasn't within a certain range of my mother. It was a strange world these dream guys had going on, but I wasn't complaining. Anything was better than dying today. I didn't want to die in my dreams. I was tired and sore from the hard labor I had put in during the day.

Despite not wanting to face the lash of death, I still found myself looking for Mr. Rhino. Here, he was called the Flying Falcon and his group of thieves was called the Bird Hunters. My group was riding horseback. I had almost expected to find myself in a fancy carriage, but the switchbacks through the forest made that impossible. There was no way to see us from above—we were hiding from the Falcon—and I could tell that I would be lost if my horse, Spock, didn't press closely to the horse before us. I tried to pull him back several times, worried that the horse in front would kick at us. Spock didn't listen to anything I told him to do. He plowed forward despite my efforts.

I examined the forest, enjoying the textures and the smells and the sounds. It was quiet here. The best part was the sun. It shone through the trees, playing upon the group of traveling horses. I didn't think things were too bad; although, if we kept our methodical pace, I would grow bored. As if hearing my thoughts, the sun shifted in the sky. I was suddenly farther down the path at noonday. The trees were less plentiful in this area, and my horse came to a stop as the horse in front of us did.

"Why did we stop?" the person behind me asked. I shrugged. "We should have reached the hill," he said.

I turned around to find the man checking out his watch as if it was the device that had shifted our time frame, and then I saw him. Standing in plain sight wearing a black, fearsome gorilla mask was the Falcon. He had come to rob us again. That would make this trip more interesting.

"There's three dead deer in the path," a shout came from in front. The person in front of me looked over his shoulder and repeated the information to pass it down the

44

line. As he did so, he noticed the gorilla man.

"Sir!" He pointed out the Falcon.

I had long since stopped holding my reins. Now I let go of the horn on my saddle as well and swung one of my legs to the side toward the Falcon, poised to jump off the horse. What level of death was I looking at?

The man behind me pulled up a bow and shot an arrow toward the Falcon. He stepped to the side and the arrow missed him, much to my relief.

"I expected better," the Falcon clicked his tongue. "I was shooting apples last night with my eyes closed and they are a smaller target. You need to work on your stance, sir."

The man behind me nocked another arrow, but didn't get the chance to shoot it. His arm was hit from behind and he screamed. Then the horses started falling. When my horse took an arrow and stumbled over, I jumped off and started to run out of the way to avoid the commotion. I felt strangely calm as I scanned the area for the Falcon. I didn't see him among the trees anymore and I looked upward. He was coming in on top of a man who was running with a sack in his arms.

The Falcon landed in front of the man and fought him for the sack. My father, The Earl of Key Hill, found my arm and started to pull me the other direction.

"It's an ambush," he told me as if I hadn't figured

that out yet. "Stay out of sight."

Staying out of sight became impossible. We were surrounded by horse flesh that blocked our path. I tried to scramble over one of the horses, but my father pushed me down, looking around and scanning the skies.

"Run for the hill," he told me, pointing ahead of us where our path was taking us. "On three."

He didn't count. He leapt and ran. I jumped up after him, running for the same hill. Before I made any progress, I was smashed to the side by a bandit. He checked my hands to make sure I wasn't carrying anything before he jumped over me and ran toward one of the men I had come with. I got up again, only to run right into the Falcon.

"Veronica," the man said my name by rolling his "r." "Are you having an enjoyable trip?"

"It got more exciting when you showed up," I answered.

I glanced toward the hill and around at the other people who were being tied up by the bandits. The Falcon held up a cord and his glaring gorilla mask made me shake my head. He grabbed at me and tied my hands together before ordering his group to leave the men right where they were. I counted ten men who were going to be tied up and stranded.

"It   seems   that   we   have   taken   away   your

46

transportation." The Falcon looked back at me. "Need a lift?"

He picked me up, and instead of taking me to the hill, he jumped into the air. I watched as the trees started to get smaller. His wings behind him, connected to his back and not to his arms, spread wide. We landed next to a large mailbox. He set me down and pulled the sack out of a pocket. Then he shoved the sack into the mailbox and shut the lid. I heard a whoosh sound from the box and I reached to check to see if the bag had been vacuumed, but the Falcon caught my tied-together arms and pulled me away.

"Do you have magic pockets? The bag was a lot bigger earlier."

"I emptied it out some. Come on. If I have you right next to me, I won't have to worry about you popping up and surprising me."

"The popping today was done by you," I told him. He rewarded me with a large laugh, the kind that could make anyone's dreams worth dreaming, before I was carried away to the bandit camp. The camp was situated in the middle of thick trees, and I would have missed it if it wasn't for the Flying Falcon knowing it was there.

"Rhino Man, can you please take the mask off?" I asked the black-faced gorilla in front of me. The mask was annoying. I appreciated seeing the faces of my captors. I hadn't ever been scared of gorillas, but this mask was a little scary. The eyes and mouth were rather mean. Where was my dreaming taking me tonight? Maybe I was subconsciously thinking about being trapped. I couldn't wait for the moment in my dream where I broke free and proved that I could rise above my circumstances.

"I don't have a rhino. I have a yeti. Want the yeti face? I also have a mean dragon, a white ghost head, or a tribal-style snake."

"Just take the mask off," I repeated.

"The mask is what you get."

"And these bonds are unnecessary," I told him, holding up my tied hands. "The next time I go flying I want my arms to spread out and feel the air."

"Next time?" I could hear the smile in his voice, but I couldn't see it. I grit my teeth. I wanted to see him!

"Please. That mask. Please."

"No. There are spies here," he whispered as he leaned in. He gave a short laugh. Then he sat back and spread out his hands behind him puffing up his chest as he looked up at the sky. I looked up too. The stars were glorious. I could get lost in the stars.

"What do you think? Are they balls of gas or smiling eyes?" I asked.

"The stars? They're guardian angels like you," Falcon

answered.

"I knew it was you," I told him glancing over at him and his gorilla face. "I see you everywhere and I love it. I feel more alive when I see you in my sleep than I do when I'm awake. Of all the people I could dream of I'm glad it was you."

I wasn't sure why I said it. This guy had gotten me to die for him a few times. I really shouldn't enjoy the thought of him, but I *was* enjoying it. It was better than the boredom of the mine. The Falcon looked back and almost removed his mask. Then he laughed again.

"You're good. Very clever, Veronica. To make me want to see you. That was a cheap and dirty trick, actually. Nice."

He stood up and walked away from me.

"I was serious!" I shouted at him.

Why did he think I was tricking him? Tricking him with what? Maybe he was married, and he thought I was trying to flirt? I shifted my weight, and then stumbled after him. I was going to ask him if he was married as the Fearsome Falcon, but before I could he turned around and stopped me.

"Don't talk so loudly about dreams or I'll give you nightmares," he told me.

I let him walk away after that. What was he hiding

from? What deep troubles had his life gone through? He felt real to me, and I realized that I knew nothing about him. I probably wouldn't ever know the answers to my questions unless I dreamt them all up to entertain myself. Could I control my dreams? I had some questions. I returned to the fire until he decided that he was done hiding and came back.

"Living is a nightmare. This is my escape," I told him when he sat back down beside me, wearing the white ghost mask. Or maybe it wasn't him. He didn't say anything, and I wasn't sure if he had switched off with one of the thieves around us to trick me. But if it was him, I guessed he was trying to wear a less scary mask for my benefit.

"Do you ever just wish you could be the hero of your own story for real? I can't get it out of my head that everyone else seems to have stopped trying. There's so much more out there. I, for one, am going to see the sun again before I die."

"The sun? Where are you? How serious are you being right now?" the Falcon asked me. He shifted a little beside me. Ha. It *was* him. I made him talk again.

"I'm stuck everywhere: in my life and in my dreams. Only in my spirit am I free like the uncatchable wind."

The white ghost mask stared at me. The stare behind the facade felt more real than all the nails I had hammered today. That work had been conducted in a haze. Why did sleeping feel like the only real part of me?

50

"Don't make me regret this."

He reached over and cut the cords on my hands. Then he held onto my hands for a few minutes before he abruptly stood and started ordering his men about. There was some slight arguing about plans for tomorrow. I tried to listen in, but when I got close enough to make out what they were hissing about the Falcon jumped into the air.

"I am going to stop this!" he told his clan. "Don't lose Veronica."

I watched him fly off into the night, losing him rather quickly with his black gear. Then I blinked. I had thought I was done with changing dreams so quickly, but it happened again. Why had I left Veronica? I liked that dream. I wasn't liking this new one. I was wearing a red dress which I didn't like. I felt too visible. I didn't spot Mr. Rhino or the Flying Falcon. What I did see was the thief that had been wearing the black cowl. What had his name been? I'd heard someone mention it. Maybe it was William. He didn't have the cowl or the same face anymore, but I was sure it was him. I wondered how I could tell. Was it the way he stood? He was wearing shorts and a t-shirt and he was staring at the end of a bucket of tar that was about to be poured on him.

What a bummer. I shoved him out of the way as the bucket tipped from the top of a roof. William met my eyes, and in that moment I felt like he was more scared of me than he was the tar that he had missed. I didn't stay long.

I blinked again, only to find myself standing on the deck of a gallows. I wasn't the person that was about to be hanged, but I was next to the guy who was. He promised to buy everyone French fries if they let him go. That sounded like a good deal to me. I grabbed a sword from a nearby soldier and cut the rope. The man dropped free and ran, but someone in the audience got mad at me and hit me on the back of the head.

The next time I blinked I was standing inside a circus ring with three tigers. One of the tigers was crouched down, ready to attack a woman that was holding an unlit ring of fire. I rushed between the tiger and the woman as the tiger jumped. I was beginning to think that I could write a book about obscure ways to die.

Chapter 6

Sebastian

"Stop following me," I growled, stepping into the hallway. I hadn't even left work yet, and I had picked up a stalker. It wasn't Nick—he would make himself known. I didn't know who it was, and it was making me nervous.

"What are you doing, Seb?" the mysterious voice asked concealed by the corner. "Did you send her?"

"What? Send who? What are you talking about?"

"Veronica," the mysterious voice told me. "Don't send her again, or I'll come after you in every version of reality you can think of."

"Whoa, dude, chill out," I told him.

I was still trying to place him and found myself failing, but he had to have come from my simulation if he was talking about Veronica. That could only mean that I wasn't the only real person in the group of thieves working to stop the Earl of Key Hill. Lucky for me, I wore my mask on the job. I was unlucky enough to be identified anyway. But send Veronica where? I hadn't sent her anywhere, and when she showed up in random places, the only thing she did was die. Had she died? Had she shaken this man's socks off, seeing her in multiple places?

"She's on our side."

"She doesn't work here, Seb. I know all the employees. If you're letting the enemy infiltrate us, I will stop you."

Okay this was getting intense. I still couldn't place the voice, so perhaps this person wasn't anyone I knew. But who knew who everyone was? The only person coming to mind was the company sniper. Great. I was talking with the company sniper. I couldn't think of anyone else who would be able to identify Veronica when she assumed the face of the avatars she invaded. Someone was getting scared. I was going to be late going home tonight. I wasn't going to set one foot on my real street until I was sure I had lost the sniper. And now I knew for a fact that the girl playing angel didn't work here. So where did she work?

"I'm not the one sending her, but I'll figure out what I can. What did she do?" I asked as innocently as I could.

"She shifted her stream multiple times," the sniper answered.

"And died, probably," I mumbled.

If she had shifted her stream more than once that meant that she had shown up in other people's visuals and interfered. Why was she doing that and getting herself caught? I really didn't think she worked for the Vikings—or rather the Earl of Key Hill. But she had to have something that made her able to sneak through our system and die all over the place. If she didn't work for the Earl, then I wondered if the Vikings knew about her yet, because she was sneaking through their system too.

"Maybe she's an independent hacker?" I mused.

"I'm watching you, Seb," the sniper told me. He let me hear him walk away, but I was still going to try to throw off any followers on the way home tonight. I hoped I would be able to get some sleep. I didn't like the thought of a sniper trying to find the real-life version of my angel. I couldn't get her words out of my head.

"I feel more alive when I see you in my sleep than I do when I'm awake," she had told me. Really? I could make someone want to live? The person who kept dying for me wanted to live *because* of me? It didn't make sense, and yet the idea that I could inspire another person was taking hold of my heart. Whatever I had done, I felt like I had made a friend. She was a confusing sniper or hacker, but I wanted to own the friendship. I could see this working out. If I had a friend who could visit in my sleep, then it wouldn't matter

where I moved to. We could still be friends.

Thoughts of my angel stayed with me all night. The company sniper must have been thinking about her too, because when I showed up to work the next day, it looked like Nick had been alerted to her presence. He was standing in front of my door. Leer was tapping his leg behind him seemingly anxious because Nick was holding testing gear. But I had to be safe. If Veronica had been spotted in other people's visuals that meant she wasn't tagging *me*, right? I had never heard of a sniper tagging multiple people and dying *for* them. She just liked to be around me because I made her want to live. She wanted to be the hero of her own story. She felt trapped in real life. This was her version of escape. Whom and what was she escaping while she played hero risking her real identity being discovered?

Nick held out the breath tester. I had previously taken this test before, along with multiple others like the stamina test and the IQ test. I figured I'd gotten this job because I had passed those, although I was never allowed to see my final numbers so I could compare them with anything. Whatever my score, my job was fun. I was hired to be a spy that sorted through virtual games and removed hostile objects placed there by hackers.

"Hey, Nick. Just so you know, I've never drunk an ounce of rum," I told him lightheartedly.

He cracked a small smile and held the breathing

device out to me. I blew into it and touched the hand wipes. The guy was testing me for drugs. I hoped it was a routine thing, but from the look on Leer's face he didn't think so. I wondered for a moment if Leer always watched my visuals and knew everything that I did. I had been told that my spy missions were too important for others to be given such a view. The company had to trust me to carry out the tasks I was given or they were in trouble.

"Clean. Fantastic." Nick nodded. "And you slept last night?"

I nodded. Yes, I had slept last night even with the angel sticking to my mind like duct tape. Maybe some people had been too stressed to sleep after seeing her. My first experience with her had put me on my toes, but I was too pressed for work to give anything up. When Nick walked off, I entered my room, looking at Leer and his shaggy black hair. He was in charge of monitoring my heart rate and cutting me out if anything went wrong. He didn't have the most exciting job. Mine was more fun.

"What was that all about?" I asked Leer as I got on the memory foam table bed.

"We've already had two people not show up today," Leer told me. "Nick thinks they ran."

"So he's testing *me*?"

I was slightly late myself, having taken a longer route

in to work because I wanted to make sure I was not being followed from my house. Leer gave me a trying smile, and told me he was glad I showed up for work. I hoped we hadn't lost anyone too important. I wondered if they had seen our company sniper as well and hadn't been able to take the pressure. Maybe our company sniper had done this on purpose. If they couldn't take the heat they had better leave the fire.

Leer hooked me up to the machine, and I groaned when my first mission flashed on the screen. I wasn't the Flying Falcon. Had I lost my chance to be that, or was I taking on another guy's workload? I was running through normal missions. My job included finding a certain object and buying it or taking it. Then I would find a terminal and put the item inside for examination. These missions had been kind of fun in the past, but now that I had tasted the Flying Falcon I was spoiled. With him I could delve into his character and be somebody awesome. I loved the fact that it was just as important to connect with the people around me as it was to get the missions done.

The mask hid the grin on my face when I finally reached the Flying Falcon again. I could picture Leer recording that my levels of joy had spiked. I was really glad that I had not been kicked out from this role. I reached my hand up to test the mask, the wooden dragon one, and then looked around. I wasn't given the names of the people around me, which was unusual. Maybe I had been here enough times that I was supposed to remember them. I recognized the few thieves that I had spent more time with: Steph, William, Phil, and Samson.

Steph was poking a knife into a log over and over again, looking antsy. Phil was jumpy and jittery on his feet. Samson was sitting and staring at a tree blankly as if his character was out of service for the day. William was pacing in circles around the campfire where Veronica was crossing her unbound arms and glaring at me. Had I just done something?

"You're a real jerk," she told me, which confirmed it for me. I had just done something, but no words appeared on my screen to tell me what.

"I try my hardest," I snapped back, matching the mood of everyone around me for a second before shifting. "But as a protector of the skies and hunter of smaller lesser birds, this falcon knows how to apologize. I am sorry."

She looked back at the campfire, not commenting on my mask or anything else. Great. It was time to figure out what was going on. Had I left her sitting outside all night and she had slept on the ground in front of the fire? Had I threatened to tie her up again?

I approached William and he stopped pacing in circles. He was really tense, and I wondered for a second if William was real. Was there a person behind this avatar? Had he seen the company sniper last night as well? It made sense if he had. All the men were tense and aggravated today. I put a reassuring hand on William's shoulder, sliding into my role as leader of this group. I found it strange that I would have been chosen for the lead role when I was rather new to this job. Why not William? Then again, he was stomping around aggravated.

"What part of my actions upset the Amazon Princess?" I whispered to William, testing my theory that he was a real person. I expected confusion from an NPC. William looked at my snake mask and his facial features relaxed looking relieved. I could hear the hallelujah chorus from his expression: the captain was back on the deck, no one panic.

"She wants breakfast," William told me. "You told her she would have to wait."

"Quite right. A little patience never hurt anyone."

I gave him a short hug before I went to check on Steph. He was eyeing me as if I were an intruder, and the first words out of his mouth revealed that he had known long before me that there were other real players.

"Everyone is acting weird today including you. I don't work for you."

"Sure you do," I told Steph. "Who else is going to help you tie your shoes? Your laces are undone." He looked down at his shoes, and I flicked his nose. "Gotcha."

Steph backed up and then he looked over at William, who had stopped pacing. Did Steph take his cues from the man? Had they worked together before I'd taken over this role?

"Will is going to spin his head in circles," Steph commented.

I looked around the group again. There was no way to get anyone to cooperate with me if they suspected my character wasn't genuine. My late start on the day was costing me a little reputation, but I was going to get that back. I clapped my hands together and shouted, getting the attention of the group.

"Energy," I started. "That great motivator that can drive a man up a mountain or bury him under his own weight. You guys are filled with it. It's time to run that in circles. Everyone up. I want three laps from all of you around the camp. That includes you, pouty peach," I told Veronica. "And you, Samson," I told him giving his player a hard look.

Samson blinked back at me before he stood up. He looked nonresponsive staring at the tree, but he moved now so his character was working again. Apparently, he had just been reading something on his screen, trying to make sense of a situation. Perhaps he was new and had replaced one of the two missing men that Leer had mentioned. I was working with all real people. How had I not noticed that before? Why did their faces not update to show who they really were? Maybe mine didn't, either? Even so, I wasn't going to take the mask off and find out. I needed to remain hidden.

I ordered them about, sending them running in circles. A few of the guys heckled each other and raced. Veronica seemed to enjoy the activity. She ran an extra lap, grinning when I ran that extra lap with her. We needed a chat. She was making the guys nervous and costing me my men. It was time to see how much I could pry from her.

"Samson," I ordered when I got back to the center of the camp. "Breakfast for two in my tent."

That would give him a good introduction to what was around him if he had to interact with the men. I was sure he was going to spend a little while reading names on his screen as he looked over all the characters before he decided how to magic up breakfast.

"Evil archenemy's daughter... Your breakfast is now coming," I told her, "and you will not get me to take off the mask."

"I don't think I need you to right now," she said, clearly relieved that I was back in control.

I was relieved too. I had work to get done, but I wasn't exactly sure of what sort. We had destroyed the necklace that had been letting the Vikings hack into our system. I had stopped them from creating a new one last night by stealing their supply of metal and throwing it into the river. Maybe they had found the missing metal and were back to making a new one? How were we going to stop them from repeating their behavior? It was disastrous that they had infiltrated all the worlds we were working on and killing off our spies. How did that necklace work, anyway? Wouldn't it need to be connected to our system database somehow? What did it connect to? Where did their information come from? Was there a double spy in our midst leaking information?

I approached Phil and asked him if we had any direct plans for the day. He didn't know of anything, either. I doubted we had been sent here just to goof off. Maybe we were here to crack down on Veronica. If that was the case, she was my responsibility. I was the one who had kidnapped her out of curiosity, wanting to see what she would do.

She was standing at the entrance to my tent, which was a beautiful work of deep brown cow hides stitched together. This alternate reality world was rather fascinating. I could see how the Vikings enjoyed it enough to place their probe here. Maybe this world connected to many other ones? What if this world was the center point where we told everyone where to go next? How would we kick out the Earl of Key Hill? He was part of the programing. His character was, in fact, the main one. To take him out would be to destroy the whole thing, but I knew that the Vikings had him. They had stolen the main character.

"Come inside. It's prettier on the outside, but the inside can be cozy," I told Veronica, holding open the tent flap so she could go see for herself.

Everything inside was set up camping style. I had a sleeping bag on a flat camping pad. A small chest that held the masks was beside one edge next to a backpack filled with clothes and other traveling equipment. For the fun of it, I decided to search the backpack. I pulled the backpack toward me while Veronica looked around. She sat down on top of the sleeping bag.

"Veronica, why are you here?" I asked her.

"You told me to come inside," she reminded me.

"No I meant..." I trailed off as the new Samson announced that he was bringing in breakfast. He'd managed to produce scrambled eggs and pancakes at a surprising speed. There was also a hot cup of cider. I thanked him as he set the food down. Veronica was already eagerly crawling over, which I found strange because she wouldn't really be able to eat it. Her character could, but it wouldn't do anything for her. I thanked Samson, and he hesitated before he walked back out.

"Sir, the sooner you get through with your mysterious plans the better," Samson told me, reminding me that the men outside the tent were all antsy. I thought I had calmed them down, but perhaps they were grumbling that I was holding a private interrogation. Well I wasn't going to invite them. I didn't know where this was going to go yet. I had no idea if I was going to get anything or just waste my time while the tagger who was controlling Veronica laughed at me. I still felt a strange sort of ownership over the girl who called me Mr. Rhino. She was my angel. I wanted my friend, even if that friendship was only going to last for the next three minutes.

"Why the interest in fake food?" I asked her when Samson was gone.

"Anything is better than canned soup and packaged bread," she answered.

She started in on the breakfast, sighing with each bite as if she was in heaven. I could only stare at her. Was she being serious or playing games? I didn't think the Earl of Key Hill would have canned soup to feed his daughter. Was she starving in real life?

"It won't do much to satisfy you."

"I was hoping it would be better. I missed breakfast at my dad's house."

"At your real dad's house or the Earl's house?" I wanted to know.

"The Earl of Key Hill. Have you ever been to Key

Hill? Is it key-shaped?"

I continued to stare at her, trying to decide if she was really laughing at her question or ignorant of it. She was playing the Earl's daughter. He had a key that would unlock the hill and reveal the well of magic that this world used. That key he kept on him at all times to keep the hill locked. That was the entire point of the game. He defended the hill while other players tried to steal the key and magic. Recently he hadn't been stopping anyone's attacks on the hill but had instead been building probes that we wanted to destroy. I wondered of the consequences to getting rid of his current character.

"I wish I could taste it," Veronica told me as she tried to smell the cider before drinking it up. "I guess my dreams can't be that good, but other things feel real. You seem real."

She reached over and touched the hard, wooden surface of the repulsive dragon mask I was wearing. It was red and black and looked tribal. My dragon bow was far cooler than the mask. I frowned at Veronica. She sounded sincere. She hadn't known about the magic inside Key Hill. She didn't know that she wouldn't be able to taste the food. Did she honestly think she was dreaming? Maybe I needed to stop thinking like a spy and try to figure out where she was coming from in a different way.

"When you're not dreaming what do you do?" I asked her.

"Try to think up ways to escape," she answered.

Again she looked and sounded like she believed everything she was saying. I pulled off the dragon mask to get a clearer picture. The eye slits in the mask didn't give me the best view. I couldn't picture her lying right now.

"Escape what, Veronica?" I asked her while she smiled at me.

She ran her eyes over my face in a familiar way as if yes, my avatar updated my face when I was here. She settled on my green eyes. Then she glanced down at my lips before laughing at herself and looking away. I hoped I wasn't making it up, but did she find me attractive? What was I supposed to do with that? I had no idea what she really looked like. I thought we could be strange friends...

"I'm trapped in a mine someplace and my name's Millie."

Again, my gut feeling was to believe her. She was trapped. She'd told me yesterday that sleeping was her escape from reality. What if she didn't know that she wasn't really sleeping? What if she was so desperate to escape that she was slipping into our games, drawn by the heiss? Heiss was the substance that was right now dripping into my arm so I could stay asleep and work in this game. Some people found themselves addicted to the drug when they got a taste of it, and could slip into alternate realities when they were really low in heiss because their bodies craved it. For others, it was simply hereditary. I had been warned that surfers often slipped. If they didn't get enough, they could "ride the waves" so to speak, of anyone who was using a lot of heiss. Snipers did the same thing. That's what they used to find people. They had a sixth sense of where to locate the stuff, and when they located a person consuming it, like the people who I worked with, they could tag them and hunt them down. Snipers could read an individual's heiss wave like a license plate. It identified a specific user. Maybe I was dealing with an addict here that was indeed trapped in a mine. But if so, why had the addict not asked everyone she met for help?

"Have you ever had dreams like this before?" I asked. "Ones that feel this real? Are you sure that you're dreaming?" Maybe if I just alerted the addict to what she was really doing, she would decide to stop on her own. I would lose my strange friend, but it had been an interesting past couple days.

"This has to be a dream," she laughed at me. "None of it is real." She looked at my mouth again, and then looked away sheepishly. She crossed her legs and lowered her head, trying to stop herself from laughing.

I couldn't help the small tingle of anticipation, even if I knew everything wasn't real. It was flattering and a little alarming that a heiss addict was flirting with me. But as long as she wanted to stay friendly and not come and kill me—or any of my coworkers—I didn't see the harm in it. Maybe she wasn't an addict. Maybe she had *never* had heiss before and that was why she had no idea what she was doing. That would explain why she hadn't asked for help to escape the mine. She didn't know she could get help, because she didn't think I was real.

I leaned over and kissed her cheek, wondering if the change in my emotions was going to show up on my work feed. I was feeling a little giddy. There was a girl someplace—my little angel—that thought I was cute. I wondered what the real Millie looked like. I hoped she was hot, although it probably didn't matter. If she died in her mine then I'd never see her again. That made the kiss bittersweet.

"Does that seem real?" I asked her.

"Does this really count as kissing?" Veronica, or Millie, asked with a laugh. She met my eyes again as she blushed, shook her head, and giggled. I had tamed the person everyone was so scared of. She was not a spy. She was a surfer, who was riding waves of heiss. I felt a whole lot better about everything now that I knew that. The only sniper I needed to worry about was the one on my own team, who could be just as deadly, but wouldn't hurt me out of spite.

Millie looked at me again and I had to change the subject before I found myself kissing her avatar a second time. I couldn't start up a dream relationship with some random person who was drawn to the heiss it took to pull me into these games. Maybe she kept coming back because I was using too much. Maybe my heiss threshold was larger than normal, or maybe she just thought I was cute and would die for me. I tried not to laugh at that. Wasn't it usually the other way around—that girls imagined boyfriends who would be willing to die for them? Okay, I needed to change this subject.

"What does Veronica do all day?" I drew back from her, looking at her face, wondering how much information she had gathered so far.

"She has a really strange foot," Millie told me.

What did that mean? As a surfer, Millie wouldn't completely understand the system. She only knew what she had seen without any commentary. I pushed the backpack away from me that I still hadn't searched and grabbed for the cloth facemask. I tugged that on. It still concealed who I was, but allowed other people to see my expressions and kept my mouth unobstructed. I tried not to laugh at myself. I should not be thinking about virtual kissing. I used to think that there was no way I would ever be able to find the idea appealing. So maybe I was a bit more normal than I thought. I had better remember that I was at work and that virtual relationships were not satisfying.

I stepped out of the tent, drawing the looks of all the

men who expected me to calm them down—or rile them up. Still no words of commentary greeted my directional gaze. Maybe it wasn't only Nick that wrote on my screen. Leer could do it too. So what was he doing instead? Was he monitoring someone else? He did have other people who worked under him, but I just suspected that he was watching me, since everyone was worried about Millie. Maybe he had been drawn back to my side by my change in emotions?

"Words," I demanded. "Words can change the perspective of the day."

That got someone's attention. The words came back, and I scanned the names around me looking for a level guru. Who had been here the longest and knew clues about feet? There. Tod was the expert on the current world. I thumbed him over.

Behind me, Millie emerged from the tent. I gave her a short glance and stood confidently as I registered the men's expressions. Some were still nervous like Tod, but William was back in the game and ready to follow my lead. Millie's expression was the most telling. She was looking at me like I was the hottest guy on the planet, and her expression made me feel smug. Who doubted me? I so had this.

"I want to know everything you can find about feet or a foot," I told Tod. I laughed at his confused expression. "Think hard."

71

Then I met the eyes of the more hesitant while I left Tod to search his database in the air. The others were slacking. If they had work to do, they needed to do it instead of stare at me and watch me do it for them. With some direction they wouldn't be as scared. This Veronica that we had wasn't going to hurt us.

"Did the delightful devils detect the detour I left for them last night?" I asked Steph.

"And that detour was..." Steph trailed off.

"They have not dredged the river yet for the missing manufactured metals if that's what you're asking," William answered me. I gave him a smile for playing my game and he smiled back.

"How do we best stop the reptilian king from repeating his offenses with his coiling necklace?" I posed the question.

The answers came in. We could cut off all his suppliers. We could find the person he used to make the necklace and get rid of him. We could alter his programing or snipe him from the game, although we couldn't really kill the Earl when the entire game was called the Earl of Key Hill.

"Hand and foot!" Tod barged into me, grabbing at my arm excitedly like he had won the lottery.

"Like the sickness or the game?" I asked him.

72

"No. There are two people who are candy pops in the world. You know, written-in hidden features. One predicts the future and the other tells the past. One works through their hand and the other one through their foot. The linchpin is that they have to be close to each other for the ability to work."

So which was Veronica? Was she the future or the past? We had one of them, and if finding the future or the past was programed into the game, we were disrupting something important by having her. I thought about it and realized that this was not just important, but major. What could I expect a person who told the future to be but a program that sent other characters messages about the game play? The person who told the past had to be a database that stored every action taken by game players. We had an unexpected advantage over the Earl by having his daughter. We could reset the game by disrupting the magical hand and foot and changing the data.

"We're eating dessert early," I said loud enough for everyone to hear.

I turned back to Veronica, who was still standing at the tent entrance, ready to pry further into her comment and what she knew about it, but William stopped me.

"What are you doing with her? Can we end her yet?"

Kill Veronica's character? And here I thought that William was getting over his fear. It wouldn't stop Millie. He had no idea what he was dealing with. Millie would find some other character to inhabit and come back regardless of what happened to Veronica. Having her take over Veronica was invaluable. I needed to work on other ways to help Millie stop surfing.

There were two kinds of surfers. One surfer purposefully played through games illegally without paying for them. They connected to the world by searching for heiss. We had a company sniper that would kick those surfers out of games. The other kind of surfer held a job that helped legal snipers hunt for cheaters in games. The difference between the surfer and sniper was that hired surfers didn't hunt for people in real life, while the snipers would if they felt it became necessary to stop the law-breaking citizens. A lot of people called these surfers "snipers" as well, since they were still hunting for people. Millie was in a third category—playing through games without the intention to deceive anyone. She didn't realize what she was doing. How could I help her when I had no idea where she was? It wasn't like I could give her any heiss.

"Do you pull a linchpin before you set up the strike?" I questioned William. "This is great, Will. I'm going to use this. Give me a few minutes and we'll have a plan of action."

It was short work after that to learn Veronica's counterpart was her future-seeing mother named J. Lilly.

The woman had been taken by the Veterans, a group of players who had been playing in this game since it first started. Since J. Lilly's usefulness had been been discovered by this other party that was also against the Earl, it meant that the Veterans also had an advantage over us. I didn't like the idea of the Veterans holding all the game instructions that normally helped to direct the Earl's actions. What did the Veterans plan on doing with the person who directed the future in this game?

"Listen up, boys," I told everyone when I huddled them all together. My eyes moved over their names, their profiles.

"We have a chance to win a golden apple. We just need to close up the distance." I explained what I had in mind. We were going to capture J. Lilly from the Veterans and keep her apart from Veronica, thereby disrupting the message relays that the Earl could receive. "We know who is driving this train and where it's at. We just need a plan to go in and grab it."

"You're awesome," Phil told me. And then he took over by getting the men to look up maps and share information about where the Veterans would hide a person like J. Lilly. I glanced back at Veronica. She had sat down and was resting her head on her knees. I threw a rock at her.

"No sleeping," I ordered. "You'll get too comfortable and not wake up."

She made a face at me, but held her eyes open. She was surfing, which meant that in the real world she was not getting enough heiss to meet her body's demands. If she fell asleep here, I feared she would decide to never wake up. I had to keep her awake. Maybe some lively music was in order, just as soon as we finished plans to find her virtual mother.

Chapter 7

Millie

I just couldn't keep my eyes open in my dreams. I had found the energy to keep going this far, but I couldn't do it anymore. I missed the sun. I missed the open air. I missed seeing my family. My head was light. The dirt I was sleeping on was filling my nose, and I could feel the dryness start the nosebleed back up. I wiped at my nose and sat up.

"Go back to sleep," I heard the order from the guard on duty. I looked at him with my head swimming and my body wobbling, weary. I fell back onto the dirt, narrowly avoiding the sleeping form next to me.

"Stay awake!" This was from the Falcon. He pulled me to my feet. He was still wearing the black facemask, and I swayed on my feet before him too. "Listen, Veronica, you have to stay awake!"

"Okay," I answered unsure why my dreams and

reality were mixing.

I planted my feet wide, finding the ability to stand up at least in my dreams. I looked at the sky, really wanting to see it one more time in real life. This was as good as I was going to get. When the Falcon went back to his group huddle, I sat back down and shut my eyes again only to return to the hard floor of the mine. The dryness of the air around me made me wish that dreams were real.

My nose was really bleeding now. I wiped it and pinched the bridge trying to control the flow. I looked back up at the guard on duty in the mine. He headed toward me.

"You're not going to make it are you?" he asked with the slightest hint of concern.

"I'm fine," I answered.

I wanted to tell him that I wanted the sun. I wanted to tell him that I was tired of all the dirt and digging and blasting and nailing. He felt my forehead, and I realized that his hand was cold in comparison. Did I have a fever? Was that why I hallucinated so much? The blood was still running from my nose. I felt the guard grab one of my legs and start to drag me away.

Then I felt a sharp slap on my shoulder as if my dream had claws to snatch me back from reality. I had to be making it all up. Were last moments always like this?

"What did I tell you?" the Falcon demanded as his

78

arm retracted from his strike. This only served to remind me that I had no idea who he was or if he frequently hit people. I didn't know the man in my dreams. I didn't know anyone. I didn't know anything. My head was swimming.

"To stay awake."

"That's right."

The Falcon pulled me toward the campfire, demanding I stoke the fire to stay awake. Then he went back to his huddle while he continued glancing in my direction. I managed to stay awake only because I was so nervous that in reality my body was being dragged away. Where did the guards put people who had a fever? Where was I going to end up? I wasn't going to make it this time, was I? I returned the Falcon's gaze every time he looked at me.

I could see his eyes when I replayed the kiss in my head. It was my first kiss. I grinned at the thought of it. My first kiss had been fake. It had *felt* real. At least I had a good imagination. I could pretend I had gotten my first kiss before I died. Is that what was happening? I just had to know.

I closed my eyes when the Falcon wasn't looking at me effectively transferring my mental functions into my living body. My face was hot! The fever worked *that* fast? I had just realized the start of it. I opened my eyes, but couldn't see anything for the blinding light. This heat could not be a fever. Was this death? No way. I was awake. I shielded my eyes, trying to make out where I was. When I sat up, I screamed. I was in a pile of bodies inside a deep hole. The people in the mine had left me to die! I wasn't going to die! I ignored the bodies and the smell as best I could. I kept my gaze up and didn't dare think of what I was stepping on as I moved around the hole and found a way to climb out. Already my skin was drying. I could feel the start of sunburn. I hadn't been touched by the sun in ages.

It took most of my energy to climb out of the pit, and when I did, I looked around for shade. There were some trees off in the distance. I was on a mountain. That made sense. Where else did you find a good mine but in a mountain? Where was the entrance to the mine? I didn't want to be found wandering back that direction. I crawled my way to the shade of the trees until I found enough energy to walk.

My walking was shaky and I could feel my fever sapping the energy from me, but I pressed onward. I reached the trees and considered stopping, but knew that if I did, I wouldn't keep going. I had to get off the mountain and find some help. Maybe I could locate a trail and follow it down.

I walked for ages. Clouds came over the sun and covered it up. The air started to turn colder, and I wished for the heat to come back. I began to shiver. How had the temperature changed so quickly? I whimpered when the first snowflake hit my face. Then I stood in awe as the clouds dumped down a torrent of snow all around me. I was in a blizzard far away from shelter. I had to find some trees. I forced my feet to move until I felt a bucket of water dumped on my head. The added chill had me cringing. I shut my eyes only to be taken back to my dreams. This was so unreal.

"I mean it. You can't sleep here," the Falcon told me holding a dripping—but nearly empty—bucket. Veronica was soaked. I wanted to tell my dream man that I wasn't sleeping, but the only thing that came out was a plea.

"Too cold. It was too hot and now it's too cold. Maybe the mine was better than this. How did it get so cold? It was burning. Can you get a sunburn and snowburn at the same time?"

"What are you talking about? I have to go do something." He jerked his head to the side. "Whatever you do, don't fall asleep here."

I looked around to find that it was night in my dreams. The time and weather could change so rapidly. I nodded, and he walked away to his tent. Then I shut my eyes again, because this couldn't be real.

Too cold! I had fallen over, tripped into the snow that was now seeping into the tops of my shoes. But the good news was that from this position I could see a tree. It was over the ridge, and I couldn't imagine what I might be slipping on to get down there to reach it, but I was going to try for it anyway. I needed something to help me. I wished I could find a trail, but with all the snow covering the ground the thought felt fruitless. My only hope was to head down. There had to be something at the bottom of the mountain.

Chapter 8

Sebastian

"Morning, Nick," I said, calling the emergency number I had been given. I instantly recognized Nick's voice and was doing my best to keep this conversation light because my mom was in the room scrambling together breakfast for my little brother with the food I had brought home the previous night.

"You're going to die?" Nick asked me with a flat voice.

"No. I need to change my work hours," I replied.

I didn't glance at my mother, Ellen, a tall woman with dyed blond hair. We didn't have money for hair dye and her red roots were starting to show through again. I knew how she was going to take this. She was holding her tongue, but she often questioned me about where I worked, and how I got the money. It made me feel like being able to provide for my family was a *bad* thing. Mom was out most days, still looking for a job. It was hard to find good-paying work when our living accommodations testified that we might not be staying long.

"What's going on?" Nick asked, more at ease since I didn't sound like I was being attacked or driven out of hiding.

"I need to help a friend. So I just need to shift my hours. That's all."

I had hardly slept last night. A bad night's sleep was one of the worst things I could have for this job, because it was deadly if I fell asleep while working. Some people couldn't wake up if they became unconscious while on heiss. I had no doubt that Nick would probably come and slap me, and then send a very small rescue team in after me if I failed to wake up. I would be fine, except that changing my hours was a long shot. Part of the job requirements was to get sleep. I had stayed awake trying to think of ways to help Millie. I knew that I wasn't the only person she followed, but she was riding my waves. When I was on heiss, her starving body would search for it. She was more prone to slip into dream worlds when I was there, because she had tagged me—locked onto my wave. I contributed to her problem of confusing reality with "dreams." She was in trouble. After all the times she had died for me, I couldn't fathom her dying in real life. I had thought about her all night long

84

puzzling out her situation.

"What time are you coming in?" Nick asked.

"Six," I answered. I ignored looking at my mom. She had frozen, perhaps trying to decipher who my employer was.

"At night?" Nick's voice was low as if he couldn't quite believe what I was asking. "Just for today?"

"Well uh… for the week, maybe."

"Seb, if I say yes to this, and you don't show up at all…"

"I'll be there. I promise. You know I need this job, Nick. I just have to help someone."

"I'm not your counselor, but this in an emergency number not the 'my dog is sick' hotline."

"This is an emergency," I insisted putting all my resolve into that statement. "I will be in at six."

"You only get today," Nick told me. "You get that emergency straightened out and get in here as soon as you can."

Nick clicked the call short, miraculously sending my heart rate back to normal parameters. It had been slowly creeping up the longer I talked with him. I was scared he would tell me no, and Millie would die leaving me to be the only one who knew about it. That would eat at my conscience for the rest of my life. I was determined to find where she currently was from the small clues she had given me. That was what I would be doing today if I could keep myself awake. I could do it. I had to do it for Millie.

"What friend?" Mom asked me.

I looked at her, still poised with the turner in her hand ready to stir the eggs. Even Triton, my younger brother, had decided not to move. He stared at me too, with his hands on the table, his red hair curling around his ears, as if I were Dad telling everyone that I was going out to look for a job and never coming back again. I wasn't that person. I wouldn't leave them. I wondered if Dad, or should I just call him Regis, had taken this same job and run away from us before a sniper made the connection between him and us. I pushed the thought aside.

"Guys, you don't need to worry. Nothing is wrong."

"Nothing is wrong?" Mom could level a guy with a glance. Her steel expression, the anger and tears she was holding back in her eyes… Yup. She could bulldoze me over.

"Not with us. There's nothing wrong for us."

"So who's the friend?"

"Just a friend," I shrugged. "I need to get going so I can get to work."

"Where do you work, Seb? Don't tell me you've been out gambling."

"What?" How could she think that of me? I stayed away from that part of town. I hoped she did too. Besides, gambling didn't give you a consistent amount of cash each day. "No! This is a different sort of friend. She only needs me to do a little research. I'll be in the library."

"You're losing your job because of a girl?" Mom asked. She slammed the turner onto the table with the effectiveness of a flyswatter. I was pretty sure I was supposed to be the fly. "She's nothing, Seb. Do you hear me? Don't lose your job because of some girl. This is your family, and I won't have you walking away from that. I've been quiet about your questionable job, your dodgy attitude, but I can't keep quiet if you're ruining our life for some bogus research. I didn't raise you to be a quitter like your father."

"I need to get going," I told Mom before she could stab me with her fears any longer. "And I'm coming back. I promise. Oh, I heard that there's a lady on Sumac Street that will give you work if you give her a marble."

"The Dowager?" Mom asked, trying to sound interested while I backed up for the front door. "That's how you get her work?"

"It's worth a try. See you later. I'm not going in to work until six, so I won't be back until tomorrow morning sometime."

"Don't let me down, Sebastian."

Mom glared at me as I turned the door handle and escaped out into the light of the day. I ran to the library. Nick hadn't sounded that accepting of me changing my hours. I had to figure out where Millie was as fast as possible. There was no one else who could help her.

Chapter 9

Sebastian

Since I was late, I jumped straight into being the Falcon wishing to find Millie and confirm that she was alive. I didn't start in the tent, and I wasn't standing off on my own. Instead, I was in front of battle plans to capture Veronica's mother. All the plans had been written up and were laid out before me. We had located exactly where J. Lilly was being held—inside a tower in the Veteran's base. It would take us a short jump to reach the location and then we were fighting the war.

I looked behind me to see more men than usual. Their names flashed over my screen, telling me that I had known them for long periods of time. I didn't believe it. My eyes focused on William, Step, Phil, and Samson: the people that I actually trusted around me. The rest of the men were new and only here for this battle. I should have expected different people since I had changed my work hours. The other people would have gone home by now.

I glanced over at the campfire, and then around at everyone else quickly. Where was Veronica? She wasn't there anymore. I held down my panic as I walked over to William. He always seemed to know what was going on.

"Where's Veronica hiding?" I asked him.

"She's not," William told me, straightening his spine. "She fell asleep last night and when she woke up, she was horrid, so I took her out. Whatever you were using to control Veronica broke."

Millie. Millie was no longer trying to inhabit Veronica. I would have to pay close attention tonight to spot her controlling a different avatar. How likely was it that I would recognize her when I was going to be concerned with this battle? Then again, she was easy to spot if she saved me.

"Where have *you* been?" William asked me. "I don't want to hear any flak about Veronica."

I shrugged. It didn't matter much that Veronica was gone. I should have seen that coming. If Millie wasn't taking over her character, then Veronica's real programing was going to come through. We had no more use for Veronica, and so it made sense to destroy the database when we had it in front of us.

"Are there any last-minute preparations we need to take, Steph?" I asked him as he stepped over to us.

"Only one," Steph answered. He drew a knife and lunged at me.

Was he kidding me? Who did he think I was? I grabbed his arm, wrestling to keep him off me. He tried to knock off my mask. Is that what his deal was? He was trying to unmask me. I wasn't about to let that happen. No hidden sniper was going to unmask me.

"You're going to turn into fried chicken," I told him as I pulled my head away from his arms.

William came up behind him, and chopped his head off. I stood there watching as Steph's character fell to the ground and then disappeared. We were not playing games today. If he was attacking me, the person playing Steph was probably not the person I had spoken with the other days. I looked around again at the other men and my eyes found Samson. Half his body was starting to deteriorate. He was looking down at himself, aghast.

"Don't get close. I have a virus," Samson told me.

That was obvious and I didn't want that spreading. Where had it come from? Someone around us wasn't who they were supposed to be, which meant that we had been invaded. Was this the work of the Vikings or the Veterans? I felt my heart rate pick up. The war was supposed to be at the tower, not here in our own camp. Had I messed this up? When Millie had left Veronica did it give the Vikings enough time to figure out where we were? Did they know all of our attack plans already? Was I going to start fading away? We had taken out Veronica, and the Vikings were trying to pick us apart. No one was safe except perhaps for William, who was looking at me with caution as if I wasn't me, either.

"Sorry about this," I told Samson as I ignored William's attention and my own unease. The Falcon was already decked out for the mission to reach the tower. I pulled my bow from around my back and made a hard decision. I shot Samson. Then I aimed it at the guy next to him and shot him too. I wondered if my real body was flinching. It had been unnerving to be sent in after Dean and wake him up after he thought he was dead. I hoped that Samson would be able to wake up after the abrupt change in his thoughts.

"Hey, I am on your side," said an avatar that I didn't recognize.

"Can you prove it?" I asked, and then I shot him too.

William and Phil took up their weapons and started in with me. A few people blinked out before we reached them. Other people grabbed their weapons and started attacking anyone next to them. To say it was a blood bath would have been accurate, except our game didn't show blood. My blood pressure was skyrocketing. I could feel the need to start running in real life, and yet I knew I was stuck to the table dreaming. I was probably twitching as my fight and flight response was activated.

I had no idea who was on my side. The men were tearing each other apart obviously unsure of the same thing. Lots of people I didn't know ran at me head on, trying to smash me down. Phil was whacked on the head by an unknown avatar. I shot the guy who got Phil and grabbed William before launching into the air and flying toward the tower. The people down on the ground grabbed bows, trying to shoot us down.

"Just you and me. How do we need to modify our plans to get Veronica's mother?"

"You know, I'm still trying to figure out what just happened," William told me.

"Our group of bandits is down to two," I answered.

"But Phil…"

"Phil and Samson were still on our side," I agreed. "We need to press on Will. Got any bright ideas?"

"We can't invade with just two people," William told me.

"Alright. I'll concoct a new plan."

I got to work on thinking about the plan we already had established. J. Lilly was in a tower. Our previous plan was to draw out all the guards with a few explosions and bomb arrows. We were going to light things on fire, but that had changed.

"It wasn't real," I reminded William below me since he was still breathing heavy. I wondered how I was doing in real life. I had to be awfully tired, but I couldn't feel it while hooked up to the heiss—not unless my energy levels started getting really bad.

We closed in on the tower, and I could see the drawn schematics that I had just looked at were correct. The Veteran's base was encased in a wall with archers. I could make out battering rams and foot soldiers. They had yet to spot us, as they were looking toward the east where we had planned to come in from. I had taken us to the west side. It wasn't as close to the tower as I would have liked.

My plan was to charge the tower. We were going to get hit, and I didn't think that Millie was going to jump into the air with any strange avatar and save me.

"They would have moved J. Lilly, the mother," William said below me. He, too, looked at the tower and the fortifications that were set up to stop our advance. "You have your plan?"

"Capture Veronica's mother," I told him. "That's who gives them instructions. We need to stop that."

"Where would they have moved her?" Will wondered. "What does it look like they are protecting the most? We've got two chances with this. I'll go in first, and if

I fail, you'll follow."

"You know you're going to get hit, right?" I asked him.

"Yup. I've been hit before. It's not pleasant, but I'll wake up. How about you?"

"I don't think I can answer questions like that," I told him.

William looked up at me with a grin on his face. Did he think I was funny for getting him to admit to being a real player? We were both obviously real players, and even though William wasn't on my team with Leer, I guessed he worked in the same building as me.

He told me to drop him off at the center of the fortifications. He pulled out a bomb arrow as I flew him over, and then he shot a bucket of ammunition next to a battering ram. The bucket on the ground exploded causing a large distraction away from where I was setting him down. I dropped him and zipped back to the air while the soldiers raised cries of alarm.

They jumped to their posts and started firing into the east, apparently hoping to hit at things they couldn't see. I watched as William fought it out on the ground, bringing another crowd his direction as he tried to reach the inside of the central room. I didn't think we were doing this right. If they'd known we were coming and then they planned on fading some of us out with the virus, then they could expect us to try to rethink our plans. They might expect us to not show up at all. They were making it look like the center was the place they didn't want us to reach, but my gut feeling was still set on the tower.

I mentally wished William luck and landed quietly on top of the tower. Using a bomb arrow that my character had previously packed, I blew a hole in the top of the tower, and then before I could lose my nerve I jumped through. There she was. J. Lilly was looking up at the hole, surrounded by a group of outfitted soldiers—two of them were archers. They shot me as I fell into the room, but I didn't blink out right away. It took me a second to realize why. My character was written into the program. I wasn't invading the system. The bird watchers—us—had taken over control of the avatar and I couldn't be destroyed with a single hit. That wasn't a good thing. I was filling up with arrows and I could *feel* them. That only happened if my mortal body was exhausted, right? Where was Millie when a man wanted an angel?

I reminded myself that I wasn't real and pulled out my bow, though I never got off the shot. One of the soldiers lunged at me. I dodged his attack while he called me a demon. And then, since my one chance was fading quickly, I used my ability to fly right over Veronica's mother. There was no time to grab her and carry her away. My plans were changing yet again. I had to disrupt the communication of this game to stop the Vikings. I pulled out my sword and shoved it down; grateful again that gore was not part of this system.

The soldiers around me dragged me down as J. Lilly fell. The walls started to fade away, proving that I was correct. We could reset the system and kick out the Vikings if we disrupted Veronica's mother, who held the instructions for this game. One of the Vikings tried to pull off my mask. I clung onto it as the entire world became black. I was floating in darkness, trying to piece together my confusion. The instructions had stopped. For William's sake, I hoped his character had been kicked out before he reached the floating black darkness that I was in. How did I get out of it?

"Seb!" I heard the scream. I felt the slap to my face as well.

"That worked," I told Leer.

I would have yanked myself upright if I could, but my body refused to move that fast. I opened my eyes and patted my chest, trying to calm down my beeping heart. Why was it still beeping? Was my armband still on? Was I making up the fact that I had woken up? Was I really still asleep? I looked at my armband only to find it off. There was another band on above where the heiss cuff usually fit. So Leer hooked me up to things when I wasn't aware of it. What did this additional band do? I didn't like that.

"Sorry," Leer told me.

He shut off the beeping sound, and then rushed back to my side. I could still feel my heart racing thinking about what I had just seen and done. I knew I had done exactly what I was supposed to. I had stolen the Viking's database, Veronica, and we had destroyed it. I had infiltrated the Veteran's tower, and terminated the instructions program. But it didn't make sense for the Vikings to let the Veterans take J. Lilly so easily. Why had the Vikings not destroyed their own program earlier when they had been invaded by two different groups—unless the Veterans were the ones who belonged to the game and the Vikings had been invading? Where was the flaw in my logic?

We had won, although I didn't like the idea of the Veterans, whoever they really were, having gotten the upper hand on us first. Even with the victory I still felt like I had let the men down. I had started them on killing each other. And now that the system was down I was questioning what I was doing. What exactly was I shutting down? What kind of spy was I? Was I in the right, or was I really the enemy here destroying something that should be left alone?

"It was only a game, Seb. It wasn't real," Leer told me. "You did a great job. You did more than a great job."

"Did they wake up?" I asked him. There was no way to send in anyone to wake up the men if the level was terminated and they thought they were asleep there. "Did I fail them?"

"Is that what you're worried about?" Leer turned back to his monitors and started typing while I tried and failed to get a grip on what I did for a job. "Just fine. Yes they all woke up. You did great."

Leer talked me through a few mental regrouping exercises. I thought he had a boring job, looking after someone like me and making sure I didn't scare myself silly. He was really nice. He turned into a good guidance counselor, and even though he suggested I could leave work early, I decided to stick it out. I hadn't found Millie.

My next missions were nothing like working the Flying Falcon. Maybe when I got enough money, I would buy that game myself. Playing his character was something I looked forward to, and I had reset the game now so I doubted I would ever go back otherwise. The Earl of Key Hill would be a fun game to play. I wanted to charge at the Earl and try to steal his key. Maybe I would manage to get some magic from the well and turn myself into a bandit wizard. I could think of lots of chaos that a bandit wizard could create.

Instead of fun, I was left to walk around a dungeon infested with oversized worms and long-toothed rabbits, searching for a secret chest that was generating money. Since the money wasn't supposed to be there, I needed to destroy the chest. When I finally found it after hours of searching I was sent to a haunted house. I passed a crying ghost four times before I realized that the voice belonged to Millie.

"Do you need help?" I asked her. "How can I help you?"

"I'm hungry." She looked down at her ghost form, apparently realizing that even in her dreams she wouldn't be able to eat anything this time. "I'm cold too."

"I think I know where you are. Just stay awake."

"But I am awake," she told me before she faded from view.

I wasn't sure if she faded because she was a ghost or because she had died on me. I felt helpless. I didn't know what else to do when I couldn't reach her. Maybe once I got off work, I would be able to find something—if I could manage to keep myself awake.

However, when I unplugged, staying awake was harder than I'd imagined. I was going to fall asleep on my feet and Nick knew it. He was in the room when Leer disconnected me from the armband. He didn't say anything. He didn't even glance at my screen. Perhaps he had been in here for a while wishing I hadn't been late today so *he* could go to sleep. I sat up, my energy ebbing away as a sick feeling entered my stomach from confusing my body's rhythm. I wasn't hungry. I couldn't fathom being hungry. *Millie* was hungry.

I gave Leer and Nick a nod and headed for the

hallway. I could change my clothes, go home, and sleep. That's all I wanted to do right now. On the way to the changing room I stopped by the vending machines and grabbed a water bottle.

I took a sip of the water, hoping that would help keep me awake. Maybe if I needed to pee really bad on the way home, I wouldn't be able to fall asleep on my feet. I was one step away from my clothes, and seriously contemplating sleeping on top of them in my changing room, when I saw Nick standing in the way, talking with a well-built dark-skinned man. His voice matched that of Will, so I scanned the rest of his face, noting his stubbly chin and dark hair and steady legs. He didn't look as exhausted as me. Great. I was glad that he had woken up, but I was under orders to never talk with my coworkers outside of my work room. I put on my game face, refusing to look tired as I stepped closer. Where did Will work? What was his angle, coming to talk with Nick?

"Tagged?" Nick asked with a short glance at me.

I didn't answer, and he looked back at Will. *Please don't make me lose my job, Will.* I lost my composure, letting the tiredness show. Will was turning me in. Maybe I had time to defend myself before I lost my job. Mom would never forgive me if I lost this job. Where was I going to get work?

"The south floor is calling her Sleeping Beauty," Will

told Nick. "I was hoping you could spare a guy to approve contact. What's this guy doing?" Will nodded his head at me, making it look like we had never met before. I gave him a smile before I took a few steps to the side so I could push my tired body up against the wall for support.

"That guy is going home to bed—if he even makes it that far."

"Well I like him," Will stated. "He looks capable. I could use a little sleep myself, but not as much as I could use that kid."

"Something came up." Nick shrugged, covering for me.

"The Vikings don't know that Veronica isn't on their side anymore. This could be exactly what you're looking for to turn the tide. When we find Sleeping Beauty, we can get her to switch sides. We'll send her into the Vikings and she can stop them."

Veronica. They were talking about her, and we hadn't stopped the Vikings for good. That put a dampener on my already sad spirits. Where had the Vikings regrouped? I almost corrected Will to tell him what Veronica's real name was. She was Millie. I had no idea where she had come from, but from my research today, I was guessing she was working in the Doldrum Mine. It was the only mine that experienced such vast temperature changes, and was close enough to our area that Millie would be able to find our heiss by being there.

"She's in the Nashville Mountains," I told Will. I was risking it, I knew. I had no idea if Will was out to kill her, but she would die if she wasn't found, and what was I going to do about it? Besides, Will had saved me today. He had stopped the infested Steph from pulling my mask off.

"I, uh…" I looked at Nick as he turned to me with his hands on his hips. "I spent all day researching her location. She's got to be there. That's the only place that experienced such a vast temperature drop that also has a mine nearby. She's freezing near the Doldrum Mine right now. It's the only mine around."

"How much do you know about this?" Nick questioned me. He narrowed his eyes. I had seen him give that same look to Dean before, resulting in Dean getting suspended for a day. I wondered if Dean had started to question his workload too. What did we get rid of exactly? Despite my fears, I couldn't afford to lose a day of work at the moment. I really wanted to go home and sleep.

"You promised you weren't tagged?" Will wondered.

"I'm not." It must have been my great fatigue because I heard myself giving out the information that I had been withholding. "She's surfing. She's been following our heiss signatures here at Visions. She jumps to my side when there are more connected people around me, because she's

103

pulled by the wave. I must be using a lot of heiss. It's not the same as being tagged. She's not working for anyone," I told Will. "She's escaping the Doldrums, and she's freezing."

"Sounds like your kind of person, Nick," Will told him. "We got a surfer who doesn't know anything. We can send your security boy in after her, tell her to meet us, and get her out of the Nashville Mountains."

We were going to help Millie? I pushed myself off the wall, looking at Will and then at Nick hopefully. I could hear my mother's poisonous words floating back to me. I was not to lose my job because of Millie. She was nothing to me... but she was. She was my angel. She was keeping me from losing my job by saving my life so I could work. She was helping me protect my family.

"You willing to work overtime?" Nick asked me after he shook his head at Will.

"You're sending me?" I asked Nick. I resisted plopping back against the wall, but it was hard. "He said security."

"You *are* security. Get back to your room and get some sleep. I'll wake you up when we have a location for you and Sleeping Beauty."

"I..." Nick glared at me. He'd told me when I was hired that I was playing a game to get information. He'd told me I was a spy. He'd said nothing about me being security for the system.

"I can't be security. I have a family to protect," I protested.

"You're good at it, Seb." Nick glared again. "Don't tell me that you're not. You identified a surfer without panicking, and then," Nick coughed, "you made the rest of us change our work plans so you could turn into a sniper and hunt a person down."

Nick talked about my actions with a lethally detached voice as if I was an actual sniper that he had hired. I wasn't the kind of person who hunted down real living people and attacked them for pay. I knew that surfers could turn into snipers, but not all of them did. I could hardly believe that I was working security. Bad things happened to people who worked in security. They were the first ones that snipers went after, but how was I going to find a different job?

"She was freezing," I made my lame excuse.

"Go get some sleep. I'll wake you up when we have an idea of how to find Veronica."

"Sleeping Beauty," Will provided.

"Her name is Millie," I told them.

They both glared at me, and I pushed myself back the way I had come to the bed I wasn't supposed to sleep on—ever. I didn't care right now. I had to get some sleep before I was hooked back up, even if sleeping here risked confusing my body. It didn't look like Nick was concerned. He had to find a way to connect me with so much heiss that Millie was pulled under my wave and brought into my visuals. Was that safe to do when I was tired? I didn't think so. I stumbled back to my work room so I could get all the sleep I could manage.

Chapter 10

Millie

I was hallucinating. I was walking along, one step at a time, and there he was standing in front of the frozen path like the grim reaper. Only he didn't look cold. He didn't move, either. So where was the weapon of death that was going to strike me down? Was it the cold hand of icy air? Was Rhino Man put into my dreams to be a warning to me that I didn't have much longer left to live? How did I reconcile that with him telling me never to fall asleep in my dream world? I believed I was awake and not sleeping right now. But he was here, so I had to be asleep. I was blurring the lines of asleep and reality — again.

"Sorry, Millie," Mr. Rhino told me. "Great graphics you have going on." He looked around the snowy mountain, taking in the atmosphere that was going to kill me. "That's Settler's Pass. We have a direct match. Yes."

Mr. Rhino looked like he was reading invisible words in the air. I was losing it. He turned in circles and pointed out more landmarks: a boulder, a drop off, the frozen trail head that I had missed. I had found a trail? Maybe I was making it all up just because I wanted to find one so badly. I sank into the snow, the drifts covering me up to my waist. I closed my eyes and let the snow take me. He yanked me to my feet.

"Don't you fall asleep!" he shouted at me. "I know you're cold. You have to stay awake. Stay right here. Build an igloo around yourself and stay right here. There are people coming to help you. Start building and don't stop until you can block out the wind and crawl inside. Don't stop," he ordered again.

"Is this real life?" I asked him as he pushed some snow into a snowball and set it next to me. "I can't do this."

"You *can* do this. I'm counting on you and you haven't let me down yet," he whispered into my ear as he grabbed my hands and helped me to form a snowball.

I made a second one, and then blinked and all my work was gone. I stared at the flat snow coming up to my waist. Yes, I was finally losing it. I couldn't tell the difference between being awake and asleep. I pushed together another snowball, however. I had no idea where the energy was coming from, but I could hear the wisdom in the words. I had to keep going. I had to make this work. I had to get myself warmer.

I couldn't feel my hands anymore. I blew warm air on them, and even that I couldn't feel. I blinked and he was back again with a snow fort built halfway up already. The sight of it made me cry. It was mocking me. Which was the real fort? Which attempt at getting warm was the one that was going to save me? I dug back into the snow continuing to stack the walls.

"The team is sent out, Millie. You'll be looking for men wearing bright yellow. If anyone else comes to get you, run away. Only go with the guys wearing yellow, got it?"

"At this point, Mr. Rhino, I would follow a bear into his den."

"No you will not. You will only follow the people wearing yellow."

He moved over to me and wrapped his arms around me. I could almost feel the warmth, but when I leaned forward all I got for my effort was to find myself face-first in the snow with no living soul around. I wished I could sleep instead of stack snow. I was too tired to work, and every part of me was freezing. I stayed where I was and dug straight down. Who cared about building a fort, anyway? I was going to build a cocoon.

I had a small circle made for my body when I found myself standing again, looking at a completed snow fort. Mr.

Rhino was there with his back to me. He still didn't look cold, but he seemed shaken, as if he was staring at a grave.

"It doesn't have a tombstone yet," I told him. He spun around, scanning me over with a smile that told me I was way worse than he expected. He looked great with his brown hair, wide eyebrows, and perfectly pink lips. See, he wasn't blue. He couldn't be cold. He was a dream.

"You're going to make it. They're almost there."

"None of this is real, you know," I told him.

"Just don't fall asleep." He had to be talking to himself, because he closed his eyes and vanished.

"I have a visual!" a man screamed.

I turned to look at the stranger in bright yellow snow gear. So this was the end, then. Mr. Rhino was gone, and his words were coming to haunt me. I was going to fall asleep in the snow and never wake up again. The rescuer in yellow jumped to my side, preventing my brilliant escape – sleeping—from any version of reality by grabbing my arm. He slung me over his shoulder and I screamed.

Chapter 11

Sebastian

"Seb!" the sound hurt. There was a light on and that hurt too. After a loud ripping sound, I felt the pressure of duct tape being pulled off my sore arm. It felt like this had been going on a while. My arm was turning red.

"Stop," I mumbled. I just wanted to sleep. I wasn't going to make it home to get to sleep. Mom was going to be worried. I was already working late. I'd told her I wouldn't be home until the next day, but what would she think if it was two days until I managed to get back? She was going to worry that I had left her. I was still coming back, just after I got some sleep.

"He stabilized," I could hear Leer saying.

"Sometimes I need a less stressful job," Nick commented.

"He'll make it."

"Think I can pull off being him in the simulation today?" Nick asked. "Stable does not mean he will be coherent enough to work his normal shift."

"I don't think anyone can act like Seb can," Leer answered.

Maybe that's because I wasn't acting. Everything was real. I heard the falseness of my words as I voiced them in my head. I was just overly tired and overly stimulated. I had pushed my body to the max so that I could save Millie. I smiled at that. There you go, Millie. There's a random guy that will nearly die for you. I felt my emotions flare up with the thought, and I could hear the beep that came with it on my monitor.

"He's fine," Leer told Nick. Did Leer wear the monitor with him? He sounded close, and it didn't sound like he had turned to look at the screen.

Nick had managed to blur reality really well for Millie. I was probably using sniper technology to assist him. I had never seen this extra equipment that could help track a person's heiss wave by locking onto it, although I guessed it looked like a box with an armband. The device was super expensive and rare. In some places it was illegal to own one. When I'd gotten my instructions on the screen, after not getting enough sleep, I was told that I should be looking at what Millie was projecting as her reality. From that, I could figure out how it worked.

Nick and Leer had given me so much heiss that Millie was pulled toward me since she had tagged my heiss signature. Instead of pulling the players into a normal game like most armbands did, this device created the game by stealing into Millie's confusion. It tagged *her*, and she unknowingly gave away her location while she attempted to control herself in her real surroundings by fighting against the dreams and her reality every time they shifted. She created the game.

The snow and the mountains were a good giveaway for her position, and she was tired enough that everything worked. Not sleeping could really kill you. I promised myself that if I ever did have a sniper chasing my trail, I would get enough sleep so my reality couldn't give me away. But it was saving Millie, and I had finally gotten to see what she looked like.

That had been a little nerve wracking. I was scared that I would find myself looking at some sixty-year-old lady. Wouldn't that be embarrassing because I had kissed her? Why had I done that? I kept repeating the conversation in the tent and how I'd wanted Millie to realize the difference between reality and virtual reality. She knew the difference. I'd just wanted her to see it, although I probably hadn't helped anything.

Millie was not a sixty-year-old lady. She was a beautiful, freezing girl with color-changing hair. I thought

Nick was doing it on purpose to throw me off. I couldn't figure out if she was blond or brunette. The length of hair stayed the same just past her shoulders. Her blue eye color stayed the same as well. I hadn't noticed a ring on her hands when I'd asked her to build a snow fort. I had looked for one several times, wondering if she was married or single. I just wanted to make sure that I hadn't kissed anyone creepy, although it was a virtual kiss so it didn't really count.

I heard my monitor beep again as my emotions picked back up. I liked Millie better than Veronica no matter what her hair color was. I wondered if I would ever see her again, because I wanted to. What if I never saw her again? There was more beeping from my monitor as I started to worry.

"It's alright, Sebastian," Nick told me. "You're not losing your job for sleeping on the job." He laughed at his own joke. I went back to sleep.

Chapter 12

Millie

I was sitting in a modified dentist chair. The comfortable chair could lower down into a bed. I had been given a lot of lotion, which was nice, and food—which was even better—and warm clothes, which were heavenly. After being carried down the mountain, I had been taken away in a van. Then put on an airplane. Then I was helped into a warm car. I tried to not ask too many questions. Mr. Rhino had been right. He had actually sent someone to come save me. I wished I could thank him, but I hadn't been able to find him yet when I shut my eyes. Whenever I tried to search, I was pulled awake again as the doctors around me placed a pressure cuff on my arm. They kept looking at me like I was an anomaly. I thought my blood pressure was fine. All I wanted to do was dream up Mr. Rhino and find out why my dreams had leaked into my reality. That had never happened before.

"What are we at?" a lean man with spiky blond hair asked as he came into the room. The doctors straightened and made sure they were looking busy as he walked over to the screen. "What?!" he asked. He looked at me, and then back at the screen. "Shut it off."

"That's a bad idea, Nick," the doctor that kept placing the pressure cuff on me told him. He looked at the screen too, and then stood by the cuff to keep it right where he wanted it. "She goes under when it comes off. There are too many waves directly around her for her to stay awake."

"Everything you just said was really confusing," I told the doctor.

"This is really expensive," the new person, Nick, told him. He reached over and tore off the pressure cuff.

Hey, I could shut my eyes again. I closed them back up, trying to find Mr. Rhino among my dreams. I found myself in a business meeting. There was a person standing before a poster that had a report featuring employee performance rates. I was sitting at a long table with a lot of other people looking at the poster. The presenter looked like a bodybuilder who had been shoved into a suit. His arms were almost too large for the sleeves—his long black hair threatened to tumble into his eyes.

"And the outlier line? That one is new," a man wearing a striped gray suit said. He had gray hair and a nice smile, but I got that his smile was not entirely real. He wasn't happy about the outlier.

"That is new. We're working on that," the reporter man answered.

"I can see the asterisks at the bottom of it. We tagged one of our own people? Is this person dangerous?"

"No. In fact, that person is my personal responsibility, and like I said I am taking care of it. Shall we move on?"

"Why have we tagged our top performer?"

The presenter flipped to a new poster, and I hadn't spotted Mr. Rhino, so I blinked, hoping to change my dream. It worked and I found him. It may have been two days since I dreamed him up. But maybe he wasn't a dream?

Mr. Rhino was playing chess against a ninja. Both men were wearing gear that hid them completely, but I could find Mr. Rhino behind any mask. I waved, and I guessed he could find me too, because he looked at his opponent worried. I wondered if the man was going to jump across the table and stab him. I shrugged, not willing to jump in the way, and gave Mr. Rhino the sign language for thank you. Mr. Rhino kicked his opponent's chair so that the man looked down. He apologized to the man for the kick, and then quickly blew a kiss in my direction.

I woke up with a smile on my face. Nick was in my face too. The pressure cuff was replaced and Nick looked back at the screen with a scowl.

"Where did you go?" he asked me.

"I don't know," I told him. "What makes you think I went anywhere? I was just dreaming."

"No, Millie. You don't dream. You surf. You know what virtual reality is?" I nodded. "You keep breaking into our gaming world and stealing into top security profiles. You're hacking our system every time you fall asleep. You are not sleeping—you are capitalizing on the energy of our heiss."

"What's heiss?" I asked. So I wasn't making up the dreams? I was... doing what? So Mr. Rhino was real? "Can you say all that again?"

"Describe heiss," Nick told the doctor.

"Heiss is a chemical that normally puts your body to sleep so you can enter the virtual gaming world. In your particular case, you've been starved of the stuff, and *not* having it puts you to sleep."

"I'm on a drug right now?" I asked, looking at my arm. That's what they were putting into my arm: heiss.

"More or less." The doctor shrugged. "I believe you'll stop needing it soon. You've been surfing in your sleep trying to find it, which makes me believe you're a natural-born sniper." The doctor stopped talking about snipers when Nick nudged him.

"In any case, a normal person who doesn't jump into dreams has a heiss level of twenty. Nick here won't hire anyone that can't handle up to fifty."

"Sixty," Nick interrupted. "If they can't handle sixty, I haven't been hiring them. I raised the bar a few weeks back, which might be why we got stuck with Millie."

"And you, Millie, have passed sixty," the doctor told me without any sign that being stuck with me was a bad thing. "We're at eighty-five," the doctor winced. "It was seventy when Nick came in."

"It's supposed to put me to sleep?" I asked, looking at the screen, which was still climbing. "So why is it not working again?" It was doing the exact opposite. The heiss was keeping me awake. The doctors looked at each other with uncomfortable smiles.

"What's it looking like?" The body-building man who I had just spotted presenting the posters entered the room. He looked at the screen—and then at me awake—and nearly swore. I gawked at him. My dreams were leaking into my reality even more now. This was getting confusing. I had just seen him while dreaming.

"I thought you would be too busy to show up. You ever see this before?" Nick asked him. "This is Leer," Nick told me. "Once we convince you to work for us, you'll be assigned to him."

"Work for you? I can't do that," I told Nick. "I have to find my mom and dad. I have no idea if they made it out. I'm not working here."

"Yes you are," Nick told me. "To put it nicely, you will work here if you want to stay alive."

"Okay," Leer told Nick, pushing Nick behind him to cover up the urgency of his threat. "I'll handle this. Yes I have seen this before, but only once."

"When we take her off the heiss, she waves under," one of the doctors told Leer as if I was a strange phenomenon. I gave the doctor a glare and Leer gave me a smile.

"She'll do that until she maxes out. Should be any time now." He glanced at the screen, which read ninety. "Here's what I think we're looking at. It happens from time to time that a person who handles heiss really well meets another heiss guzzler in a virtual world and they fall in love. They run off to, say… Ocean View?" Leer didn't guess my hometown correctly, although he did pick a place that was low on technology.

"No one follows after them because we think they got scared of a sniper and hightailed it out of there. Then they have a kid. We're looking at the kid. You're going to be just fine, Millie, but I don't think you're going to find your parents very easily. If you want to locate them, you'll have to train to be a better surfer and hunt them down the hard way. They'll have run away where there is so little heiss they can't be tempted to wave. And if they didn't find another spot without heiss, then they might have taken up working for some other company hoping to hunt *you* down. It's in your best interest to work for us so you can meet your parents. And as Nick pointed out, you'll find it rather hard to say no."

I shook my head at them and glanced back at the screen. The number hadn't changed, and I didn't feel tired at all.

"I want to find my parents," I said again. "We got stopped before crossing the border, but I promise we're all legal citizens."

"I will help you achieve that goal one step at a time," Leer told me. "Where do you want to start?"

"I'm going to start by getting out of this chair."

I pulled off the arm cuff myself and jumped off the seat. Would they block me from running? I had no idea where I was, and I had no money to buy a bus ticket. I understood what they were saying—I posed a threat to them, and they were making it impossible for me to do that again, but I hadn't meant to do anything. I walked to the door, looking at the people behind me. They were not running to stop me, but I ended up stopping myself. Coming right toward me was a man with swarthy skin and short, dark brown hair. His muscle mass was large, but other than that, he was short for a man of his age.

"Hi, Millie," the man smiled at me causing my brain to spin. I had heard the voice before while working with the Flying Falcon, but once again the face was different. "Is Nick in there?"

"William!" I connected the voice to the name of his character. "I'm really confused."

"Why did you leave Seb?" Leer asked while Nick stepped around me to see Will.

"Yah, about him. He's refusing to wake up. I tried my best, and he walked off on me. I think it has something to do with him spotting Millie. He's trying to find her."

"So try something else," Nick told Will.

"I think the only thing that will work is sending in Millie. When I said *walked off*, I meant he jumped waves. He's not done that before. He's looking for Millie."

"He started surfing?" Leer asked with a lopsided grin on his face. Nick didn't look nearly as happy with the news. He looked frustrated.

"We can't send in Millie. She's maxed out," Nick told him.

Will took a glance at the screen, and then performed a double take, whistling about my numbers being beautiful. Nick reached over and shut the screen off, but was too late to hide my heiss level.

"That's confidential," Nick told him.

"We can send in Millie," Leer told Nick. "She doesn't need the heiss. She can ride the waves without it, as she has shown us all before. Would you be willing to tell... what does she call him?" Leer looked over at Will.

"Could you go tell Mr. Rhino to wake up?" Will asked. "He's been maxing out the last few days and I'm worried he'll get himself hurt. The last time he did this he could hardly walk out of here on his own."

"He's real?" I asked them.

I already suspected that Mr. Rhino was real, but this would confirm it. After all, Will was real and standing right in front of me. If I didn't know for a fact that I was awake, I would have been very, very confused. I could jump into virtual worlds by falling asleep and looking for these strange heiss levels. If talking was an indication that people were real, then maybe it had been my dad who had grabbed the back of my dress and asked me if I was alright while I was being Veronica. I wished I had known this sooner. I could have talked with my dad.

"Are you sure you want me to look for Mr. Rhino? Didn't you just threaten me?" I asked Nick.

I wasn't the bravest person. I typically avoided confrontation. Me jumping in front of all those blows for Mr.

Rhino was not anything I would ever really do. I had only done it because I was dreaming.

"No," Leer tried to correct Nick's earlier statement. "We offered to help you find your missing parents."

"How long has he been on today?" Nick asked William.

"He asked for overtime," William replied. "Leer wasn't there to tell me to stop him."

"Come on, Millie. Go wake him up," Leer told me.

He took hold of my arm and put me back on the chair. I stared at him until he reminded me that Mr. Rhino's living person might suffer a heart attack. That didn't sound good. For all the times I had stepped in the way of the blows meant for him, it was strange to think that I could do it in real life too. I sighed and sat on the pressure cuff to make sure it was not put on me before I shut my eyes.

I started off back in the business meeting again. I was sitting in the same chair, but the topic had shifted to a game screen that was replaying a man sneaking up on a wolf. I blinked to get out of there. I found myself standing at the edge of the ocean. There was a boat coming in. I could see a dock and people there waiting for the boat. I walked over to the dock, looking for Mr. Rhino. Nope. I found the man who had been playing Phil. I didn't let him notice me.

I blinked again, or as my new terminology would tell

me, I rode a different wave until I came to a swing set. I walked around the swing set and through the park, looking at the people walking dogs. There were a few joggers. I moved to the middle of the grass and turned around and found him. He wore the face of a Spanish man, but his vibes, or heiss level, felt the same. He had found me first. He was standing with his hands on his hips and a large grin on his face. No mask. The smile was enough to sweep me away. As it was, it didn't sweep me. It rooted me to the field while Mr. Rhino walked over.

"Do you stroll?" he asked me, sounding exactly like himself.

"Stroll? Like you and me around the park?"

"Anywhere, really," he answered. Then he laughed. "I might need a mask right now." He was blushing. I could not believe it. He had been riding waves through a strange game world to find me instead of waking up.

"You need to wake up," I told him.

"I wanted to make sure you weren't cold anymore."

"Not cold. Confused, but not cold." Mr. Rhino grinned. He took a step closer.

"Listen, these guys told me that you need to wake up so you walk out of... wherever you are."

"Where are you?" Mr. Rhino—or was his real name Seb?—asked me.

125

"Standing right beside you."

He grinned at me again. Then he laughed. "I'm sorry. I just can't. Have you seen yourself yet?"

"What?"

I looked down to see what I was wearing. I was in a jogging outfit that was rather horrible. I had a bright yellow shirt cut off at the middle. Underneath that was an orange shirt, and below the shirts were a few layers of pants. I tugged on the first layer just to check that out, and Mr. Rhino burst out laughing again.

"Shush. At least I found you," I told him.

"How quickly?" he asked, and his smile turned serious. "How many other places did you go first?"

"Two?"

"Where are you?" he asked me again. He grabbed onto my arm and looked around, as if expecting that we were being watched.

"I don't know. Wherever you are, I think. I have no idea."

"But you're okay now?"

"I guess..." I trailed off and pulled a face, thinking about that Nick character. "I've already been threatened, which wasn't fun. Do you think I have to do what they tell me to?"

126

"Uh…" Mr. Rhino looked around again, then rubbed the back of his neck. "I'm not supposed to mix work with personal life."

"This is your job?"

"You know what…. I can't…" He let go of my arm and stepped back.

"Okay." I shrugged. If he was working with Nick, I didn't doubt that he was hesitant to say anything. "I'll figure it out. You need to wake up now."

"Right. Save me a stroll sometime." Mr. Rhino smiled. I stood there until his character started stretching. It was then that I knew he wasn't being this other jogger anymore. I put my jogger back where I had found her and then woke up.

There was something stuck on my arm, even though I was still sitting on the pressure cuff. I tugged it off to find that everyone was looking at me. Leer was biting his lower lip. Nick was holding his arms together, looking at William. William was shaking his head.

"What's this thing?" I asked, holding up the armband.

"That allows us to ride the wave with you," Leer told me. "We can see what you're doing when it's on. That wasn't too bad," he told me, and gave a look at William to ask him to stay quiet. William didn't look like he was going to say anything to me. He turned around and left the room. So Seb and I were being spied on. Nick, Leer, William and the doctors had all watched Mr. Rhino laugh at me.

"Please don't linger in the conference room," Nick told me. "I'll leave it to Leer to show you around."

"I didn't agree to work for you," I reminded Leer.

"Not yet."

He smiled at me.

Chapter 13

Sebastian

Millie was here! I woke up to find that, for once, no one was in the room with me. My bands were off. There was a piece of wadded-up duct tape on the bed beside me. I hoped it wasn't used, because my arm was still sore from when I had passed out at work two days ago. I still hadn't managed to get home yet. I had been sleeping at work, and they had me running my job as soon as they thought I could handle it, which was right now. But I was doing better, and I really needed to go home to prove to my mother that I hadn't left her—just as soon as I found Millie.

I anticipated seeing Millie's startled reaction when I found her. I also wanted to see her hair color. Was she blond or a variation of brown? Who knew the answer? Had she been the one to change the filter over her hair, or had that been done to keep me from knowing it? I wasn't a sniper. I wasn't going to go hurt Millie. I just wanted to meet her in real life. I could, couldn't I?

I paused on the edge of my bed. She had found me in two wave jumps. That was pretty fast even for a sniper. I had been reading about how to surf waves at the office, since I hadn't gone home yet. Leer had let me borrow the material, because I was curious to know how Millie did it. It was supposed to be impossible for some people to surf. You had to be able to handle a lot of heiss in order to tell your body to look for it. I actually didn't think it was going to work for me. Everything had been fuzzy for a while, like a blurry dream. It took quite some time for anything to come into focus, and when it did I'd actually panicked. I had no idea how to stop the dream. How could I tell myself to stop looking for something that I didn't expect to find?

Then Millie had found me and reminded me that I could wake up. I knew how to wake up. I had woken up lots of times after being connected to the heiss world. I woke up rather easily. Now I wanted to go back under—I wanted to find Millie. They wouldn't let me see her, would they? Why did I expect to walk into the breakroom and just see her there?

I looked at the door as Nick opened it and came in. He was not happy, but I had to ask anyway.

"Can I see Millie?"

"No," Nick snapped. "And don't come in to work tomorrow."

Nick knew how to get my attention quick. I had just stayed at work for two days. How was I going to explain to my mother why I hadn't been home, and then why I couldn't go to work? Why *couldn't* I go to work? Nick couldn't know that I had illegally surfed that quickly, could he? My bands were off. No one was watching me talk with Millie.

"Nick, I'm fine," I told him.

"You are never, ever, ever, ever, with lots of evers, to go looking for Millie again. If I ever find you doing it, you're fired. Surfing the system is illegal, Seb. You know that. I don't care what your excuse is. You're suspended for a day."

He made a note of it on my chart, and I stared at it, wondering what Leer was going to tell me when I came back after my suspension. Maybe Dean had been suspended for surfing. How had Nick caught me that fast? I watched him close up my screen with a lump in my throat. I was a day without pay, my mom was going to be frantic, and I wouldn't be able to see Millie. This was the worst. For Nick to have caught me, our company sniper must have told him. He said he was watching me. Everything I did at work was monitored, and now I had lost Millie.

"No protest?" Nick asked me turning back around. He noticed the wadded-up piece of duct tape. He grabbed it off the bed and threw it away.

"I wanted to see Millie."

131

That was a fine protest, Seb. Yeah. That would really get Nick to change his mind. I was so doomed.

"I thought you didn't mix work with your personal life," Nick told me, nearly quoting my own words. Had he watched me? Was Nick our sniper? It might not matter exactly who it was. I was still busted.

"I don't," I answered. "It's just... I just... I didn't expect that to work."

Nick shook his head at me. I really wasn't doing well at this. What was I supposed to say? Sorry? I wasn't sorry, because I had read the company policies before I accepted the job. I couldn't see Millie outside of work if she started working here, and I couldn't see her *in* work if I didn't go find her. I might not ever see her again, yet we would only be a few floors apart at most. I just wanted to meet her once for *real.* Her words were already coming back to haunt me. She had been threatened and didn't know if she had to do what they told her to do. What had they threatened her with? What did they want her to do? I wanted to see Millie!

"Get out of here, Sebastian," Nick told me. "Your glare could cook a pancake."

"Can't you make an exception?" I asked him, hopping off the table. "Just once? I just want to see her in real life once."

"No. That's a horrible idea. You already saved her.

132

What more could you want?"

"I want to know what you threatened her with."

"Get out," Nick directed between clenched teeth.

I headed toward the door. Maybe I would ask Leer when I got back from my suspension. He might be lenient enough to let me see Millie just once. I sighed at the door. No he wouldn't. I should have asked to meet her someplace when I had the chance to talk to her as the jogger. I was never going to see her again. I already missed my guardian angel. Maybe... maybe she would come see me?

Dream on, Seb. She would be told not to do that as well. They'd convince her somehow that I wasn't worth the risk. I wanted to look back at Nick and protest—*Really* protest, but I didn't want him to fire me. What I *should* do was just forget about her. I needed to get home.

"See ya," I told Nick without looking at him. Then I made my way to my dressing room. The sniper was going to be hot on my tail, wasn't he? He would be making sure that I wasn't surfing the system messing up other people's work and getting in the way of missions that I didn't know how to complete. Yes, I knew why surfing the system wasn't a good thing, but I still wished the rules were different about me seeing Millie.

I ran the idea of Millie through my head all the way home until I got sick of the subject. I might be worth the risk, but maybe she wasn't. I really didn't know anything about her. I had no idea how she had ended up in the Doldrums or even how she had gotten out. These were puzzles that bothered me. Forget about it. I had to forget about it.

I opened the front door to hear my brother crying. I didn't think the company sniper had found my house. I had been really careful. Nothing would have threatened Triton, so why was he crying?

"Triton?" I called out, thinking not for the first time that I wished my mother had a different favorite movie and that her hair wasn't naturally red. It was easy to get picked on when we had names like Triton and Sebastian.

"Seb?" my twelve-year-old brother asked back. I heard him running out of the single back room next. He rushed into my arms, giving me a full view of his messy red hair. I pictured his tear-stained face since I couldn't see it. He shoved it into my stomach.

"What's wrong?" I asked him.

"No… one…" he bawled, "came back."

I felt my wind leave my chest. No one?

"Where's Mom?" I asked, but I already knew.

She'd thought I was leaving her. I hadn't come back in two days. She was out trying to find a job so she could feed Triton. What was I doing trying to save Millie when I needed to save my own family? I had butchered everything.

Had Triton been left alone for two full days, or only one? Had he gotten anything to eat? Was he starving?

"I'm so sorry," I told him, hugging him tightly. "Let's get a pizza and find Mom. I wasn't leaving. I got stuck at work."

Tears came to my eyes unbidden. We had two day's pay to work with, and I wouldn't have anything for tomorrow. Mom was right. What chance did I have to date a girl? I couldn't afford it. I couldn't be anything to Millie.

"Come on," I told Triton, dragging him out the door. He clung to me, still crying and not letting go. "Let's get you some food. I'm really sorry. I'll do my best to not let that happen again."

Triton was still clinging to me when we got the pizza. I had us eat it outside because he was still sniffling and I didn't like all the attention that brought, but I wasn't going to tell him to stop. He'd felt abandoned. I couldn't tell him not to feel that way. It was my fault. I should have known better.

I was still kicking myself when we finally found Mom. She had given up on the work idea yet again and was standing on a corner holding a sign and begging. Triton almost didn't want to walk up to her with me. His pride got in the way, but he was too clingy at the moment to let go. I glanced around the street, wondering how bad this was going to be. My eyes caught sight of Will and I looked away.

He was probably out shopping. He wouldn't have a care in the world for my struggles.

I dragged Triton over to Mom and handed her the pizza box.

"I told you I was coming back. I promised."

Triton started crying again. I started crying again. I purposely told myself that I had no idea who Will was. Actually I didn't. Will wasn't even his real name. That was his character name in the Earl of Key Hill. I didn't know his real name.

Mom looked at the both of us crying and bawled too. She grabbed the pizza and pulled me into a hug.

"I'm really sorry," I admitted.

There was no way I was ever doing anything for Millie ever again if it involved the real world. I couldn't stand to see the pain it caused my mom and brother. She was on her own. I didn't think I could hold up anyone else but my struggling family right now.

"You got everything fixed at work?" Mom asked me. She started to reach for me, but the pizza smelled too good. She propped the box on top of Triton's head so she could open it with one hand and grab a slice.

"Here," I said and helped hold the box before it fell off Triton. "Yeah. Work will be fine."

At least it better be. I would beg Nick to take me back if he decided to fire me. I didn't know how I was going to explain not getting a paycheck tomorrow. Maybe I would end up trying to get work from the Dowager on Sumac Street.

"Let's go buy some marbles," I told Mom. It might help her out too. Then if anything like this happened again where I was stuck at work she would have something to fall back on. I couldn't let this happen again. It caused way too much stress.

We had fun picking out the prettiest marbles we could find. Triton and I played with them while Mom went into the store and spent most of the money I had brought back. I held my tongue about the expenses, since I was thinking about paying the rent and the energy bill. We'd make it work somehow.

Chapter 14

Millie

"Alright, tell me about the border," Leer said once we had walked down to a room that didn't contain any dentist beds. It contained a lot of chairs. Leer sat down on one randomly and draped one of his strong arms over the back of the chair beside him. His dark hair was already plopping into his face. He didn't brush it away, but if I was him, I would have.

"The border? I can't tell you how to cross it. Obviously we didn't get it right, because we never made it. Our guide had us walk down the Millennial Trail—you know the one that's so long it goes everywhere. Then we took the shortcut into the desert and crossed that for three days. That sucked. Then we reached the old shanty town that was supposed to be a rest stop and we got attacked. Everyone was separated from each other, and then we were put to work in the mine. I'm still trying to figure out why.

Does the government do that or was it some illegal operation?"

"I've never heard of it." Leer shrugged at me. "But I'll alert the authorities."

"Which ones? The ones here in Sanatonia? What would they care if border crossers didn't make it?"

Leer didn't answer me. He just gave me a smile, and I knew that I was right. No one here would do anything to get my parents back. *I* had to.

"You were born here?" Leer asked me.

"I was born in a home on Pickney Street inside a little green house with yellow shutters. That's what my parents said. I won't have hospital records. They used a private doctor."

"Which makes sense, because you could turn into a sniper. How about we find your citizenship records and go from there?" Leer posed.

Leer opened up the computer that he had brought into the room with him. He powered it on while I frowned at him and tried to come up with an argument that might work. I was not a sniper. I couldn't hit anything. Not being able to sleep correctly did not make me a sniper. But I didn't get the argument out. These people had rescued me, and I *did* need to prove that I was legal to stay here. Maybe I could find out where my relatives lived and get them to help me

140

find my parents. My Uncle Phillis was supposed to be around.

"Where am I?" I asked Leer.

"Can I get your citizenship number?" Leer asked back.

I told him and scooted around so I could see his screen. Whatever program he was using brought me right up. Then it brought up my parents. They had a different house in the area that the program claimed was their residential address for the past thirty years. I had never been there. My parents were listed with having jobs that I had never heard of. I was listed as graduating from my online college. Maybe if I found this house, my parents would make it out of the mine and find me there.

"Millie *Ankerton*." Leer blinked with awe. "I didn't expect to know you." Leer made a point of shaking my hand before he showed me why I was famous. It wasn't me. It was my dad.

"Jessie Ankerton masses thousands in a single game release," an old newspaper clipping reported. "The Earl of Key Hill is an innovative multiplayer game with riveting characters, hidden magical trails, and new secrets to unlock daily."

I guess that made me rich. Had my parents decided to hide away because of the money, or were we not hiding, and my parents had just decided that since money wasn't an issue we could work out in the middle of nowhere on hundreds of volunteer projects? Had we been hiding that far away to escape heiss?

"What's wrong with the game? It's being attacked? Is that because my dad's not there? Does crossing the border have anything to do with this?" I asked, thinking over the game I had been inside where I thought I had found my dad. Why shouldn't he be there if he had made it? Why had he never mentioned this?

"Most likely," Leer replied. "That game is his most famous work. He has about seven others that link to it from hidden locations inside that one. *The Lost City of Arabold, Whisps, Terraria's Journey, Day Seven, Scales of Justice, Rendippidy*, and *Breath of Sulfur*. There are a lot of online forums for posting hints for those games. The largest forum is called *Seize the Day*. The most vocal players don't give out cheat codes, but they do give some very detailed hints at times. I've managed to play through *Scales of Justice* before. I had to give my code to J. Lilly, Veronica's mother, in order to connect to the world. That game was intense, but oh so good."

J. Lilly as in Juliet Lilly Ankerton, my mom. That was Veronica's mother. She had been captured before. She was the portal to entering all the other games that my dad had made. Was that why she was said to tell the future? I tried to not assign symbolism to that but it was hard. The Earl could be my dad, and J. Lilly could be my mom, and Veronica could be me. Did my dad see the worlds as his children in a way? I didn't.

"Wow," Leer, said looking at me again. "We will take good care of you until we find your parents."

Without my permission, Leer started to hire me for the job. I complained, but didn't get anywhere. As he pointed out, if my parents escaped the mine before we got to them they would start looking for me and this would give them an easy way to find me. Plus, Nick would be mad if Leer didn't hire me, not to mention that Leer was going to convince me that I was working for the greater good of everyone on the planet. In addition to that, how else would I get money and food and shelter while furthering my search for my parents if I didn't have a job?

He got me there. I didn't have any idea. Maybe I could find my Uncle Phillis, but I would need money to get transportation, or at least cooperation to use a phone to call him, and since we'd never met, I fretted that he wouldn't believe me over a phone. Why would he come pick up some girl he had never met? What if he hadn't known that my parents had even had me? I made sure to ask about the company policy for quitting.

"You don't show up for a few days we assume you quit," Leer told me. "If that happens, we'll try to find you.

143

We'll send out a sniper or two to hunt you down. This business is rather competitive and we don't like losing anyone, but it does happen."

"You're hiring me to be a sniper?" I asked with the most appalled voice I could manage.

"Not. Exactly. We're hiring you to be a surfer. All snipers start out as surfers, but some go bad, you know. Bad snipers work for hackers. The hackers pay them to stop people from foiling their plans. Bad snipers will go after anyone that stands in the hacker's way. At our company, we have good snipers who hunt down the illegal surfers, and snipers, before our men get hit. Our snipers also stop surfers who are playing games without paying for them, like you were doing."

I did my best to wrap my head around all the new terms. "So what you're saying is that snipers take out surfers no matter where they come from, and you want me to be a surfer?" I didn't see how calling me a surfer instead of a sniper made much of a difference if I was going to be hunted down either way. Maybe it was the idea of it that counted. I wasn't going to actively hunt anyone down myself.

"We need you to infiltrate and stop a group of highly successful hackers," Leer continued, already messing up the way I viewed the terms.

"So I'll be a sniper," I pointed out.

"No. Unregistered snipers that work for hackers are illegal. Surfers aren't. No one is putting a gun in your hand. You won't hunt anyone in real life. You won't be a sniper."

"So to make sniping legal you call it surfing?" I asked still confused. Leer rolled his eyes at me.

"You won't hurt anyone, Millie. Surfers look for people in games. Snipers hunt for them outside of games. We need you to locate a group of hackers while you're sleeping. You're perfect for the job, because you've already hacked them. You assisted the Flying Falcon in disrupting their communications for a few hours, but they're back again. I'll have William explain the rest of that to you. You won't need to do any sniping outside of being asleep."

We left the conference room, and I was given a black shirt and pants and an ID badge that was white and could open the doors to get me in to work. I found myself staring at Leer. Didn't he want to run a background check on me to make sure that I wasn't a terrorist? Didn't he want to ask me if I had ever had a job before? I hadn't. I had worked with non-profit organizations on habitat projects, and had never been paid before. Wasn't he going to tell me the name of his company? Show me a picture of the boss? Anything other than shove me into a scary job that I had not asked for?

He unlocked a room where a guy was sleeping and told me to stand there and not touch anything. Then he walked out on me and closed the door. Was this a test? I was so confused. I looked at the guy, didn't recognize him, and tried to open the door, but I was locked in. I pressed my ear to the door. I could hear Leer. He was next door talking to someone. Was he simply putting me out of the way? I went to look at the guy whose closed eyes were moving back and forth. I looked at his screen, searching for the one thing I had been shown earlier: heiss levels. This guy was at fifty. Right as I was about to find out what he was seeing, by placing the special armband on him, Leer opened the door and motioned for me to follow him again.

"Sorry. I'm supposed to be working right now. I've got people to wake up and send home. My next guy is in ten minutes. Let's find Will."

Chapter 15

Millie

I was finally told the information that I had been trying to spot on the office pens. The company I had just been hired by was called "Visions," and they worked for developers and large game firms to monitor their games and stop hackers that found ways to place cheats into games. In some private circles Visions was also known as the Bird Hunters, a term that I had heard before. They were known for fabulous instincts and quick solutions to large problems. Typically, people on the fourth floor could find the troublemakers and identify what objects might be causing the problem, like extra money being generated, or a paper list of cheat codes, or players that agreed to give out rare goods to their friends. Then the people like Seb on the other floors were sent in to remove the problem. Each floor had its own sniper, and that person usually handled the troublemakers and issued warnings against their illegal

147

methods. They would kick them out of games or block them for a time, depending on the severity of the infraction.

Will gave me the impression that Visions' version of sniper was used in a much more appropriate way than other places. Illegal snipers would attack players in real life, sometimes making them owe large debts. They were enough of a scare to make players give up heiss forever. In extreme cases, an illegal sniper would really kill a player before the player had the chance to reveal who the sniper was or worked for. It was the best players who usually received that fate, since they were the ones who could scare snipers. I blinked a few times when Will told me that, because it sounded horrible to die. Will followed it with a reminder that I wasn't going to be told to find anyone in real life. Visions just needed me to stop a group of hackers called the Vikings who were taking over a large host of games.

"But you find people in real life?" I asked Will.

"Not usually, and if I did accept a job to hunt a real person it wouldn't be to hurt anyone. Currently, the guys have me working around the clock," William told me. "My normal boss is Pauley, and I work on the fourth floor. However, Leer has me following Sebastian around while he's playing games, and Nick has me following him after he gets off work. I don't think the two of them realize yet that they're both using me." Will grinned. "You'll get used to them. They're always in each other's business."

"But anyway, it looks like I have also been assigned to help you. Here's the most important thing you need to remember. Never, ever, tell anyone your real name while you're surfing. You don't want snipers finding you. I'm assuming you'll recognize your parents, and that's alright, but don't give yourself away to anyone else. I'd also advise you not to share your real name with people you meet outside of this office. It is very, very bad for a surfer to give away his identity. My name's Casper," he told me as his white teeth contrasted against the color of his deep skin. I snorted at him. Was I supposed to believe that?

"What you need to do is poke at the Vikings. We haven't been able to figure out who is behind their attacks. This isn't your typical case of smart kids trying to cheat at a game. These guys are professionals who are making a lot of money by disrupting normal game play. We've been forced to invade companies that haven't asked for our help, because we've spotted the Vikings in their games. For example, the Earl of Key Hill did not want us to be there. That's why we got the three opposing groups: us, the Vikings, and the Veterans. The Veterans run that show, but Seb thought that perhaps the Vikings were controlling the key characters and had us terminate them. That took care of the problem for a while. He was right about the Earl. The Vikings stole the Earl and most likely Veronica. They had to have had some influence over Veronica's mother for the game to crash like it did when we found her.

"The point is that when we go into games where we haven't been invited, we can't use our regular people because their avatars will reflect who they are. We have to send in snipers or surfers who can sneak into the game and hide their true face, otherwise we get player battles. We're a little stretched on snipers. There's me, Rory, Tabitha, and Lex. We wouldn't normally use Sebastian for a surfing mission (especially since he's so new) but as our top performer for the quarter it only makes sense to use him on our hardest job. Besides, the kid clearly loves it, and he jumped waves just the other day to find you. So there's the possibility that we can move Sebastian into a surfer mode, eventually.

"That move is a little contentious at the present. Leer thinks he could handle it. Nick doesn't, but I think that's because Nick's been cheating with Seb. Sometimes he sends Seb into unpublished games without any instructions, just to see what he will do. That always gets Leer a little angry if he notices.

"But aside from those two," Will said, shaking his head at Leer and Nick's personal struggles, "our other snipers (Lex and Tabitha) have been handling all the other smaller cases this week. Rory was following Seb until Seb got moved to me, because he has a sniper. I'm trying to put this nicely, but Seb's sniper isn't you. Obviously you were making it known that you were a real player and Seb picked up on it. But we were thinking he was tagged even before you showed up. His presence is easy to pick up. That was why we thought he had come from some rival company and the sniper from there was hunting him down for leaving, but that's not the case. He's never worked on virtual games before.

"This goes without saying, but any information about Sebastian has to stay in this room," William told me. "He's our special case. He's the employee that is so perfect for the job that it's ridiculous not to hire him. He maxes out at seventy-three and doesn't leave anything unfinished. He's great, except that he lied about most everything. The only contact information we have on him is his phone number.

"It took us a long time to find where he lives, and that only happened recently because he was emotionally compromised in that moment and didn't make following him around difficult. He is the sole provider for his mom and younger brother. His mom can't find a job, and his brother can't go to school until they can afford to move. The school in their area charges an enrollment fee. Seb will do anything to keep his family from begging on the streets. He's hit the hardest when he doesn't have work, so he gives work everything he has," Will told me. "Technically he's not legalized to work where he is, but we can't bear to fire him. He puts his whole heart into it. How can you fire someone like that?"

Yes, how could you? Who would want to get rid of

the top-performing employee just because he lied on his paperwork? Why was I being told all of this?

"I'm glad you hired him," I said. If it wasn't for Seb doing his job, I wouldn't be here at all. I'd have frozen to death.

"Everyone is glad that we hired him, except for the people who are not." William smiled. "That's where we come in. We've gotten a lot more hacking problems since he started. He's become a rather large target for the Vikings. They are trying to find him. He's stopped most of their infiltrations and they're getting a little mad. We need to find the Vikings before their sniper locates Seb."

"So you want me to save Sebastian?" I asked. Wasn't that funny? I had already started in on that job. I guess it wouldn't be too different from what I was already doing, except that now I would have a purpose and paycheck along with the madness.

"*My* job is to save Sebastian," William told me. "Your job will technically be to infiltrate the Vikings and expose who their real players are. Then it will be Rory's job to make them stop hacking and infecting systems. Tabitha will tell you that your job is to find the Viking's motive. She's all about motives. Nick and Leer will tell you that you're only playing games. But as a personal side mission, if you happen to find anything that will help save Sebastian I'd appreciate it as much as him. Currently I'm under an obligation to put myself in the way of anything that would hurt Seb in real life, which, I'm not going to lie, is the part of sniping that no one in this office likes."

"Why are you telling me all of this?" I asked William, completely overwhelmed. "I'm just a girl with an early college diploma. I've never had a real job before, and Leer didn't even ask me. Nick just said I had to work here. I feel bad about Sebastian, but I need to find my parents."

Did I mention that I didn't want to end up getting hurt? I was not going to be put under any obligation to get hurt. I had not signed up for this. Is that what happened to most immigrants who crossed the border without support? They were taken in by whatever company wanted to exploit them?

"Here's your reason," a woman with the curliest, short light-purple hair said. She plopped down a piece of paper in front of me. William introduced me to Tabitha, the sniper on the third floor who worked with Nick. I wondered how she made herself inconspicuous when her hair was so glaring, but I didn't ask. Instead I glued my eyes to the paper. It was a legal document defining a prison sentence for anyone associating with illegal border crossers. It would be waived if I worked with Visions. I probably had been beside a few illegal people, but could they prove it? Will tossed the paper into the trash can, but I was sure that Tabitha could print up another one.

"We don't need that. Leer's going to help her find her parents."

"Is he?" Tabitha rolled her eyes. "I've been assigned to check out their mailing address, as if anyone will actually be there when Millie has already told us that they're mining in the Doldrums. So I'll be out next week. Rory's going to be working my job while *you* watch the babies."

"They're not that much younger than us," William told Tabitha. "Enjoy your vacation."

"I will." Tabitha offered a wide smile. "If you ever need anything, honey, I'd be happy to help you," she said looking at me.

"I've got it," Will deflected.

"Sleeping Beauty is wanted downstairs," Tabitha told us as she walked out of the room, leaving the threat of jail in the trash can.

"That's you," Will told me, and before I could complain, I found myself marching down the stairs after Tabitha to find Leer. He did indeed have a job for me. He wanted me to look in old databases for anything that might show my parents had worked there. He was under the impression that I might recognize them by some code name or something, particularly my mom. Tabitha laughed at my job and told me that Leer just wanted me awake all day long so I wouldn't mess anything up.

154

"Rory will be around to watch you ride the waves later and offer some instruction," Leer told me sweeping his surfer-style black hair out of his face for once.

"Between the three of us that's a bad idea," Tabitha told Leer. "Nick thinks Rory is the reason for Dean's demise in the Wild West."

"He is not," Leer picked up the old argument. I had no idea what they were talking about. I turned to the computer and started to search for my parent's names. My dad made games. Where had he met my mom?

"Some insider source was responsible for that probe and my gut tells me it's Rory," Tabitha stated.

"Millie," Leer said. "If you ever find evidence that Rory is helping the Vikings invade places, let me know."

My fingers paused over the buttons. Could this be happening? I didn't feel mature enough for all of this. Will wanted me to save Sebastian's real life. Nick wanted me to stop hackers. Tabitha wanted me to find the Vikings' main motive, and Leer wanted me to expose corporate saboteurs. Was this my job? Golly gremlins!

"A sniper had to have placed it."

"I agree," Leer told Tabitha, "which leaves you, Rory, Casper—" that was Will "—and Lex as prime suspects, since you know the ins and outs of this system. However," Leer held up a hand before Tabitha interrupted with the sentence tickling her tongue, "there are other people around us capable of surfing, something which Sebastian proved just the other day. Anyone who can handle over sixty heiss could have placed the probe. I have personally checked out every employee's heiss level on that day to see who could have been capable. No one was starved for heiss except for Millie, and she doesn't count because we already knew where she was. That narrows down the suspects to about ten. Sebastian is naturally excluded from placing the probe. He was already being watched by Rory at that time and then by Casper, and if I'm not mistaken you and Lex also went into the Earl of Key Hill along with Grant."

"It's totally Rory," Tabitha insisted. She took up a chair and sat down. "And you can't prove anything about Grant. Besides, one day's data is not enough. The necklace could have been placed a few days before your search."

"Tabitha dear, I call Grant for help all the time. I know his actions. He was playing Samson."

"Grant wouldn't place a probe."

"Well if it wasn't our own snipers it proves that there's a sniper close enough to hack in. If you find out who placed that probe Mille, let me know," Leer told me next. I looked at him as he walked out of the room to chase after his beeping monitor.

"What probe?"

This was so confusing, and I couldn't possibly solve everyone's problems. Who did they think I was? Tabitha filled me in about the probe that I had actually helped to destroy. It was the necklace that the Earl had hid in Veronica's room and I had handed it to Sebastian. It had the strange ability to let people from the Earl of Key Hill invade the other places that Visions was trying to fix. Just hearing that sent up a red flag. The Vikings were targeting Visions to kill off all their players. What would they do if they got most of the players down? Get worse? Destroy the whole company? No wonder everyone around me was panicking.

Nothing came up in a simple search for my parents. Tabitha gave me a rule book and walked me through the steps of normal work. She left me with Rory when he came into the room. She waggled her eyes at me as she walked out, and I sighed. She expected this guy to be evil, and she was leaving me with him. I didn't find anything evil about Rory. He looked young, with a lean frame and brown scruffy beard that he was growing out. He did hook me up to a monitor to watch my interactions and had me perform a few simple missions that I thought were simulations and not real. It was strange when words flashed across my vision. The first time it happened I tried to touch them, until the words told me not to do that. I couldn't help it. Floating words in the sky? It was so unreal.

Chapter 16

Sebastian

"You're late," the voice on the phone told me. I hadn't expected to hear from Nick. In fact, when my phone went off I was considering how expensive keeping a phone was. I would have gotten rid of it, but I had to have a phone for work. I couldn't really lie about my phone number.

"It's Wednesday," I reminded Nick. "You told me not to come in today."

"And now I'm telling you that you're late," Nick redirected. "Just as long as you promise not to repeat your poor behavior I could use you today."

I looked up at my mom, who was playing marbles with Triton. She had been eyeing me, wondering why I hadn't left yet. I had yet to offer her an explanation, because I couldn't come up with one that was good enough. I didn't want to tell her that I had broken company rules and gotten

159

suspended right after they had me nearly dying for them, although the lack of sleep was my fault. I was considering hiding away in the library and coming up with a different excuse for why I didn't bring any money back. However, not going into work sounded better than risking my mom thinking that I had been fired, so I had stayed.

"Yes, I promise," I told Nick. The words slid off my tongue fast. Nick didn't need to repeat himself. "I'll be right there."

I met my mom with a smile. She was justified in looking relieved, because we had bills to pay soon. I wondered if she would try her luck with giving a marble and wondered what Triton was going to do if Mom went out. Triton could use a friend. I didn't want him to end up working like I was, expending himself in being security for a company that would much rather not say their name than otherwise. I didn't know how they kept afloat and how so many people had heard about us when we didn't advertise our services to stop hackers.

Either way, I ran to work. They were still paying me to keep at this, so I was going to keep at it. I was hooked up right away under Leer's guidance. He didn't say anything about me almost losing a day of work. He acted like everything was the same, so I did too.

"Special request from the west floor," flashed across my screen, drawing me into the problems for today and why

Nick might need me. "Solve the riddles."

That was as much warning as I had before I was standing in front of a sphinx with glowing red eyes. I would give my left big toe that those eyes could laser me with harsh powered photons. There was one person standing next to me, a short boy with blond, nearly white hair. His skin was as pale as his hair and he had several red spots on his neck. I didn't ask.

"What do I need to do again?" I asked, assuming that I had been given another man's job. Had he failed? Was I going to fail?

"Defeat the alphabet," the lad told me. "Starting with 'A' you have to make sentences with four to five words, all with the same starting letter from A to Z."

Sentences? Bring it on!

"Can I get an example?" I asked, just to make sure that I had this right. The lad grabbed my arm and backed me away from the sphinx and down the hill so he could give me an example.

"One person said that the barber bakes bubbled baskets."

The corners of my mouth churned upwards. Now that I could do. I could bake bubbling baskets any time of the day. I raced back up to the sphinx with my first sentence already formed.

161

"Amazing antelopes ate artificial artichokes."

The sphinx's eyes lit up. His left eye glowed the letter "A" and his right eye glowed with a number. Was that my point total? I looked at the lad as he caught up to me. He told me that the first one was easy. The other letters were hard. Hard? This was going to be like prancing ponies pecking picnics. I laughed as the words flowed through me. I had billowing buffalos burst bubbles while confused cantaloupes crossed catwalks. Jagged jumping jellies jeered jubilees and zooming Zachary zigged zealously. The hardest letter for me was "X," but I had played numerous games of scrabble against my brother and had my answer perfectly picked before I'd even started with "A."

"Xaviar Xeroxed xanthous Xyst." Now if it was only possible to photocopy yellow-colored patios I was going to win. I wished this game I was in celebrated my vocabulary victory with a display of ferociously festive fireworks, but instead all that happened was that the sphinx turned to stone and a door opened between his legs. Talk about anticlimactic. I voiced my annoyance at the lack of celebration as I sauntered into the building with the albino beside me.

We entered into a room that was likewise devoid of instructions. I looked at my young guide for information and he shrugged, telling me that he had never gotten this far.

"What's our ultimate goal here?" I asked, scanning the room that had multiple puzzles along the walls. I didn't want to start touching stuff without knowing anything about it.

"We have to rescue my sister," the albino told me. "The love of your life," he said to prod my memory.

I grinned at him. "Have you a picture of her that will keep my heart yearning to find her down yonder?"

"Are you tall enough to reach that?" the albino pointed up at the ceiling where a key was hanging from a chain. Now we were talking. I winked at the kid and started circling the room so we could puzzle our way through it. Each puzzle built off another one. Sometimes I needed extra arms and had to instruct the kid to hold certain buttons on a wall across the room to lower the chain and key. It was funny, but once we got the key, nothing happened. The kid could only tell me that he once again had never gotten this far yet. I gave him a few more lines he could say instead and laughed at him when he actually started to use them.

After waiting for a good ten minutes a door finally appeared that we could go through. It should have happened sooner. I noted the slow response and told whoever was watching me, if anyone was, that they should report the slowness bug in this game. I spent the rest of the day calmly pushing through the puzzles to reach the "love of my life" that I learned did not look anything like her little brother. She had been researching an ancient artifact that a cult didn't want her to get, and they had trapped her in this tunnel of doom. I pointed out that we hadn't seen any of these people and they should do a better job at protecting the people they kidnapped.

"Here you go." Nick handed me a fat envelope of cash before I left my room. Leer looked at him, curious, but otherwise didn't say anything.

"What's this for?" I asked Nick, making sure that he could see what he had just given me. Maybe he had mistakenly given me everyone's money for the day.

"It's an advance on your paycheck," Nick told me. "We thought you could use it."

Will. Had Will told on me? He had seen me with my mom and brother crying over a pizza. Had he told Nick? It was probably fine. I didn't need to panic. Will was alright and Nick wasn't going to hurt us. He was giving me an advance on my paycheck. This would make my mom feel a lot better. We wouldn't have to scramble to pay the bills this month. Moisture beaded my eyes as I held the money. I hadn't expected to get work today, and here I was getting more than I normally would.

"I'll work for all of it," I promised. I wasn't going to run for anything. I was indebted to him.

"I know you will. Have a good night, Seb," he told

me.

As I walked down the hallway, I heard Leer ask about the money. He commented that it sounded like it meant a lot to me and he wanted to know how I was doing. Nick of course told him it was confidential and walked out behind me.

Chapter 17

Sebastian

I expected to see Leer impatiently standing by my door to get me hooked up to my monitors, but my door was shut. Was I late? I checked the time on my phone and I was spot on. So what was the deal? I walked closer to the door to try the handle and noticed a paper partway under the door playing peek-a-boo with me. I slid it out to read that we had a team meeting. Unusual for the day, but I wasn't going to protest. A team meeting might let me see Millie.

I made my way down to the meeting room and added my body to the congregation in the hall. The door was open to the meeting room. What was everyone's problem? I looked at the usual talkative individuals—Dean, Justin, and Nikki—who exchanged looks with each other like a round robin. Well, I wasn't about to put my head on a pole. Why was no one going in? I shoved my way through. Dean put a hand on my upper arm to stop me, but dog-headed I reached the door and looked through.

Millie was in the room. She might as well have been in the direct center since her presence was a beacon of sunlight. Instead of letting the room envelop her, she was at the far left edge. Her feet were propped on the seat of the chair before her and she was playing with her light brown hair. Now I knew exactly what she looked like. She grabbed a section of it and I waited for her to twist it around her finger. Millie didn't twist. She nestled the hair into her mouth. Was she going to suck on it? No. She tilted her head toward the sky and spit the hair out of her mouth in sections, creating a unique series of quiet thwaping noises. She repeated her behavior while I stared at her, wishing she would look at the door and bring me in with her orbital focus.

Then again, did I need her to look at me? Maybe she wasn't looking at anyone because she'd noticed that no one would enter the room if she did. Ah. My teammates were scared. I could fathom their swirl of thoughts and gut-wrenching emotions. "Have I ever seen her before? It's a sniper! What do I do? She's in the meeting room! Run for it, river rats!" I winked at Dean, and then strode inside, bursting with anticipation.

"Are you on our team now?" I asked Millie. "I cannot begin to tell you how excited I am."

Millie spat her hair out of her mouth alongside a

joyful reply that increased my own heart's pattering. "Seb! Did I ever say thank you for making me question the delusions of reality?" She got up off her chair and gave me a hug. Real-life hugs were way better than virtual ones. For one thing, I could feel it. For another thing, I recognized her emotions as genuine. She was excited to see me. There was no guessing involved.

"That rascal reality. You'll show him who's boss," I answered.

Dean crept into the room after me followed by the rest of our team. They treated my center of gravity like an opposing magnet. Each of them pressed to the edges of the room, south poles to the north pole of Millie. That was fine with me. I had her all to myself.

"I'm not exactly on your team. I report to Leer, but I'm working two floors down with William, which isn't his real name."

"Say no more or I might start calling Will the sneaky sister stealer, the female filcher, the rival renegade—"

"Or the best-looking guy in this dump," Will announced his entrance. He strode into the room, ignoring the finicky coworkers at the edges to join my inner circle. I wondered if any of them recognized him. His age, height, and dark skin caused him to stand out, but while that made my coworkers nervous, his presence made me calmer.

"When it comes to looks no one can take their eyes off me," I responded.

"That's because you're so funky," Will told me. "You have a lopsided personality."

"All the better for fooling those hackers," I told him proudly.

Millie's eyes lit up. She looked between us and I could picture her watching us as the Flying Falcon and Will the thief. I didn't think I was ever going to live that game down. In fact, maybe I would live that game up.

"I expected most of you to fail this test." Nick strode into the room without a clipboard, but with his usual air of authority. "And I'm not surprised that you passed it, Seb. Have a seat, everyone."

"What test?" Jared asked as he took the closest seat available near the back.

"Life. I'm sure Sebastian can explain that to you."

Me explain about life? I could take a bite out of it. "All of life is a test. You're born, you live, and you get spun around with the Earth's orbital rotation. If you don't keep your head on straight, it might get flung to the wall."

"We're not in the games yet, Seb," Nick chided me instead of being taken in by my brilliance. He pointed down, so I took up the seat right next to Millie and copied her by putting my feet up on a chair. Was she always this relaxed at work? Will elbowed me and I looked to the front to find that Nick was still staring at me.

"Did you want another life analogy?" I asked him.

"I want your attention," Nick requested. That was going to be a hard one. Millie was sitting right next to me and I wanted to stare at her. However, I gave Nick a nod instead of catering to my personal fantasies.

"We have a new team member," Nick broadcast. He pointed, but he didn't need to. Everyone had already seen Millie. "Millie will be showing up from time to time. She is in training. You are not to ask her to do anything relating to your missions. She has her own." Nick looked directly at me while he said this.

"Come play with me, Millie," I whispered from the corner of my mouth. I watched her stifle her gleeful reaction.

"We also have the monthly performance records ready. Leer will discuss with you your contributions today. We had a good month." Nick ran through the rest of his prepared speech. He might as well have run the treadmill, his mouth moved so fast. Will kept glancing at me from the seat next to mine. I asked if he wanted me to take notes, since he didn't look like he was paying attention.

"I have an ear for the important stuff. Everything else I block out. It's a shame we're opposites in that regard," he whispered.

Before I could give Will a retort that would leave him laughing Nick cleared his throat at us.

"Life analogy?" I blinked.

"You're about to play musical chairs," he told me. "Be serious, Seb. We're not playing games yet."

"Life is a game and I'm an overachiever," I muttered when Nick looked away from me.

"Come on, Millie," Will apprehended my newest life interest. "Time for work."

I pouted as they left the meeting early because I still felt like bantering with them. I wanted to play hooky from the meeting. Why did Will get to play with Millie? Was there a chance I could run across them in the breakroom?

Chapter 18

Millie

I stood at the front of the building with a map in my hand and everyone's problems running through my mind. On the forefront was trying to figure out all my coworkers who had signed up for this gig. Was one of them bad like Tabitha thought? Were all of them good? Rory was under the impression that I was not effective at working my job if I didn't know the people in the company. I had concluded my time with him today by learning the employee's names and faces. I still felt it ridiculous that everyone suddenly trusted me to know all this stuff when it sounded so important.

Also, did they not realize that I had never lived in a city before in my life? We had been out on plantations and middle-of-no-wheres. I was out of my league to have a map in my hand, a key in my pocket to an apartment, and complete control over whether I made it to the place or not. I was going to be realistic. This was going to take me a while.

I stared at the map so long that another person exited the building behind me, striding out into the world like the pro she was. Cool. I would head that way, too, until I ran out of roads on my map that kept me in a safe boundary to the people that had rescued me—or rather bullied me into working for them. The lines were a little blurry, unlike Visions slogan: "Clearing away the sludge."

I called what I was doing stalking. I followed the woman—whose name was missing from my overly full brain, but who worked on the first floor—until I ran across another person I recognized. Then I followed that person. Neither one looked back at me. Neither one seemed to realize what I was doing. I hardly knew what I was doing, but doing something was better than sitting around alone in a strange apartment. It was funny how many people I recognized. I would start getting bored with following one person, and then another person would suddenly show up across the road, giving me another target. It was strange how none of them recognized each other. I had read in the rule book that they were not allowed to interact for safety reasons, but I wasn't sure how well *everyone* followed that. These people took that stipulation seriously. How did they make friends without talking to coworkers?

One man had a second job. I followed him to the employee entrance of a fast food joint. He inspired me to enter and buy dinner from him. He didn't look like he recognized me at all. Tired of stalking, sniping, whatever, I

174

finally found my way to my apartment. It was hard to enter knowing where my parents were sleeping. The room was sparsely furnished, but it was much better than the dirt of the cave. I locked the door behind me and collapsed onto the mattress. It had taken a few days, but Leer had found me this place to live instead of living inside Visions' work building. I think I preferred the building. It was lonely here without my parents.

I lay down on the mattress ready to sleep to pass the time. However, sleep was elusive. This place was strange. The walls were a bare white. The kitchen connected to my bedroom and the front door. I had one small table and two chairs. Off to the side of the kitchen was a very small bathroom. Visions was a quiet place, but coupled with the lack of people, the absence of sound made me nervous. I wanted to escape my situation by sleeping, but the moment I closed my eyes, I found myself back at work.

"This is ridiculous," the man in front of me said. I agreed. I wanted to sleep, not surf the waves all night. But I stayed for a moment to figure out what was taking place. If I was being pulled into a place without me trying to go there, or blinking to change my destination, that had to mean that either a strong user of heiss was here, or that more than one heiss user was meeting together, pulling me in toward their collected source.

I was standing in the middle of a dirt road, which

made me remarkably more comfortable than the city I had traversed in real life tonight. Hopefully I wasn't supposed to say anything. I was part of a circle with a group of seven other people.

"Profits are falling. You promised results," another person answered. I started memorizing faces. I didn't have a camera to take pictures, but this sounded strange. Actually, one of these people I knew. The gray-haired man that I had spied in the company conference room was the CEO of Visions. Was I in the middle of another work meeting? They were not in the conference room. Nick had told me to stay out of that room.

"What you are asking is proving harder to correct than we thought. There's an organization of hackers that are calling themselves the Vikings that have infiltrated half of your games. We've been following these guys for a while, and although difficult they are stoppable. We're working on it," the CEO promised. Ah. I was orientated now. Our CEO, Berk Bergstrom, was trying to convince these people that we could stop the Vikings. One of the guys in the circle jerked backward.

"June's overrun by a sniper!" he cried and looked at me.

"Sorry. This jump was accidental," I told them. I blinked my way out of there. June, who I had overtaken, must have sent the guy a message on his screen. Hopefully she wouldn't panic. I didn't want her to think her life was being threatened.

Was I sleeping this time? No. I was looking at a man who was wearing a top hat and bow tie and lazily signing a piece of paper about war. He reminded me of a president and mumbled something about the number of troops. His voice was woefully familiar. This was the guy who had overtaken the Earl of Key Hill, and called me Dove. Had I found the Vikings already? That was easy. This person had to be using a lot of heiss for us to keep bumping into each other. He was someone I was supposed to find.

Now I just needed to make sure that the character I had taken over wasn't one that was vital to anything or needed to respond to anyone around me. I didn't get my wish—I was the only other person in the room with Mr. Top Hat. I was holding a clipboard which featured more signed war papers. I didn't like wars. Was this paper necessary? I didn't know what game I had stepped into, so I wasn't sure if the infiltrator before me was supposed to be creating a war or not.

How was I supposed to hunt this guy down? If I could learn this, perhaps I could find my parents. I could follow the fake Earl in my sleep, but how did that relate to finding a person in real life? I had recognized William—or rather Casper—by his voice, but if I never met the sniper in real life how was I going to place the person's voice? I didn't want to get that close to a real sniper that actually killed people. That wasn't on my to-do list. Finding my parents, getting enough money to buy my own car, and finding a way to fit in at large cities were on my to-do list. Literally being hit by a sniper was not.

Rory had me run over the basics of finding people earlier. First, I was to focus on the time zone. When was this guy most active? It was night, but that didn't mean anything to me. I didn't know how to not get pulled into the games. This guy was always there. He could be using heiss in his basement, for all I knew. Or maybe he was like me and didn't need heiss to jumpstart any surfing session. The absence of heiss helped him find it, although Rory had said not having any at all when you got used to it was just as dangerous as having too much. That was one of the reasons why employees were monitored so closely.

If possible, I was supposed to draw a picture of the Vikings' people I found. How was that going to work? This guy was a sniper, and invaded different people's faces. If I could see him and knew that he was a sniper couldn't he see me and recognize me as one too? I assumed that there were different levels of people's sniping abilities, but this guy was a professional, so he had to be good. What was it that I was seeing, anyway? Rory had described it as reading a person's wave level, but I had yet to see waves floating through anyone's body. It was more like a sixth sense of smell, which didn't sound logical, because I was using my eyes. Actually,

178

no I wasn't. My real eyes were closed. I was using this strange new heiss sensor.

"Read me the last paragraph on the top sheet," the president directed.

I started to read off the correct spot. The president picked up his copy, shaking his head. He stepped over to compare, and before I knew it Mr. Top Hat had pulled out dental floss that he wrapped around my neck. Yes, this was exactly the sniper that I didn't like. I blinked out before I could die. I needed to find a way to follow this person from a safer distance. Was this the same sniper that kept killing me over and over again? Was this, in fact, Seb's sniper? How was I supposed to tell anyone what he looked like?

It took me a few jumps before I guessed I was back in the same game in a different part of the building. There was a picture of the president, in any case. I had infiltrated a guard in the hallway. I held my breath when I heard the sounds of boots coming down the hallway. There were three other guards near me. One looked toward the boot sound. Another one looked out a nearby window toward a flashing light. Was it a code for something?

Coming down the hallway was Mr. Top Hat. I didn't dare move or say anything as he got close to me. He was holding his signed war papers and flicked through a few of them as he walked right past me. Did he not know I was there, or could he only tell who I was if I talked? Had he already planned on terminating the secretary so she couldn't tell anyone that he was starting a war and I had just been in the wrong place? Did he really not sense me in the same way?

I looked at the other guards near me. As soon as the president walked past, the guard at the window answered the code by flashing his flashlight in a signal. I decided to follow Mr. Top Hat. I was a guard, after all. I had several weapons. Would I get in trouble if I shot the president?

He entered a room that had green as its main color. There was green wallpaper and green lamp shades and green rugs. The walls and border trim were white, but I didn't think it provided enough contrast. Inside the room was another player that I recognized from playing the Earl of Key Hill game. This man had been one of the people that had been left on the hillside when the Flying Falcon had taken me away. I memorized his face before the door was closed. A while later Mr. Top Hat came out, walking beside the man who was now holding the papers. Neither one seemed to guess that I wasn't supposed to be there. I guessed that starting a war really wasn't the wisest thing to do in this game. I didn't know how to stop it, though. All I could do was try to remember what Mr. Top Hat's companion looked like. I wasn't sure how I would ever place Mr. Top Hat's voice to a face.

Mr. Top Hat waved the man goodbye when he

reached a car, and when the car pulled away the sniper in him was gone. The president character looked around to locate his current position, and then turned around and headed back up to his room where he was supposed to be. I watched the commotion break out when the secretary was spotted. Everyone scrambled around because of the security breach. I didn't bother to tell the computer characters that a sniper had been the cause. I blinked, trying to find the sniper again. When I failed, I wondered if I could find a way to get myself to sleep tonight.

Chapter 19

Millie

"What are you doing?"

There was something pressed to the back of my head. A book? The question felt familiar, the book was new. It felt like the corner of a book, anyway, and the voice was low, male. This wasn't supposed to happen inside the work building. I wasn't good at merging the dream world with the real world. In my opinion it should never be mixed up like this. Why did such things as snipers even exist to cause other people so many problems? Then again, my actions at the moment were a little stalkerish.

"Working," I answered the mysterious voice as the book was pushed closer to the base of my neck. What was that book going to do? Could I turn around now and see who was threatening me?

"Who gave you permission to be in here?" the voice

asked me.

Was this a man or woman talking? I could almost recognize the voice, but with so many things to focus on right now, I couldn't place it. Was the person behind me using a voice filter? Could I track the sound of the voice, assuming that I got out of this unscathed? There shouldn't be attacks at work. Then again, I had just proven to myself that my employee record had not made it into Visions database. Had I not been hired? Maybe the person holding the book to my head knew the same thing. I was in the records room, the one place that didn't seem to house a sleeping body in this building. I had researched my own records, nothing, and then looked up people by their heiss level, trying to figure out which ten people were capable of surfing into the Visions system. They needed to be able to handle a heiss level over sixty. Leer had only named five names along with Seb's: Casper, Tabitha, Lex, Grant, and Rory. I was missing four. I didn't personally think the problem was any of the employees, since I had gotten in by riding waves, but I still wanted to know who could hold the most heiss in this place.

I reached over and closed the screen that I was looking at, although I was sure whoever had snuck up behind me had already seen. Still, though, I logged out as well, just in case this turned south and they were trying to steal their way into the records that I had been searching.

"I have a lot of permission to be in here. Who are you? Do *you* have permission?" I asked.

"You better not be looking up Sebastian Tinsley," the voice threatened even lower now.

I wasn't, but why did everything have to be related to Sebastian? Why did this person care if I was trying to find information about him? There was nothing wrong with Sebastian, except that he didn't have his correct address posted.

"Nope," I told the person behind me. "I have no intention of looking up Sebastian," I said into the silence, because I already knew his heiss levels. "But why shouldn't I?"

Wrong question. My vision went dark, and it wasn't like I could blink and fix it. I felt the tip of a needle at my neck. I wanted to ask mystery person what book he was reading, to try to keep the conversation light, but that didn't happen. Why did reality have to mix?

When I opened my eyes again, I was stretched out on a picnic blanket on a grassy field. Beside me rested my shoes. My feet were bare and I couldn't see my socks. I was awake, right? I tried blinking just to make sure, and yes I was awake, but where? Whose grand idea was it to drug me and make it look like I was sleeping on the edge of a field? I had been dragged out of work. Could I find anyone's fingerprints? I looked over at my shoes. One of them was buzzing. I reached inside and pulled out the phone that Will had given me. I recognized the number, because Will had given me a bunch. Nick was calling me from his personal phone line.

"Hi," I answered.

I stood up to look around and found myself still a little woozy. The back of my head hurt. I rubbed at it and found a lump. *The drug wasn't good enough? You had to hit me on the head and dump me too?*

"What makes you think you can leave work early?" Nick asked me, full of impatience.

"I didn't. I was drugged, smacked, and dumped on a picnic blanket. When I figure out where I am I will come back to work, although I really shouldn't. Someone there just kicked me out."

Nick was quiet on the other end of the phone. I wondered if he was at work himself, since he had called from his own phone and not his work line. Why was he looking for me instead of Leer or Will? Was he the one who had dumped me here and he had called me to wake me up and pretend like he'd had nothing to do with it?

I checked my shoes to make sure there were not rocks in them and then pulled them on. Then I rolled up the blanket to bring as evidence. The closest building that I could see wasn't too far. I moved toward it.

186

"Okay. I am standing in front of the Go Lucky Wok," I told Nick. "Smells like Chinese food."

"Stay put. Will is coming to get you."

Nick hung up on me. Of course Will was coming to get me. I looked at my phone to see that I had fifteen missed calls from Leer, Will, and Nick. Had Nick used his own phone because they thought I was avoiding answering the work lines? Well I wasn't. I was still trying to figure out why anyone would dump me because of Sebastian. I ran the question past Will when he showed up in a black car with the license plate knocked off. I didn't tell him that it was illegal to drive his car like that. He told me I was lucky that I hadn't been killed.

"I was at *your* work," I told him. "This shouldn't have happened."

At least I wasn't far from work. I had been left only two blocks away. Nick was standing outside waiting for us. He unlocked the door and we stepped inside, continuing our conversation.

"My work?" Will asked. "So you're trying to quit?"

"That's not what I said, but I have no employment records. I don't work here."

I tried to find myself in the database as soon as Leer had walked out the door. I wanted to know what kind of information they had written down about me. I had told

187

them everything, and they had bullied me into a job because they thought I had seen too much and that I would be back again anyway—so I might as well put my dying practices to good use and earn money for it. Maybe it was Leer who had dumped me. Where was he?

"You do have records," Nick answered while he looked at the professionals that guarded the front desk. They didn't let in weirdos, but I was pretty sure that they had missed one today. "With the threats to our system security we haven't uploaded your records to the main database. You *do* work here, and you are not to run away. We will find you, Millie."

I looked at Will and rolled my eyes. No one but Nick threatened me. So was he really behind my attack or not? It hadn't sounded like him, but he could have concealed his voice. It could have been Leer. It could have been Will, too, trying to see what I would do if I woke up in an unfamiliar location. After all, I wasn't that far away. They all could have been spying on me the whole time.

"What's the deal with everyone being against Sebastian?" I complained. "I like Sebastian, but it's not like..." I stopped talking because the door between the workrooms and the front opened. Speaking of Seb made him appear. I checked the clock on the wall to see what time he got off work. It was six. Well I knew where Leer was. He had been waking up Sebastian.

Sebastian looked pretty good when he woke up. This wasn't my first time seeing him in person, but I still liked how his own body fit him versus a few avatars he had been. He was taller than I'd first expected by a few inches. He was wearing a gray shirt with the picture of a dragon on it. I smiled, thinking about the dragon mask he had worn before. He had blue jeans and clean white shoes. I was already familiar with his brown hair and green eyes that could mesmerize me.

"Oh!" I told Will as I thought about shoes. "I lost my socks."

"You could have lost way more than that," he reminded me.

"It's not *my* fault!" I told him. "Maybe you should check my phone for fingerprints." I shoved my phone at Will. Then I looked back at Sebastian, who hadn't moved an inch after closing the work door.

Seb was staring at me with something running through his head. He glanced at Nick and Will puzzled. Maybe he was trying to figure out how I could have lost my socks. I still didn't know. Of all the people at work I could suspect, the one person it clearly wasn't was Sebastian. Who kept picking on him?

"Have a good night," Nick dismissed him.

Nick started to walk toward the door, so Will and I

189

followed. Seb stepped to the side still trying to look like he wasn't interested in our conversation. He failed when we got closer. He burst out with a smile, the same one that had stopped me several times. I came to a halt again and smiled back.

"I was a midget today," Seb told me. "There's nothing like being short to remind you of being a little kid again."

"If you took up residence in a world of giants, you could feel little all the time," I answered, wondering if he was trying to use a code word that I was missing. He had thought about it long enough.

He looked between me and Nick before he took a step toward the front door, but only one to put distance between himself and Nick.

"Did I see you today?" Seb asked me. Did he think I had been a midget with him? That would have been nicer than napping on a picnic blanket exposed to everyone around me and the sock thief.

"Just coming in," I told him, even though I wasn't supposed to discuss my work hours, but I still didn't believe I was even working. Nick had to be making up my employment, or perhaps Leer had hidden my own name before giving me access to the database.

"And you're going out," Nick reminded Seb. He

pointed toward the door and Seb grinned at all of us.

"Good night, Nick. Good night, Will," Seb told them. He paused before he said the same thing to me. "Good night, Millie."

He rolled my name off his tongue deliberately slow and with a hint of the satisfaction that rested in his eyes. I tried to not giggle at him. I really did, but I couldn't help it. He seemed pleased with himself for knowing my name even though I had *told* him my name.

"Don't encourage him," Nick told me. He grabbed my arm and pulled me through the door, shutting it before Seb could say anything else to me. I was still trying not to laugh. What was it about Seb that one look could move me so much?

"I should not have been dragged out of the office. How did that happen?" I asked Nick and Will. "Wouldn't someone have seen me?"

"Let's not talk in the halls," Nick directed.

I followed him down to my room. We passed Leer, who had gone to wake up the next person. Will sat on the edge of my bed and I dumped the picnic blanket on it. Nick examined the blanket. Will searched through my phone. We all looked up when Leer came in.

"What?" he asked as Nick gave him a cold stare. Did Nick suspect Leer?

"I was dumped outside, unconscious," I told Leer. "You didn't happen to see who dragged me outside, did you?"

"Well gee it wasn't me!" Leer told us. "Why would I do that? I thought I was the only one trying to protect Millie instead of the company profits."

"Well you're not blaming this on me," Nick told him.

"Wasn't me, either," Will shrugged. He put my phone down, and then decided to ignore the anger between Nick and Leer. "What do you think, Millie?"

"It's tangled up with Sebastian, whatever the issue is. The person was rather adamant that I wasn't looking up Sebastian. I wasn't, by the way. Sebastian didn't even cross my mind. But he's on someone's mind, so that's the person we need to find. I almost recognized the voice. He or she could have used a voice filter. Who might have been walking around the halls at ten? Maybe I could match the pitch of the voice if I heard it again. Is there a voice filter in the office?"

"Yeah. We'll start there. Let's go see if we can find that voice filter."

Will jumped off my bed and passed me my phone. I put it in my pocket and followed him out the door. Nick and Leer were still glaring at each other. I expected them to exchange heated words as soon as no one else could hear them.

"You'd think *they* were dumped outside," I mumbled as I followed Will into the breakroom. He started opening drawers, so I did too.

"They're just scared. It's one thing to get told that there are people sabotaging their employees in virtual reality. It's quite another when it starts happening in real life right beside them. Whoever it was, they didn't think you much of a threat yet. They might come against you again."

"I'm not hired. I could just run away," I told Will.

He paused to tap his fingers against a drawer before he told me that if I ran, he would be sent to hunt me down.

"You could just let me go," I voiced.

I slammed closed a drawer that was filled with paper cups. I didn't have much hope of finding my parents like this. They were either stuck in the Doldrums where I had just come from or, as Leer had suggested at first, so far away from any existing heiss that I would never find them through it.

"I can't let you go. That would mess up Sebastian," Will answered. He kept his face angled away from me while I glared at him.

"What is it with everyone and Sebastian?!"

"Seb's cool," Nikki told me as she stepped into the

breakroom. She worked on his team with Leer. Was she the person that Leer had just gotten up?

"Being cool is not enough for everyone to obsess over him." I didn't mind that I liked him, but everyone?

"I am not obsessed with Sebastian." Will glared back at me.

"I'll just be quick," Nikki told us. She looked between us as she moved to the vending machine to buy a candy bar.

It didn't make sense. Who was messing up the system because Sebastian was here? Someone had been trying to kill him repeatedly and unmask him. Was someone jealous of his abilities? If that lead didn't get me anywhere, then alternatively who was trying too much to protect him? Maybe that wasn't the right question either. Who wanted Sebastian's information to remain hidden?

"I'm going to look someplace else," I told Will.

"Call me if you find it," Will said, apparently glad to see me go.

I nodded and headed back to the records room. Leer had already beaten me to it. He was looking around, trying to spot clues. He shook his head when I came in as if he hadn't seen anything. I moved back to the computer and logged back in. Of course the first thing I did was look up Seb Tinsley's information. It was pretty much what Will had told me. He could handle a heiss level of seventy-three, and all his other information was incorrect except for his phone number. He had a mom and a brother. Maybe I could find them. Did his mom handle heiss well too?

"Do we know anything about Seb's dad?" I asked Leer.

"Not a thing," Leer told me before looking at the door with suspicion. "I thought you'd left," he said to Tabitha, who normally worked with Nick. Her purple hair was pulled up today, revealing a star tattoo on her neck.

"Plane got delayed. I'll be leaving in a minute. I heard you had an incident. I'm holding you responsible if Millie gets hurt," she told Leer.

I couldn't spot her holding any weapons, but her voice was one. The scary woman smiled while she delivered her threat. I looked at Leer, who took offense as well. She was trying to intimidate him. He stood up to his full height and briefly flexed his muscles. If she had delivered her notice on a piece of paper, I could picture Leer throwing the threat into the trashcan the same way Will had done earlier.

"It's not happening again. Have a good trip."

She left, taking with her a sigh from me. Leer gave up his search in the computer room to reinforce his statement telling me all the ways that the work building was secure and how he would personally see to my safety. I was going to be locked into my room from now on, which meant

I couldn't wander.

After Leer's explanation, and a few breathing exercises that Leer made me do, Will had us meet him in the men's bathroom. He had found my socks and the voice filter in the trashcan there. His theory was my socks had been used as gloves to conceal the fingerprints of whoever had tossed me out. I had been thrown out a window. There was footage of me tumbling outside headfirst from an outside camera, but no footage of whoever it was that had pushed me. There was also no footage of who had picked me up and moved me. So whoever had done it had known enough to delete the inside cameras and the outside cameras but had forgotten one.

"Could it have been Rory?" I asked just to put it out there, since that would be Tabitha's first guess.

"I'll find out who it was and take care of it," Will promised as he handed me my socks. I hoped they were not too dirty because I had no idea where to do laundry. That would be on my agenda tonight once I got off work.

"The important thing is to make sure that you and Sebastian are safe," Will asserted. He must have caught my annoyed expression. "I don't like you being questioned about him."

"Could Seb's sniper get in? I was right next to him last night in my dreams," I fretted. I had been stopping his sniper by getting in the way. Wouldn't that make the guy want to stop me too?

"Which proves that when you first started surfing, you were following the sniper," Will pointed out. "Keep it up. The person might eventually slip and give you a clue about his or her location."

"Has he found Seb?" I asked Will worriedly. I didn't want anything to happen to Sebastian. I also didn't want anything more happening to me. I needed to get better at my job.

"What makes you certain that his sniper is a man?"

"His voice? I can recognize his voice, although I can tell it's him before he talks. It's like a weird sixth sense."

Will nodded and claimed that he hadn't heard the guy talk since he started following Seb. He thought he had spotted him a few times, but he wasn't sure yet. Then he told me that I needed to get enough sleep and to not work overtime outside of the building. When I had come in this morning, I had reported sleeping maybe a total of four hours last night.

"I like to assume the best about the people I work with," Will said waving the voice filter in his hand. "Since knocking out an employee is the same as putting them to sleep, perhaps the person who tossed you out the window was helping you."

"What?" I asked him, looking at him like he was

197

crazy.

"So you could get some sleep," Will pointed out. "It's a health benefit using desperate measures."

He shrugged when I remained skeptical, and Will mumbled that it was a train of thought he was pursuing. I could have been tossed out by anyone who knew I was staying up too late. That would imply that the person who had tossed me out wasn't actually evil. I wasn't feeling as forgiving as Will.

Chapter 20

Millie

"If I don't max out on heiss, then I'm always at work. It's aggravating. I feel like I'm stepping on everyone's toes all the time or bumping elbows or rubbing shoulders," I told Rory as I sat up. I eyed the heiss machine next to me. I had only been in the room for a few minutes before Rory had entered.

"Not rubbing shoulders. You are smashing toes," Rory agreed.

"How do I sleep?" I asked Rory, trying to see if he would give me any indication that he had thrown me out a window to put me to sleep yesterday. "Do you have this problem? I don't try to have this problem, but the waves pull me under. I can't break free of the riptide."

I was already yawning and it wasn't even lunchtime yet. I hadn't gotten much sleep the night before, even if I

199

hadn't seen much of Seb's sniper. The sniper had found me once, waved, and that was the last I had seen of him.

"Follow me. We're only going to the kitchen," Rory promised when I didn't make a single move out of my workroom door. I was tired. I walked after him anyway, and lingered at the edge of the door so I could see down the empty hallways.

"You need something that will ground you in reality. I would suggest ice. Train yourself that when ice is touching your arm you shouldn't ride the waves."

"Train myself? How?"

I caught the ice pack that Rory threw at me. He was the first one to come see me after Leer had left, and I got the sneaking suspicion that he wasn't supposed to be talking with me. I was supposed to be locked in my room. Rory had woken me up when he entered.

"We practice. The medical team informed me that you averaged four hours of sleep a night when you were here. How do you think you did when you were out of the office last night?"

I shrugged. Four hours or so was probably accurate yet again. I had spent my night trying to locate anyone that would be playing in the Earl of Key Hill. What that amounted to was running across people whose pictures I had been memorizing from work. I was certain that I had seen Rory a few times too. He had been walking in a game with clouds. Watching him had been nauseating. The ground beneath the clouds was nonexistent and dangled over a fathomless chasm. I wasn't sure who Rory was following, but I had not followed him for long.

"When you locate Berk you are to leave right away without lingering," Rory told me when we made it back to my room. I was glad that he left my door open.

"The CEO Berk?" I asked, sitting on the edge of the bed and holding the ice pack. "I didn't mean to, and I didn't see him last night."

Rory sighed and sat down beside me. "This is why they still call you Sleeping Beauty," Rory told me. "You're not to hunt for Visions' snipers."

"Are we talking about you now?" I asked him.

Did he realize that I had found him a few times, or had he just told me yet another company secret and our CEO was a hidden sniper? That added another person to my list of people who could place a probe. If our CEO was a sniper, then perhaps the person I thought was Berk was really an avatar and not the real person. I would have to try to track Berk sometime to find out. That might give me some idea of how to locate real people.

"I was trying to sleep," I said, wishing I was still doing that. I feared that being too tired would make me miss something vital in the search for my parents.

"You were following me?" Rory questioned.

He grabbed the ice pack from my hands and jumped off the bed to make his way to the heiss machine. I insisted on Leer being the only one touching it, since I still had my apprehensions about Rory being in my room.

"You need practice, Millie," Rory told me, ignoring my request with the machine. "And Leer doesn't have the time to sit in your room and help you sleep. He wakes people up. What's your max?" Rory asked me.

I shook my head. That was confidential. Had Rory come in here trying to steal my information? I didn't let him put the heiss to my arm until he called in one of the doctors to do it who already knew my stats. Then I grudgingly agreed to learn how to sleep by using an ice pack.

"Won't I get too cold to sleep eventually?" I asked Rory. "That won't help me sleep."

"This is only practice. When you can stay asleep and not surf for ten minutes on demand, than you can graduate to an armband. A lot of snipers sleep with an armband so, don't go thinking it's for babies. You're not the only one with sleep issues. Everyone else is just too busy to deal with them."

I was to lay down and try to get to sleep while the ice pack was on my arm. We were going to try for a half hour before Rory would tell the doctor to max me out on heiss to prevent me from surfing. I already knew that it wasn't going to work. I closed my eyes.

Tabitha was the first person I found. She didn't have purple hair, but I knew it was her by the way she handed off a threat to the person standing with a box of chocolates beside her. I blinked and found the person who had played Steph in the Earl of Key Hill. Last night he had shot me when I'd scared him by inhabiting a person right beside him. Maybe I should figure out who he was. He had to be a sniper. I knew Rory was awake. I had just identified Tabitha's waves, and I could instantly place Will. That left Lex. I hadn't met Lex in person, but he was the sniper on the first floor. It had to be him. There, I'd done it. Easy.

Rory was right beside me, so I could place his waves by default, and yes I had followed him last night a few times on *accident*. I could probably make a rather good guess at who had been at the Earl of Key Hill. Lex had been Steph, Casper was William, and Samson was Grant, so Phil was played by Rory. I wasn't sure which character Tabitha played. I tried not to think about how Rory had just told me not to hunt for Visions' snipers. I had just run through all of them already in under a minute.

Blink. Grant. Now this was new. Grant was the person that Nick used to find problem areas for his team to take care of. I knew he could snipe due to Leer and Tabitha's conversation on the probe problem, but right now he was using his real face. I wondered what the problem was. I wanted to ask him if I could help, but I wasn't supposed to bug Grant *ever*. I blinked again and smiled.

"You can take out the rodeo, but not the road," Seb was saying to a cowboy. I looked around for Will. He would be around here someplace, trying to sort over who was sniping Sebastian. A pair of eyes blinked back at me and it wasn't Will. I didn't like who it was. I knew the wave signature of this person a little too well.

"Howdy." I nodded and found my voice raspy. I looked down to see that I was wearing boots without spurs and a pair of jeans. That was new that I could change my voice now. Maybe it was a feature of this game.

"The art of riding is lost, but you're practiced at rhinos," the guy told me.

I froze. Did he recognize me? He hadn't seemed to recognize me the other night when he'd walked past me carrying the war plans. In this game I couldn't place his voice. Could he place mine, or was he recognizing my wave the same way I was guessing that he wasn't Will? I looked around again and started inching toward Seb to protect him, but I found that I couldn't stay awake.

"No!" I complained, yanking off the band that was giving me heiss, because I was failing my practice using the ice pack to keep me awake. "That was him! That was Seb's sniper. Dang it." I tried to go back to sleep, but it was of no use. I couldn't make myself tired enough to surf. I was tired, though. I should probably sleep.

"Casper will handle it," Rory told me, talking about Will. "But don't forget that wave if you think you found it again."

"No!" I screamed at Rory.

He rolled his eyes at me. I wondered how often he found himself in my shoes, overly tired, with too much on his mind that when he needed to sleep, he found himself unable to do so.

"Millie." Rory pulled me partway off the bed to shove me close to his face. "You haven't gotten a decent night's sleep in more than a week. Guess what that does to your brain? You can't help anyone like this. You need to find a way to stay asleep."

"I don't care! I can't sleep. I just can't. It's impossible."

Rory looked over at the doctor, who shook his head.

"That's illegal," the doctor told him. I wondered what conversation they had had while I was surfing.

"Try," Rory directed me again, dropping me back on the bed. "I'm taking this up with Leer. He's reasonable, you'll see," Rory told the doctor.

Rory walked out of the room and I tried to sink back into the dreams again. "Can you take heiss out? How does it go away?" I asked the doctor.

"You don't. You need to find a way to sleep. He's right about that. Your readings are erratic." The doctor showed me my screen that had lines all over the place. I didn't know what they meant, and I didn't ask for him to explain. I tried to find Seb again. Instead of succeeding, Rory came back with Leer. He looked at the readings and frowned. I looked at them and heard them beep at me while I grew angry again.

"Okay," Leer told Rory. "Here's what I'm willing to do. I'm willing to let you wake up my people and I'll handle Sleeping Beauty."

"She needs to sleep, Leer," Rory insisted.

I glared at him. Why did he want me to sleep so badly? What was he planning on doing when I was sleeping? Leer handed Rory his monitor that connected to his side. Rory shoved it back to him.

"You have no business here," Leer scowled.

"Do you have any idea where she gets to unsupervised?!" Rory screamed back at him.

"Millie is a registered employee of this company just like you. I don't need to sit here and supervise. She knows her job."

206

Oh yes. I had many, many side jobs.

"You're going to kill her. Have you ever explained what happens when people don't sleep?"

Leer gave him a smile that reminded me of Sebastian. It clearly said that he was in control and Rory was out of place and not winning for anything. Leer pushed Rory and the doctor out of the room and called Nick. He told him to make sure those two got back to where they belonged. I started complaining right away, talking about Rory breaking in and trying to make me sleep. Leer agreed with everything I said, even that Rory was probably up to something and didn't care about me at all. That was the last thing I remembered. I think Leer put me to sleep. Was that illegal?

Chapter 21

Sebastian

I hadn't missed the exchange or the fact that Cassie the cowgirl was starting to edge toward me. I didn't think that was in her normal character, and that thing about the rhino... that had her on edge as well. Was it Millie? It didn't last long if it was. Maybe Leer had kicked her out of my feed again like I suspected happened a lot. All the same, I spun around with my gun out toward Jim who used to be Will. Was it not? Had the sniper kicked out Will? What was Will doing? Trying to find me again?

"I'm coming for you," the sniper told me. I shot him. Then I looked around for anyone who might be Will. Had he seen that? No, but Tory was still right next to me. I'd needed to ride his bull and not fall off for ten seconds so I could win the ribbon that was messing up this game. I had just messed that up.

"You better start running because the sheriff is going to kill you for your cold-blooded murder!" Tory screamed at me. Yup. I had ruined that chance. We'd have to find something else. This sort of game was so broad that you couldn't reset it. There were other players involved in multiple places. I wished I had the powers to reset the level. There wasn't anything I could do about Jim lying flat on the ground, but I aimed my gun at Tory next. I wasn't a moment too soon. He raised his gun at me instead of running to the sheriff, and I shot at him too. The sniper had switched to Tory. I heard a laugh at my side and I swung that way next.

"Look at that. I can turn you into something insane," a little kid told me. He was holding a pistol. Where did he get that?

"What's your problem?" I asked the sniper, still wondering if Will was coming to help or not. Was my monitor beeping like crazy? Where was Leer? I was pretty sure I was trembling. I felt really cold.

"Only you," the child grinned at me.

It was hard to do, but I pulled the trigger on the kid, and then started running. I was too much in the open and my chances of winning the ribbon were over. I might as well just steal the thing and get out of here. I knew where the ribbon was. I broke the window on Tory's house, climbed in, and stole the box that he kept the ribbon inside. I ran again after grabbing the ribbon. Gun shots followed after me. A stampede of cattle started in toward me and I was running for my life when Leer pulled me out. Finally.

"What was that?" Leer asked me. "You scared the cows that bad?"

He hadn't seen the sniper. I really had one. I had suspected there was someone after me, and now the person was giving me verbal threats. What was I going to do? I had gotten an advance on my paycheck and felt obligated to work for it. Besides, if a sniper was really after me was it in my best interest to move my family and run? I would be leaving all the people who understood *why* a sniper was after me.

"I think I lost Will," I told Leer as I rubbed at my arms, trying to figure out what I was going to do.

"What?" Leer played stupid, but I knew he allowed Will to follow me.

"Seriously?" I asked Leer. He rubbed at his eyes as his monitor started beeping at him again.

He grumbled, and then pulled me to my feet. I followed him down the hallway into a room that he unlocked and pushed me inside. He looked over his shoulder, making sure no one was watching us enter the room. I looked, too, before I realized where I was.

Millie. She was asleep on the bed and her heartbeat pattern was flashing. Was she hurt? She wasn't hooked up to anything.

"Just stop trying!" Leer screamed at her.

He slammed the door shut, and then I realized that she *was* hooked up. She had a thin cord on her ankle instead of her arm. Leer took the cord off. Along with it came a needle. He shook his head as he picked up the armband that allowed him to spy on people. He put the spying armband on Millie and looked at the screen. Millie jumped right in. She flashed into a screen, looked around, disappointed, and flashed out again.

"What's she doing?" I asked. It was surprising how fast she could change her position. She ran through five more games, jumping all over the place like crazy.

"She's scaring the company snipers. *That's* what she is doing." Leer sighed.

We had more than one? She rushed into a game with flashing lights and squares that a guy was catching. He looked at her and punched her face, screaming at her to go to sleep. I looked over at Millie in real life. She didn't even flinch. Her monitor beeped again and she was off.

"I've got to get her to sleep," Leer tapped at the monitor that was beeping on his side. "Then I can get back to you. The ice didn't work."

Leer explained to me that the ice was supposed to keep her grounded in the real world so she would sleep for a few hours. Wasn't it illegal for us to sleep in our beds at work? I shrugged. I had done it before. Leer slipped the heiss band onto her arm, and I couldn't help but look at the levels. She was at eighty-seven, which I'm sure was high. He didn't start the band working, though. Instead he typed into the computer and Millie skidded to a halt at the corner of a block where a snarling dog was barking at her. Leer told her to find a way to go to sleep. She screamed back at him that she wasn't going to.

"Why doesn't she want to?" I asked Leer. He told me that information was classified. I snorted at him. I knew I had told myself to not help Millie, but she made that hard. I could do something, right? It wouldn't impact my family. Leer changed the screen to a street that caused her to skid to a halt again. She looked over the place and then screamed that it wasn't real.

"It was worth a try," Leer mumbled. Was that where Millie used to live? Was he trying to give her familiar images? He tried a few more places that only made her madder. I stopped looking at the screen and turned to Millie. She looked really tired, so I took her hand. There was a momentary beep from her monitor, and then her heartbeat steadied out.

"Hey," Leer told me. "If she's stable for five minutes remind me to tell you that you're a genius."

"You can tell me again right now," I bragged. Then I

213

inhaled. Millie gripped my hand. She gave out a sigh and the other levels on her screen started to level out too. That lasted for only two minutes before she was jumping again, however.

"He's fine!!" Leer wrote on her screen. Who? Who was Millie looking for? She jumped around a few more times and I squeezed her hand back.

"Millie, you should go to sleep," I told her. She stopped jumping again. She stood still in the game she was in, not the best one to stand still in since she was crossing a road. The cars honked at her relentlessly. "Remember? You have to sleep in real life," I tried again.

"I can't!" she screamed from the screen. She had heard me? Was she mixing reality and games again? How could she still have this problem when she was overly tired? She knew the difference. Maybe it was a surfing thing.

"That's wrong. Use your real mouth."

"I can't sleep!" Millie shouted at me from inside the room instead of only inside her head. Leer filled his mouth with air and then blew it out. He waved me on, saying that was the best progress at getting her to realize where she was yet. She clenched at my hand again, and then forced herself awake. She jerked upwards. As she did so Leer shut off all her screens so she couldn't see them.

"Hi," Millie said, looking at our linked fingers.

She threw the vision viewer cuff across the room as she let go of my hand. Then she hid her face and complained that nothing was going to work. I pulled her off the table as an idea came to me. She had been sleeping on the dirt in the Earl of Key Hill.

"Can we try the floor and a weighted blanket?" I asked both Millie and Leer. "Millie doesn't like to be cold and, let's face it, the floor is hard. She'll realize where she is on that."

Leer called to bring in a weighted blanket. I guessed that someone had to go buy it. While we waited Leer turned into his psychology mode, telling Millie that she was fine, but she needed to sleep. He probed her for how she would sleep as a child, and we all smiled when she mentioned using a rattling baby book.

"It got lost somewhere in the desert," Millie sighed.

Leer sent someone to fetch a book that contained crinkling plastic film between its fabric pages. I started telling her bedtime stories that I had practiced on Triton. When the items came Millie laughed at the whole thing, but it worked. Ten minutes later she was curled up peaceful and cute. Nothing flashed on her screen from the armbands.

"Is that going to work every time?" I asked, and Leer told me not to jinx it. He escorted me back to my room, where Will was frantically pacing himself in circles very similar to his actions when I had been late being the Falcon.

215

Leer passed off my absence before strapping me back in. Was that safe? I had a sniper. Who was going to destroy the ribbon, or had it already been destroyed from the stampede?

"Come in right behind me," I told Will. He nodded to me like he knew exactly why I wanted someone watching my back. It wasn't going to be Millie. She was sleeping on the floor with a baby book. Her adorable features flashed across my mind, drawing out a short beep from my monitor as it registered my increased level of alertness. I smiled, thinking about her, before I was back in my own problems.

Chapter 22

Millie

The door opening woke me up again. It was dark, and I couldn't figure out where I was for a while. It felt like I was still traveling through the great unknown with my family. I had a warm sleeping bag and my baby book wasn't lost. Oh right. I smiled again at the baby book and sat up. Leer was standing in the doorway, letting the light trickle in.

"You did great!" Leer told me, always the optimist. He turned on the light, causing me to squint. It had been dark and quiet. How long had I slept? As he flicked on my monitors to review the data, I came to stand right behind him.

"How... how did you gather that data?" I asked Leer. The pressure cuffs were not on me, and I was certain that no one else had come into my room while I was sleeping.

217

"It's on your right arm," Leer told me. "You make it impossible to use the normal cuffs. I have to use that. It's short range, Millie."

What was? I shoved up my sleeve to find a plastic square on my arm. It was amazing that I had not noticed it yet. Leer explained it to me, answering my questions before I could ask them. It kept track of my temperature and blood pressure. I could take it off by peeling up at the corner. Most people didn't use them, but he was trying to help me unobtrusively. He asked me to always leave it on unless I was taking a shower or swimming. I pulled off the device to make sure I could and then put it back on when Leer made a face at me.

"Work's over for the day. Leave the blanket and take the book and tell me if that gets you to sleep tonight."

Would I be able to sleep tonight? I had spent all day asleep missing every opportunity to look for my parents. I actually wanted to find the CEO (or at least Rory) before going back to sleep. What had Rory done in that amount of time? I left the building with the city map in my hand again. I wandered for a while until I spotted Sebastian. Seb was standing in front of a train schedule board, looking it over. Since he was adorable, and I was rather alert and off work, I brushed away my other concerns moving in closer to Seb.

Just in case he was going to get on a train, I added money to a train card. I followed Seb into the train station, noting all the people who I worked with. Seb walked right next to a few people on his team, and they didn't even blink at each other. When Dean looked at me, I waved to him. They could be so aloof. That wasn't something I could ever see myself being. I liked knowing people. My parents had worked a lot leaving me on my own. Now I wondered how much of that work included creating games that other people played far, far away from us.

I eased my way onto Sebastian's chosen train glancing at the route number so I could find my way back. He met my eyes once, but it was with a glazed-over expression that left me feeling lonelier than I had been before. I had thought that we were friends. He had told me all those stories earlier today easing me through the fright of not being able to sleep. I know the cure was the baby book, but the cure to everything felt like Seb. I loved how he could step outside his own problems to share mine. My parents were often too busy to listen to complaints.

Sebastian was selfless, but here on the train I had to look away before anyone else noticed my disappointment. My eyes strayed to a couple that was talking about what they wanted to eat for dinner as I scanned the rest of the train. A lot of people met my gaze, including a man in a business suit with a white and black beard, but Seb ignored me every time my eyes moved over to him.

I stepped off the train before Sebastian did. It felt like

he was blowing me off which, after reading over the company rules, was exactly what he was supposed to do. I headed toward a newspaper stand, grabbed a free paper, and skimmed the headlines.

"You take the train?" Seb stepped up beside me. I nearly jumped. He wasn't blowing me off? Had I made him miss his real stop? He was hiding behind a newspaper as I was doing. I almost put mine down so I could see him. The newspapers felt like masks, barriers between us.

"I'm wandering. I'm used to small towns where I know everyone. This town makes me feel alone." I hadn't meant to let that slip out. "But I can do it," I added, before he thought me incapable. "I can soldier on and help my parents escape the mine."

"I know the feeling," Seb told me. He reached one hand over to touch the side of my arm. It was such a simple touch, but coming from Seb, I felt like he truly understood me. I pulled my newspaper mask down to scan the side of his face properly. "I'm helping my parents, too. Sometimes the pressure is like holding a ticking bomb."

"Like, I'll miss the number hitting zero and lose everything?" I whispered. He finally lowered his newspaper, thoughtful, searching.

"No. Like you're the energy that makes the bomb tick, and if you *stop* trying to help, then it all explodes."

I smiled at him. He saw things is such an interesting way that I would never get bored of being around him. Could we do this again and find a way to be together? Despite the thought of ticking, he already had my earlier disappointment cured. More than that, my entire body warmed at that sight at him. Seb took his hand off my arm and pointed to the paper as if we were discussing it.

"I was really bad at science, Millie. That chapter on kinetic energy and all those formulas to calculate it... man. I nearly failed science every year. Don't tell anyone. We're supposed to have perfect grades for our jobs. I was not a star student."

Even with knowing that he lied on his paperwork, his reveal took me by surprise. "Honestly? But you're such a genius."

"There were some geniuses that were bad at school," he countered, offering me a wink.

I smiled back still stunned with the open honesty we had going on right now. It was impressive that Visions had hired him. It was equally impressive that he was trusting me with one of his largest lies like we were confidants. I suddenly wanted to tell him everything to prove that I trusted him just as much.

"The worst lie I ever told was on my birthday. I told my parents I was going to see a kid movie and saw something else. I never finished the movie because I got scared and ran out. Even worse, one of my friend's parents saw me leaving the theater room and told on me."

"Well," Seb remarked, shaking his paper. "I'd never tell on you even if you're breaking a few rules like right now."

I was talking to him outside of work. Yes, that was breaking a rule, but since we were breaking the rule together, I wasn't going to say anything. Seb seemed to read that on my face because he smiled again.

"I never told anyone else about science," he said. "But I was really good at math even though it was all formulas designed to make you think *inside* the box." He said that as if he was brilliant for doing things his own way. I admired him for his confidence.

"And I never told any of my friends about the movie," I replied.

We smiled at each other, and it felt like we were passing that ticking bomb between us. The last person with the bomb would have to be the first person to step away. I was the last to speak, I was holding the bomb, but I couldn't move.

Seb took the bomb back. "I always passed gym. That said, I'm late for my evening run."

"I took ballet for seven years," I blurted out not wanting him to go just yet.

"Me too!" He passed me his newspaper and pulled his arms above his head so he could stand on his toes pulling off a pirouette. Once completed, he sank into such a graceful bow that I almost believed he really had taken ballet. When he ran off, I was pretty sure that he had left a piece of himself with me. I didn't feel as lonely anymore. But once gone, my other problems came back. The man with the black and white beard from the train passed by me. I needed to move, too.

I located a large, overwhelming grocery store. People flew past me clearly experts at playing the game of shopping. It took me a good half hour to find the prepackaged sandwiches.

At least I was better at finding my apartment now. After eating, I moved to my mattress on the floor hoping that the timing was right enough to find my parents in a game. The way I saw it, if the heiss around me was strong enough to pull me into a game when I had never had it before, it had to be strong enough to pull in my parents even if they fought against it. It was only a matter of time before they let the heiss take them. I had to be there, in those games, for when the right moment happened. There was no telling when they would wave under, so I felt pressured to be on the lookout always.

I pulled out my baby book, but kept it at a distance as I closed my eyes. How was I to wake myself up if I used the book? Like usual, it took little effort to transport my thoughts into the gaming system. I ran across Visions' CEO. He was playing a racing game and didn't look up to notice me as he sped past me in the stands.

I found Rory following one of the people I recognized as a security guard from the president game. Is that all he had been doing today? Following hackers and trying to scare them away? I followed along behind him watching our leader escape all the traps.

We made it to the other side, and up a vine wall where the man started to discuss a cheat code for some other game. Rory left the game after the code was passed over. Did he have enough evidence to block the cheater? I moved in closer to see.

"You promise this is legitimate?" a black-haired teen with a large nose and skinny chin asked. He was holding a small statue of a monkey, the item with the code.

"That will get you to *The Lost City of Arabold*," the code-passer told him, naming one of my father's games. He was going to say something else, but his character froze and words flashed through the air, telling the skinny teen that the code passer had been removed from the game. That was Rory at work, all right. The teen shoved the monkey into his pocket, ran a few steps, and then left the game. I continued searching trying to follow anyone that would have a strong heiss signature.

Chapter 23

Millie

"There's no one as beautiful as you," Will said as he walked closer to me. I tried to ignore him. He wasn't supposed to talk to me, and I was waiting for the bus, but gee he was getting closer. I had a strange moment where I considered how alone I was and all the things Will could probably do to me like toss me out another window.

"Can a man's beating heart take any more hits? Not this time. I just want to pull you into my arms."

"I have a crush on someone else," I told Will, surprising myself for verbally admitting the truth. I took a step backward, which put me in an even worse location nestled into the backboard of the bus stop. "Go away!"

Will shook his head at me as he continued to get closer. I took another step and hunched sideways when I realized that I wasn't alone at the stop.

"You're scaring the locals," a woman's voice said from behind me. I gave her a brief glance, and then Will pushed me to the side. She was beautiful with braided black hair and green eye shadow that made her brown eyes pop. Her cocoa-colored skin reminded me of caramel and chocolate.

"Let them tremble under the hypnotic power of my stare," Will laughed. "Besides, the local has a crush for someone else." He shrugged.

Will pulled the woman into his arms and started kissing her. I heard the bus pull up, and then I let the bus leave without me because I couldn't do anything but stare. Will was flirting with this woman. Who was she? She seemed to know him rather well—intimately. I had never seen anything as sweetly revolting before. My parents didn't kiss in public places.

"Maybe you should get a room," I told them. Will braced himself against the bus stop backboard, and then he turned his head over his shoulder to look at me.

"This is my wife. I haven't been able to see my wife in weeks. Why in tarnation did you not get on your bus?"

Will was angry at me. I shrugged. It wasn't *my* fault. He was the one who had made it look like he was trying to hug me, and I'd wanted no part of that. He was the one explaining his relationship, not me. It was his own fault if he was going to reveal his life to me. He could have waited

226

until I left before he started with his wife.

"Maybe that wasn't her bus," his wife told him, trying to draw him back.

"That was her bus," Will, or rather Casper, assured the woman. "Get out of here."

"She's just some random kid," his wife told him. "Let her be."

I left the bus stop and made my way down to the next one. I was going to be late to work today, but Will could tell everyone it was because he'd scared me away. I checked the bus schedule and waited the seven minutes until the next one came.

As soon as Leer had locked me into my room, I was back to my search. Jump after jump left me feeling frustrated that I wasn't finding my way into the Earl of Key Hill. The only players I knew who I could follow to that place played when it was nighttime.

I stopped moving when I ran across the CEO with Rory. Why were they meeting in a setting like this instead of in the real office? Wasn't it more dangerous to hold conferences virtually? I checked to see what I might be, and realized that I didn't have hands. I tried to look down and failed at that too.

"Did it work?" Berk asked, looking directly at me. I felt exposed all over.

"Maybe?" Rory answered. "You're the one who determined the numbers of her wave form."

Berk held up a piece of paper that contained a set of numbers and an equation I couldn't make out. "It's not a guaranteed thing," he told Rory. "Lots of people can entice surfers to join them, but that doesn't mean that they'll stay when they realize they've overtaken an inanimate object. She can just jump out again."

"I wish she would stop jumping," Rory complained. "They're not giving her enough direction. I doubt her floor monitor spends any time checking her work during the day."

Were they talking about me and complaining about Leer? How had they gotten me to jump into an object that couldn't move? Could I do it again on my own? How did it work? If I could sneak into things that no one suspected to have ears, I could gather a lot of information that way, not to mention find new venues for searching for my parents. I blinked myself awake and pulled off my arm monitor, knowing very well that it would start beeping at Leer. When he came into the room asking me what was wrong, I asked him if it was possible to inhabit things that couldn't move. What characters, exactly, could I jump into?

He left me with a short book on advanced wave jumping and told me to put the monitor back on when I was ready. I read the whole book forward and backward. I couldn't jump into just anything. The object had to hold a certain amount of intelligence, but sometimes that could include non-human characters like aliens or dogs or locking mechanisms. Those jumps were harder to make and took a concentrated effort. They normally required understanding how the game in question was programed in order to determine the level of intelligence a particular avatar could hold. It was fascinating to learn.

I tried shoving myself into an abnormal character right away. It was hard, and I wondered if Leer knew what I was trying to do when words came to my screen with a list of uncommon characters I could jump into. I found one of the characters, a scarecrow, and tried to animate it. After a few unsuccessful blinks, I looked down to find that my hands were made of straw. I also heard myself yawn. It was rather tiring to use a character that wasn't exactly designed for it. I moved the scarecrow around for a while until my curiosity got the better of me and I opened my eyes.

Leer wasn't there but I had been wearing the pressure cuffs. Could he monitor me remotely? I pulled them off, stopping the visual feed of whoever was typing to me. It probably also alerted Leer to my actions again, but he didn't step back into my room. Maybe Berk had asked that my jumps be monitored. I glanced at my heiss levels to check them, seventy-six, and compared it to the level that I had started with. Jumping into inanimate objects drained me of heiss. That was interesting too. If I ever wanted to get

229

myself empty so I could search for a particularly hard thread of heiss, all I had to do was jump into inanimate stuff first.

It was a remarkable find that helped me understand my surfing abilities better, but I *still* hadn't made any progress with my parents today. I minimized the computer screens that were open. No one had ever told me explicitly that I couldn't use the computer for a public search. Perhaps my parents were in one of their games I had not discovered yet. I resumed my search on my dad's worlds, perusing the forums that Leer had talked about.

After I was more familiar with my dad's games, I moved on toward finding the players. If I could find one of these players in a game, then I could get in. I was sure I wasn't the first person to have ever had this thought. I scanned the forums for recent posts, lingering on the people who got feedback. The largest informant was a guy who used the name Platonic. He was everywhere. He gave out tips as well as posted links to sites where people could buy things from him directly. If there was any name I needed to remember it was that guy's. I had usernames. All I had to do was get into them. Rory had given me a brief overview of how normal people were connected to certain games, but I needed a password that I didn't have in order to connect myself into Visions' system. I wished I found it easier to sneak into characters without needing to be drawn toward another player's heiss.

As it was, I had to surf in order to play. Leaving the pressure cuffs off, I got back on the reclining chair, and let the strongest heiss around pull me in. I found myself as a chicken, of all things, looking up at the man who liked to cut me down: Seb's sniper. Could I tilt my head side to side and get away with being a staring chicken, or would he notice me? He wasn't standing alone, and that's what had me instantly drawn to his devilish side. He had to be using heiss to connect to this particular world and send himself into a certain role, although the role concealed his face still. He wore a farmer's overalls and was standing next to a farmer's wife. She was slowly swinging a dead chicken in her hands. I was glad I wasn't that one.

"How close are you?" the wife asked the farmer.

"It will be a simple cut job," the sniper answered, "finished by the end of the week."

"Fantastic. Who would ever play this game?" the wife asked, throwing the dead chicken toward a group of pigs that squealed and scattered.

"Boring farmers?" the sniper asked, looking around. "Or people like us who need only two possible characters in the entire programing. There's no way to sneak up on us."

I had the chicken look away, just to be on the safe side. The other chickens around me were walking, so I started that up, too, doing my best to keep these two from thinking that no one could sneak up on them. Who were

231

they? I recognized the bringer of death, but not the wife.

"I hear they have some really good snipers this time around," the wife brought up.

"Indeed."

"I hear there's one that keeps getting in your way."

"It won't be a problem," Mr. Evil answered.

"Don't get it wrong," the wife told him before she left the game.

Mr. Evil exited the game shortly after. I decided to flutter my wings just for the fun of it before blinking. Here was yet another distraction from finding my parents. I needed to find that other person who sounded like a boss. Would I find her, or him, or had the boss kept the visit short to minimize the possibility of being traced? I jumped around, searching, certain that if the boss person was still connected, I could follow the trace. I couldn't find anything. I couldn't find the sniper again, either. I found Seb. I identified Will, watching him toss a bunch of hamburgers out to customers. Since all traces of finding the Viking's lead characters were failing, I went back to trying to find my parents and failed at that too. Why were they so hard to find? Didn't they think I would look for them once I figured out how? Which game were they hiding inside?

Chapter 24

Sebastian

I had told my mom and brother that I would be working late today. It was a small little lie that I hoped wouldn't backfire. I really shouldn't risk losing my job because of Millie, but she intrigued the heck out of me. Compliments from Leer telling me I was smart was part of his job to boost morale, but Millie? She didn't have to say that yesterday. She had no idea how her taking me seriously while still being able to joke around had me swooning. Usually those two things didn't go hand in hand, but everything about Millie made me feel at ease, and I craved the feeling. I wanted to see her again.

I was following behind her, nearly mesmerized. She had me taking a new path, and I admired her for the tips on a fresh route. Before I knew what I was doing, I had bought both of us a burger for dinner. After I paid, I held the two burgers in the bag and stared at them realizing that I would take the risk of spending my hard-earned money on this girl. There was no denying it now. Both in work and out of work, she meant the world to me.

I watched Millie unlock a door to a small rental room, looking lonely and distraught, and I knew I had found her current place of residence. I hoped I could make her night better. I waited a few minutes so she could have some time to unwind before I went to her door and knocked. When she opened the door, she didn't slam it shut. Millie smiled, looked around the street, and held the door open for me to come inside. I passed her dinner.

She opened the bag, looked inside, and I swear her eyes started to tear up. It wasn't from sadness, but gratitude, as if she realized how large of a gesture this really was. She covered her mouth before she looked up at me.

"Thanks, Seb! You're the best."

I had earned another compliment, and I was proud of it. I took the remaining burger as I moved in toward the kitchen out of habit and leaned up against a counter. Millie was right beside me.

"Want to play a truth and a lie?" Millie posed as she opened up the food and took a bite. I nodded as I scanned the small area. It was barely furnished. She had a mattress on the floor and one small box of clothes. She gave me a smile that started at her mouth and moved to her eyes as the stress from her day was pushed back.

"You first," I directed, partaking in the spoils of my dinner as well. I enjoyed talking with her yesterday and learning that she liked ballet. I loved dancing. The more I learned about Millie, the more I wanted to be around her.

"I once broke into my high school, or I had a pet cat."

"I'm going with the cat as the truth," I guessed.

"Nope! I'm allergic to cats. I broke into school to get a textbook from my locker."

I had learned two truths from that. It was my turn. "I once went a full week pretending I was blind, or I taught myself how to sing the national anthem backward so I could throw everyone else off."

Millie was already grinning at me. She laughed when I revealed that they were both true. But thinking of throwing people off plunged my mind unpleasantly back into work.

"Millie, how do I know if I'm doing the right thing? My missions are always so vague that I'm left to wonder if I'm being the good guy or the bad guy." I asked the question before I could stop myself. It had been on my mind for some time, and she made me feel safe, so safe that I could share any secret at all with her. No one else had that power.

"For example, with the Flying Falcon I completely shut that program down. Am I defending what's already ours, or destroying things that I shouldn't? I feel like I'm shoved up against this gray area. They don't tell me things for my own protection, but it sure makes a guy suspicious of his job. Do they watch me all the time?"

"Watch you? No. That's why Will has you tagged. Since you're the top performer, being tagged bugs the company CEO. Leer is hardly ever in the room with you. He's normally someplace else. He staggers people being awake and asleep and doesn't stare at you."

"I'm alone in the room?" I asked, feeling more uneasy about that than if Leer was watching me all day. I had woken up alone once, but I hadn't realized that I was that way all the time. "So anyone could find me sleeping and stab a fork into my arm or something?"

"No. There's a security guard," Millie told me.

I snorted. "The company sniper? He's already threatened me before. Am I doing the right thing, Millie? You mentioned the CEO. Who is that? What side am I on?"

"Leer locks your door. If you were ever to wake up before your shift ended you'd find yourself locked in. Your job is difficult to describe. Sometimes you are the bad guy and sometimes you're not."

"What do you mean?" I asked, confused.

I was security. How could I be both bad and good? Millie leaned up against the counter beside me, which was all the support that I needed to not feel like I was breaking company rules by asking her these questions. I hadn't planned on asking her anything like this.

"We're a security company that other people hire. Most of the time we are procured by small businesses and game owners to fix their platforms after hackers take them over. The hackers normally change codes and do things like sell fake memberships to the games, or cheat codes, or give out unfair advantages. You take that out and make the game safe again. But sometimes we enter games we've not been hired to search as we track down these hacker gangs. So you're both helping and invading at the same time."

"We can get sued for that," I told Millie. She shrugged.

I had invaded games before—I was sure of it. Could I be held responsible for that? I was stopping hackers, so wasn't that a good thing? This blurred the lines of legal acceptability in my mind. If the company didn't explain this to people working in security, at least not on Nick and Leer's floors, what was Millie's job title? I wondered if she would tell me.

"I don't want to put my family in danger," I moaned, thinking about how much trouble we were in. Why didn't I know when I first started that I was going to be security? The back of my mind told me that I should quit, but I had that pay advance, and I couldn't see myself being dishonest enough to run with it. Plus, we would use it up sooner rather than later and be back where we had started—

without jobs. The gnawing desperation of that refused to let me think about leaving.

"Okay," Millie shrugged as if there was no real threat to any of us.

"We need this job, but I don't want them to be in danger. So what should I do?" I asked. Should I run? I could find another job someplace else. My brother wasn't situated in school yet, and I didn't think too many people would blame me for running while I had a chance, but that would put us several months behind and jobless.

"Don't do anything," Millie told me. "We're going to stop that hacker for good so you don't have to worry about the person trying to discover you."

"And that's your job?" I asked her. How was she going to find the person who had tried to pull my mask off? She wasn't there when it happened to the Flying Falcon.

"I can't tell you my job. I can only tell you that there are people helping you."

"Millie." I tried to entice her job title out of her with a pout. She only smiled back at me.

"Honestly, I don't know what my job is. It tends to change on a daily basis depending on the mood of the employers. Seb, while it's just the two of us here, I still haven't found my parents. We got stuck crossing the border. I might have run across my dad once in a game, but I haven't seen him since. I keep thinking that if they were in need of heiss there should have been some sign of them by now."

I hadn't heard anything, but she did have a point. If she had been desperate to find heiss, then her parents would have turned up if they were close by. What if they were the ones who were doing this? What if they were the people who were hacking into everything and messing it all up? After all, the problems started up when Millie got close enough to surf our system, and she had come with her parents. At least one of them had to be a surfer since she was. Maybe I was looking at everything wrong again.

"What are your parents' names?" I asked her.

"That would be mixing personal life with work," she teased. How easy it would be to tell each other everything if we didn't have work rules in the way. Millie had just told me that Will was following me. He'd get suspicious if I stayed too long. Maybe I should just go before he decided to report my work infraction. I couldn't lose this job.

"I wish we could spend more time together, but I don't think Will would approve."

"I wish that too." Millie leaned in closer to me. A hundred thoughts flashed across her face. Was she thinking about dinner or other people who had taken her on a date?

She swept her eyes over my face and inched closer

239

with that cute tugging smile that she always tried to hide. Her eyes seemed to grow bigger, reminding me of large-eyed stuffed animals that subconsciously made me want to protect them. In Millie's case it was working on me just the same. I scooted my back along the counter, bridging some of the gap, which caused Millie to look down and giggle.

"Truth or dare?" I asked her, judging what she would say expertly. She played into my game asking for a truth. "Are you in love with anyone?"

Her flushed cheeks were totally worth it. I wanted to pull her into my arms, but she beat me to it surprising me at her speed. As her arms wrapped around me, my pulse picked up, and then dropped just as quickly when she crossed out of the small kitchen and held open the front door.

"Maybe," she answered, coy. "There's no telling how close Will might be." Millie looked out the door, probably trying to spot Will. I nodded. I hadn't even been able to hug her back she was that fast. I winked at her as I left her place, pulling off what I thought was an impressive cover for my disappointment. If we didn't know that Will was around, I would have stayed longer.

Chapter 25

Millie

I felt something cold on my arm and blinked awake. It was a small ice cube. I sat up abruptly, looking around my room to see what could have caused this, because ice was supposed to keep me asleep and it didn't do anything. Was someone trying to keep me quiet? Had someone read the information on my sheet that said ice was my sleeping trigger? I noticed that Leer hadn't updated the information. He kept it that way so no one else would know how to put me to sleep. I sat up and found that Leer was face down on the floor beside the heiss band in my room.

"Leer!" I panicked.

I jumped off the bed and rushed to him. He didn't wake up, and I didn't spot any wounds on him. He was still breathing, which I took as a good sign. Still, I was scared to move him or even touch him. Had he thrown the ice cube at me? I could hear his monitor beeping as my heart rate spiked. I tore off the plastic monitor on my arm and placed it on my bed, wondering if the sound would stop when it couldn't find my erratically beating heart, but the beeping continued.

"Leer!" I tried again.

Apart from disconnecting myself, I had no idea what to do. My brain froze, giving me zero possibilities, and I fretted that I was wasting the precious time I had to act. Why was I doing this in real life? Why? I wondered if I had woken up right away or if I had taken a while. Was there a sound that I should have heard that would clue me into what had happened here? Who was attacking? Was the person still around?

I grabbed the ice cube off the bed and placed it on Leer's head, wondering if it would work for him. My door was unlocked, mocking me. My air was sucked out when I noted that the door next to mine was ajar. It was like stepping into a silent horror film. Where was the suspect and what was I to do? I took a quick peek inside the room next door to find Sedona with her armband attached. The monitor in her room was beeping. Her blond hair looked sweaty and her face looked ashen. She needed to wake up. I glanced behind me at Leer once before panicking again.

"Hold on, I'm coming," I told Sedona even if she couldn't hear me.

242

I rushed to her screen to find out where she was the fast way, and then yanked off her armband. If she didn't think she was dead the missing armband would have already woken her up, but she was still beeping with thoughts of being dead. Resting my back against the wall in her room, I traveled into her world. I hoped to find her quickly, because I was scared. Leer wouldn't leave the door open and crash on my floor. We were being attacked from within, and Leer had the keys to the doors. He had the key to Seb's door…

Sedona was in a forest. The white trees and purple sky did not pass along their serenity to me. When I didn't see Sedona in two seconds, I gave up on her. She was probably close to whatever character I had taken over, but I was unsettled and jittery. I was more worried about Seb.

I jumped waves until I could locate him, all the while hoping that no one in the real world was blaming Leer or Sedona on me. Seb was a mountain climber comparing a map in his hand with his location.

"You have to wake up!" I grabbed his arm.

I didn't care who saw us. He was hiking with a group of other men that I didn't glance at. This was an emergency. I needed him awake. I had a horrible sinking feeling in my stomach. I had just told Seb yesterday not to do anything, because there were people looking out for him. But I was wrong. I could handle being wrong, but I couldn't handle Sebastian getting hurt because of me, and I couldn't think of any other reason for why Leer would be laying on the ground and all the doors hanging open. How had the attacking sniper gotten in? Was he the same person who had tossed me out the window? Who had lost their badge to get into the work building, allowing the enemy inside—or had Seb's sniper had inside help? I still had no idea who this guy even was.

"He's coming for you. We're being attacked. You have to wake yourself up!"

Seb's face turned white. I knew he had a fear of this exact thing happening. He had just expressed that fear to me yesterday, and I hadn't done anything about it. Why not? Hadn't I heard sniper man telling his boss that he was going to get the "cut job" done by the end of the week? I'd had every warning I could possibly get, and I had failed this mission!

I wondered how many other rooms were beeping from Leer's monitor right now. I had to do something. I had to fix this! I should have said something!! Why hadn't I said anything? Why had I let myself get distracted by trying to find my parents?

"I don't know how!" Seb grabbed onto my avatar's arm, already shaking. "How?!" He looked like he was trying to wake himself up, but he was still hooked up to the heiss. The last time he had woken himself up after jogging he had already been disconnected. There was only one thing I could think of that would jolt him awake. I grabbed the hatchet on his side and cut his avatar's head off. His character faded from view, and I gave off a relieved sigh, hoping that he would be able to handle the real-life stuff better than me.

I woke myself up, glad that I was still sitting upright in Sedona's room without guards blaming me for the incident. Sedona was not awake, and while I knew that her beeping meant she needed to be, I couldn't bring myself to search for her yet.

I ran back to Leer, checking his pockets for his keys. I didn't find them. Should I try to revive Sedona, or help Leer, or run to Seb? I had too many options, and I got the feeling that if I ran down the hallway, I would find more people to save, only adding to my list of things to do. I already couldn't make up my mind. It was frazzled. What if I got it wrong? What if I didn't save the right people first? I couldn't start all over again.

I chose to run down the hallway. It was selfish of me, I supposed, but I wanted to make sure that Seb was fine. As expected, I found a few more open doors, and when I glanced inside the people working there were still on their beds. Not all of them were beeping, which was good. That had to mean that they hadn't died in their dreams and they were still functioning normally. That gave me fewer people to save in the dream world, but there were still lots of people in the real one that needed help.

I turned the corner and crashed into the exit door that led to Seb's area. I yanked open the door, wanting to scream for help, but I wasn't sure who was attacking us, and I didn't want to be in the way of getting hit. I could hear Nick's voice talking, and I dashed that direction, hoping that he wasn't the one I was trying to avoid. He was waking up a person in a normal, easy fashion. My crashing into the room made his talking stop abruptly and the person he had just woken to mutter "whoa." We had crossed paths before in the real world. I had done that on purpose out of curiosity and boredom and my need to feel connected to people when my parents were lost.

"Leer's face down in my room!" I told Nick, feeling my breath pitch up. I really wasn't good at the whole "scared to death" thing in real life. "And half the doors have been unlocked in the hallway. I unplugged the girl next to me because she's in a sleeping death, and Leer has lost his keys. I've got to reach—"

"No you don't!" Nick told me. He jumped at me, and I bolted down the hallway, trying to escape his reach in case he had something to do with it. He reached me right as I was going to yank open the door that led to Seb's floor.

"I'm not risking you. You stay here. And stay awake!" Nick pushed me behind him and ran through the door himself.

I looked back at Thomas, the man Nick had woken up who was standing in his doorway, and decided not to do what Nick told me to do. I sat down in the hallway, putting my back to the wall, and let the heiss wave me under. I couldn't find Sebastian anywhere. At this moment he was off heiss. He had to have woken up, which was good. I went back to Sedona and ran through her world, searching for her until I found her. I wasn't going to let these people be stuck asleep. I knew how it felt to be unable to control sleeping, and it was aggravating.

I picked Sedona's character up, and then dropped her a few times simulating the dream of falling over and over again. Her eyes blinked open briefly before she lost the connection to her game. I wondered what she would do when she found her door open and no one else around. But I didn't wonder for long. There were still a few more people to look for that I had passed in the halls, so I headed in to save them too.

Nick prodded me awake and told me what I expected he had told everyone else when they realized that Leer was out of commission. Leer had gotten sick, and his workers needed to go home because he wasn't available to wake them. I wished he was sick. I looked at Nick hoping for a better explanation, and got it. He tapped the back of his head. Leer had taken a blow to the head and passed out? Where had his keys gone?

247

I raced my way back to my room, noticing briefly that Leer was no longer there, before I continued running toward Sebastian's. Nick ran along behind me, waving away the guards who were flooding the floor a little late.

"Will said he got him out," Nick told me as I braced my hands between the doorframe of Seb's empty room. I glanced back at Nick as he thumbed over a phone message from Seb's bodyguard. He looked at Seb's bed, where Leer's ring of keys rested. Nick pushed me aside to pick up the keys, shifting his eyes all over the place.

"Will wouldn't..." Nick trailed off, apparently trying to figure out how the keys got in the room. Was Will responsible for bonking Leer on the head and taking his keys to open Sebastian's door? Why would he unlock the other rooms while searching for the right one? I didn't share my theory about Seb's sniper. I found myself trying to keep Nick calm.

"Will would have stopped whoever hit Leer on the head," I voiced, "then rescued Sebastian."

That was his job. Will was going to save Sebastian. Who had hit Leer? How had he gotten in? I scanned the room again. Nick nodded his head a few times, agreeing with my short explanation, and then told me to go home as well.

"Can I review the security cameras?" I asked Nick.

He shook his head at me and called Grant, asking him to get on the cameras and find out who had hit Leer. A few minutes later Grant's voice was telling us that all the cameras were blocked. I walked back into the hallway and stood on my tiptoes. There was gray putty over the camera that I hadn't noticed as I'd rushed down the hallways. I got a chair so I could reach it and removed the blockage while a guard told me I was messing with evidence. Grant's voice echoed over Nick's phone, telling him that he could see me now. He fretted over the state of the camera woman, who normally was watching the feed here. After calling around, the woman was located in the bathroom with diarrhea, cleared from being the person who had sabotaged the cameras.

Grant promised to keep looking for clues. Nick told me to leave again. I slowly made my way to the changing room, but I had no intention of leaving. I was going to surf again. What if someone else needed help? All the other snipers were busy, and besides, I wanted to stick around in case those clues were revealed to me.

Chapter 26

Sebastian

Millie had cut my avatar's head off. That was the first time I had died, and the shock of it left me so confused that I didn't realize I was *still* dying until it was too late. Strong hands were around my neck. I was strangled back into unconsciousness from lack of oxygen. I had no idea how long I had remained unconscious, but I was awake now, trying to understand where I was.

The first thing that hit me, after gasping for air on a rather late reflex, was the sensation of my entire body trembling. I had felt shaky like this before, so I realized what it was. I was hooked up to heiss. I didn't think I was at work. Nick and Leer were more careful with heiss, and I couldn't hear any emergency beeping sounds. Too much heiss was just as dangerous as having too little. I hadn't made it. My sniper had gotten me and was flooding my body. Where was Will? He had been right beside me when Millie had cut my head off. Surely he had raced to my room. How could Visions have such a lack in security when we were a security company?

I opened my eyes, focusing on the fake world that was being fed to me. I was looking at a large Samoan character with wavy black hair. In his hand was a massive, black prototype gun. I squirmed, only to realize that I was tied to a brick wall. I wondered which would kill me first, the thought of dying again, or actually dying. My sniper was going to explode me with heiss while shooting me. What a way to go. Did he like torture? Did he need to scare me?

The terrifying gangster lifted his gun, and I just couldn't do it. Normally I felt heroic, but when it came down to last moments, I was only left with regrets. I shut my eyes against the onslaught. I wished my final moments were something happy, instead of the dread I felt for letting down Mom and Triton. They deserved better, and they'd ended up with me. What good was I for them? I couldn't tell them my real job. I couldn't tell them all the steps I had taken to protect them from my actions that I knew were going to hurt us all. I guess I had finally lost the last needle that would stitch us all back together.

The gun shot, but I didn't feel the sting of it. That was fitting. I was already so far gone that nothing could hurt me anymore. Plus, this wasn't real. This part was just to torment my mind into making me think I was dead before I was. Maybe the heiss wouldn't hurt me if I already thought I was gone.

"What are you doing?!" the gunman screamed.

I opened my eyes, confused. Me? I was just tied up here waiting to die before I really died. I was waiting for the torture and doing a good job of giving it to myself with my emotional dialogue. Maybe the gunman was right. I should tell myself that I was awesome. I shouldn't spend my last moments drowning in personal failures.

"Dying," a voice whispered.

I looked down at the ground where the voice had come from and I couldn't utter a word, although my mind was screaming. There was indeed a random man dead in front of me. My throat felt like a hand had grabbed hold of it to strangle me a second time. Maybe there was a hand trying to suffocate me in real life, or maybe it was a delayed mental reaction from being strangled earlier. I couldn't work words around the shock.

"Idiots," the gunman muttered.

He took aim again, and right before he shot, another man jumped down in front of him, blocking the shot from hitting me. No. I was going to die anyway. I didn't want anyone to get in the way. I didn't want my last moments to be remembered like this.

"Are you dying too?" the gunman asked this next

person. "It won't do you any good, you know."

"I don't care," the new man standing in front of me answered, and I knew it to be true by the sound of the unwavering conviction. "I'll die a thousand times for him."

It couldn't be. Millie had told me to wake up. How had she found me here? What was happening in the real world around her if she had found me here? This had to be Millie. Who else would be foolish enough to jump in the way every time?

Bang. The shot dropped the avatar to the ground. The gunman tried to get off another rapid shot, but another avatar was already falling in my path taking the bullet again. I felt my eyes prickle in every version of reality that I was in. I hadn't expected the hope to come. I was just going to stay there and give up, feeling like I had lost everything, and yet here was my angel reminding me that I had more life left to live. I started to struggle with my bonds, although it seemed pointless. Another person fell into the way of the bullet.

"Hey!" the gunman screamed. "You can't take over that character!" He looked around scanning the area for the next hero. Since Millie was surfing right now, why didn't she kick the sniper out and then cut me loose instead of dying? Could she do that? Could she take over a character that was already taken?

"What about this one?" A new person stepped in the way. I couldn't see where the people were dropping down from. I tried to look up and find out, but I couldn't decide if there was a mass group of people watching from above or not. The gunman hesitated with his next shot, then out of anger he pulled the trigger. Before the avatar fell, there was another one lined up.

"Get out of here!"

That avatar fell too. I couldn't look. I closed my eyes again, only faintly hearing the next avatar show up.

"Please don't, Millie," I pleaded. "I don't want my last thoughts to be of you dying. I'd much rather remember the time I almost kissed you."

"Almost?" she questioned.

"I never actually kissed you."

"So stay alive a little longer and you can."

"I'm sorry. I'm going to disappoint you."

Millie didn't agree with me. My cheek stung with her slap. I was so surprised to have felt it that my eyes betrayed me as they snapped open. Was my mind confusing the real world with this one so that they both felt real now? If that was the case, I didn't want to get shot. Millie was inhabiting another man, and he was glaring at me, fiercely.

"You're not going to disappoint me. You're going to live. That's what you do. You live."

"I'd much rather live without you dying," I said, and

Millie's avatar's fierce determination swapped away for confusion. Millie spun around to look at the gunman, wondering what was taking so long. I looked at him too. He had the gun still up, but it looked like he had stopped functioning. I tried to wiggle out of my bonds, only thinking of myself. Millie, of course, thought of everyone else first. Oh, how I loved her. How I wanted to tell her.

"You stopped?" Millie asked the gunman. She took a step toward him, but then pressed herself back into me, not willing to give the man an inch between us to get a shot magically over her head into me.

"Why are you here?" the gunman asked her.

His hand wobbled on his gun and I took the moment to look around, trying to figure out how I was going to get myself out of this. Now would be the time for a brilliant plan. I needed an ingenious idea.

"I am going to stop him from dying. If you were to kill him right now he wouldn't wake up. That's unacceptable. In fact, if he does die, I am going to hunt you down and make you pay. The hard way."

"Wait no!" I screamed, giving up on devising a plan. My head was starting to feel sluggish. My limbs were protesting. Couldn't Millie see that it wasn't worth it? I was already gone. I was wasting my time instead of telling her everything that I wanted to say. I would never get another chance!

"Don't turn into a murderer because of me. Please don't do that," my mouth spoke those words instead of the words I most wanted to say. Dang. Maybe there was still some time left to say what was on my mind. When a man lay dying the most important things were jarred into focus. For me, that meant I needed to talk to Millie. I tried to ignore the weariness. I forced myself to stay awake. I had done it before. I had made myself stay awake for Millie and I could do it again.

"Is your name Millie?" the gunman asked.

He lowered his gun. The avatar before me, Millie, trembled a little and I groaned. I had used her name. I had revealed her identity. My last dying moments had doomed her to be discovered so she could die too. I hated myself. The tears in my eyes flooded out, and once again instead of telling her what I wanted to, I found myself apologizing. How could I have done that? How could I have killed her? I couldn't let this happen! I yanked on the bonds holding me to the wall. What an idiot I was to destroy something as precious as Millie. I had to get myself out of here so I could save her.

"If you dare touch her at all, I will make you suffer so much that you'll bleed out of your eyeballs!" I screamed at the gunman.

"Who are you?" Millie asked, instead of recognizing my anger at how unfair everything was. All I wanted to do was save her. Just once more. It wasn't fair that she was the one saving me all the time. I didn't deserve anything like that. Not so many times.

"If you're Millie, then I'm…" the gunman trailed off, and then set his gun on the ground. He started to walk toward her and I felt a new rush of fear. What was he going to do now that the gun was down? Would he snap Millie's wrists off? Hit her a million times until she was so abused that she dropped? Was he going to torture her? I couldn't take that. I couldn't.

"If you touch her, I will find a way to make your death worse than crucifixion!" I screamed at him. Millie turned around to glance at me with a sad smile on her face. I screamed at her too.

"Don't look at me! He's coming!"

"What is your mother's first name?" the gunman asked. He stopped walking closer. I would love to think that it was because he could see the anger in my eyes. How dare he ask any personal questions?

"Juliet," Millie answered.

"At least I'm not the only one with a tricky name," I said before I could stop myself. I wondered if Millie was going to reveal that her father's name was Romeo. I always felt like my name was hard to take seriously when it resonated so closely with the thought of a crab. The name

"Juliet" had an equally strong connotation.

Millie looked at me again and laughed. How could she be laughing right now? How could she find humor in the face of death itself? There was no end to her amazing me. I had to tell her right now. I couldn't wait any longer.

"She named you Millie," the gunman said as a mere whisper. Millie stopped laughing to turn around and look at my murderer again. I wished I could tell her to ignore the gunman, but from the expression on his face I couldn't. Millie hadn't lied. She was telling the scoundrel the truth.

"No," I begged her again. This time the fear coiled on so thick I felt myself throw up in real life. My avatar heaved with the pressure. "Don't tell him anything. Don't sacrifice yourself for me."

"Of course I will!" Millie turned her back on the monster yet again. How could she keep doing that!? "I've never been good at being the hero of my own life. You know that. There's only one person I'm good at helping—"

"You help everyone!" I screamed at her and heaved again. I could almost smell the vomit that would be all over me. Really, why was I wasting my time with these words instead of just telling her? "Don't do this!"

"It's keeping you alive!" she screamed back at me.

Please not like this. I couldn't stand for my last words with her to be an argument.

"I love you," I told her. The tears pooled into her eyes next. My tears had never left. I had said it, but I wasn't done. "You are the most heroic person I have ever met. You're such a hero for your own life that your extra heroism oozes over onto everyone else."

"Oozes?" Millie questioned.

"Yes. Your heroism is a thick mucus substance adhering to the walls of everything it touches, leaving snot of unmovable heroism. You can't blow that kind of bravery into a Kleenex and toss it out. It clings to everything like tar."

Millie snorted. Then she laughed again. "How do you think these things up?" she asked me.

"Really goopy green snot." I smiled at her.

I faked the smile for her. The gunman was moving closer again. If he was going to hit her, I wanted the last thing she remembered of me to be a smile. I couldn't leave her with anything less. I had to leave her with my best. She reached out and touched my face, which would have been fine except that she was inhabiting a man and I was having trouble looking past that to the Millie I knew was in there.

"Wake yourself up. You've done it before."

"I..." How could I tell her that I couldn't? The heiss was still pushing into me. I would wake myself up if I could. I would smash down the jaws of twelve thousand alligators if it helped me reach Millie.

"I will. Just as soon as you're out of the way," I told her with another forced smile.

"I'm not leaving you!" she insisted.

"I'm not leaving you, either," I retorted, although I could feel the truth. I *was* leaving her. I was leaving her really fast. I could feel my body shutting down. Any moment now and there would be nothing that could keep me awake. "Live, Millie," I told her as my avatar's eyes started to blur over. She had to keep going. I couldn't be what killed her. I couldn't be.

"Not without you!" she screamed.

I prayed for her forgiveness and her soul if she really did decide to ignore my dying wishes and turn herself into a monster in real life by seeking revenge. How could I have revealed Millie's real identity so the sniper could kill her next?

Chapter 27

Millie

Seb slumped over and I knew without a doubt that he had struggled to stay conscious as long as he could. He was the one who told me not to fall asleep in the dream world, and here he was passing out. This had to be bad. Where was Will?!

"Come back," I ordered Sebastian. I could hear the tone in my voice betraying my inner emotions. After all this time of trying to save him, Will and I had both failed.

"Where is he?!" I spun around toward the sniper, who was looking like a three-hundred-pound Samoan. At least he had dropped the gun. I knew this was not his real face, and he knew it wasn't mine, either. The Samoan walked closer, as if he expected to find me underneath the avatar I had taken. If this sniper wasn't going to tell me where Seb was then I was going to make him. I jumped at him and just like that, he vanished, taking Sebastian with him.

"No!" I cut myself awake with the sound of my own voice. I was still in the changing room at work. I had no idea where Sebastian was, but he wasn't safe with Will. Where was Will? I called his phone over and over again for five minutes straight until he answered with a text telling me he was on it and to not disturb his concentration. A second later he wrote again telling me not to mention this to anyone. We couldn't have lost Sebastian. He had been in the same building as us. How did this happen? I knew it would be impossible to find Seb by searching in a game if he was no longer hooked up to heiss.

Well, impossible was going to have a bad day because I wasn't going to sit there and give up. I was going to find him too! I fled the changing room and started searching everywhere. I ran for hours, searching the streets and every exit I could think up as an escape route from Visions. I checked out the place where I had been dumped once. I vainly ran down several random paths, crying so hard that many people asked me if I was okay. I didn't dare answer a single one because that would give them my voice. It was dangerous to give that away. No wonder my parents lived so far away from this. Talking to the man at the grocery store could be the thing that condemned me. I had no way of knowing who was friendly or not.

I also had no way of finding Seb. While I knew that, I couldn't help the crazed rush that had come into my legs or the way they drained of all energy several hours later. I plopped down on the sidewalk, rather lost bawling my eyes out. When I could move again, I started over by barging into Visions and searching for clues.

"Will you go away?" Rory asked me when I found him still at work too. I opened my mouth to protest. Couldn't he see that I had been crying? Seb was missing!

"Leer slipped on the ice. There is video evidence of him falling and hitting the back of his head in your room. You don't need to look so frantic."

"But—"

"Do you even know what your job is?" Rory asked me, shaking his head.

"To save people," I told him.

He wiped his face down, starting at the top of his forehead and smoothing over his brown beard that wasn't looking as scruffy as the first time we had met.

"No. Your job is to report anyone you think is working for the Vikings."

Right. That was my job. I was yet again getting all my many side missions tangled together, but this was really, really important! When Rory asked me if I had gotten any sleep, I gave him a short smile and let him follow me to the

265

front door of Visions and halfway into the street. I ran away from him, knowing that I wasn't going to get any information from the building. I didn't believe that Leer had slipped. That was one delicately fabricated accident. What excuse did they have for the covered cameras? Was Rory working for the Vikings? How could he believe the footage?

I couldn't sleep nor could I believe Rory. I called Will several more times without getting an answer. When night switched to day, I returned to Visions, hoping that I would spot William. Had he found Sebastian yet? I was glad that Rory didn't appear before me. When I reached my room, I met Leer and asked him if he had really slipped on the ice. He nodded. He believed that story too?!

"I was coming to wake you up to tell you that Tabitha didn't find anything revealing at your parents' house. I had to have slipped on the ice."

"And the cameras?" I persisted. "Your missing keys?"

Leer sighed. "You tell me, Millie. I can't vouch for your actions."

"I didn't do it!" I protested. I wished I could say more, but I didn't want to mess up what Will was working on.

"Stay in your room," Leer insisted.

He closed the door on me after tossing me back my

plastic arm monitor that I had left on the reclining chair yesterday. Why did I get the sense that I was being blamed? I had tried to save his life! I had saved most of the people on his floor. Leer was being ridiculous. I vainly called Will again before trying to wrap my head around the job I was supposed to do.

I couldn't help but think of Sebastian instead as I randomly wandered worlds looking for him or his sniper or any Viking. No love interest had ever told me that they loved me like Sebastian had. It seemed a little rushed, but I was feeling the same thing. It didn't matter if we hadn't gone on a real date. I knew Seb's real character, and I loved him. Waiting to hear back from Will was eating me alive.

Since I'd had such a rough night, my monitors were beeping the instant they touched my arm. The sound kept waking me up and ruining my focus. How could I have slept when I hadn't been enough to save Sebastian? I was on edge all day, scared that Rory would come into my room and force me to sleep. I was glad to only see Leer, but he wasn't glad to see me. He hardly said anything when he dismissed me for the day.

With work finally out, I wasn't sure what to do. I was about to run away from this entire place. What was the point in being here? No progress had been made with my parents yet. I had enough money now to leave. Of course, with Sebastian missing maybe that would mean that Will was following me instead, and he would stop me if he realized my intentions.

I paused before opening the door to leave the building. Just because I hadn't seen Seb or Will in the games today didn't mean that they were dead. I had to believe they were both still out there alive. I vainly felt a ray of hope as I gripped the door handle, trying not to burst into a torrent of tears.

Should I run? How many people had asked that same question at this very same door? I felt like I had faced the worst failure in my entire life. I hadn't saved Sebastian. I shoved open the door and stepped outside before I could internalize the thought. What if I couldn't save my parents either? I couldn't become a puddle right here. Keeping my gaze on the hard, unforgiving gray ground, I let my feet do the guiding while my mind worked through the stages of denial.

"He's at the Muller Hospital," Seb's sniper's voice spoke from my left.

I trembled at the very sound. I had never known a voice that was scarier. Was I next? Was he going to kill me right in front of the work building? He had taken Seb from the building. He could probably do the same to me. Why was he talking about hospitals instead of capturing me next? I had been getting in his way for days. Did I dare hope that the man I thought was Seb's sniper wasn't actually the same person who had taken him in real life? No. Of course it was the same person. I slowly raised my head to see the speaker. He was a man in his fifties with a salt-and-pepper beard, a black business jacket, and gray slacks. I had seen him before. He took the same trains as Sebastian to get home…

"How do you know that?" I asked. I knew I should keep my mouth shut. I should walk away without saying anything and not give myself away, but did it really matter? I was already caught.

"You're Millie, aren't you? You look like your mother. I should have noticed it earlier. Is she here? She said she'd never come back."

He wanted my mother? Was Seb's sniper the same person that had gone after my mother? Had he gone after my dad? I glanced at Visions' welcoming doors behind me, ready to run back inside. I didn't know why my legs were not moving. If I wasn't being myself and was sleeping, my legs would have done what I wanted. My real body felt stuffed full of tingly water, unable to respond.

"Millie, I would never hurt you," the man told me. "In fact, putting the Flying Falcon in the Muller Hospital was an act of pure selfishness on my part. It's my only ticket to begging your forgiveness. I lied about him for you. Whatever is going on between the two of you clearly shows some kind of relationship. I'm not stupid enough to break that and ruin my only chance to get you to listen."

269

I managed to take one step backwards. I was pegged as being in a relationship. What did that mean? What did the sniper want me to listen to? He had been going after Seb since the moment I had first met Sebastian in my dreams. He could have been after my mother since before I was born. I couldn't trust him.

"Please, just a minute of your time. Juliet told me she never cared for me, but she named you Millie, so she must have."

"What?" I asked.

What was going on? What did this guy want from my mom? Furthermore, if he had already found Sebastian and knew what trains he took home every day, why did he attack him at work instead of when he was alone outside? Was he just proving that he could? Did he take pleasure from terrifying people? Regardless, I had to verify the information about Seb. I pulled out my phone, watching the sniper nearly jump at me for it.

"Just give me one chance!" the man begged, going down on his knees. Um... I didn't want to assume I knew what was going on because I hadn't a clue, but on his knees was fine with me as long as I could still see his hands. I desperately called Will again and thanked my luck when he answered.

"Did you check the Muller Hospital?"

"This late I don't have a hope of finding him," Will sighed. He hadn't shown up at work today. I assumed he was still out there checking for any signs of Seb.

"I found a clue. Check the hospital, alright?"

"You found a clue? How? What did that cost us?"

"I don't..." I trailed off. I didn't know. The man before me was still on his knees. His eyes were tearing up. What?

"I told them to watch you closely. I knew you'd do something stupid about this. What did you do? Where did you go?"

"I didn't do anything stupid," I told Will. I had slowly plodded around one of my dad's secret worlds today, not finding my parents again. My actions only left me feeling despondent, especially since I couldn't find Seb either. Leer had given me a short hug before he'd discharged me for the day. He probably knew exactly what I was feeling. I wished he would offer me some comfort on the subject.

"Check the Muller Hospital and call me right away if you see him."

I hung up on Will. Then I looked back at the crying man. Snipers could cry? Really? This guy literally killed people for his job. How did he have any sort of compassion?

"I don't know what you're talking about," I told the

271

crying man. Behind me, Marcus came out as he got off work. He looked at the kneeling man, and then looked back at me as he worked up the nerve to ask a question. I didn't give him the chance.

"This is personal so..." I held up a hitchhiking thumb and jerked it to the side, asking him to move along. I really didn't want more people getting mixed up in this. I would feel horrible if I knew that I had caused my entire work building to be threatened even if I had never talked with half of them. Marcus was one of those people, but I had followed him a few times before.

"Oh sure. What else would it be but personal to find a guy crying in the street?" Marcus looked at us again before he shrugged and walked off.

I waited for him to be well out of the way, but I knew I would have to say the exact same thing another twelve times or more while everyone got off work. Maybe I could move this to a different sort of crowded place where the sniper wouldn't decide to hurt me. I started walking along my normal path toward the bus station. Sure enough, the man jumped to his feet and started to follow after me. It reminded me of Seb telling me not to turn my back on the guy, but I couldn't see how it mattered. He knew how to find me in every version of alertness and grogginess that I could face.

"I just want one chance," he told me, "or maybe two

if I've already lost my first one. I saved him for *you*, Millie. You owe me a few minutes."

"I didn't think you'd want to get interrupted by everyone coming out," I told him.

I looked over my shoulder and he sped up enough to match my pace. He wiped at his eyes. I considered doing the same thing even if mine were not tearing up right now. What had I ever done for... no. Why was I even special to... A sniper saved Sebastian for *me*? But would it even work out? We weren't allowed to be together. What was this sniper's angle? He had been following Seb on the train for several days, maybe longer. He had been planning his method of attack, and I hadn't noticed anything. I was passable as a surfer, but I made a rather bad sniper.

"Where's Juliet?" the man asked.

"Who are you?" I asked the sniper. I took in his business suit again and frowned, wishing that I had suspected this man of being the stalker earlier. I could have told Will, and then he could have stopped him before Seb had ended up in the hospital. Was Seb going to live?

"Just forget the rule that says you can't tell me personal information, because I'd never hurt Juliet. I've loved her forever."

I stopped walking. I wasn't where I was planning on being, but I was in the middle of a sidewalk on a busy road, so if anything were to happen there would be a witness. Why did this man love my mother and why did he think my name had anything to do with it?

"She's not here with you, is she?" the sniper asked.

"Did you make her run away?" I questioned him.

"No I..." but I could see the answer lying beneath his words. Yes, he had. He influenced my mother's name for me and then she had run away where he couldn't hurt her anymore. The sniper swallowed. He looked around, making himself look suspicious, before he begged me for a third chance.

"What did you do to the Flying Falcon?" I asked him.

"I... *he* overdosed on heiss," the sniper told me, trying to avoid the blame. "But he's still alive. Your friend will call you back and confirm it, I swear. Look, about your mother—there was this sniper after her. Not me, but when she learned what I was, she didn't believe me. If you could have honor among snipers, I'd be the best one. I..." He looked around again before wiping at his eyes and choking on his words. "I fake all the accidents and then let everyone run. I told your mother that I'd help her, but she didn't want to believe me. She couldn't see past the job to the man, even though she didn't have a problem with me before she knew."

"So you dated my mother?" I asked him. This was

weird talking to some long-lost man my mother had never mentioned. And why would she? She thought he was trying to kill her.

"No. I'm your uncle."

He must have seen the horror on my face, because he was back on his knees begging me to tell him where she was. No. Why would I tell a sniper where my mother was, even if she was in a dangerous situation right now? My uncle was a sniper? This couldn't be my Uncle Phillis that I was supposed to meet after crossing the border with my parents. This had to be a different uncle.

"I have no right to impose myself on you, but if you could tell your mother that I was never going to hurt her... or you... Not telling her about my job sooner is my largest regret. If I could have another chance... I would do anything to help you with the Flying Falcon, if that's what it will take."

The man was crying again. I wished Seb was here. He would be able to say something right now. I couldn't bring myself to talk. Impose? Like the guy standing next to me thought I was his niece? And he was trying to bribe his way into my life.

"Do you know what happened to his dad?" I asked. "The Flying Falcon's real dad," I tried again, because the man before me was stuck in self-pity and hadn't understood me. I knew Seb had a mother and brother, but I had not

275

heard anything about his dad.

"He's working as a trucker and is on the road a lot. He puts up missing-person photos of his sons and his wife wherever he goes because he can't find them. The photos are a few years old."

Seb. I felt like crying for him. His father was trying to find him. My father was possibly trying to find me too, but I couldn't reach him. I had looked and looked and failed to find my parents in their games. I didn't know how else to find them. I had no idea what their waves looked like. When I had seen my dad I hadn't known how to look for anything like that. I hadn't paid any attention. My parents were lost, and I knew how much it hurt. I didn't want Seb to have the same problem.

"Could you get his contact information to the Flying Falcon?" I asked the sniper. He nodded, then met me with a look that told me I needed to uphold the deal he thought we were making. His information for mine.

"My mom's lost. We were put to work in the Doldrum Mine after failing to cross the border. I only got out because they thought I was dead when I started surfing and my nose had been bleeding for a few days so..." I shrugged, not wanting to relive the memory. "I don't know if she's there or got away. If you find her..." I trailed off. A sniper wasn't the best person to pass along my personal heart-felt messages. "My dad was..."

"You were all stuck in the Doldrum Mine?" Mr. Sniper wiped at his eyes again before getting up off his knees.

"I've been trying to find her. Honestly, I've been hoping that she'd start surfing and I could find her. That's how I was found, but she must know how to control it so... I don't know how to find her."

The sniper gave me a short smile. "I'll find her," he resolved.

"But if she's there, they won't let her out unless she drops down and looks dead..."

"I'm the master at that. I'll find her."

"But what if she... what if she's still scared of you?"

"Maybe she'll make an exception if I'm saving her life. Besides, I can tell her where her daughter is."

The sniper put his hands in his pockets and I backed up, worried what might be in there. He looked around at the street again and then crossed to the other side when there was a break in the traffic. I tried to decide if I wanted to watch him leave or run after him. Then my phone rang, and that made my decision for me.

"Is he there?"

"He's here, Millie," Will told me. "He's going to be alright."

I felt a pressure float off my chest that I hadn't even realized was crushing everything about me. Seb was alright, and maybe I was too.

Chapter 28

Sebastian

I was not going to be alright as long as I was kept in the hospital bed. My mom and brother had to be worried sick. At least no one had tried to contact them and tell them that I had overdosed on heiss. The nurses looked at me like I was an addict. I wished I could tell them the truth. I was nearly dead, and then somehow I was here and breathing again and Will had shown up. He took one look at me, and before I could say anything he was on the phone calling Millie. How did he find me? I was conscious again, but I felt horrible. How soon until I was going to be released? Did I need a clean bill of health first? Maybe Millie would let me crash at her place so that my mother would never find out about this. I closed my eyes, pained at the thought. Was my mother going to think I was working late, or leaving her? *Please think I'm working late.*

Will sat down on the side of the overly large bed. I

wasn't sure how I'd ended up with such a large mattress. My bed at home felt five times smaller. Will looked ragged and tired. He eyed the mattress, and I smiled. He didn't need to ask. He could take a nap on the bed. I wouldn't mind. I wasn't about to fall asleep.

"How did you find me?"

"Millie," Will said. He took me up on my silent offer and stretched out beside me closing his eyes with a sigh of relief. "She told me to check for you here. Said she found a clue about your whereabouts. I have no idea what she had to do to find it. She didn't say more than that."

"Where's Millie at?" I asked him, worried that she was doing exactly what she said she was going to do: hunting down a sniper. I had to stop her, only I still felt like I couldn't move. Maybe I could move. I tried to sit up, but my limbs were heavy. I got part way up and then fell over onto Will.

"What are you doing?" he asked me, pushing me back down. "I don't want to be your nursemaid. I was up all night trying to find you. You're not fit to walk yet."

"I have to reach Millie," I told him, trying again. I got even less distance before Will constrained me. He grabbed one of the pillows, placed it on my stomach, and then laid back down. A pillow and a head were stopping me from reaching Millie? No way. I tried moving again, nearly laughing at my own efforts.

"You need to lose some pounds," I told Will.

"Don't strain yourself. She'll be coming."

"I can't let her hunt down the sniper for revenge. She said she would. I have to stop her."

"Do you know what the sniper looked like?" Will asked me, not moving. He folded up his legs and made himself more comfortable. I strained against him one last time.

"No." I had to admit that I had never seen the guy's face. One minute I was waking up at work, and the next I was hooked up to a table and everything felt wrong.

"Could you uh... well, here's the catch, Sebastian. You'll be fired if anyone learns of this. I'm keeping it as quiet as possible. I told Nick that I removed you from the work building before he realized it wasn't me. The only ones who know right now are me and Millie. She called me to find you."

"I can't be fired!" I struggled fruitlessly again, and Will looked at me, but he didn't give me an inch of room. He still kept his head flattening me down. It was only one head on a pillow!

"So when Millie gets here we'll tell her never to tell anyone, and you can keep working your high-risk job and I can go back to sleep. That is... until Millie tells us how she got her clue about you, and then I'll probably end up working off the record to keep her out of trouble."

"I'm going to save her," I told Will. I didn't struggle against him, though. It was pointless. My limbs were soggy river bags. Will told me to wake him up when Millie arrived.

I lay back on my bed with a sigh. My high-risk job. I hadn't signed up for a high-risk job. I needed something stable. Maybe I could find something else? I could look into changing careers while I worked this job, hoping that no one found out about me being caught by the sniper. But what else was there that I could be hired to do? It had to pay enough that I could afford housing and food and necessities for my family.

I was barely holding things together. I could picture a scene where a beggar walked up to Millie's father, shook his hand, and asked him if he could date his daughter. That beggar would be me, and I would have to tell her father that I had nothing to offer her. He would tell me I had no future and kick me out. I moaned. I knew that money wasn't everything and didn't make a man, but if a man couldn't make enough to afford a single date where was this going to go? Nowhere.

I was still bemoaning my nearly jobless state when Millie walked into the room. She looked wonderful, wearing the same thing that she had been brought in with. Maybe she didn't care if I didn't have much. What did she have? A broken home, missing parents, a mattress on a floor. We could both save up together and...

"They let people sleep in here?" Millie asked me as she looked at Will, amused. "Perfect."

She walked around to the other side of the bed and climbed on, squishing up next to me on her side. I tried to move over, but everything screamed at me. I wasn't going anywhere. How was my captured state going to be kept between us if I couldn't move? I had probably missed work. Millie placed her head on my shoulder and I wished I could move my arm around her. As it was I was stuck, mad, and angry at feeling like a paraplegic. She was tired, too, and closed her eyes as well. How long had she been awake? What had anyone said about me at work?

"Please don't take revenge, Millie," I begged her. "I couldn't stand it if you were—"

"I know." She shivered all over her body, and then curled up just like William, making herself comfortable next to me. "At least we don't have anything to hide from each other. Imagine that conversation..."

She sat up, met my eyes with a smile, and then snuggled in again.

"I can't move," I whimpered. Just one arm. I just wanted to move one arm around her.

"Did he hurt you? He said he overloaded you on heiss."

"You talked to him?!" I hissed. Will sat up to look at her. I wondered if he had ever really gotten to sleep yet.

"We made a deal," Millie said. I felt sick. I had caused this.

"I'm so sorry. Are you next?"

"What? No. Seb, you probably saved my life. You saved your life too. If you hadn't said my name... well let's just say this particular sniper has a thing with my name."

"Which is..." Will prompted.

I felt too sick to talk again. I felt like throwing up, which would be a bad idea considering the two worn-out people who were using me for a bed.

"You know I think he... he's... I think we're related. Once I find my mom I can know for sure. He said he wasn't going to hurt us, so we should be fine. He's going to help find my mom too."

"I don't like this," Will said. I nodded my agreement.

"Does your wife know what you are?" Millie asked Will. He had a wife? Was I the only one that couldn't afford a family?

"Millie..." Will glared at her and then looked back at me. "That's no way to apologize for interrupting."

"You were the one kissing her," Millie defended. "All I meant is that my mom apparently didn't know about

284

this guy's job until it was too late, and then she got scared and ran off. You should be honest with your wife."

"The wife is fine. Do you suspect your mom used to be a surfer?" Will asked her.

Millie nodded, and Will pulled himself up further, glancing between us until his brown lips formed an "O." I could almost feel his heartbeat pumping through his veins.

"Well shoot," Will declared. He plopped back down on top of me. Will had used the past tense. So Millie's mother no longer surfed waves into virtual games. If she was trying to stay far away from heiss, she would take Millie with her. She might be running from a sniper. Yeah. Shoot.

"Don't tell Nick or Leer about the sniper," Will advised Millie. "Don't tell anyone, or Seb loses his job. I called them up today to tell them that Seb had food poisoning and was going to be out for the day. I told them he was staying at my place after throwing up. That way I could claim I was looking out for him. I didn't know what else to say. I knew you'd find something, Millie."

"I might throw up again," I moaned, feeling my stomach churn. Will jumped away from me. Millie told me that she'd find me a bucket. She brought me an empty trash can, and I had to look away from her as my pride took over. What a way to impress a girl—by throwing up in front of her. Maybe Will would hold the trash can? Nope. No time. I heaved it up.

"Remind me never to overload on heiss," said Millie.

"I've done it before. He'll be fine in a few hours. He'll just throw up some and feel like a one-hundred-pound weight."

"Five hundred is more accurate," I told them.

Millie set the trash can down next to me and resumed her place on my shoulder. Will moved the trash can before taking over the pillow again. Both of them closed their eyes. Mine were wide open, worried that I was going to splatter them with the foul contents of my stomach.

A new nurse walked in holding a clipboard. He shook his head at the sight of my sleeping companions and rubbed the clipboard on his salt-and-pepper beard. He checked my readings, changed out the trash bag for a new one, and tucked an envelope into the top of my shirt.

"You have a wonderful family, sir. I hope one day I'll be as lucky."

Millie flinched as he walked out. Will risked a peek at him, but was too tired to do more than that. Millie breathed faster for a while as she wrapped her arms around me. I hoped the envelope contained discharge papers especially when both Millie and William fell asleep. I was left to churn through my thoughts by myself. The people with me were not my family, but I guess it could look that way. My napping friends were looking out for me. They stuck around even through the terror of snipers. They stood in the way of my bumps, helping me keep my job. I loved them a lot. Yeah, maybe they did feel like family, the kind that never walked away no matter where you were. They were the kind of family that made everything better when you reached rock bottom.

Maybe instead of sitting here feeling sorry for myself I should focus on the positive. William wasn't going to mention the sniper. Millie had saved me despite the fact that I had nearly ruined her. Any other sniper and it could have gone worse. Maybe Millie had been put in my life for a reason. I had never met anyone who would stick around through so much. She just kept coming back. Did she love me, or was she just tired? I looked over at her curled up around me and smiled. I could get used to that, just as long as I could *move…*

Will helped me throw up the next four times. Millie was out. She plopped against me each time I moved, but with each time I started to feel better. The first thing I did when I could move was put my arm around her. William laughed at the look of triumph that crossed my face. But then he pointed out my forgotten envelope in my shirt. I pulled it out and opened it and my face drained. That was not a regular nurse. Why would a nurse give me the mailing address of my dad? Regis was in Aperton according to the paper. Had the nurse figured out who I was and was going to bill my dad for my hospital stay?

"Who is paying for me being in here?" I asked Will.

He shrugged, and then left to go find out. I stared at the paper, trying to decide if I wanted to tear it into tiny pieces or memorize it. Dad had left us. He had walked out and not come back. We'd sold everything to keep afloat and when that hadn't worked out we'd had to leave. It wasn't easy taking on the load for the family. I did my best, but look where that had gotten me?

I looked down at Millie. At least I had that right now. She was one of those rare people that was easy to be friends with. If we hadn't moved, I never would have met her. But that didn't change what my father had done. I could still see the devastated looks my mom cast out the window every day, waiting for him to come back. I decided to dwell on it later when I wasn't injured. I didn't tear up the paper and do something that I would regret. I put the paper into my pocket, which was the smallest movement I had done in a while, but it woke up Millie.

"You're warm," she sighed and hugged at me again.

"Thanks for saving me," I told her.

"The world needs people like you in it," she replied. "Where did Will go?"

I told her, and she skipped off to find him. When Will came back he told me that Millie had gone home for the night. I asked him if I could do that too.

Chapter 29

Millie

I was trying to sleep. I honestly was. I didn't want to run into my uncle again right now. I had just gotten away from him in real life. Why was he back here haunting me wherever I went? I was just about to blink away after noticing him when he spoke.

"I got your parents out," my uncle told me with a voice that didn't send chills into my body. What it did do was command my attention. He was dressed as a dragon slayer, but he was less scary in a way. There were not very many games that changed a player's voice as well as a player's face, but this was one of them. We would both be hidden, which was why my uncle had been standing here waiting for me to show up when I couldn't sleep. He knew my schedule too well. What had my uncle done? How had he found my parents so fast? My heart leapt at the sentence and pounded once inside my chest. Leer hadn't made any progress that I knew about.

"They have a few bruises and blisters, but they'll be fine. They'll be making contact with you shortly. We shut down that mining operation rather quick, don't you think? I was pleasantly surprised at the team in charge."

No way. I continued to stare at the sniper. My parents were going to make contact with me? I had been waiting for that to happen. I'd spent days trying to make it happen, and yet this guy had pulled it off in under nine hours. That wasn't fair! My uncle was probably always going to be a better sniper than me.

"Are you sure you found my parents?" I asked, not wanting to find myself in an elaborate trap like he had pulled off on Visions earlier. This guy had serious talent.

"I have arranged for a meeting." My uncle nodded. "They should be coming this way soon."

I looked around, waiting for my eyes to train themselves onto a wave form that I didn't recognize. Maybe he hadn't gotten my parents out of the mine that fast. He had simply found them and gotten them to agree to stand in the same virtual world as me to make contact. Still, that was more than I had managed to accomplish.

We were in a dragons and dungeons world. I could see a dragon flying off in the distance, circling around the turrets of a stone castle. Drums sounded through the air, alerting the people in the game to the challenge. I wasn't dressed for attacking the dragon. I was standing next to a thatched-roof house wearing a scratchy dress. I was glad I couldn't feel it.

I focused in on one form that jumped several times, strategically drawing closer. Was it my mom? If it was, she chose to overtake a shopkeeper's avatar after she opened a bag by the avatar's feet and pulled out a crossbow. I looked around again, catching sight of another person who was walking toward me. Was it my dad? His actions seemed a little familiar, but I couldn't be sure when I had never paid much attention to him the first time.

"Is it you?" I asked when he stopped short of reaching me. His character had several weapons of destruction, including a barbed whip in his hands. That thing could hit me from where he was. Would my dad really swing it?

"Were you the person who told me to read Veronica's magic?" I asked my dad. "I had no idea what was happening at the time. I thought I was dreaming. I've been looking for you ever since. It is you, right? Are you alright?"

My dad nodded, and I arched an eyebrow at him, still not wanting to be taken in by a gimmick presented to me by my uncle. He had either really found my parents or had hired people to play the part. I wasn't taking chances.

"So say something," I demanded. Then I

remembered that in this world our voices were changed. Tricky. Even if he talked, I wouldn't know for sure if it was him.

"You prove it first," he answered. He shifted his eyes around, drawing them over to what might be my mother and then to my uncle.

"How? I want to hear you." I pouted. "I'll meet you at the Earl's house? Can we meet there?"

"Too crowded, but I have an idea. Follow me?"

"I've been trying to," I sighed.

He vanished. I looked to my mom, who wasn't taking off after him. The male shopkeeper I suspected was her walked toward me until he was standing right in front of me. My skin crawled with goosebumps. I wanted to hear these people! I wanted proof!

"What's my nickname for you?" the shopkeeper questioned. I didn't like the voice. I wanted my mother's voice.

"You don't use a nickname," I told her, trying to think up a nickname. My parents called me Millie. They didn't call me Mill-Mill like a few of my past friends had. I took a step back from her and blinked, searching for the wave of what could be my dad.

I found him sitting on a park bench watching a Ferris wheel load up passengers at a state fair. I sat down beside him and tried to see my father by looking into unfamiliar eyes.

"Oh, please say something!" I begged again. Even my virtual character, who was now a janitor, was full of the jitters.

"The sniper is right? You made it out? You're not hurt at all?" my father's voice asked me. I squealed and wrapped my arms around him. He hugged me back fiercely, wiping his eyes off on my shoulder.

"I'm so sorry he was the one to find you. We've been trying to keep you away from him."

"I'm fine. I'm just fine." I hugged my dad tighter. "I made it out of the mine a long time ago. He's my uncle? Which one?"

"Not here, Millie," my dad whispered. He looked around the fairgrounds apparently expecting us to be watched. His gaze lingered over everything and everyone searching—questioning as if he had trouble telling real characters apart from fake ones. Did he? I pulled back to scan the area. The only person I could see appeared in the heiss levels of my questionable mother. I waved to her. She was standing inside a woman with a baby carrier on her front. The woman unclipped the baby and set it down on the ground before hustling over. Her eyes were brimming with tears, her face beaming with hope.

"You left a baby on the ground?" I asked her, pointing to the infant that lay sideways. It was trying to crawl out of the carrier.

"It's not a real child," my mom's voice washed over me. I grinned while feeling disappointed at the same time. I hoped she hadn't ever left *me* on the ground. "I can't feel bad about a program, Millie. If I did, I couldn't focus on what's most important: my real baby."

"I'm not a baby," I protested.

I didn't get anywhere. My mom pulled me off the bench to wrap her motherly arms around me while she called me her baby a few more times. I rolled my eyes in my dad's direction. He laughed and joined in the group hug. I never wanted the hug to end. I grabbed both of them, smiling and trying to control the tears.

"I looked everywhere for you!" I told them. "Why are you so good at hiding?"

"To protect you," my mom told me. "It will be a little stressful, but we'll get you away from Dante, I promise. I don't know what he's trying to do, but we'll be with you soon and everything can go back to normal."

"Normal?" I asked, thinking of how we had lived our lives hiding away from heiss and everything else. "Is Dante my uncle's name?" I smiled at that. Seb would have fun with a name like that. My mother glanced up and around the area in search of my uncle. She didn't answer. "So are you out of the mine?" I asked them.

"Yes, and we're coming. We'll see you soon. We promise," my dad told me.

I gripped at them harder. They weren't going to leave me yet, right? I looked up into their avatars' eyes and whimpered. Fake people or not, I didn't want them to vanish on me again so soon. The last time I had seen them we had been pulled apart.

"Don't go!"

"We have to, so we can travel to your location," my mother told me, using that adult voice that tried to tell me her actions were for my own good. I shook my head, and she looked at my dad.

"Soon. We'll see you soon," he told me.

"No don't...!"

They left. I let go of the fake avatars, and because I couldn't leave a baby on the ground, strapped it back on the fake woman before I turned away. My eyes brimmed with tears through the entire process. They had left me. I knew they were coming to find me, but I felt like they had stranded me. Maybe they hadn't really left. Maybe they had gone into a different game?

I blinked rapidly, searching for their waves now that I knew what to look for. I didn't find them. Instead I ran across Rory dressed for the beach. Rory was standing next to Lex who held a surf board. Rory had his arms crossed and was tapping a foot.

"Hey," Rory said when he spotted me. I froze. I was still sad about my parents' eagerness to leave me in one setting to find me in another. I wished we had never been separated. But as sad as I was, it was strange to find Rory next to another sniper. The last time he did this, he had wanted me to be drawn to his heiss and stuck in an inanimate object. Was he trying to get me to find him now by standing beside Lex? I was naturally drawn toward large usages of heiss or collected heiss signatures. Did Rory have information about Seb's attacker? Was he going to tell me to go to sleep? He'd better not. He wasn't my dad!

"I'm going to get you fired for this," Rory told me.

"For what?" I asked him, eyeing Lex. I couldn't think up anything.

"Giving our company equipment to the Vikings!" Rory explained. "Where did you put it, Millie?"

"Put what?" I asked him, bewildered. "I never gave them anything."

"Don't play stupid. Why don't you wake up? You're going to face the consequences of your actions."

I jerked awake with my heart pounding. Rory sounded like he suspected *me* to be working for the Vikings.

I had a large suspicion that it was *him*. By pretending that his only motive to sneak into my room had been to clear out the Vikings, he was keeping himself away from the possibility of being evil—unless Rory was never evil. I wasn't. Had I misjudged his earlier actions? He hadn't tossed me out the window? Why couldn't we get along? My eyes were still wet from crying over my parents. I wiped at them, realizing that I wasn't alone in my apartment. How had I missed people breaking in? This was scary. At least I knew the person.

Lex was there. I had never seen him in real life, only in pictures. He had a large nose and an aging unforgiving face. He stood up, as he had been leaning against the wall while he surfed. He accused me of working for the Vikings and kicked me out of the apartment, taking my key. He told me I was fired as he searched my entire place. I wasn't sure what he was looking for. Proof that I was working with my uncle? How many people had seen me talking with him? They couldn't have known who he was. What was I being accused of? I wondered if this had something to do with Leer thinking that I was the one who had blocked the cameras during Seb's attack.

I had nothing in the apartment. Lex tossed out my one bag of clothes, closed the door on me, and told me not to come back to work. He told me if I did, or if they found the evidence they were looking for, I was going to jail. I had never felt so stranded or scared. What now?

297

I needed to stay close to where my uncle could find me, so that I could meet up with my parents. I wondered how they were traveling toward me and I headed to the train station to wait. It was the middle of the night and nothing was open. The trains were running two to three hours apart. I spent a few hours sitting on a bench trying to decide what I should do. My parents had made it out of the mine, but their games were still being broken into. I had to stop the Vikings for them. It felt like the only thing I could do. I had all the available tools, didn't I? I could surf my way through games and people and inanimate objects. I had cash in my pocket to buy train tickets or taxis. I had no obligation to show up at work in the morning.

I leaned against a wall of the train station, looking like a sleeping homeless person. I could now sympathize with a few characters I had portrayed in the games. I was going to be sleeping on the hard ground tonight. That was going to keep me awake. How long would it take before my parents came? I was feeling a little insecure with my surroundings, but if anyone were to come at me, I wanted documented proof of their actions. The train station cameras could provide that. Where else could I get a free security system?

I jumped into my father's games, following around a few people who worked for the Veterans. Did they have any more clues about the Vikings? I doubted they would share anything if they did. I avoided the Earl's house because it was so fortified that I didn't think the Vikings would use it to strike again.

I blinked through the levels, looking for anything that might have changed since the last time I'd run through. I stopped moving randomly when I found myself in another one of those worlds that contained only two players. Instead of being a chicken, I was pretty sure that I was a mounted talking fish on a wall. I could see a brief reflection of myself in a lamp. *Thank you talking fish, for providing me with this sniping opportunity.* I hoped it wouldn't last too long because inanimate object jumps drained me of heiss.

It was unfortunate, but I couldn't see who was talking. I could hear them, though, and I was pretty sure that one of the players was the same person my uncle had talked with in the farmer game when he said that he would have his cut job done by the end of the week. This was possibly the Vikings' boss. His or her meetings were always hard to find, but I could do it.

"I tested the firewall. The Bird Hunters can't get through," one of the voices spoke. I tried to link the voice up with any person that I had ever met before. They were talking about Visions' players being blocked.

"Great, thank you. You'll be compensated shortly," the voice of the boss replied.

"You'll stay out?" the other voice asked. "You promised."

"Oh yes. We got what we wanted. Just keep your other twits out of the way and no one else needs to get hurt."

"No one can get through the firewall," the voice promised.

"Then you have nothing to worry about," the boss said.

I felt the boss's presence leave, and I blinked as well, trying to find it again. When that failed I tried to find the other person. I was not going to take this as lightly as I had the first meeting. This was serious business. Someone had just stopped Visions from being able to reach anything that the Vikings were doing. Who was going to stop the Vikings if Visions couldn't get in?

The person who set up the firewall had to be scared after the recent security breach on the building, even if Leer and Nick were downplaying the event. How had that person contacted the Vikings to ask them not to do anything like that again? Was it a first contact I had just seen, or was this the person who had let my sniper uncle into the building to start with? Was the deal to let Seb get caught and save everyone else? Who was the person in charge of picking what games Seb faced? This person had led my uncle to him. It wasn't Leer and Nick. They were more in charge of keeping the people alive. It was the people on the first floor who controlled everyone's work load.

So if I could find the person who was personally feeding Seb's games, I could find who was probably behind leading my uncle to him. Will said things had picked up when Seb was hired. The first-floor person had decided to use Seb as a scapegoat. I hoped I could remember who was giving Leer's people their jobs. I ran through the names that I could think of, coming up with two. I wasn't sure which name was the one that I needed, but I had resources to help me find out.

I woke myself up, taking in the quiet train depot that was still around me and the mounted security camera. I moved to the computer station that let people look up train lines. It would give me a half hour to research. I was going to prove why it was dangerous to give out real names. But first I had to find voices. I typed in the first name on my list, Pradeep Patel, and came up with possible matches on various social sites. When I matched the face, I spent my last two seconds of time finding a friend of a friend that had posted Pradeep in a video. I pushed in more coins to bring back my search while I told myself that I would take out anything that had my voice in it. I couldn't stop being a surfer now, and this very same search could get me or my friends hurt.

The voice didn't match with the one I had heard in the games. I moved on to the next name on my list, Pete Jennings. His search was harder, and I used up lots of cash on it getting timed out, but I managed to find his voice. The

301

video didn't show his face, and he was listed on a relative's blog in the background, but it was the same voice that had been talking to the scary boss person. I was going to bet I had found the person I was looking for. Pete Jennings had planted a firewall inside of Visions. He was the scheduling coordinator for Leer's floor. I congratulated myself for figuring this out, but I still didn't have all the answers.

Was he the same person who had placed the probe inside the Earl of Key Hill? That question would be hard to prove since the probe was destroyed, but I still had ways to find out. Did Pete Jennings have his own account to play inside that game? Did he have an avatar he used that could have helped to insert the necklace?

I checked over the forums, performing a painstaking search for names that could match things that interested Pete. I located his email address and tried to match it against an avatar. It was frustrating. I couldn't prove anything like this. I gave up when the computer timed me out again, and I backed up against the station wall dropping into the Earl of Key Hill. I ran through characters with the speed of a tornado until I overtook someone who was walking right next to Veronica. My magical fake character didn't look to have a sniper in her currently. I grinned and took her over.

The first thing I did was have her sit down and take off her sock on her left foot. She was being guarded by the Veterans, but I could still get some information before they realized she wasn't acting normal, right?

"Pete Jennings," I asked, tapping the foot five times on the funny A and W mark. A character came up with the name of BSpacAlon. He usually played the part of a merchant. I ran through his player history, backing up to around the time the necklace was first found and discovered him with it. By now the Veterans people suspected me, but they weren't doing anything about it. One of them came to sit down right next to me, to watch my work without speaking to me. Maybe she thought I didn't recognize she was a sniper, but I did. Pete passed off the necklace rather quickly to an NPC. I could only guess that the role had been taken over by my uncle or another sniper at the time of the exchange. I followed the necklace's path as it was sold a few more times before it made its way to the Earl. With each sale I wondered if it was my uncle passing the thing off to himself. I looked over at the sniper beside me and gave her a smile.

"You found it. Who are you working with?" she asked me.

"The Bird Hunters," I answered, even if I had just been fired. It was because of Visions that I even cared to find the roots of this necklace. I wouldn't have known anything about it if I hadn't been brought into that company. The Veterans' sniper shifted her eyes to another team member before nodding to me. "Anything you can tell me? Any other problems like this probe popping up?"

I could prove that Pete was the person who had started the probe. I backed up in the necklace timeline to where it was first created.

"We did that too. We couldn't prove where the thing took on a sinister property," the Veterans' sniper told me. I smiled as I memorized her voice. She was probably memorizing mine as well. I wondered if she recognized it.

"Well I can. Don't lose this proof, okay?" I asked.

She nodded, and I replaced Veronica where I'd found her. I asked again if there was anything else the Veterans' sniper could tell me, but of course the woman didn't tell me where her group was focusing. I blinked out with one of the problems solved that Leer had given me. They all thought that it was a sniper who had created the probe. It did look that way, but the person had had help. I guess Visions was lacking the access to my dad's database in order to search for something like that, and the Veterans wouldn't know that Pete worked for Visions.

I could expose Pete, but I wasn't sure I wanted to yet. He was currently trying to protect everyone else from the Vikings' attacks. Maybe he really had let them find Seb and let my sniper uncle into the building. Thinking of my uncle, who was he? I was going to look that up next.

Chapter 30

Sebastian

"They fired Millie last night," Leer's voice hit my ears before I had made it out of my changing room at the end of the day. I stepped out, pulling my shirt over my head only to find Will standing there. Was Leer talking to him or me? Who could fire Millie? What had she done? She was saving us. I couldn't see why anyone would take away my angel. Is that why I never spotted her surfing into my work today? I kept looking for her, wondering why she wasn't worried enough to at least say hi.

"Why?" I asked. Will looked grave, but he didn't say anything.

Leer wiped at his nose and his eyes looking tired. "She was caught exchanging information with the Vikings."

"About her parents?" I asked. What other information was she after?

"Rory got her fired last night," Leer told me. "He had a long list of offenses to prove she worked for the Vikings."

"Of all the stupid things," Will complained. "Rory fired Millie so that the Vikings would be tempted to threaten her into working for them."

"She wouldn't do that," I protested. Right? She wouldn't? If she went to work for them, that would put her against me, against all of us. "They blackmailed her!" I insisted. Of course they had. They were trying to break us apart.

"Seb," Leer warned. I lowered my voice.

"Millie wouldn't work for them. They were killing her off left and right."

"This was a different," Leer shrugged as if he didn't care that he had lost Millie.

"Can't we help her?" I asked Leer. What was she going to do now that she didn't have a job?

"She doesn't work here anymore," Leer said before he put his hands on his hips and walked away. My mouth hung open at how easily Leer was letting her go. I looked at Will, made sure my shoes were tied, and ran for the front door.

"Who is Rory?" I asked him as we raced down the street to where Millie had lived. Would she still be there? Where would she go?

"He's the sniper for the second floor," Will illegally told me. "He's been trying to unmask Millie since she showed up. I'm honestly not surprised that he found something to hold against her. He didn't like her much. He was the one who threw her out a window. Not that I can prove it, but my gut tells me that it was him who did it."

"She got thrown out a window?" I asked.

"Yup. While working in the office. He hit her with a book to the back of the head and tossed her out. I tried to connect Rory to the recent attack on your floor, but I can't prove that, either. I'd hate to find that it really was that sniper." Will coughed as if he had no idea who had just tried to kill me. "Leer has no idea who got him. Tabitha was trying to get Rory fired, but she's away right now trying to get Millie's parents. That makes Lex really overworked since I've been following you."

"Lex?" I asked. I had never heard of these people.

"The company snipers," Will told me. "I wish Leer had told us sooner. This makes me rather nervous."

We reached Millie's door, and I banged on it with all the frustration that I had skating through my head. She didn't answer. There was a gap left open under the window shade and I peeked inside to note it empty.

"Where would she go?" I asked Will.

"I don't know. I don't have the time to spend on

Millie's personal problems. I've been watching you," Will reminded me.

I felt like breaking in the door and searching for clues. I wanted to search through the work building for answers as well. If this was a game, I would have spent all day finding out why Millie was fired and where she had gone, but this wasn't a game. This was real life, which only made losing Millie worse.

"This is going to be hard to hear, but without information we have to let her go."

"We'll get the information!" I banged on the door again, even if it was pointless. "You could get it."

"You should check on your own family, Seb," Will told me.

He had a point. It was hard to hear that I shouldn't get involved in Millie's problems. I had told myself that I wouldn't, but that was all before I managed to spend real time with her. I had my own family that I needed to protect from the Vikings threats. I also had the problem of my dad. I had looked up his location and realized that I was a wanted man. My dad, Regis, had posted the alert. I really didn't like the idea of my face being up on notices telling the world to find me. I didn't want to be found. I had to tell my dad that I was fine, and to do that I had to call him. However, I thought my mom should know, even if I expected her to be bitter about it all. My next step to protect my family was to remove my missing person portrait.

Millie wasn't here. There was no sense in wasting my time at this location. I lowered my hand off Millie's door and ran away from Will, slipping through places and people, until I'd lost him. If I could lose *him*, I could lose any other sniper trying to follow me. I did wonder if it even mattered. What if Will already knew where we lived? He would let me lose him and then show up when I wasn't looking outside.

Mom glanced at the clock as I stepped into the house, so I did too. Was I that late? I was a little late. She and Triton were waiting around the table so we could eat dinner.

"I found Dad," I told them, pulling out the envelope. I hadn't been to see them yesterday, but they didn't seem worried that I had skipped a day again. I sighed my relief and cringed at how hard this next step was going to be.

"I miss Dad," Triton voiced, looking at my mom unsure if she was going to tell him that missing Dad wasn't allowed.

"Where?" Mom asked. Already she was turning angry, hurt.

"I wasn't looking for him," I told her. "A guy from work found him and told me. This doesn't have anything to do with me liking Dad more than you or anything."

Mom scooped some dinner on her plate and started to eat it without blessing it at all. Triton eyed me before he took some too. This was rough. Mom had stopped talking for a time when Dad first left. I had done my best to be the cheerful face in the family. I had strained myself to find us a job to get us food and housing. Why did it never feel good enough?

"So we have his number and address. He's been working for the Boswell Trucking Company, and get this— he's trying to find us. I'm calling his number tonight to tell him to stop."

"You don't want to see Dad?" Triton asked me.

"I want him to stop telling all the police to find us," I answered. "It's only a matter of time before other people notice that we're listed as missing."

"A guy from work found this information?" Mom asked.

"Yeah," I answered, trying to keep my voice controlled. It was much harder to do so when I was talking to my family rather than people in games. "I work in security and one of the guys I work with looked it up."

"You work as security where?" Mom pried.

I ignored the question. It was one thing to tell that much. I couldn't tell her the rest. She would insist that we move. I didn't feel like leaving Will yet. I needed his sniping skills now more than ever. I opened up the letter that had come from the mysterious contact and fingered my phone.

"I'm going to call him," I said again. "I thought you should know."

Mom didn't say anything to me. Triton nodded that I should. I couldn't blame him. Things felt easier when Dad was around and I wasn't left to pick up the fallen pieces. I got his answering machine and the only thing I could think of to say was to ask him to call back. Disappointment mixed with my fear, and I held back the anger that produced. I was trying so hard to hold the family together, and tonight it felt like I wasn't holding anything. Millie had slipped away. I partly feared my dad would stay away too. Maybe he only put out wanted posters so the police wouldn't suspect him of having anything to do with us being gone. I grabbed food of my own and then the phone rang. He'd called back.

"Hi." I frowned. This was one of the few times I was at a loss for words. What did I say to the person who had caused us so much pain already? "Stop looking for us."

"Sebastian..." My dad's voice strained. I could hear music playing in the background and people talking like he was at a restaurant. The sounds faded like he had walked outside. "Where are you? Is everything all right? Is Ellen fine? How's Triton? Why did you guys leave me?"

"You left *us*!" I shouted.

"I didn't leave you. I got hit by a car and robbed and was in a coma in the hospital, unidentified for months. When I woke up, you were gone. You didn't even try to find me? I've been looking everywhere. That landlady said you stopped paying rent and left."

My mental functions came to a screeching halt before I got control of them again. He hadn't left us. How had we been so wrong?

I looked at Mom. I hadn't tried to find Dad. Had Mom checked the hospitals for unidentified people? It wasn't something that I would normally think about. I felt like an idiot. I had just been in this same situation, left at a hospital unidentified. I had woken up without knowing anyone around me until Will showed up. This was hitting me too close.

I passed the phone to Triton. I couldn't say anything. I was finding myself too mad. I wished this was a game. Then my brain would be thinking right. I needed time to process this in real life. Triton didn't, lucky kid. He started talking to Dad asking him questions, wondering if he had broken his leg or had any scars to show him. I stared at Mom.

"I did look for him," Mom told me as if my anger was for that reason.

I shook my head. I was mad at myself for not doing more before we moved. I had accepted the decision from my mom to leave, and then her telling me to start looking for a job, and then the multiple moves. I had put up with her silence, and the realization that it was all on me. I hadn't questioned anything. I hadn't gone looking for Dad. Maybe I would have found him.

"Ask Mom when I can come get you," Dad said over the phone. Mom dropped my stare to look at Triton. He looked at her wide eyed, the hope unmistakable. I couldn't look at the phone.

"Seb," Mom whispered. She grabbed the paper off the table that had Dad's address. "If he was in a coma, then it's me who needs to be forgiven. I didn't find him. You can go back to being yourself again. I know this has been really hard on you."

I glared at her. Then I pushed away from the table and went outside. I wasn't a kid. I know I had acted like one before, but that had all changed when I was forced to grow up and take on the responsibility of Mom and Triton. She had always looked at me like my contribution wasn't good enough. She was the maddest at Dad. How did she forgive him so fast?

I climbed over the sound barrier wall that separated our house from the road, and walked along the gutter until I reached sidewalk. With my hands in my pockets, I tried to clear my head, ignoring the sounds around me until another walker got too close.

"Rough night?" Will asked me dropping in beside my long steps. I jumped slightly when he talked to me. So he did know where I lived. I shrugged, unsure if I could tell him anything.

"I can't, Will. It's personal," I answered.

I didn't make an attempt to lose him, although I did consider moving Mom and Triton, or sending Will back to watch the house and make sure they were fine. I needed to clear my head. I put my life into words trying to sort through it without my personal emotions being in the way. Maybe Mom was never mad at Dad. Maybe she was always mad at herself. Maybe *she* felt like the one who wasn't good enough, and that's why she looked at me like she did, because she felt bad for making me work so hard.

Did that mean that we were going to move back with Dad? What would Will do? Hunt me down? It would be safer if I never touched virtual reality ever again, but the thought of not going into work tomorrow left me feeling depressed. I liked this job. How many other jobs would I ever get where I could play for work? If I left, I might never run into Millie again. I might never find out if she was okay. She had saved my life. I guess that we were even, but I really wanted to find her again. Should I stay or leave? It would be safer for Mom and Triton if they left.

"I'd look for you," William told me when I stopped on a bridge and stared down into the water, trying to decide what I was going to do. I rested against the railing and looked over at Will, who somehow managed to have a wife while working as a sniper. He risked everything for the thrill of the job. He probably wasn't the best example.

"Not what you're thinking?" Will asked. "You know I'll try to find Millie," Will told me, "and Tabitha is already doing that. I called her and she went ballistic."

"I was thinking about your wife," I told Will. He grinned back at me.

"I won't introduce you. I'm keeping her for myself."

"Selfish of you." I smiled back, finding his teasing smile infectious. Then I frowned at him. "You didn't think I was running away right now, did you?"

He had never made himself known to me when I was close to my house. I couldn't think of another reason for why he would confront me tonight unless he thought I was leaving. Did he think I would run away to find Millie, or was he thinking that I was scared of that sniper who had already decided not to kill me because of Millie? I wasn't scared of him, even if Leer thought I should be. If I ever saw the sniper again, I would look him in the eye and tell him that he was never going to rob my future. Maybe I would make it sound a bit more poetic.

"Will?" I asked him when he didn't answer.

"*Are* you running away?" he questioned. I laughed at him. He did think I was running. He didn't know that I had just called my Dad, did he? Maybe it was the look on my face. I was still considering it.

"Like I said, I'd come after you," Will told me again.

"And bring your wife with you?" I teased. Will didn't smile back at me.

"I should get back." I looked toward the house. I needed to know what my mom and Triton had decided. I wasn't sure how to tell them that I was considering staying. Would I still want this job if I didn't have them to support? Was it worth the risk if I didn't need it?

I stepped back into the house still unsure, but trying to look optimistic. The phone was sitting on the table which was clear of food except for my plate. Beside that was Mom looking tear-stained.

"Dad wants to thank you, Sebastian," Mom told me around sniffles. Triton was coloring in a coloring book that I had gotten for him so he would have something to do during the day. "You're the greatest blessing to us. You really are."

"You're leaving?" I asked her, sitting down to eat only because if I was starving tomorrow, Leer would notice.

"Dad will be here in a week. We can start over. Things won't be so hard anymore." She started crying. I remembered finding her standing on the corner trying to get food for Triton, along with a million other flashbacks.

"Maybe we should start fishing," I mumbled.

"What?" Mom asked.

316

"Nothing. I'll tell you at the end of the week if I'm coming with you." I picked up my food and took it to my room so I could eat and then fall asleep. I heard my mom start crying again. Triton climbed into the bed with me a few hours later.

Chapter 31

Sebastian

"Hey there," Leer said when I sat up wondering why my work had stopped. What had happened? I wasn't being followed by anyone. I hadn't even noticed Will around. Everything was easy and simple today, making me wonder how much Leer knew about my trip to the hospital. I questioned my work load yet again. Was I stopping anyone from attacking games, or was I being given simple in-game missions unconnected from the main mission of Visions?

"Did I miss something?"

"Did *I*? You can tell me anything, Seb," Leer told me.

"I'm fine," I answered.

I lay back down, unwilling to talk about it. My readings had been erratic as soon as I'd been hooked up this morning. I had initially refused to be put to sleep when Leer hooked me up. I was scared that I would find myself dead if

I let my eyes close. I was fighting the heiss, and it was hard to do. Maybe Leer had decided that I needed a break. I was still struggling with myself, searching for a way that I could wake up while on heiss like a surfer could. I never wanted to find myself in the hospital again.

"I am not in here," Will told Leer as he opened the door and snuck inside. Leer looked ready to punch him, but he muttered a few of his mental regrouping exercises and calmed himself down.

"That thing about her uncle," Will told me. He pulled out a picture of a man that I had seen hundreds of times on the train. "You're not going to believe this, Seb. Millie's last name is Ankerton. Her dad invented the Earl of Key Hill and this guy, Dante, is her uncle. He's also the guy who tried to kill you and left you with that envelope," Will said, not looking at Leer. "What did that envelope contain?"

I looked at the guy with the salt-and-pepper beard and made the connection. It was the same nurse who had given me the envelope. That was Millie's uncle? Why hadn't I recognized him when he'd emptied out my trash can?

"Wait so does this guy work for the Vikings or the Veterans?" I asked.

So many connections were firing around in my brain. Millie's dad had made the Flying Falcon. If we were in the game without her dad asking for our help with the Vikings then it made sense for the Veterans to work against us,

320

which they had. We had infiltrated his game. He probably thought there were two groups of hackers after him. Was that the reason why Millie's parents had moved closer, or had they been coming closer to meet Dante and assist him in clearing out hackers from the game? He was taking me down, because he thought I was in the wrong, and I probably was for breaking the game.

"Is that a sniper?" Leer asked William. He nodded. "You found Seb's..."

"He's always known, Leer," Will told him with a roll of his eyes when he didn't complete his sentence.

"Who does he work for?" I asked again.

"Vikings, Seb. This guy is not your friend."

"So is Millie in trouble? I've seen this guy a hundred times. Will he hurt Millie?"

If her uncle wasn't working for her dad, then he wasn't after me because I'd crashed a game I wasn't supposed to be in. He had to be after me to keep the Vikings' evil plans intact. Was he going to use Millie against her parents so he could gain all the access to the game that he wanted for his clients? Where was Millie?

"I don't know. What did the envelope have?"

I shook my head. It was personal. Millie had been fired because her uncle had shown up and probably talked about her parents. What was going to happen to me if

321

Millie's uncle told me that he was saving my parents? They were getting back together again.

"Seb, for your own safety please tell me," Will begged.

"No, it was nothing."

"Did he threaten you?"

"I can take care of it," I answered. "It really was nothing. The envelope was empty."

"I *saw* you read the paper from the envelope," Will reminded me. "Whatever it was, Seb, we're not going to hold it against you. Just tell me what it said."

I groaned and flicked my pressure cuff off the bed so I could swing my legs over. If they were going to fire me, then at least I wouldn't have to run and Will wouldn't come hunt me down.

"It was my dad's address and phone number. I called him last night. He had been lost in a coma, which was the reason why he never came back to us." I choked on the words. "He's coming to pick us up at the end of the week."

"You're quitting?" Leer asked me with a large gulp. "Don't do that. You reminded everyone that this job could be fun. Even Nick likes you."

"I haven't decided yet," I told them honestly. "I have a week. Are you going to help Millie?" I asked Will to shift the subject off my personal problem. If I was here next week, they would know my answer, and I would either feel great about striking off on my own or horrible for leaving my family after I had spent so much time holding them together.

"I'll keep looking," Will promised. "I just had to make sure that you were going to be all right first when I realized who that man was. He got right next to us." Will shivered. "He must have talked with Millie outside of the virtual world."

"I wish I could talk to Millie," I sighed. "Not going to fire me?" I asked Leer. "For sharing too much personal information," I pointed out when he looked at Will for clarification.

"No. Get back to work. Tell me if you see Millie," Leer directed.

I grinned at him and pulled the heiss cuff back onto the bed. Maybe Leer wasn't so bad when it came to being tagged by a sniper. He was trying to keep me around even at the risk it posed. Didn't that scare him? He had moved my room. Everyone had been given a room change, and the security guards down at the front were moving around the halls monitoring everything. Our rooms were going to be switched up every day from now on. The locks on the building doors had changed. The windows had gotten a second alarm system. It was surprising how fast those things could be installed.

"I need to talk to you," Leer told Will.

Leer followed Will out of my room, leaving me with the option to connect again or not. I knew how to do it, but the whole thing of being alone still got to me. I tugged on my bed, shifting it close to the door. If anyone opened the door they were going to ram it into my bed and wake me up. I made sure to leave enough room for Leer to slip inside, or rather crawl under my bed through the small crack in the door, so he could wake me up at the end of my shift. I wanted all the security I could get. It wasn't going to be easy to reach me. Only then did I go back to work, and the main reason for it was because I hoped that Leer's words would come to pass. What if I saw Millie? Then I would know that she was still alive. I really wanted to see her.

Chapter 32

Millie

I was making more progress than I'd expected. I had to move myself away from the train station when all the people crowded the place for work. I couldn't imagine that they would just leave me to lie on the ground like I was asleep or dead for hours. Plus, I was hungry. I bought a bunch of snack foods when the stores opened, and then hid underneath a bridge.

From there I forced myself to get some sleep. It was really hard to do, especially with the sun shining and the fear that someone would find me and call the police. I had run across the Vikings' boss again the night before by taking over a cat. If I was working, I would have checked my heiss level, and no doubt hooked myself up for more, but I wasn't working. I tried to look on the bright side. Low heiss only made it easier to steal into the Vikings' mastermind's hideaway. He wasn't talking with Pete Jennings or my uncle. I found him in a secret game room relaxing with choreographed music. He also used the room to make personal phone calls. I had listened to everything he said.

Selling other people's work wasn't this guy's only job. I felt like screaming for joy when he mentioned a company merger going on with his actual work. Baljing Electronics was merging with Logic Core. From there I had looked up the news. Then I discovered the company employees, and it was only a matter of time before I found him. I wasn't going to hop on a train and run down to his work place in Cinpinati to spot his real face. No. I was going to shove coins into a payphone and call every single person that worked in Logic Core until I heard his voice and found him. His voice was the only thing I knew. It would take a while, but I was going to do it. I hoped that I would identify his voice quickly and that it didn't take all week.

First, though, I needed to find a better place to hide. Once again, I found myself wishing I was more like Seb. He would have been able to think enough to find a better hiding spot. I stretched and peeked out from under the bridge, spotting Tabitha and her bright purple hair right away. Why was she here? She couldn't have gotten back from finding my parents' house that fast, right? I slunk out of the way making sure she didn't spot me and got moving again. I was determined to take down the Vikings before my uncle realized how close I was, and before he found my wave again to tell me to meet my parents.

I had spotted my uncle, Dante, handing off restricted items to random players, but I had left him alone. I wasn't going to worry about the smaller things right now. I was going to reach the head of the organization and watch it crash from the top down. Besides, I didn't want to waste my heiss. I was only going to tap into the games at night when boss man was there. I had to be careful. I knew what it felt like to tremble from the lack of heiss. Getting too much made Seb throw up. Having too little made me exhausted. I hoped my parents were going to understand that I was suddenly a rather expensive person now that I had discovered how heiss affected me.

Chapter 33

Sebastian

"Gone in yet or just got here?" I asked my dad as I jumped down from over the edge of the protective wall that tried to shroud the noise from the road away. He was hovering half in his truck with one hand on his blond head and the other one on his back.

"Sebastian!" he called out as he closed the door of his familiar truck. I wasn't surprised that he'd taken up the truck business. He always did like driving. "I've missed you a lot."

Dad held out his arms and I shrugged my way into a hug before trying to go inside. He was still taller than me, and always would be. He stopped me with a "hold on," and I frowned at the look on his too-serious face. He'd just gotten here. Maybe I should have been slower coming home tonight.

"Mom said that you might not be coming with us. Why's that?"

"I got a job here." I shrugged again.

I had made up my mind, but it wasn't easy. I was going to watch them all leave me, and I'd probably cry myself to sleep after they left. I expected it to take a week before I realized how stupid I was. I couldn't get fulfillment out of life by living in games that constantly changed. I needed real people, but I had rationalized that it was safer for them to leave, and plus I hadn't spotted Millie.

"A security job?" Dad asked. "But you won't tell your mother where?"

Did Mom tell him all of this on the phone, or had he been waiting outside after already talking to her today? He wasn't holding any luggage. It was possible that he had brought it inside already.

"Will you tell me where?"

"How about we go in?" I tried to deflect, but Dad shook his head.

"I've wanted to call you every day this week, but thought this was better said in person. Your mother's worried about you. She appreciates all your help, but if you can't say where you're making the money there's something wrong with that. You can't quit?"

"I can quit," I answered. "I can leave at anytime."

330

"So are you? Are you coming with us? Triton won't be the same if we leave you behind. None of us will. We're better with you beside us."

"Dad, I have this project that I want to see through to its completion, and if I left, I'd never know what became of it."

"Sometimes you work for days. You work and don't return here to sleep. Where do you sleep?"

"At work." I gave him a short smile. "Honestly. I had a time sensitive project."

"Did you finish, and it was worth it?"

"Yes, and yes," I answered. "Every second. I saved a life. Are you sure you don't want to go in?"

Dad looked at the front door and shook his head. Maybe if I walked in, he would follow and stop the interrogation.

"I'm not going in until I know what we're going to tell your mother. I've been sitting out here waiting for you. You were being the man of the house while I was gone, and I appreciate that, but our circumstances pressured you into taking this job, and I don't want to go in there and tell her that we're leaving you."

"Sorry," I told him, attitude creeping up in my voice. I couldn't leave. I was still holding out hope that I would find Millie or that Will would figure out something and tell

me.

"Why can't you tell us where you work? Did you know that your mother has tried to follow you a few times? You take a different way to work every day?"

"Yes I do. I take a different way home every night as well."

"Whatever for?"

"Because," I answered like the contentious teen I used to be. I had gotten better when I stopped questioning everything, and look where that got me? I hadn't known that my dad was in a coma in the hospital. He grabbed my arm and opened the door to his truck, ordering me to get inside. Was he trying to ground me? I refused to get in unless he gave me the keys. I watched him turn frustrated before he tossed them to me. I climbed into the passenger side with the keys in my hand and stretched my legs out. How long was this going to go?

"Sebastian, your mother and I love you. We want what's best for you."

"I can't leave, Dad," I whined. I was still torn about the whole thing even if I had made up my mind to stay. I had missed my dad, and wanted to see him, but what was best for my family was to not be in the way of sniper attacks.

"Where do you work?" he quizzed me again. He fixed me with that stare that held no argument. I found myself smiling. I had argued back against that look lots of times.

"Please, Sebastian. You were acting like a man. Talk to me like one."

Ouch. He could spin a hard line. I could probably spin it back at him, but I was still looking at him and we weren't playing games.

"Mom would have a heart attack," I told him.

"I won't. Clean bill of health," Dad informed me.

I looked out the window to see if I could spot Will, even if I hadn't noticed him following me this week. Maybe he was going to let me go, or maybe he was taking a break so he could be with his wife before he might have to hunt me down. I didn't know, and that was the part that got to me. I didn't know what was going to happen, but I did know that if I left, I'd miss it. I had spent the week going back and forth with leaving and staying, running through every option I could think of for and against.

I told my dad he couldn't tell anyone if I told him where I worked. He replied that he would be his own judge, and I snorted. He wouldn't be telling anyone. I gave him the name of the company, and the briefest logistics of what I did erring on the forgiving side and mentioning how I'd saved Millie from freezing.

"There are snipers who work against that kind of job,

Seb," my dad informed me. I did my best not to laugh. Really?

"We have snipers who stop the snipers, so I'm pretty safe," I answered. "But I try to be cautious all the same, which is why it's better if you all leave without me."

He shook his head. I wondered if I should have not told him, because now he would envision me getting shot. I had avoided that so far. The only one who had ever killed me was Millie in the games, and she had been quick about it to wake me up. It was very effective.

"You're not invincible," my dad told me, and I played with the keys waiting for the rest of this speech. I had heard it before. I usually got the lecture when I asked to borrow the car.

"I know that, but I'm awfully good at this. I'm the top employee of the quarter," I bragged.

"I can't leave you to this," my dad said, surprising me. "We're staying with you."

"Dad, no. You guys go. I'll be fine."

"You won't be fine. You'll stay at work for days playing and forget to take care of yourself."

"I take care of everything!" I told him, gripping the keys in my hand again. If it wasn't for me we'd be rotting in a ditch. Maybe we would have ended up in a homeless shelter. I had turned responsible. Couldn't he see that?

"It's hard to take care of yourself when you're lonely, Sebastian," my dad told me, his voice suggesting that he had a hard time living without us. I felt bad for him again. I relived waking up in the hospital alone, terrified that Millie was out there hunting down her uncle to get revenge. Since I hadn't spotted Millie, or heard anything either, I had been reading the news on the way into work wondering if Millie's face would show up after she destroyed her uncle. Was she going after him? Where was she? Had she already found her parents? Was anyone ever going to tell me? I didn't think I would ever know if I gave up my job.

"I'm still thinking about it, alright?" I asked.

Dad finally agreed that we could go inside, but I didn't think the conversation was over. I knew his views. He didn't want to split up the family, and he was going to talk me around to the same way of thinking if he could.

"Dad!" Triton shouted, plunging into our father's legs and obscuring his face underneath his red hair. Dad greeted him just as warmly, sniffling a little over how much he'd missed Triton. I met my mother's eyes. She approached cautiously as if she knew the whole time that my father had been sitting outside, not coming in. She looked between me and my father, and I made the lame excuse to use the bathroom so I could step away. Why did I feel like this was my fault? I should have looked for my dad. I had done everything I could think of to hold us together, except to look for my dad. Mom and Triton needed him. Why hadn't I considered it?

When I came back out, I could see that my mom had splurged on dinner tonight, expecting him to show up. I was glad that he had made it so I wouldn't be a witness to her tears and feelings of abandonment. Everyone looked at me when I stepped into the room. My dad gave me a smile, and I could see the struggle beneath it to not revert back to lecture mode. So my job was a little dangerous? Every job had some sort of risk, didn't it? He was driving trucks. He could crash.

"Whatever we do, we're doing it together as a family," my dad said.

I wondered if my mom had already asked him if he had talked to me. I gave him a smile doing my best to hold everything together again. It was going to be strange taking the back seat instead of driving, now that I was used to it. I was going to feel pushed aside. But we'd figure out something. I offered to set the table.

Chapter 34

Sebastian

"Maybe a little help here," I asked, hoping that perhaps Leer was watching. I had gotten another of those missions where I had no idea what my mission even was. I'd arrived in a house with no instructions and figured out the first room. I had to escape. Now I was looking at a fireplace and I knew what to do, but I couldn't do it.

"I need to sing the song from that movie on the poster." I pointed to the poster that was over the mantle. It showed a ghost who needed to get a living person to fall in love with him so he could turn mortal again. I had never watched the show. "I don't know the song."

"I crawl through pathways in the dark," a familiar voice echoed around the room. "I hide away from the day. The glow stabs me through the heart." I got chills and looked around tingling with anticipation. Where was she? It sounded like Millie! She always inhabited avatars I wouldn't suspect, but I thought I was alone. Where was she?

"It's torture to want your hand. My scars are so deep you'll never understand."

There! I spotted it. A cuddly teddy bear was singing to me. I picked up the bear, turning it around. I didn't think it was supposed to be able to talk. Millie winked at me and kept singing.

"But I won't back down away from you. Your smile is what gets me through. Darling, my fire's for you."

"Fire? It's a ghost." I pointed to the ghost. "This burning inside my soul is the only thing that makes me whole," I guessed, matching the tune. The bear tried to reach my mouth to make me stop messing up the song. "We will score in the net without breaking a sweat. It's the portal to make you mortal," I sang. The bear laughed at me.

"Have fun playing. Save me a stroll sometime," the bear said before its animation stopped.

"Hey!" I shouted, turning the bear upside down and shaking it for a reaction. "Don't go."

I dropped the bear and scanned the rest of the room, picking up everything around me, frantically hoping that something else would start singing to me. I had seen Millie! I wanted to know where she was. Had she been following me long? Was she coming back? I tore through the room twice over with nothing else coming to talk to me. Oh fine. I sang the song that Millie had taught me and the fireplace swung open. I dashed into the next room, searching everything for clues to reaching Millie. Was she waiting for me at the end of this place, or would she suddenly be something else like the stuffed otter that was sitting on the shelf? I picked up the otter, and then tossed it on floor.

I had been trying to spot her for so long that it was torture to know she was surfing right now and hadn't stayed with me long. What was more important to her than being a stuffed bear? Really? Hadn't she always wanted to be a stuffed animal? I made it through the rest of the house and still had not spotted another sign of Millie. What if I walked past her and she was laughing at me for not noticing? No. That sounded cruel.

"Escape that," the words flashed across my screen. I was standing inside a glass cage with no apparent way out. My prison was set on top of a rock wall, making me want to tip the cage and hear the glass shatter. Below me people walked, oblivious to my fate in the glass. I waved my arms, wondering if anyone would notice, and then flung myself into the glass. It was Millie! She was down there, and she wasn't surfing. She was playing as a real character in this game and her face was visible. Is that why she had left me? I banged on the glass to get her attention.

Just seeing her flooded me with a warmness that

settled around my heart. She was playing with the ends of her braided hair, pulling it toward her and smelling it for aromatherapy. I sincerely wished I could smell the scent that intoxicated her, because it was intoxicating me without the nasal stimuli. How could she smell it? This wasn't real.

I had to get out of this glass. I pressed my hands along the whole cage looking for a seam. My character didn't have anything sharp. In fact, I was made from wax. What was this? I was a statue? I shoved at the edges of the glass, my frustration peaking with every second. What if Millie left before I escaped? Why could no one see me?

"Let me out!" I shouted like I was drowning in a locked tank. I hit the glass again and dented my wax hands. Great. That wasn't going to help. I molded my left hand into a shovel, trying to break the glass. Millie wandered off to talk with another character. I'd had quite enough of this. I didn't care if it was cheating to surf my way out; I was going to get out of this glass.

I forced my body to look for heiss. If Millie was looking like herself, she had to be on heiss. It was probably the smallest trickle, but she had to be using some. It took me seven tries before I managed to surf my way back to the same street Millie had been on. Looking at my glass cage from below revealed that it was so reflective no one would have seen me. I examined my stolen character. I was wide and holding a bucket of a mysterious yellow substance. I carefully put the bucket down and ran into the street to find Mille. Where had she gone? I finally found her trying to buy boots.

"That's why you didn't want to keep the teddy bear," I said, coming up as close to her as I dared. "It wouldn't fit in the boots."

Millie jumped and looked at me. My grin was wider than a canyon. I had Millie right in front of me. She was tantalizingly close, and no doubt farther than she had ever been in real life. Then she was gone. I felt the heiss drain from my system and everything turned dark.

"Can't I get overtime?" I asked, even if my head felt fuzzy. All of me felt a little weird.

"I told you he could do it again," Leer spoke to someone in the room. "You just playing around with him or what?"

"You have to admit he's great fun to watch," Nick answered.

Gee, my head was still fuzzy. Maybe I had been on overtime already. I checked my arms and pulled off the cuffs and opened my eyes.

"Did we find Millie?" Leer asked Nick.

They were not looking at me, but rather at the screen where Millie's face was frozen and displayed. I sat up a little wobbly and checked the time. Wow. I had worked an hour over. That was my longest yet, and it didn't sound like Nick or Leer was upset with me for surfing. Had my game not been one of Visions' missions but a side quest Nick had put me on?

"Will and Tabitha have been searching for her. Will has this crazy idea that if she keeps running into Sebastian that she'll call us or something and try to come back," Nick told Leer. "Tabitha thinks we'll find her with her uncle. She's been looking for him, but he of course keeps throwing her off."

Leer looked over at me and rushed to help me before I fell. He told me to take it slow because surfing could make me woozy. I felt my hopes shatter along with the strength in my legs. It had been a week. Where was she? Leer supported all of my weight with a grunt. I bored my eyes into Nick, waiting for more news.

"She was the bear, yes?" Leer asked me.

"Yes. Why didn't you let me talk with her?" I complained.

"That wasn't her," Leer informed. "Nick created that false image."

I sighed. But I *had* seen Millie. She had come to see me, drawn to my side by me using excess heiss. Would that idea really work to get her back? Could I overuse heiss to see her again?

Chapter 35

Millie

My feet were moving on their own accord as if they knew where they were going, but they had no idea and neither did I. This was my first time out of the seldom-used storage shed at the local school. I think I picked the school as my base because of how easy it was to break into the place. It reminded me of my younger years.

Maybe I was going toward a store? I was too tired to think about where I was going as I staggered down the road. I would have kept staggering if I hadn't fallen asleep on my feet. At least, I thought I had fallen asleep when I realized that I was standing in a strange place with no recollection of going there. I had finally identified the voice on the phone. It had taken forever, but I knew who was behind the Vikings. Funnily enough, I had been able to pick up a few other voices that I had heard in the games over the phone as well. I posed as a reporter interested in the merger, so I could keep calling Logic Core back. I had a great list of people to arrest.

I wobbled, everything turning dark again. It was either I blacked out or my body was so used to running toward disaster that I had brought myself here because of the noise. Someone was getting beaten up. I could hear the shouts from inside a house and the harsh sounds of hitting. I wanted to rush inside and do something. If I was asleep, I'd have an infinite number of lives to save the person. In the real world, though, my horror over my frail, girly body started to tear me apart. I'd never hated my body before. I was fine with it until now. The screams got louder. Couldn't I do anything? I pulled out my phone to call the police, but I saw someone looking at me from the corner.

"Have you called the police?" I asked the man who was wearing baggy pants. I resisted the urge to ask him about his monetary status. He looked poor with several holes in his shoes. I was probably looking worse.

"You wouldn't if you know what's good for you," the man answered.

What was he? A scout? Would he come and beat me up if I dialed the number? Would I be next? I had never felt like such a coward before in my life. The inside of my nose started to feel moist. My eyes started to tear up. I had to *do* something! Maybe if I turned and walked away, I could call the police after I was out of the guard's sight. I turned around, but suddenly I was beside the guard instead of away from him and I had no idea how I had gotten to the other side of the street. Was I reversing reality and sleeping? I checked my hands just to be on the safe side. Mine. Why was I blacking out so much?

"He needs help," I heard myself say, although I was slightly incoherent and couldn't remember what I was trying to get help for. Then I remembered the final scream of the beating and I started to tremble. I didn't feel cold. I simply couldn't control the motor reactions of my body. I tried to stiffen. Actually, I knew exactly what my problem was. I was out of heiss.

"You need to worry about yourself first," the scout told me.

I tried to nod so he would let me go. He was holding my arm, and I was still trying to decide how I'd gotten to the wrong side of the street or why I'd even turned down this path to start with.

Did I fall? My elbow hurt and I could smell blood. It smelled closer to me than my elbow, but I couldn't make out where it was coming from. All I could tell was that I couldn't stop shaking. The scout thought it was funny. He told me that he hadn't even gotten started yet, but I had no idea what he was talking about. What I did know was that I was in trouble. Could I sneak into Visions while out of heiss again and find help?

345

I was standing somehow. I tried to get my legs to start running, and maybe I did get them to function around the uncontrollable trembling, because the next thing I knew I was down on the ground, not out in the street, and my side hurt along with my elbow.

Wow, I needed heiss right away. I tried to blink into Visions' except that another kick on the same spot on my ribs brought a scream out of my throat. I wished I could pretend that I was good at dying. In reality, I was still horrible at it. If I was asleep, nothing would really hurt. I wouldn't feel the pain. It would just be a blank dark slate on which I erased a program and I could start over again. Suddenly I wanted to believe in reincarnation.

"I didn't do anything!" I begged, rolling over to protect my sore side. I hoped that this guard, who I had a strong hatred for, didn't decide to hurt my unbeaten ribs next.

"Oh yes you did."

The voice only increased my trembling. It was not the voice of the scout, but it sounded familiar. I screamed as my shoulder throbbed next. Who had recognized me? Was this the Vikings? Did they have more than one sniper? I tried counting my blessings to pass the time. At least I kept missing the hits because I kept blacking out. I stopped counting my blessings when the smell of blood became overpowering. It was running down my nose. Was that all?

I'd had nosebleeds before. I'd be fine, right?

My brain woke up enough to place the voice. The man towering above me with cruel malice was the same man who had shoved me and all those other people crossing the border into his cars to work in the mine. I had been so busy thinking about unreal worlds that I'd forgotten I had problems of my own in the real one. This guy probably knew that I had escaped and could guess that it was me who had snitched on his unfair empire. I wondered if my body was going to be tossed onto a heap of other likewise tormented flesh—for a second time.

I wanted to run. I wanted to take a few pictures of the villain with my phone and show it to the police. I wanted to tell Will to snipe this guy down for me, because I didn't have the guts to do it. Maybe I didn't have the guts to even ask. Maybe I did ask, because suddenly my legs started hurting too.

I found myself wondering what Sebastian had been thinking when he thought he was going to die. All I could think of was how sorry I was that I wasn't saving him or saving my parents. I couldn't save myself. What business did I have trying to save anyone else? I opened my eyes, and for some reason I realized that there were six beer bottles tossed on the floor next to four pieces of crumpled paper and one blue pencil without an eraser. Useless details. Maybe in a game something like that would help me, but in the real world I couldn't think of any use for it.

"You picked on the wrong person," another familiar voice swept through my delusions.

It was the same voice that had pressed a book to the back of my head and knocked me out before. Will knew who this person was, so why didn't I? I tried to stay focused, because the detail seemed really important. The next thing I heard was the gunshot. I would have flinched if my body could stay still long enough to pass the message along.

"Why didn't you sleep last night?" the cold voice asked me.

I was so dead. Did I say that out loud? I became focused, again sprawled out on a mattress. *My* mattress. Yes, the person who got me now was a sniper and knew where I previously lived. I had been kicked out of that place. Why had I been brought back? I needed to move, except that I had no idea how. I couldn't make myself walk anywhere.

"I said stay down!" the cold, deep voice knocked me to the floor. I had to leave. I had to get out of there. Again the sniper smashed me to floor, reminding me that whoever he was, he didn't care for me one bit even if he had just saved my life.

"Keep your eyes on the floor. That's all the heiss I'm going to give you. What do you think you're doing?" the person asked me.

I finally understood the second time. He didn't want me to look up and figure out his secret identity. But if the person didn't like me, why was I not dead yet? Why bring me home? Had I gotten heiss? In my room? Everything still felt fuzzy.

"Have you any idea what you are saying right now? Who overloaded on heiss?"

Woah. Was I talking? How was that possible when I couldn't make sense of anything? How badly injured was I? Was this going to happen *every* time I ran out of heiss? What had happened to the man who had kidnapped me to work in the mine? Who was helping me?

"You're a bloody mess. What happened?" That was Will's voice. I was on my hands and knees, but Will was here. Why was Will here? Oh well. I could stop trying now. I had to get some sleep so I could function tonight. I had to find a way to turn in all my hard work.

"Millie…" Will's voice shook me awake briefly. "Don't you ever go on a real sniper hunt again."

"What?" I asked, trying to make out my location. By the bed. I crawled my way to the rest of the bed. It rattled. Someone had placed black trash bags all over it. Was that to protect it from my blood? I hadn't the energy to clean it up before I collapsed back onto a pool of red. Had I stopped bleeding yet?

"Don't you ever! Why did you snipe out the man who caught your parents?"

"I didn't," I answered Will.

I closed my eyes. I couldn't think like this. Someone else had to find the rest of the Vikings, because I couldn't function. At least the rustling of the trash bags was similar to the sound of my baby book. It was wonderful. Every time I felt myself waking back up I heard the rustling and I went back to sleep. Would they let me sleep forever?

Chapter 36

Sebastian

I didn't like waking up still attached to everything without Leer's face there to greet me. It wasn't like I had been killed and the separation of a mental connection had woken me. I wondered if I was starting to get used to the timing of when I was done for the day. Had I gotten myself to wake up while connected to heiss after a week of mentally telling myself to figure it out?

I checked the clock from the safety of the bed just to make sure I was right. I was. Then I noticed that my door was slightly open. Chills traveled over my arms. My question of why I had woken up was answered when I heard the voice coming through the slightly open door. It was the person who I had first thought was our company sniper. The low voice was the same person who had threatened to torment me in every version of reality if I brought Millie into Visions. I hadn't heard from the man

351

since he'd hid from me in the hallway, but I had been responsible for getting Millie into Visions.

"She's a traitor," the voice grated.

"She wasn't. It's your precious Rory that unlocked her door. I didn't like him sneaking into the room and spying on her," I heard Leer say. "I won't tell you anything."

"You're not the only one," the mad voice replied. "And it's your job to tell me about these people."

"I'm sorry. Who made it against the company policy to not talk about employees like this?"

Leer's monitor started beeping at him. He silenced the sound and shut my door. I yanked off the rest of my monitors and rushed to the door so I could keep listening. I heard his monitor beeping again, informing him of what I had just done. I put my ear to the door to try to hear more, but Leer moved off as he realized he was being too loud. Were they talking about Millie? I didn't want to assume, but it seemed everything was about Millie all the time. Maybe Will would know? I called him to see if he had woken up yet.

"Know what happened to Millie?" I asked him.

"Did you see her?" William asked me.

"No, but Leer is talking with a guy in the hallway that I thought was a sniper, and it's making me suspicious."

352

William hung up on me. I vainly asked "hello" a few times before the disconnected chime came to my ears. I sighed and sat on the edge of my bed, waiting to be let out. Both Will and Leer came into my room when the door finally opened.

"Free to go," Leer told me with a shake of his head. "Please stop what you're doing, Sebastian."

"What do you mean?" I asked. I had been sitting here for fifteen minutes, locked in my room. I hadn't been doing anything.

"You woke yourself up. Yes, you would be super helpful if you trained yourself to act like a surfer, but I can't defend your hide right now. I have too many other problems."

"Is it Millie?" I asked. And it wasn't my fault that they were training me to surf pestering me enough to make me jump waves. I guess I could only blame Nick for that.

"Go on," Leer told me.

He turned around and left without more than that. He was in a bad mood. It must have been that company sniper. I shut off my own computers for him and raised the reclining chair. Will didn't say anything to me. He stared at the wall. I walked past him without saying anything, either. I hadn't told my mom that I was going to be home late, but maybe she would be alright if I wasn't too long.

353

I looked behind me frequently as I took unusual trains until I reached the place where Millie had lived. I stared at the shut blinds. I had banged on the door last time, but I hadn't tried to open it. Maybe she hadn't really moved. I glanced over my shoulder again as I tugged the door open.

"Oh," I said and shut the door behind me before anyone else could see what I had just walked into. Will was standing in the room with his gun out in a standoff. He was facing the fake doctor, who was my personal sniper, or rather Millie's uncle Dante. Both of them were trying not to blink and miss their shot. I should have felt scared, but both of these snipers had saved me before. There was no way either of them would kill me when they looked so intent on killing each other. Both of them were sweating. Neither one looked at me, and I wondered if they recognized my voice.

"I don't think you want to shoot each other," I told them.

Why were they doing this? I looked toward the floor and dread swept through my body. My heart felt on fire. Lying on the mattress, covered in blood, was Millie. Why would her uncle... I looked between Will and the sniper again before I rushed to Millie. I took in my observations quickly. She was still warm. She was still breathing.

"She's alive," I reported. Maybe while Will distracted her uncle, I could carry her to the hospital on my shoulders. I didn't care if it got my clothes bloody. I'd find something to explain the mess to my parents and brother. I ran my hands around her head, looking for the source of her wounds. Why had she been fired? If she had been at work today, she would have been in a safer location.

"Is she?" her uncle asked. "What's bleeding?"

"It was only her nose," Will told him, "and I didn't do it."

"You didn't do it?" Dante asked. "I didn't do it either."

"I know," Will answered.

"So why do you have your gun out?" her uncle asked.

I looked back at them now that I was certain that Millie was still alive. I didn't want them to fire and change that status. The two snipers were still not blinking at each other. How did they manage that for so long?

"If I put my gun down would you hurt us?" Will asked the Vikings' sniper. I felt oddly calm to be standing around Dante. Will was more nervous about all of this than I was. I guess I realized that the man had already had one chance to kill me and hadn't done it. I didn't think I had done anything new to change his mind.

"I'm putting my gun down," her uncle told us. "Don't shoot me. I only stopped by to check on her. You know what happened?"

355

"Millie took the wrong end of a sniper hunt," William answered.

He gave her uncle a nod, and they both lowered their weapons at the same time, but they didn't take their eyes off each other. I ran my hands over Millie again, checking out anything visible while I tried to decide if her only injury was a bloody nose.

"Her shoulder was popped out as well," Will sighed. "I shoved that back in earlier. Why are you here, Seb?" Will asked me.

"As if you need to ask," Dante chided.

We all jumped when the door opened again. I stared at the door startled. Dante and Will both pulled their guns back out and aimed towards the light. I was glad that they hadn't decided to gang up against me when I stepped in. I had gotten lucky. Standing in the doorway was a brown-haired man I had never met before. He yanked his arm out to the side, stopping the blond woman that was behind him. His eyes drifted around to our faces, and then he gasped on the sight of Millie.

"Jessie, Juliet." Dante nodded at them as he lowered his gun. Will lowered his gun as well when we all recognized Millie's parents.

"What happened to her?" Millie's dad asked. Millie's mother shrieked when she saw her. She ignored the snipers in the room, save to look at them with a slight hesitation, before she rushed to her daughter and started to perform the same search I had been doing. I told her that Millie's nose had been bleeding. Her mother shook the plastic bags and looked at her husband with horror. I understood the look. Millie wouldn't wake up if she was on the bags. The soft sound would put her to sleep. Jessie Ankerton was still standing at the open door like he would rather run back outside than check on Millie.

I stood up and looked in the kitchen to see if there was something I could use to clean up the mess. There wasn't. Millie didn't have a single utensil, and the cabinets were empty of paper towels. The sink worked. I shook my head. My shirt already had blood on it. I would just buy myself a new shirt for once. I pulled it off my head and soaked it before bringing it back and handing it to Millie's mother who had managed to pull her daughter off the mattress and had her flat on the floor. Will had been adamant that she pull her by the legs and not her arms. Her mother tried tickling her daughter's neck and hands before looking back at her husband with another shake of her head.

"Here," I said.

I took my wet shirt back and rubbed it on Millie's face. I had used cold water on purpose. It was cold, hard, unforgiving things that woke Millie up. After a few moments of me trying to work the blood off her face, she convulsed, then grabbed at her waist moaning. Her eyes remained shut against the pain. I wished I had a painkiller. Her mother shoved Millie's arm out of the way and yanked up Millie's shirt before screaming.

Her husband, Jessie, finally shut the door. Millie's stomach was shades of black, blue, purple, and green. The sickly colors brought tears to my eyes. I wished again that she hadn't been fired.

"Who did that?" I asked, picking a new spot on Millie's contorted face to clean up.

Millie pinched her eyes together again before giving up on being tense. She relaxed onto the floor with a sigh of relief after hearing my voice.

"She's not broken," Doctor Will told us. "Only her left shoulder was dislocated, and like I said, I put that back in. She failed a sniper hunt."

"Sniper hunt?" her father asked dangerously. "You're using her as a sniper?"

"Don't look at me. I'm not her boss," Will answered.

"You have to do something!" Millie's mother beseeched her husband. "She can't turn into that."

"You can't stop her from being what she is," Will grumbled. "Maybe you could have protected her from it if you had ever explained surfing and sniping. It's too late now."

"What have you done?" Juliet asked Millie's uncle. Was he her brother? I looked between the family, trying to place the family traits. It could be that my sniper was Juliet's older brother.

"That wasn't me," Dante answered.

Millie opened her eyes and looked directly into mine. It didn't take her long to discover that it was my shirt trying to clean her up. We hadn't seen much of each other in real life, and it showed. Millie blushed, shut her eyes again, and shook her head as the smile worked its way up. I laughed at her, but she recovered quickly.

"Mom!" she squealed, trying to sit up against the pain. She didn't make it. "You're finally here."

"Oh darling," her mother sighed. She looked at her husband as tears came out. Jessie still didn't move away from the door.

"I looked for you every day," Millie expressed.

"We looked for you too." Juliet looked at Will and Dante and me, and then advised that they would talk about it all later. Millie sighed, finding it hard to hold back the questions she had been saving up. I decided to ask my own.

"How'd you get hurt, Millie?" I asked, ignoring the glare both her parents sent at me.

She ignored my question. Instead she flicked her eyes to my mouth and pinched her lips together, similar to the time that she had invited me to kiss her in her dreams. I couldn't help but feel the same tingle of anticipation sweep through me.

"I thought of you when I thought I was going to die," she told me. "Then I wondered what you'd thought of when you were going to die."

Couldn't she remember? I had tormented myself by not saying that I loved her. Millie scanned my face again nervous. That was all it took to send my thoughts back in time when she had told me that if I stayed alive, I could kiss her. No time like the present with her parents watching and two snipers who would come after me. I laughed at the irony of it all. There was never a romantic moment, but sure. They were going to take her away from me. I'd probably never see her again after this. The realization brought tears into my voice. I could only hope that she would come visit me in the virtual world.

"Collecting on your promise?" I asked her. I bent over and tried to kiss her cheek, but she turned her head so I missed and got her mouth instead.

"Indeed," Millie whispered to me.

"Okay, break it up," Jessie directed, moving to stand closer to me. I didn't look at him. I knew this was the end. I was going to be crying all night. The tears were already coming.

"Will it be green snot?" Millie asked me, trying to be oblivious to the fact that this might be the last time we ever saw each other. I snorted, despite the ache of leaving her. I wanted to take her in my arms, see that she got fully healed, and carry her home with me. I was attached to my guardian angel.

"Purple," I answered. "And I'll leave it to you to work out why."

"Okay, you've seen her. Millie's still alive. Now get," Dante dismissed me.

I looked up at her uncle, at his salt-and-pepper beard, and wondered why I couldn't stay longer.

"Grapes," Millie said with a gasp as she sat up. Her mother rushed behind her so that Millie could lean against her like she might relax into a portable lawn chair. "Purple grapes. You were chewing them, and then started laughing so they came out your nose. That's the kind of laugh that burns, but it doesn't matter because it's just so funny."

I smiled back at Millie as she grabbed onto her mother's arms like they were her lifeline. It filled me with hope that she could love someone so dearly, and dread, that I was being turned away. Stepping away was going to burn just like Millie's analogy suggested. How could something so sweet burn?

I was never going to get the memories of her out of

my head. She was always going to be the person I thought of when I got close to death. Even if our paths never crossed again my dying thought would be of Millie, wondering if she would save me. I was so much better for having known her and her kindness. I felt changed from her friendship, our one real kiss, and a second chance at a real life.

Millie's uncle told me to leave again. At the tone of his voice, Will grew worried and tugged me to my feet.

"Berk tossed me out the window, William," Millie said as her eyes obtained a red ring around them. I probably looked the same. We were a pair of cute raccoons. I was just about to mention that, but Millie wasn't done.

"That's who it was. I finally made the connection with the voice! The person who helped place the probe necklace was Pete Jennings on the first floor. He also placed the current firewall to keep Visions away from the Vikings because he's scared of the Vikings attacking the building. The man behind the Vikings is Walter Hammerton. He's in Cinpinati working as a media coordinator for Logic Core. He has several associates working with him there as well." Millie rambled off a few more names. Will pulled out his phone and started to jot it all down against the very angry glares from her parents. "So you can tell Tabitha to lay off Rory," Millie concluded.

I suddenly understood why she looked so tired and where she had been all week. She had just destroyed the

Vikings. All of us glanced up at her uncle, wondering what he was going to do about that. He wasn't looking like any of it mattered to him. I wondered how fast that would change.

"I'll do that. Thanks for everything, kid," Will told her.

He teared up, which surprised me, and pulled me to the door. I didn't want to leave. Millie hadn't told us what happened to *her*. If it was just the two of us I was sure I could have gotten the information. Then I would hold her against me and make her impossible promises until she laughed herself silly.

"Bye." Millie trembled with her tears coming down when I reached the door. She was breathing faster and faster the closer I got to walking out on her. This was ridiculous. Even if the count was two parents and a sniper uncle against one rather poor me, we'd find a way to see each other again.

"Have fun with those talking teddy bears." I winked at her.

Then I turned around and pulled open the door. Will shut it behind us, and we both stood there for a while listening to the sounds of her parents chew her out for sniping. I hated to leave her to that. Will cringed a few times. I couldn't stop crying. Then he took me by the arm and bought me a new shirt even if I could afford one on my own. I hoped Millie kept my shirt. Part of me wanted her to start sleeping with it.

Chapter 37

Millie

I wondered if my parents knew I wasn't listening to a thing they had just said. Dante knew. I had closed my eyes as soon as my parents started in with the "you can't be a sniper or surfer" speech. How could they dictate what I should be when they created games for these people? Had they really thought that keeping me away from heiss would help? I had been so desperate to see them again and now I was mad at them. Couldn't they hug me, tell me that they missed me as much as I missed them? Was all this verbalized stress because my uncle was still in the room? They were safe, and out of the mine, and my heart was bitter and twisted. It made me want to cry.

Why had my parents never told me anything? Why did they think that a lecture would help? I already knew how dangerous sniping was, but living and running away from heiss had been just as dangerous. It was the border

365

snatchers that got me in the end, not a sniper. Why couldn't I just hold on to Sebastian a little longer? He wouldn't scream at me. He was going to patch me up. He had already started by washing away the traces of my accident. Sebastian would find some way to tease me about not sleeping, and I'd play along trying to get him to rock me to sleep by a warm fireplace.

Instead of paying attention to my lecture, I had discovered a super effective technique of ignoring my parents. I had jumped waves and found Rory, which proved that I hadn't been completely incoherent earlier. CEO Berk really had given me heiss. He had guessed what my real problem was: no heiss and exhaustion. Actually, maybe I had told him. I couldn't remember what I had been rambling about. Maybe Berk didn't actually hate me even though he'd fired me.

I had told Rory my findings about the Vikings, explaining that I had also told Will, and that I wasn't going to be around to help much longer. He had rolled his eyes at me and had told me to go away, but I knew he was grateful. Maybe he would stop thinking that I worked for hackers. He was in a position to take immediate action against the traitor to the company, and from there they could scare the living pants off the Vikings.

By the time I came back to reality, my uncle had his hands on his hips, shaking his head at me, totally aware of what I was doing—what I couldn't stop doing now just because my parents told me to not be what they bred into me. Maybe I should go tell Berk my findings now that I realized he was the other sniper that I hadn't been able to place. Had he been scared of me or was his main motive to put me to sleep when he tossed me out the window? I had no idea how he had found me after firing me. Had I walked past him on accident? He hadn't taken any action against me for all those times I'd snuck into his business meetings. I smiled at the thought of surprising the CEO, and my uncle narrowed his eyes.

"That's enough," he told my parents. "You can't take the heiss out of Millie. You can only put it in."

I gaped at him. They wouldn't, right? If my parents continuously put heiss in me, I'd be maxed out all the time and couldn't surf. They couldn't keep me full of heiss. I had to see Sebastian again. I couldn't stand the thought of not knowing what he was up to. Whatever it was, it was going to be fascinating and full of energy and life. He hadn't said goodbye to me. He had asked me to steal into inanimate objects, ones that shouldn't have a voice to them. He had asked me to use my ultimate, secret, superpower to see him. That was impossible if I couldn't jump waves. My parents couldn't keep me on a constant heiss drip to make sure I stayed ninety. That was expensive.

"This whole thing is a major disaster!" my dad

367

bellowed. "And you won't be seeing that boy," he told me.

I thought about arguing with him, but I could only muster a smile. Seriously, how was he going to keep me away from Sebastian? I could see him in my sleep. I'd leave secret notes throughout Visions' system so Seb could find them if that's what it came down to. I giggled, thinking of all the fun that would cause the company snipers. They were going to wish they had kept me.

"Millie," my mother's weary voice got me to look at her. I didn't need a fully functioning body to see "that boy again." All I needed was more than four hours of sleep. I yawned just thinking of the word. I knew it was important to sleep when using heiss, but sleeping was still hard.

"I'm starving," I told my mother.

She asked me how I'd gotten hurt. I opened my mouth to explain, but I could still remember it like it just happened, the trembling, my lack of focus, the pain that still coursed through me, and then the gunshots after Berk Bergstrom murdered the people who had captured me in the desert. Had they died, or had he simply sent off a warning shot? I wanted to think that those men deserved it, but I couldn't think that way. I didn't like thinking of anyone facing death. It was hard. It was merciless. Had Berk called Will? His was the next voice I remembered. Did Berk think that Will would know what I was doing? He thought I had gone on a sniper hunt. How would I actually snipe out people who didn't use heiss? I couldn't picture the men who stole immigrants using heiss. It was just really bad luck. Maybe Will knew that. Maybe he was just protecting my image to Berk.

I closed my empty mouth and complained about being hungry again. My mother looked at Dante to ask him for more details about my injuries. He, of course, didn't know. He had gotten to my room and found me out cold with a sniper hovering over me. What was he to assume from that? He wouldn't give out details about Will and Sebastian when my parents asked. I almost zoned out again. The hunger in my stomach was making me woozy.

"The kid's a surfer, right?" my dad asked, looking at my mom and then my uncle. "Did you ever see him, Juliet? I saw him a lot. I saw him jump waves before. Did you ever see him?"

"I saw him too," my mom confirmed, leaving me with a sigh, "and Platonic. He wouldn't leave me alone. He got annoying."

Who was that? Oh, right. I had looked up his name once. Platonic was a major gamer who posted on the forums, giving people hints. He was in my parents' games all the time. He had beaten every game they'd ever created. Maybe my parents did know that I hadn't been listening to a thing they'd just told me. They didn't like surfing, but they could still do it. And this proved they had done it, and I had failed to find them every time I looked. I knew what to look for now. I was now prepared.

"You *both* saw Seb jump waves?" I asked them. So he could find me! I knew he had tried to find me before when he'd gone to the jogging track, but I hadn't heard of him doing anything like it again. This proved he was practicing.

"He's nothing but trouble, Millie," my mom told me, looking me in the eye to make sure I was listening. Oh if only she knew how much trouble. I laughed at the thought. That only made her grow more stern.

"You can't trust surfers," my dad informed me.

"So I shouldn't trust you two then?" the retort was out of my mouth before I could stop myself. My parents squirmed, and nothing they said next made an impact against the accusations lying under the surfaces of my beaten skin. They claimed that they never used their ability in a harmful way. They had never lived such a dangerous lifestyle, and I shouldn't either. They pointed out that surfers could eventually turn into snipers and betray me.

Well, there was nothing they could do about it. I was rather acquainted with a lot of other surfers already. Whether my parents saw me as one or not, those other people would always see me as one. If I stopped acting like one anything could happen—like them all hunting me down to find out where I had gone and finding my parents. I had to keep up at least a short presence in the gaming world.

"You understand why it's dangerous for me to just disappear, don't you?" I asked my uncle.

"I can make it look like you died," my uncle answered. "Just as long as lover boy and his lackey don't believe it, you could slip out of here."

"I don't really want to find out what overdosing on heiss feels like." I shook my head picturing myself throwing up for hours. With my current wounds that would hurt immensely.

"That's not how I would kill someone like you," my uncle answered.

My parents got on his case right away. They didn't want me coming close to death. I wasn't one of his sniper hunts. My mom told him he should have never found me at all. My dad told him that he had been disowned from the family and should have stayed that way. I thanked my uncle for getting my parents back, and he laughed at me. Then he told me he would be right back with food.

As soon as he left, my parents finally released some of their stress. They both came to hold me tight telling me how worried they had been. But thinking of worry put them right back to it. They told me that I couldn't like my uncle. Didn't I know the murderous person he was? Yes, actually I did. I had seen the dark side of him too clearly, but I had also seen his good side, and heard him beg for me to accept him as family. I wondered who had first disowned my uncle, but I saved the question for later.

"Why are we here?" I asked my parents. "Didn't you think that I would find heiss at all? You could have said something."

"We were located, Millie," my father sighed. "I made a game once."

Once? I shook my head at him and named off a long list of his games, including the current one I had found a few nights ago that he had written last year. It didn't look like it had come from him, but I could tell by several clues that it was his work. *Walk the Backdrop* had really good graphics, the ability to add in magic, extra players, and a large playing field. My mom didn't look like she knew he had made it. My father covered his eyes and asked what they had done to me.

"And it was safer coming closer to the people who had located us instead of farther away?" I asked my dad.

"This was the fastest transfer location to our real destination where the snipers wouldn't find us. We were going to be with you the whole time. It was only going to be a few hours of you being here. You would have stayed awake and not noticed the heiss. Just forget about it, Millie. Nearly dying all the time is not the life we wanted for you."

I couldn't argue with that. Nearly dying was not the life I had ever pictured for myself, either, but who was going to watch out for Sebastian? He was too easy to follow unless he started getting better at jumping waves and turned into a surfer. Visions no doubt already realized that. If they were going to keep him as an employee, they needed to hide him. He already had one sniper almost take him out.

"I'm staying here," I said, even if this apartment wasn't the greatest. I'd lived in humbler conditions. I couldn't imagine what my life would be like if I left all the heiss behind. I'd constantly worry about Sebastian, and other snipers picking up his trail. I'd worry about people finding my parents through me. I knew it was Will's job to keep Seb safe, but it still felt like *my* job. Seb had saved me from the snow. His smile alone comforted me through the confusion of surfing, and Dante knew my heiss wave. If he could learn it others could. I could lead snipers right back to my parents again.

"You are not staying here. Just look at you!" my mother protested. "You'll die here!" She started crying.

My dad huddled beside her on the floor, holding her in his arms while he looked at me like I was tormenting my mother. I felt bad about it, but I was a threat. How could they take me with them? How could I leave Sebastian? I couldn't help it. I was drawn to him on so many levels. Maybe I could get my uncle to hide me, but then my parents would disown him even more… No. I couldn't do that to him. He was trying to make things right between his family. Besides, what kind of person walked up to a sniper and asked to be erased? I didn't want to be erased. I wanted to stay.

I looked at Dante sadly when he came back with food. My parents were a little hesitant to eat it, but I didn't care. I was starving, and how could things get much worse? They wanted me to leave Sebastian and heiss. Wasn't I old enough to decide where I wanted to live? Maybe what I would put my mind to was spotting the snipers who got too close to my parents, and tipping off Visions about potential problems. Maybe I would start being better friends with the Veterans as well.

"Like I said earlier," Dante looked at Jessie, "I am not in your games to hurt you. I'm only there to figure out where you are."

"Don't believe anything he says, Millie. Someone's been trying to attack us since before you were born," Juliet gave another hesitant glance to Dante who shook his head. "You can't trust snipers. They enjoy torment and torture. Who did this to you?" My mom pressed for information.

"Not him." I jerked my head toward my uncle. The more I looked at him, the more I could see the family resemblance.

"At least you forgive me right, Millie?" my uncle asked.

"If you keep Sebastian alive for me," I answered.

He frowned at me, but he had heard what Sebastian said when he was about to die. He couldn't be surprised by the request. I'd feel better leaving help behind me.

"Millie, that's Will's job. He'll kill me if I interfere again. You'll have to trust Will to do his job. Sorry," he told me.

"You know what you're doing is wrong, don't you?" I asked him, suddenly questioning the state of the food he had brought like my parents were doing. I looked at it again, but shrugged. I was starving. I chomped down more.

"So you decided not to forgive me? I didn't kill your lover, but you'll treat me with the same contempt regardless, just like your parents. I should have guessed. They raised you, after all."

Is that what had happened with my parents? My uncle had tried to kill my dad and they took off? Is that why my dad was slower to move past my uncle than anyone else? I looked between my parents, who were passing each other secret sentences that I could read. It was time to go. They were going to pick me up and carry me between them if I couldn't walk on my own. They were still scared of my uncle, even if he had been the one to come rescue them. But Seb had almost been killed by my uncle, and had faced him without a single tremble. I smiled at that. Fearless Sebastian could take on the ferocious cook in the kitchen and escape all the same.

"Why don't you switch sides?" I asked my uncle.

"Let me know if you ever change your mind," my uncle told me before he gave a nod to my parents and walked out.

"Can you stand, Millie?" my dad asked me.

I shrugged and looked around the apartment, not willing to leave it. What was going to happen if the Vikings' sniper heard me tell Will... Yes, I could stand. I stood up, grabbed Seb's shirt, and ran out the door past my uncle, who shook his head at me before pretending he had no idea who I was or why there were two grownups hard on my heels. I ran for the bus stop and slid around anyone in my way, ignoring the burning that caused in my stomach. I spotted Will's wife before I spotted him. When he saw me, he grabbed his wife's hand, and ran as hard as he could away from me. I skid to a halt, the tears coursing down my face. Trust William? He was going to run. He was done. He was scared that Dante would go after him next now that the sniper knew his face and his connection to Visions. There was no one protecting Sebastian, and it was all my fault.

I pulled out my phone and called Nick. "Will's running," I told Nick in as quiet a voice as I could. "You can't let Mr. Rhino work the normal way. Can't you get him to jump waves and connect through surfing instead of heiss? Please, Nick," I begged.

"Sorry," Nick told me. "He's on his own. For his own

good I just fired him. He's a smart kid. He'll be alright."
Nick tried to sound assuring, but it hit me as a fist in my
already wounded gut. I doubled over. Seb was not on
Visions' system anymore? Would he ever touch heiss again?
He didn't have the money to get a gaming system. If he
didn't learn to surf in his sleep, I'd never see him again.

"Bye now." Nick hung up on me first.

My parents caught up to me, grabbing both my arms
and asking what had gotten into me. Now father away from
my uncle, they were back to being my loving parents, asking
me how I was doing and how they could help. Could they
help? I had just lost Seb. I had just lost heiss. I tried to
picture my life without Sebastian Tinsley and found it
incredibly lacking. We got on the next bus, and I could
picture Seb running away too. Had I really saved anything?

Chapter 38

Sebastian

"What's this?" I asked Leer, since Nick was already in my room.

"Millie says that Will quit yesterday," Nick told me.

He had seen Millie? When? Had he been able to see her last night in a game while I had to sit at home pretending that nothing was wrong? I'd failed at pretending. I'd skipped dinner and went into my shared room and sulked. I'd cried all night long. I wasn't surprised about Will. At least crying got me out of explaining why I had a new shirt. No one had asked me anything.

"Seb, if you're going to keep working here you can't use heiss. You're too easy to spot. You either become a surfer or leave right now," Nick contended.

I didn't know how to get into a game with no heiss at all. I was basically fired, and Will was gone, and Millie was

379

gone. I looked at Leer, defeat on my face. My dad had said he would stay for me, and now I was no longer good enough to work. I couldn't think of anyone else who would take me into their gaming system if they ever found my past history. It would be too dangerous to join in games on my own with old snipers out there that already knew my face. Nick was right. I was done for.

"Did we at least stop the Vikings?" I asked him, hoping he wasn't going to play dumb with me about everything I had been doing. Didn't I deserve to know?

"We arrested the leader of their group and a few others but not everyone Seb. We didn't get their annoying sniper," Nick answered.

I looked down at the floor, because I knew about the sniper in question. Will had let him walk free yesterday because he had let me go and he was related to Millie. If Millie's uncle was done with me he was probably going back to where he came from. Maybe he was stalking after Millie and her parents as they ran away. But we had made an impression on the Vikings. Maybe they would stop their enterprises now that their boss had been taken away. I wondered what Will was going to do.

I suddenly didn't like my job. I had lost Will and Millie. I couldn't imagine all the other people I might lose if I got close to them in the games. This was why we weren't supposed to mix work with personal life. This was why Leer kept most of his people in the dark about what their job actually was. I used to not understand my job fully either, but now I did and I had tasted the pain.

"You've surfed before." Leer nudged me while looking at Nick concerned. "You don't want to try it at least for a day? You might see Millie," he tried to entice me.

I shook my head and turned toward the exit. I could go back with my dad to his job. He didn't have to quit because of me. We could stay together where he had already found roots. I wouldn't be the head of the family, or the one who was going make my brother cry if they left me.

"Millie left with her parents yesterday," I told Leer. "She won't be there."

"And you know that because...?" Nick questioned, frowning at me.

"You don't think that would keep her away, do you?" Leer asked me. "She can be here whenever she closes her eyes."

But I couldn't. I didn't know how, and Millie's parents would take her out of range for the heiss to work. Even she had a limit. She had to be close by in order to find the heiss by surfing. Otherwise, she would need to be hooked into the game like everyone else.

"Besides, with the Vikings under wraps their sniper will decide to leave you alone. What's in it for him when coming after you won't do any good or generate a profit? You are sniper free, Seb," Leer told me with another annoyed look at Nick. "So he can use the heiss," Leer calculated.

"Only to supplement him while he learns how to be a surfer," Nick contradicted.

"You need this job," Leer kept going.

"Actually, I don't anymore," I told Leer. "I got my personal issues taken care of—mostly."

I was going to miss it if I stopped working, but at the moment the benefits to walking away were greater than staying. If I stayed it would only be because I personally liked my job, which I did, as long as snipers didn't get in the way of it.

"You're good at this, Seb," Leer tried again. "We can't afford to lose you and Will and Millie at the same time."

I sighed. I had lost Millie. I had little hope at seeing her ever again, unless I found a way to surf the waves. The wound was still fresh enough that it would have made Leer's monitors beep. I stood there, staring at the exit, trying to decide if I was selfish enough to make my dad lose his job so I could keep mine. I had heard him talking about it last night with my mom. He wasn't going to stay with the trucking company if we stayed here. He'd find something else so he could be around more. That would make me the one feeding an extra mouth for a while until he did. We were still living off the advance that I had gotten from Nick.

"Why are you doing this?" Leer asked Nick. "We need Sebastian."

"Look who's only thinking about company profits now," Nick retorted.

"Get out of my section," Leer ordered. "You've been messing around with my people for too long. I don't want to see your face over here again. You and Rory are the worst."

"Shh!" Nick hissed at Leer for using Rory's name. They both looked at me and I shrugged. I wasn't supposed to know who Rory was, but Will had told me.

"I need to think about this," I told Leer and Nick. "I'll let you know by the end of the day."

I didn't want to turn them down if my dad had already called his previous job and quit. I wasn't going to make that kind of decision and ruin everything. I trudged home to talk with my dad and see what he thought. I shouldn't have wondered what he would like me to do. I already knew what he thought.

Chapter 39

Millie

My mom had not named me Millie. My uncle had. That's why he knew the name. My mom was already pregnant when my father's second game was to be released. There were a few people back then that had tried to break into the game development. My dad had gotten scared, mostly because of my uncle, who had been the one breaking into his games. My dad confronted Dante about the issue. Not much later someone had tried to kill him, and he had fled.

I had a large looming "why" hanging over my head. Why would Dante try to kill the person that created the games he made money off of? That was just stupid. Wouldn't it be the other way around? Wouldn't he want to keep the game creator alive so he could continue making money off it? My uncle had been calling my mom's baby bump Millie up until then. My parents had kept the name—

and kept me far away from my uncle.

I knew he had done something to scare my parents when I first met him. He had scared me, too, and virtually killed me too many times to count. I wasn't sure how repentant he was if he was still the one breaking into my parent's games and using them after all this time. I wondered if he really was the mastermind behind getting the Vikings set up. Walter Hammerton was just a person he got to take the blame. Dante would be back with a new threat, but I was certain that threat was for money, not death.

My parents, although uncertain, had agreed to meet with Dante when he'd claimed to know where I was. They had still been in the mine at that point, but not working for the miners. They had found a way to sneak out of the group and meet up, and they were stealing food to stay alive while trying to find me and break up the slavery at the same time. We had left our previous home because Dante had been spotted coming closer to our location. I wished he had never been that close to Seb.

The team my uncle had sent into the Doldrums had chased the miners out. That was why my parents' captors had ended up in the same city as me, running away from getting caught. But they had still been caught by Berk. I guessed Berk was stalking me to determine if I was working for the Vikings since that was what I was accused of doing.

He probably thought I'd been working for the Vikings the whole time with the way I had taken over Veronica and snuck into his work meetings—only he couldn't prove it. While I didn't agree with most everything my uncle did, I agreed he was right about heiss. My parents could not take the heiss out of me. They could only put it in. I had never had withdrawal symptoms from a drug up till now, but they were awful. I could hardly keep my eyes open. I shut my eyes, trying to find Seb, and kept using up all my reserves, which then left me wanting more heiss, so even without trying I was surfing again looking for more.

My mom told me I would get over it in a day or two. While I worked on that, my parents worked on moving us closer to my Uncle Phillis. We were going to hide away on a plantation. When they said that, I pictured endless fields of corn or flat grasslands inhabited by natives.

I asked for heiss constantly. Nothing. My parents hardly acknowledged that the word existed. The lack of the substance turned me into a monster. I screamed at my parents for denying me the drug. The only thing they would tell me was that the feeling would pass and I would be grateful that they were keeping me from living such a dirty lifestyle. I screamed some more. There were lots of people who used heiss appropriately. Why did they think I was going to abuse the substance? The only time I had done any sniping was when I *wasn't* using heiss. I wished my psychology worked on them. It didn't. After two days of trembling and screaming I finally started to be able to control myself again, but nothing was better. Seb was still out there without protection. I couldn't see how ignoring heiss like this was ever supposed to save any of us. I started coming up with a few plans of my own. I had survived a few weeks in a city alone before. I could do it again. I loved my parents, but I couldn't give up everything the same way they did.

Chapter 40

Sebastian

"Julia." I smiled, standing even taller than usual by bouncing on my toes. "What's the rest of that name?"

I held out my hand to lead her to the dance floor. She accepted, and I could already feel the electricity buzzing the air. I had been eyeing her for a little too long. Even Triton had picked up on my fascination. He kept telling me to ask her to dance. With her normal partner run off to the bathroom—her little sister May—now was my chance. I could picture Triton behind me, laughing into his hands. That's what I got for taking my brother to youth dance classes. But it wasn't all that bad. The last ten minutes was a free for all should any of the kids want to improve their steps. Triton usually sat down and snickered to me about the girls who would partner up with each other and show off.

"Julia Veronica Herring," the beautiful redhead

whispered into my ear right before I swung her around. My arms clamped up. My feet refused to move after they completed the single circular motion. Around us the other dancers continued forward, unaware of my predicament. My heart lashed open with the violent force of a knife stabbing a baked potato. Veronica. I knew that it was impossible to forget that girl, but this was incredibly cruel. How could Julia's middle name be Veronica? How could she remind me of Millie?

I knew nothing about Millie, I reminded myself for the hundredth time. Soul mates were not real, I told myself. I had managed to go months without pining over Millie and feeling cravings for heiss. This had been my best month yet. Now it was all ruined in one eventful blow. Why had I bothered to ask Julia's name?

"Did you want to try the salsa or tango?" Julia asked me.

I shut my eyes. Neither. There was no way to forget Millie. I would never know if she was tangoing away with someone else. I would never know her middle name. I did my best to hold back the tears before all the water leaked out of me. Was it always going to be like this? Would I always pick up right where I had left off, crying over Millie because I hadn't said goodbye? I should have made the decision final and realized that everything was going to change once her parents showed up. Millie had said bye.

"Are you alright?" Julia squirmed backward against my arms, looking at my silent features. I wished Millie was looking at me. The way her smile perked to the side filled my soul with a light that refused to be snuffed.

"Fine," I answered. I opened my eyes, wishing Julia wouldn't say anything about the fine layer of mist that had formed there. "Sorry. It's just that you said Veronica, and I knew a Veronica that changed my life. You deserve a better dance partner than me."

"You can't dance, can you," Julia laughed with a shake of her head. "You just wanted to get me to yourself."

I wished that was still the case, but she was wrong. How long was it going to take before I got over Millie? It had been six months. That was half a year. It didn't feel like half a year at all. I could still see Millie's wounds and her struggle to sit up and her desire to banter with me. She was leaving. I was leaving. There was nothing left that was going to hold us together besides the memories we had carved with knives into each other's minds.

"I can square dance," I told Julia, trying to put the smile back on my face.

I needed to get better at living a normal life. Everyone had noticed the shift in my mood since we'd left Sanatonia. My dad thought it was because I resented him taking back the authority of the family. My mom thought I hadn't wanted to quit my job. Triton didn't say what he

391

thought. I had talked it over with my dad, and we agreed that if I had a clean slate to break from my dangerous line of work, I should take it before things got worse for my family. I knew I'd endangered them, but it was hard to put it behind me.

The second day as we drove away in my dad's car I'd felt as though I was leaving my soul behind. I had notable mood swings. I hadn't been trying to be cranky, but all I wanted was to be hooked back up at work. I guess the overtime stuff was getting to me. I craved heiss like it was an addiction. It didn't help that I had once been overdosed on the stuff. I knew I couldn't have it. I couldn't ask for it. I couldn't look for it. I had to leave it all behind me to protect my family. That's what mattered. I didn't resent my dad. I had started to resent myself for wanting something other than my family.

"I'll start with my left foot and you can start with your right," Julia directed.

I slid my feet around the room, matching hers without thinking about it. It had taken me two months to stop craving heiss. It was taking a lot longer to stop craving Millie. I had gone through a hundred scenarios where I would strap into a game and Millie would pop up beside me. It was only a matter of guessing the time when she would show up. I had pictured myself playing the Earl of Key Hill and her father turning up and running me off. Then

Millie would show up again where I had skipped off to and tell me she was coming to find me...

"Ah, I've seen better dancing out of you when you were with your grandma!" his familiar voice pierced the room. I staggered to a halt and looked at the door all gloom chased away instantly.

"Will?" I asked, astonished to see him standing there in blue jeans and a plaid shirt. All he needed was a cowboy hat and a southern accent and I'd ride my horse with him into the sunset. No. I would turn into the horse and be the one running. I was so excited to see him that my body felt like it would burst from the joy. I was nearly screaming the emotion out my nose.

"You going to show that filly how to think outside the box?" Will asked me, nodding his head toward Julia and our rather slow, boring square dance. "Or did you lose your mind when you lost your fat paycheck?"

"Hey." I laughed as Will strode into the room like he owned it. Was it too much to ask him for heiss? We could go run off to see Millie together. Maybe he knew where she was already. Maybe she hadn't been able to stay away as long as I was doing.

"My legs flash circles around my grandma."

"That's where all your baby fat went." Will winked at me as he sat down next to Triton and kicked out his legs

393

to lean back into the chair. "It's in all those leg rolls."

"I'll show you what these legs can do," I retorted, greatly missing his commentary on my work. Triton looked at Will like he was an alien.

I wasn't sure how good of a dancer Julia was, but I could lead effectively. I had led my own pack of thieves against the Earl before. A few dance steps were nothing. I looked at Julia to judge her reaction to Will's intrusion. She gave me a short smile and a shrug. For all she knew, Will was my uncle stopping by to visit. I returned Julia's smile and started to liven up the room.

I led Julia around in a swing dance while she laughed and giggled. Will stomped his feet to the beat of the music while he told me that he was never letting me meet his wife. My moves were too smooth to resist. The younger kids in the class all scooted out of the way to watch the show. Even the teacher gawked at us, clapping her hands as I twirled Julia around the room. It wasn't until I started picturing Millie's face instead of Julia's that I stopped.

I finished off the dance a little early, to the applause of my younger audience and the rapture-thrilled face of Julia. I yearned to see Millie. Actually, I wanted to scream for Millie. I was going to storm out of the classroom and scream her name until she showed up to stop me being a maniac.

"Where did you learn to dance like that?" Mrs.

394

Woodlin, the instructor, asked me. Her hair was still neatly pulled in to a blond bun. Julia's red ponytail was slipping apart. The necklace that she was wearing had shifted out of place and now rested on her back instead of her neck. I reached over to fix it while I answered the dance teacher.

"High school."

That was as far as that answer went. The longer answer made me blush. Me and my buddies had quickly learned two things. One: girls fell for you if you could dance well. Two: girls fell for you if you could play a musical instrument. I wasn't one for musical talent, so Rob and I had taught ourselves to dance. Rob made a fabulous dance partner. I wondered if he still thought of me and laughed.

"You really dance around your grandma?" Julia asked me as I finished adjusting her necklace. I gave her a short smile and looked at Triton. Then I panicked. Will was gone! Why? My stomach felt like churned milk: a little clumpy and uncomfortable.

"I don't think my grandma knew how to dance," I informed Julia. "But you're fabulous."

I looked back at Triton again, who wasn't doing anything to come to my rescue. He was looking at me steadily—he was mad. Great. What had I done? I had him collect his things so we could get out of there. Julia cornered me before we reached the door, asking if I wanted to dance with her next week as well. I shrugged and gave her a noncommittal answer pushing around her to get outside so I could search for Will.

"Why did you do that?!" Triton accused. He glared at me and took off running toward the car, which was parked as far away from the dance studio as possible. I had been feeling cranky when we had arrived, and I had been hoping that the extra steps from the car would count as exercise and change my mood. Now I wished we'd parked closer because I couldn't look for Will when my brother was dashing across the road.

"Triton!" I screamed his name instead of Millie's like I planned on doing. He reached the car safely. I was the one standing in a dangerous location, frantically spinning in circles and trying to find Will.

"Did you see where he went?"

"No," Triton retorted. "You make me mad. You're never happy anymore, but Julia and that weird guy made you happy for five minutes. You never smile at *me* anymore. Can you really not get over that girl?"

"What girl?" I gave up on looking for Will. He wasn't anywhere in sight. Maybe he would find me again. I moved to the car, gritting my teeth, trying to stifle my questions so I could be there for my family.

"You said you saved a girl's life. You've not been yourself since you left her," Triton told me.

So now I knew what Triton thought of my behavior. He was pretty smart for a little brother.

"I miss her like my lungs have been ripped out," I told Triton. I glanced around one more time and found Julia. Shoot. She was standing a few cars away staring at me. I had just messed that up. She wasn't going to want to face my personal demons again.

"Why don't you ever talk about her?" Triton asked me.

"Her parents didn't like me," I told him.

"I like you even if you scream at me," Triton said. I didn't like myself when I screamed at my family. I needed to do something to make up for it. I handed Triton the keys. He looked at me with his eyes wide before his teeth sparkled into the light.

"Oh cool!" he cried. "We're not going to tell Mom and Dad right?"

"I'm not saying anything. You know how to drive it, don't you?"

Triton wasn't old enough to drive, but he did know how. I gave him a lot of tips and pointers as we pulled out, but I think they came out of my mouth more for my own safety than because he couldn't drive. He did great, and I made sure to tell him—with a smile. I knew I had started something when he asked to drive home next week as well.

He was suddenly looking forward to dance class. Mom had talked him into it. She really just wanted him out of the house and meeting people because he was floundering at school and not making friends there.

When I got into the house I waited until Triton got busy with drawing his favorite anime characters before I searched for ways to get heiss that didn't include actually owning a gaming system or paying a fortune to use a public one. I wanted to find Will again. I wanted to find Millie. It wasn't long before I was questioning the legitimacy of a black-market deal claiming that it sold heiss in shots medically, which were used for aspiring snipers who were weaning themselves off the stuff. I was as weaned as I was going to get. I ended my search, deleted my search history, and closed my eyes.

I waited like that for a long time, trying to come up with an excuse I could use for leaving the house so I could search for Will. Why was he here? Was Millie in trouble? Could I pretend I needed to fill up the gas in the car?

"Someone at the door for you, Seb!" my dad called nearly three hours later. I hadn't realized it was that late and he was home. Mom hadn't called me to dinner. Maybe Triton had told them that I was moody again.

I reached the door, puzzled to see who would be calling me. It was Nick, and he wasn't "at" the door. He was past that position and already inside my house. I glanced over everything to determine what level of threat this posed. Nick had seen my whole family! They were standing right there just waiting for me to tell them who Nick was. I swallowed. I wanted to go back sooo bad, but not at the cost of my family.

"I told you it's a very competitive business," Nick started right in. "I don't like losing able-bodied employees, especially not ones that make themselves indispensable. You were the best, brightest employee I've ever met, and I think I've finally found the very thing that would convince you to come back."

Nick held out a wooden box to me. I wished this was all a game. I would take my family out of the room, and they wouldn't have to witness how badly I wanted to betray them for my addiction. What was in the box? I crossed the room to take it from Nick's hand and opened it up, careful to keep the contents hidden. The first thing I saw were heiss shots, the same kind I had just looked up. Heiss for snipers. I was more prone to believe the shots were legitimate coming from Nick. Had he been watching my computer history? The next thing I saw in the box was a company card for Engines: Intellectual Reality Games. I looked up at Nick confused.

"Leer and I branched out," Nick informed me. "He insisted he had to be around to keep my employees alive and me honest. Actually, he kind of insisted we partner up when he made me tell him that the games I had put you on were ones I was creating. A lot of your special missions were from me. You're a very effective game tester, Sebastian. I can offer you competitive wages. You can work remotely if you want after the first two weeks of training. Everything will be completely safe, and for my trump card I can offer you William. Millie's not available yet. No one can find Millie, but I'm betting she will stagger on in as soon as you show up again. I can give you two days to think it over if you promise to use that box responsibly."

I looked down at the heiss in the box, ready to jump right back in. I had never wanted to stab a needle into my arm so badly before. I was sure that the greed was written all over my face. Use this responsibly? Could I use it right now? Was Millie asleep? Did I really get a second chance at playing games for a living?

"You snagged Will?" I asked. "Is that why I spotted him three hours ago?"

"Three hours ago? Funny you should ask that. Will had been missing for a while. I just found *him* about three hours ago. I was going to ask *you* to help me find Will, but he turned up when I was coming to find you." Nick chuckled. "I guess he couldn't give you up, either. He's been floating around you this whole time. He delayed me coming to talk to you by a few hours being nitpicky over company rules and contracts."

Will had been with me the whole time? What kind of

person ran away from their well-paying job to chase after a guy who wasn't going to pay him anything? What money had he been living off while he watched me for six months? What had he done with his wife? I could hardly believe that Will was still protecting me like this. Would he have shown up to stop me if I had broken down and tried to go into the public virtual games center? Or would he have followed me in, sat down beside me without me knowing, and joined me?

I looked at my dad, who had fear and concern on his face. He was the only one who knew what security company I had worked for. I hadn't told him my bosses' names, though. He wouldn't recognize Nick or Leer, but I was guessing he was worried that the person in front of me might not be as friendly as he sounded. My mom, Ellen, was looking at Triton with her lips pursed. Triton had his hands behind his back. His mouth looked full, and there was chocolate on the side of his face from a stolen cookie.

"This is my old boss," I introduced to my family. Nick waved. "I don't need two days to think about it," I answered. "I'm in. Do you have any idea how hard it is to ignore heiss?"

Nick shrugged. "The first few days of withdrawal symptoms are usually hard, and technically Leer was your boss, only he never liked giving out his number, so you got mine."

"Two months," I told him.

A few days I could have handled. My sullen erratic moods had nearly left me in a puddle and they still came back at times. I pulled out the first of three heiss shots and twirled it between my fingers. The elliptical motion was beautiful. Triton asked me what it was.

"Two *months*?" Nick asked me, shocked. "We worked you overtime a bit, but I never overloaded you on so much heiss that it would be a problem. That's unethical. How did you stand it?"

I tossed the heiss into the air and caught it with a grin. Nick had no idea that Millie's uncle had nearly killed me with heiss. Leer could probably guess. He had heard me talking with William. Did that make me more of a surfer than I thought I was? Could I use the heiss right now and sink into a game without being connected to anything? Had Dante's effort to kill me really enabled me to keep the life I wanted?

"How much is in this?" I asked Nick.

"That would give you ten minutes. It's to entice you into working for me again. It's not a continuous drip of—"

That was as much as I heard before I sat down and stabbed myself with the heiss. I didn't care what my family thought of that. I craved it too much, and I had to see Millie. My world was dark at first—fuzzy—as I tried to find something to grab onto. Where was it? What could I smash into? The shapes slowly started taking form around me, and

I was pretty sure I cheered out loud when the images focused.

I was standing behind a booth, looking out at hundreds of people streaming past me. Was this a flea market? I glanced around my particular booth, only to realize that I could send people into a game by stepping on the button by my feet. Had I really just taken over a non-player character? I had done it? I was surfing! I had traveled to a place that contained a lot of waves of heiss.

"Is this one any good?" a girl asked me as she stood before my booth with her friend.

"The best one around," I told them.

They stood in front of me debating if they wanted to play the game for a good five minutes. I was starting to get irritated. I only had ten minutes here to work with. They were clogging my booth! But I couldn't get frustrated with them and tell them to go away. I wasn't supposed to be real. At least their chatter told me that I would send them to a skiing game *if* they ever made up their minds. One of the girls was scared that she would get motion sickness. They finally gave up and left. No sooner had they left than a sporty couple stepped up and plunked a few coins into the box on my left. When a green light appeared, I stepped on the button on the floor and the two of them vanished.

"Like a magician," I said, peering over the edge of my booth.

"Can you magic me two hot dogs, two orange drinks, a couple of breath mints, and a blanket to watch the fireworks show over there?" a gypsy asked me. She was wearing a purple skirt that jingled, lots of bracelets and anklets, and half a shirt that revealed a belly button ring. I could only hope that this wasn't a joke. What would my current character say to that?

"If you bring me my magician's hat I'll do my best," I promised.

"I left it behind with the teddy bear," the gypsy told me.

Millie! I was going to scream her name if it was her. It was either that or start crying again. I knew what the real me would start doing. Could it really be her? How had she found me that fast with all these other waves around me to distract her? How was I going to know for certain if it was her or someone else entirely?

"I know you didn't blink out," the gypsy told me when I didn't answer. She dropped her hands and rolled her eyes. "Mr. Rhino?"

I tried to scramble over the counter to reach her. That was all it took to make me want her in my arms right then. My character smacked up against an invisible barrier that I beat against before I looked around, wondering how to turn myself into someone else so I could be with her.

"See, that's what a good training session prevents." Another character stepped up beside her. This person was a beast of a man with a loin cloth and a whip slung over his shoulder. Gypsy Millie couldn't contain herself when she looked over at him. She burst into infectious giggles that had me grinning and crying at the same time. I really was going to cry forever until I could see that girl in real life again. I had never said goodbye. I had never wanted to leave all of this. Was the person beside her Will? She wasn't doing anything about him other than laughing.

"What took you so long?" Millie asked me, wiping at her eyes and looking at me.

"Come work with me," I beseeched. "I'll get down on one knee and beg, but I'm not sure you'd be able to see me if I did that."

It was a tall counter and my time was running out. I could feel myself struggling against the heiss vanishing. I was using it up faster than I had expected, as if my threshold for the stuff was higher than it was before and it moved through me quickly. Maybe it was because I was surfing and had only used a shot instead of a drip. But Millie didn't need the heiss. How did she do it? Yes, I wanted that training session with Will.

"You're proposing?" Millie asked me, placing her hand on the invisible barrier that was between us. She pushed on it, and then placed her other hand on it as well, leaning toward me looking just as desperate as I was to break through.

"It's a work proposal." I nodded. "With me and Will and our past two bosses." I had no idea if that sentence was safe to say, but I had to get it out there. I had to present the chance that we could be together again. It was the only thing I had wanted over the last six months.

"If you call me, I'll give you the details," Will said from beside her.

"How do I not leave?" I whined, trembling to stay in the game.

"And you think this is safe?" Millie asked Will. She gave me a sad smile.

Will shrugged. "Safe for two of us. You're always a risk when you show up. I've met your dad maybe two hundred times and he always asks me to send you home."

"Where are you?" I asked Millie, placing my hands right on top of hers.

"Always right next to you," Millie told me.

My body pulled me out of the connection right at that moment.

"No!" I screamed, lunging for the box that Nick had brought. He kicked it out of my reach.

"Nick!" I shouted at him, leaping around my parents

for the box. They were blocking me. I guessed they had rushed me after I'd injecting myself with a mysterious substance. Triton was standing there with his mouth hanging open, revealing the stolen cookie.

"That was too fast," Nick fretted. "You drank that up like soup. We should get your levels reassessed."

"It was Millie!" I told him, trying for the box again. Nick shoved me out of the way and grabbed the most tempting box in the universe off the floor, telling me again that I needed to be hooked up first. I considered punching my boss. I needed Millie way more than heiss. That stuff I could put behind me. It was my guardian angel that I couldn't clear away.

"Millie was that fast, was she?" Nick smiled, trying to get the box out of my sight by putting it behind his back. "You three really are inseparable, you know that? You'll need to work on that. Finding one of you brings the other two."

"Give Millie back, Nick," I sneered at him, holding out my hand for the heiss. I was really going to jump him. I started to, but my dad grabbed my arm and held me back.

"Calm down, Seb. You know she'll show up," Nick told me, pocketing the heiss and tossing me the empty box. I let it drop by my feet.

"She's by herself," I cried.

She had run away from her parents so she could reach the heiss again. I had stayed with my family to avoid it. At least I assumed she ran away with what I had just heard between her and Will. Her father was looking for her. We had made very different choices up till now and I really hoped that we were going to make the same one this time. Why had Nick taken six months before perfecting his job offer? I had no idea how long Millie had been alone. Was she calling Will right now to get the details of where we were? I wanted to see her even more.

The front door opened and Will walked in. He looked at the scene of my dad holding me back from punching Nick, and Nick waved him forwards as if Will would protect him from my mood swings. I pinched my eyes together recognizing the moodiness for what it was and apologized. My mom decided to grab Triton and hold him back from the craziness that I was bringing right into the house.

"She ran away four months ago," Nick informed me, giving me a smile that perked upwards like his blond spiky hair. Millie had gone missing around the time that I stopped my cravings for heiss and gave up on it. Had she known? "I got a call from both her parents about it. She'll be my hardest employee to hire, due to her particular background, but it'll be worth it. Seb saw Millie," Nick told Will. Will gave Nick a laugh.

"You're running behind, Nick," he answered.

Leer was through the door next, looking like he always did with his black hair half in his face. My mood swings were all over the place. I teared up again just seeing Leer. Gee, I was a basket of noodles.

"I see we found Casper." Leer smiled at Will. "So we're only missing one." Leer tossed me a small piece of plastic that I caught one handed and looked at in confusion. Will explained that it was to monitor my heart rate. I pushed it onto my left arm and Leer's monitor at his side started beeping at him instantly. I cried again just at the sound. How I had missed that sound.

"Emotional at all?" Leer asked me. "We'll get that taken care of. What do you say to starting right away? Your levels are way too low," Leer told me after glancing at my stats. "At least you're not Millie. She can't quit cold turkey like that."

"If you fix my mood swings and give me back Millie I'd do just about anything," I answered.

"The thing about Millie—" Leer started to say.

"Her parents don't like me," I stated.

"Her parents don't like anyone," Will added.

"I'm telling you we've got an offer even *they* can't refuse," Nick promised.

"Can I get that drip now?" I asked Leer.

"You worked as security in *what*?" my mom asked me. I had almost forgotten that she was there. I was rather consumed with the idea of ending my mood swings and searching for Millie again.

"This is much safer. You have nothing to worry about," Nick gave my mother a false smile that I failed not to laugh at. "We've even got an exercise program lined up for him."

"It's gaming virtual reality," my dad told my mom. "Seb will be fine."

"So were you a…" my mom trailed off as she looked at Triton. Then she told him that he was never allowed to do what I was doing.

"Seb's not a sniper," Will tried to sooth. My mom didn't look like she believed him. She had just seen me inject heiss and connect to Millie without being hooked up to anything. She had just heard Nick say that two months of withdrawals symptoms was unethical and talk about overdosing me.

"I'm sorry," I told my family. "I'm not a sniper, but sometimes I can surf. I've done everything I could to keep you out of it."

"There was never any threat to your family. I saw to that," Will said, more for their benefit than mine. Thinking of family, I couldn't resist asking Will where he was keeping his wife. When he told me she was in a pumpkin shell, I could not stop laughing. Leer shook his head at me, took me by the arm, and claimed he was going to cure my moods. I followed him out of the house like a sticker stuck to the bottom of a shoe. It was going to be hard to pry me away.

Chapter 41

Sebastian

I was in the back of Leer's converted camper, but I felt so much better. My brain could think again, the symptoms of depression lurking inside a dark corner of my being were put to rest for once. I wasn't scared that I would suddenly turn moody and scream at people. I had just run through a full session of one of Nick's early games. Parts of it I recognized as things he had put me in before, but they were slightly different, and I had tried to break the entire thing as best I could looking for loopholes. I had crashed it twice.

"Here comes a hard question," Leer said when my eyes opened back up and I gave off a content relieved sigh about being in control of my emotions again. "Will you get bored if you test the same thing every day?"

Good question. Part of the allure of Visions was that I

didn't know what was coming at me every time I touched down. It was a new adventure each time. I could see myself getting frustrated working over the same level again and again, but I didn't know where else I was going to go to find another job like this. Now that I wasn't moody I was fired up. I was starting to understand Will. I knew why he had followed me. It wasn't just because he liked me—it was because he had to. Millie's uncle had faked my death, so if my face appeared before the wrong crowd Dante's deception was going to get discovered. It would then be Dante's life or mine. I didn't think that there would be anything accidental about my next death if I scared Millie's uncle. I couldn't show my face or work with heiss unless I could learn to be a surfer and hide who I was.

For that matter, I couldn't see how both Leer and Nick would have been allowed to "branch out" on their own together in what they correctly called a very competitive business for employees. My gut told me that Will had informed Nick and Leer what had happened to me even if he had told Millie to keep quiet about it. Perhaps her involvement was kept quiet, but *his* wasn't. I was still his job. I suspected that Will was still working for Visions and his "run" from the company had been to confront Millie's uncle, not to leave a place he loved working at. Which meant that Nick and Leer had been sent to maintain me as an employee in the only way they could think of: turning me into a surfer, and what better way to do that than test Nick's games? I would be off all public channels. I didn't think they would hook me up to anything public ever again until I could surf. If I had tried to use the public gaming rooms, I bet Will would have come to stop me and tell me not to get myself killed. Nothing had changed. I left, and Will had hunted me down just like he said he would.

"I might get a little bored, but it's worth it to protect my family."

Leer gave me a nod and didn't answer. So I moved onto the next problem and nearly hit my head for not thinking it up sooner.

"How can you have a plan that will entice Millie's parents if she's not with her parents?" I asked. Will had said no one could find Millie, but I'd found her without a problem. She had to have heiss in order to surf. When she had nothing at all, she got shaky, and exhausted and she hadn't been either of those. She had been alert and teasing me just like always. But she'd also been sad. Was she worried about me? It hadn't been my face showing.

"Who has Millie?" I asked, already dreading the answer.

Was it her uncle? Had she gone to work with him? Would we one day battle against each other? That wasn't going to work. I was pretty sure I would cave if it came down to that. If she was with someone equally competitive as Visions I had no hope that Nick and Leer were going to get her back. Was it worth it to work for Nick again just to keep my mood tamed? Probably, but could I handle it all without crying every time Millie popped up? She could break into anything. I was guessing that she could find me even in one of Nick's games if she was close enough.

"We think she's with Platonic," Leer told me, "because he's the only one not telling her parents to get off his case. He claims that he hasn't seen her, but if he does he will hand her over to her parents. That is not what anyone else is saying."

"Who is that?" I asked, completely confused.

"Surfer." Leer shrugged. "Millie's parents have turned her into a celebrity. They've been asking every sniper and surfer to find her, so of course they have tried. But here's the thing, Sebastian. Everyone claims that they haven't seen her, which is highly suspicious. We've run across hidden messages intended for her, asking her to work for various snipers and surfers alike that give her ridiculous benefits and impossible incomes. The person with the best offer is Platonic. She has to be working for someone. Visions is capable of stealing into Millie's mental perceived visuals if she gets low on heiss. Every attempt has been unsuccessful, which proves that she's getting heiss. She has to be with someone who can provide it."

"Everyone's seen Millie," William startled us from the door of the camper. Leer and I both jumped, then laughed at each other for not having heard him open the door. Will stepped inside, pushing away a canister of heiss so he could sit on the edge of my makeshift work chair.

"You're right that she's getting heiss. I've failed to tap into her wave as well. She's not letting herself get low enough. That doesn't prove she's with Platonic. But wherever she is, it is working. Millie's current actions are passed off as her being a rebellious child. She just happens to be in the same place as another sniper or surfer because she's drawn to the heiss and can't stop herself. That way everyone thinks she's harmless. Visions, of course, doesn't believe it. Rory and Berk can't overtake her visual field, so they assume she's working for someone. She still hacks her way in and hands over objects to Visions' snipers."

"Why did Visions fire her?" I asked, scratching my head. So what if she talked with her uncle? How could they really fire her for that?

"They thought she'd stolen expensive company equipment," Leer told me. I looked at Will. He looked extremely smug all of a sudden. I had no idea how Millie would steal equipment from Visions. She had nowhere to put it, but Will... he probably had a car as well as a hidden wife.

"You jerk," I mumbled, testing out my theory.

"What?" Will stretched out his legs, clearly unintimidated by my statement. "It was safer for Mille and easier to get her back to her parents. I totally thought Millie had figured out I'd framed her when she chased me to the bus stop. When Dante blocked all the cameras he gave me the perfect chance to set Rory onto Millie. I didn't think Dante would get to you as fast as he did. Sorry, Sebastian."

"Wait," Leer said, catching up on the snippets of conversation he had heard us discuss earlier. "Sebastian was really caught by Dante when the cameras blacked out? And you let him get away because you were busy framing Millie?"

"It all worked out." Will gave Leer a large smile. He tapped me on the leg and asked me if I had any hard feelings.

"Yeah, I might have a few," I answered as I tried to sort through what I would have done if I was William. I probably would have saved *me* first, and then stolen the company equipment, but maybe he hadn't expected Dante to find my room so fast.

"You got lucky, Seb. You had more than one sniper after you, you know. There was another man—we shall call him Berk—that connected your employment with the Viking attacks. He had his suspicions and may have anonymously threatened you."

A man named Berk may have threatened me? Besides Dante, my other mysterious threat had come in the hallway at work. It had to be Berk Bergstrom, our company founder, who had threatened to haunt me if I let Millie into the building. Leer looked boggled by this information as well.

Will continued. "When your name came up tagged during a performance review, Berk thought he was correct in his assumptions. He would have attacked you that day if not for Millie. He decided that Millie was either acting on her own or working with you. He threw Millie out a window trying to prove his ideas. That day you were both kept away from Viking activity to see if anything would change. Nothing did. I assured him that you were not working for the Vikings, but I couldn't prove as much for Millie. Berk set Rory out to follow Millie, but she's near impossible to follow. They even used sniping technology to calculate her wave form so they could track her. I got Millie fired before Berk did anything else to her. He was tracking her through her phone after she was fired which was why he was able to save her life."

"The day she got beat up. You know why it happened?" It had been hard to see Millie like that. I still couldn't get the image from my mind. Will nodded.

"She was caught by the people who tossed her into the mine. Since she was in bad shape, Berk had me come over. He wanted me to make her confess that she worked for the Vikings. I managed to let her slip away and reveal the real culprit."

I looked to the door of the camper as Nick stepped inside. He smiled to see us all sitting there together and asked the question that was on his mind. What was my current heiss level and how did it go unnoticed that I'd overdosed?

"Seb's sniper overdosed him on heiss." Leer shook his head. "These two just admitted it."

"You found the sniper?" Nick asked, alarmed. "What happened to him?

"I took care of it," Will whispered.

"And how have you taken care of Millie?" I asked him searching for more deception. Will was good at fooling people. I didn't see how Millie was with a mysterious person named Platonic. She trusted Will more didn't she? He was hiding her.

"It is not safe for Millie to make herself known until her parents stop telling everyone to find her," William told me. "What's your plan for that, Nick?"

"We'll have to assure her parents that she's safe and convince everyone that she returned home."

"Through Platonic?" I guessed.

"Yes exactly, but it only works if we have Millie."

"We have Millie," I answered, certain of the fact.

"Not completely, but I'm working on it," Will smiled.

420

Chapter 42

Sebastian

"You used to be at a top level of seventy-three," Leer told me, glancing at Will, who was looking at my numbers. Will gave him a shrug as if he'd expected everything he saw. "Now you're not," Leer simply said not telling me what I reached.

"I'm assuming that I'm higher now—so it's easier, not harder, for snipers to find me?" I asked. This only added complications to my life.

"The average Jane uses twenty," Will told me. "Visions won't hire anyone that can't handle fifty to sixty, because of how long you have to work. You have to be able to handle it. You were perfect for overtime when we could push you to seventy-three. I'll tell you a secret. Millie maxes out at ninety. When she reaches that she can't surf. She's too full to do anything."

"That's confidential," Leer reprimanded Will. He shrugged and pointed at the screen that Leer was sighing about.

"Look, Seb was never fooled. He knew he was tagged the whole time. Not telling him his own stats only limits him. He's got to understand that he has a limit where he can't surf. Let me show you two something."

Will pulled out his phone and revealed a picture. It was a medical report on a screen that he had stolen. I read the report before reading the date. The person it was talking about was DOA—dead on arrival. Resuscitation had been attempted for the next twenty minutes. Another emergency had come up, leaving the dead body in a room alone for a half hour. When the nurses came back the dead man was awake. He had been moved to a recovery room where his cause of death was listed as an overdose on heiss. The miraculous recovery had one conclusion: the dead guy's desire to surf which drained him of the extra heiss. The conclusion at the end of the report called the person a sniper and listed a bunch of codes I didn't know. DNR. DNLMR. DNLNN. I looked at the date recognizing it right away. It was me. I had *died*. Millie's uncle had really killed me and I had come back to life.

"What do the letters mean?" I asked Will while Leer glanced over at my screen again seemingly rethinking his policy to not tell me everything.

"They mean do not resuscitate, do not leave medical records, do not list nurse names. Basically, the hospital is scared of you and doesn't want to get in the way in case a sniper comes after them next, or in case you come after any of them next. If you're ever found again, no one will try to save you if they find this report. You'll be left for dead, because it's too dangerous for anyone to want to help you."

"He killed me," I said into the silence, shocked at the revelation. I had brought myself back to life, desperately trying to find Millie and stop her from taking revenge. It had taken me forty minutes to bring myself back to life. I couldn't remember doing anything like that. I remember blacking out and that was it.

"And Millie found me?" I asked Will.

"She was tipped off." Will nodded. "Her uncle must have told her where to find you. That's why I've been hanging around Sebastian. Dante never finished his mission with you. Regardless of Millie, I've never known Dante to not complete a mission, even if the other people who are paying him for it have gone to jail. He used you living as an excuse to reach another target of his. Once he completes that mission he'll be back around for you."

"Will," I whispered, wondering how I was going to get to sleep knowing who was out there. It wasn't going to be heiss the next time that got me. It was going to be something worse. The thought was terrifying. Why was I even still alive? Millie's uncle had to know where I was. He could track me down at any time. Maybe he had left me alone because I had done nothing with heiss, but now I had...

"My wife spotted him earlier today. He's in town right now because everyone he wants to reach is right here. He's been trying to knock off Jessie Ankerton ever since the guy married his sister. Juliet refused to tell him who she married. She and Jessie lived in different cities for a while until it became obvious that she was pregnant with Millie, then they both ran. Strange backstory, Dante named Millie. Juliet kept the name to protect her in the event that her uncle ever found her."

"We were all in the same room together," I told Will, placing my hands beside me on the bed to steady myself.

"Yes, but he has to make Jessie's death look like an accident if he wants his sister to talk to him again. Not to mention that both Juliet and I carry guns. You may not have noticed. We'd have protected you, Seb."

"What if it's been long enough that Dante doesn't care if his sister talks to him?" I asked.

"Then we have a problem. I thought of that too. He could be here to steal Millie. She's a goldmine. She can snipe snipers. That makes her rather usable to snipers who want to snuff out their competition, or even just keep tabs on them."

"What about Platonic?" I asked. He was a surfer so they said. Assuming the guy had Millie I couldn't see him just walking away and leaving her. She had to be doing some kind of work for him.

"Platonic sells avatars that have completely beaten games to anyone who buys them. Snipers, surfers, and regular players all like him. It's nice to get into every level with every modification we want. No one wants to hurt him, because we've all bought his work," Will informed me. "If he has Millie, I would guess that Millie's been helping him find people to buy his products. She can identify anyone, and she gets everywhere. Millie is actually rather safe with him. No one would try to knock her off if she was in the business of giving them what they wanted."

"But I can save her somehow in real life?" I asked.

I had wanted to do that, but I was nervous about it. What was this going to cost me? Did Millie realize how badly she had tripped into this alternate world? I was still just starting to realize how I would never be free of it. What had I gotten myself into? At least I had Will, but was he enough to keep me alive? He had already messed up his timing on me once.

"You need to save yourself," Will told me. "No matter how careful I am, I can't protect you every second of the day. You need to snipe your sniper in real life Sebastian, and find out what he's really after or it won't matter how hard I've been working. You're a dead man."

I was dead, and Millie might be too. The color drained from my face and my heart monitor started beeping. It was funny that my pulse hadn't started up as Will was explaining to me that I had previously died. It wasn't until he said the word that my pulse skyrocketed. What was this going to do to my family? Could they escape if I didn't give myself up or do what Will was suggesting—face off with Millie's uncle before he killed anyone else? I was that poster in the movie from the song Millie the teddy bear had sang to me. I was a ghost trying to come back to life by getting the living girl to fall in love with me. How did that song go?

"Okay. I'll handle this," Leer told Will, turning off my screen and cutting the sound to the monitor. "I don't appreciate you scaring my employee. Seb is not a sniper. *You* can stop Millie's uncle before anything disastrous happens. All you need to do is kidnap Millie first. I'm sure by now she could hack her way into Dante's wave and talk to him safely from a distance."

"You want Millie feeling responsible if her uncle dies?" Will asked Leer. "We can use Seb. He's perfectly capable since he can reach eighty-three. He jumped up ten levels."

"No," I told them. This wasn't the way this game was going to go. We were not going to scare Dante into doing something reckless. "I'll find out what he wants."

I had used heiss again and had to face the consequences. I was going to play this game right—a game that could cost more than my life.

"How long do I have to think up a plan?" I questioned.

"Five minutes?" Will told me. "Millie's parents are walking up to your house."

I jumped at the window and shoved it open. Will was right. I wondered if he had spotted them before he'd come into the camper to fetch me. I was going to be thinking on my feet. I turned back on my monitor to reveal my steady heartbeat. It was show time.

Chapter 43

Millie

It was rather funny how games and reality could mix. I had just spent two hours playing a rather realistic fishing game. It was slow and boring, and I hated needing to fish in order to retrieve the plastic horseshoe that the thief had thrown into the water. That was my fake life for the day. I got the horseshoe back and left it where Tabitha would find it. Invading Visions' workload was often slow. They really should have kept me. I didn't know how Tabitha continued losing the plastic horseshoe. This was the third time I had gotten it back. If it was down to me, the thing would have been destroyed the first time around.

I didn't understand why it wasn't destroyed currently. Every time the horseshoe was put into one of my father's games and placed on a horse, a character dressed as a safari tour guide appeared. He didn't ride the horse. Instead, he opened his hat which held a truckload of money he spent on buying a large weapon. The tour guide then went around destroying every female character in his path. It was making people mad. It was making me mad too. Why wasn't Tabitha taking care of this thing? She was often next to it. I assumed that she was the one who was hunting it down. Perhaps, she had no idea what it was. I was going to give it to Rory next. He would see the device destroyed and find out who kept placing it. Since it was only girls being targeted, it made me wonder if I was the intended target. It held no distinction between real or computer characters. It took out everyone as if it was hunting for a surfer. If that wasn't the case, it was a rather annoying malicious attack.

It was making me question Tabitha's abilities when she looked inadequate against a horseshoe. What had her so distracted that she couldn't make the connection between the horseshoe and the safari hunter? My suspicions were turning deadly. Tabitha was the only sniper around it. What if she was placing the device? I didn't want to dive down that path. I would hand it to Rory if I saw it again. Heck, I'd even give it to Grant or Lex. It kept showing up where other Visions people where. This was a Visions problem. They could handle this one. I was tired of it.

But I wasn't tired of my real life even if felt fake with the way I was sneaking around. It felt funny to sneak around. I had even put on a disguise, which I thought was hilarious and wouldn't fool anyone. I was wearing a baseball hat backwards that didn't hide my long hair, with a t-shirt that would fit my dad rather than me. My pants were sagging so much that the seams were well below my hips, but I had come prepared. I had multiple layers, a belt, and suspenders just in case. If anything, it would throw off the regular people who didn't know me. It wasn't going to fool the people I was actually trying to avoid, but it might confuse them for a while if they didn't see my face. That's what I was aiming for. I would walk like a gangster because there was no other way to walk while my pants were sagging this much, and I would break into the bedroom window that was my ultimate destination without getting tackled by the two people who were around to stop me.

I moved in closer to the house, noticing the white van parked on the corner. It wasn't marked with who owned the vehicle, but with the out-of-state license plate I was pretty sure where it had come from. Dang. Make that four or more people who might try to stop me. I was only betting on Will and Platonic getting in my way. I didn't want to see Leer, or Nick, or Lex, or Tabitha, or Rory. Yeck.

I scanned the rest of the street, trying to spot Will. If he got to me before I got to that window I was going to end up facing him. I had no intention of giving him any apologies or telling him anything about who I was working for. I glanced around for the other problematic surfer: Platonic. Our relationship was weird. I was pretty sure that he had never let anyone else walk up to him and see his real face. It was like me walking up to my uncle and saying,

431

"Hey let's be strange friends because you intrigue me." That's pretty much what it was.

Platonic was the strangest surfer I had ever met. I expected him to be some really old guy, because everyone knew him. He wasn't. He was in his thirties and looked younger. He had laughed at my startled reaction of meeting him. I wasn't quite sure how he got his start into gaming, but everyone respected him despite him selling to questionable people at times. That's why I had walked up and said hello. I had asked him to help me find a safe way to get heiss that wouldn't involve hurting anyone. He asked me to follow him through several games to prove I could do it, and then he told me to meet him. I was pretty sure he hadn't expected me when he first saw me either.

Platonic had very specific instructions for everything that I did. Most of the time it was things in real life like walking down to the supermarket wearing a green shirt and buy him the newest movie release at register ten. It made me wonder if I was planting fake codes in the real world with how specific he was, but I couldn't ever prove anything, and I was good at checking to make sure that any cash he gave me was real. I wondered if he followed me around for fun, or if he was simply bored and wanted to watch a movie without risking his own face to go get it.

His instructions were similar in virtual worlds. I would go into specific characters and "wave hi" to a man at the corner or give a person flowers I picked from the side of the road. I had first wondered if I was being sent in to intimidate people, or if he was just bored and having fun moving me around. It took me a while to realize what I was really doing, and it took Platonic a while to realize how I was doing it. I had no idea what he thought when he first discovered I could get into inanimate objects, but he knew I could. I was pretty sure that he was the only one who knew that besides Berk, Rory, Leer, and Seb. Maybe Will knew. Inanimate things were super useful when spying on other players.

Once my effectiveness was discovered, I was told to stand in certain places and look for anything unusual. Unusual usually turned out to be another surfer in the area. We had mapped out a lot of surfers,' and snipers,' favorite retreats and hangouts that way. We had identified what missions some of them were working on that way too. Since Platonic sold avatars to these people, I believed that most of the time, my work helped him discover new people to create business deals with. He would legally beat games over and over again and sell his characters off to game enthusiasts and snipers alike who wanted instant stats, or the coolest features, or just easy access to any level in the world. It was a strange way to make money, but it worked for him. Even better, it worked for me, because he would give me heiss, unlike my parents. I didn't think I was ever going to change their minds.

Every other month I would find my mother and hand her a piece of paper, asking her if she thought I could have heiss yet. She usually tore it up and told me to come home before I did something I would regret. I hadn't seen my dad. I had complained about it to Platonic. By now he knew I had gotten my start with Visions and who my parents were. I hadn't told him any specifics. His usual advice about my family situation was to give them so much time that they gave in and said yes to my question. My mom hadn't given in yet.

I really hoped my parents didn't show up to stop me before I reached that window. That made two more people who could stop me that would guess where I might eventually show up. I wondered if they had discovered where Seb lived now. It would have been easier for them to do than for me. I didn't want to research anything that Platonic would notice. My only way of finding Seb was if he touched heiss again. Seeing as how Will had decided to lure me in, I was guessing that Will would pop out and stop me. Since Platonic hadn't seen the real me in the last two days—I talked to him virtually—I was guessing he would follow me out of curiosity. After briefly talking with Will, I had taken off before Platonic could stop me, but then realized at the front door that my wallet was still on the other side of the house. If I walked through the house Platonic would hear me. So I had stolen his credit card off the table to purchase a few tickets. He would know exactly where I was. He hadn't canceled his card. He had to be following me like it was some strange game.

I looked around the street, finding it quiet. Now if I could only make knocking on the glowing window unsuspicious. I crossed the yard, holding up my baggy pants even if I had taken extra liberties to not let them fall down. So far so good. No one was jumping out at me. Not a single parent or strange sniper. Not a concerned neighbor or playful child. I resisted the urge to look around a third time. That third look before knocking would give me away. I knocked and held my breath.

Zwip. The blinds pulled up, and I was looking at a curly-red-haired boy around the age of thirteen. He looked me over while I gave him a smile, and then he cranked open the window without the slightest indication that he was scared.

"Hi, Triton," I greeted him gripping my pants even tighter now in case he turned fearful that I knew his name. I grinned even more when he did nothing more than nod at me. He was like his brother. He could look potentially scary people in the face and still maintain every ounce of sense.

"Do you want to come in?" Triton asked me. He glanced up the length of the window, and then started to pull off the screen after finding the hooks that held it in place.

"You're just going to let me in? What if I'm a

robber?"

"Not dressed like that you're not." The teen laughed at me.

Well I wasn't going to complain about instant access. This was better than I had been planning. I had been scared that I would be turned away and need to knock on the front door to explain myself. Triton set the screen to the side as I climbed in the window. I had to pull up my pants to get my legs to move. My pants sagged again as I let them drop. This fashion was hard to work with. Triton left the screen off as he rotated the glass shut again and pulled the shades down.

"It will be a little while. Seb's talking…" he trailed off already guessing why I was there.

I tried to pick out Sebastian's voice, but it was quiet. I looked around the room, noticing the two beds pushed to opposite sides of the walls. Triton pointed to one to tell me exactly what I wanted to know. The bed with the computer sitting open was Seb's. Why wasn't Triton more concerned about me breaking into the house? Did Seb usually get visitors like this? I moved to Seb's bed, finding the computer on and open to an anime site.

Triton came to sit down next to me and look at the screen. I gave him a short look, wondering what he would do if I touched the computer. It was too tempting to not touch Seb's things. I opened up a text document and wrote a line from the teddy bear song: "Your smile is what gets me through. Darling, my fire's for you."

"I love my brother," Triton told me after smirking at my message. He looked up from the computer with eyes very similar to Seb's. When did I get to see Seb? "Do you love my brother?"

Umm. Okay this was tricky. I had no idea how much Seb had said about me, or if he had shown Triton a picture of me. Did Triton know who I was, or was he guessing? Could I say that I was in love with his older brother? Maybe, but we hardly ever saw each other. The last time we'd met was six months ago. I knew I was walking into a trap with the way that Will had shown up, but I couldn't help it, and it was Will, so it'd be fine. He had explained his job offer. It was tempting. I just didn't know what to tell Platonic.

"Tell me your name," Triton demanded a little late to be kicking me out. I was already inside his house, sitting in his room and waiting for his brother to show up. Wasn't that creepy? Even in the gaming world it would be creepy. I never would have let myself into the house.

"Millie Ankerton," I answered before I could second guess myself. What if Triton had met with a random sniper who knew what was going on? What if he had been paid to reveal me to my parents upon confirmation of my identity?

"I knew it." He grinned pleasantly and not with any sort of evil twitch in his eye. "Seb's in love with you."

"I think we're just friends."

Triton shook his head. "Nope. He said he missed you like his lung was ripped out."

I laughed. That did sound like something Seb would say. Why was he comparing me to lungs? Gosh, I missed him so much.

"I'll go get him," Triton offered, seeing the longing in my expression. "I will allow you to do my homework in exchange for my services."

Triton pointed to the other bed where a science book was open. I laughed at him, hiding the sound behind my hands because I didn't want to be too loud. What if the Visions' official was also in the house? They would recognize me. I agreed with the homework exchange and started sifting through the book for the answers, penciling them in lightly so that Triton could redo it in his handwriting. I had to hand it to him. Triton was pretty clever.

I was fighting the laughter when Triton's excuse for his brother echoed down the hall into the room he had left slightly open. He claimed he really needed Seb to help with his homework because he just couldn't figure it out. It was very simple, actually, and didn't take any complicated thinking. I zipped through the assignment, then looked over the textbook, wondering if I had used the same book once. It was really familiar.

I heard Seb in the hallway, whispering with his brother and thanking him for getting him out of the conversation that was going to send his pinkie toe into another realm if he had to keep pushing it into the floor to stay focused. Why had I forgotten that Seb was so funny? I was struggling so hard to not laugh when he stepped into the room, pushed by his scheming, grinning brother who shut the door behind them, that everything I planned to say never made it out.

Seb froze by the door. He looked around the room, at his shifted computer, at the window screen on the floor, at his brother, at me still laughing. Maybe it would have been easier if I had knocked on the front door, because then I could be loud. Trying to stay quiet was going to be hard.

"Have you seen what you're wearing?" Seb asked me. "Don't tell me you woke up like that? You have no excuse."

"I'm hiding from Will, and I am wearing layers," I told him, watching him for the reaction I was hoping for.

I wasn't getting it yet. Was he not excited to see me? Had I picked a bad night? He didn't look overjoyed at all. Triton was watching him too. Instead of smiling, Seb pinched his mouth together and shook his head. He crossed the room and pulled off my hat, scrutinizing my outfit as if he couldn't tell who I was. I felt the wings on my belly butterflies lose the ability to fly. My disguise was going

439

away. I would have been fine with it if Seb looked even slightly excited to see me. Instead, he teared up and tore away every practiced sentence that I had ever talked myself through.

"Bye, Millie."

His eyes brimmed with tears as if he was letting me go—or telling me to go. He didn't want me here? Did he know something that I didn't about Will, or did he really never want to see me again? I pulled the hat back out of his hands and stepped to the side, away from him and toward the window.

"That's it? It's not like I stole from Platonic to come see you or anything. It's not like I've been waiting six months for you to show up. That's just great."

I shoved the hat back on my head and made my way to the window. This was all a mistake. I should have waited. I should have asked Seb if he really wanted me around instead of assuming he'd meant his proposal when he was in front of Will. Perhaps all it had been was a moment of weakness. Will had offered heiss, and Seb had wavered, but he didn't really want to go back to the games. He wasn't going to play with me again. He had changed his mind and was never going to talk to me again.

Seb shoved himself around me to block me from reaching the window. He waved his brother to block the door. I pouted at Triton when he did so. I'd done the kid's homework. Wasn't he going to let me out?

"I didn't finish," Seb told me, wiping at his eyes. "I never said goodbye to you. You said farewell, but I never did. It nearly killed me. I just had to say it to get it over with. I can be fine without heiss," Seb insisted.

"No, you scream a lot," Triton contradicted. Seb rolled his eyes and ignored him.

"But I'm not fine without you." Seb continued. "Will's great and all, but I've never had a better guardian angel, and I never want any other angel except for you. You're the lantern in the dark, the glow beneath the door, the flashlight under the blankets—"

"I knew it." Triton grinned from the doorway. I glanced at him briefly before pulling my hat back off. I hadn't really expected this. I'd expected Sebastian to smile at me, ramble about working together again, and maybe ask if he could buy me dinner. I hadn't expected him to stand here and cry.

"Every day you're the one person I want to see. When I try to forget about you, I just *can't*. I'm changing my mind about the work proposal," Seb told me as if I hadn't already guessed. "I'm not offering a work proposal. I have a different one. I want you to keep me."

He stopped talking, and I had no idea what to say. I was confused. I looked at Triton, hoping that he had a better

441

idea of what was happening. Maybe Seb had talked to him about his change in ideas. Triton shrugged.

"What do you mean?" I asked.

"You said you stole from Platonic. I thought you were hiding away with Will. I don't care who you're working for. I'll do anything to stay with you, Millie. Keep me with you. I propose that we stay together."

My mouth was hanging open so wide a bug could have built a house in it. I hadn't expected meeting Seb again to be anything like this. He was seriously proposing. It wasn't a typical "will you marry me" proposal, but how could anyone think anything otherwise? What else would staying together lead to if not eventually a different sort of proposal? Maybe I was thinking too far ahead, but I couldn't help it. It was like what my friend in ninth grade had told me; boys accepted a date to have fun, and girls accepted a date thinking about the rest of their lives. I shouldn't be jumping straight to that.

Seb wiped at his eyes again and fidgeted on his feet, waiting for my response. I still didn't have one. I hadn't prepared myself for this. I should have prepared myself for anything. I should have gone through a scenario in my head that featured Seb tearing up and proposing to me in his bedroom in front of his brother. Why hadn't *that* occurred to me?

The closet door in the bedroom slid open behind me

and Seb jumped at me pushing me behind him out of fear so fast that I hit the wall. Who was there? Had Triton been in league with someone the whole time? I glanced at him. He was pale, so that answered that. I couldn't see who was standing in the closet. Was it Will? One of my parents? Rory? Whoever it was, it was scaring Sebastian. He planted himself right in front of me, very similar to the time that I stood in front of him in the virtual world while my uncle shot me for the fortieth time. Maybe it was my uncle.

"Who is it?" I asked Seb as I tugged off the belt and the suspenders so I could lose the baggy pants. I had a pair of shorts on underneath. I could run much better in those.

"I was expecting that you got lured into some kind of trouble," Platonic's voice reached my ears. I scrambled upwards trying to look around Seb, who was taller than me and holding me back. Platonic was standing with an unraised gun in his hand, looking more normal than I had been. He was wearing a blue business suit. He had short blond hair that he managed to tie beads into, as well as a goatee. It really did make him look younger.

"You must have been very fast at getting Millie to meet you here, sir. I missed the whole thing. Let me tell you right now that I have a really large problem with your proposal, and that problem happens to be underneath that bed."

Platonic pointed to Seb's bed. I hadn't even

considered looking underneath it or in the closet. I had been left alone in the room and Platonic was right there. What was under the bed? Seb shook his head and told the stranger that he wasn't moving for anything. I could see his shoulders shaking, and I guessed at the horrible thoughts running through Seb's mind. He probably thought we were going to die. Before I could say anything, Triton beat me to it.

"He told me I couldn't tell anyone he was in the closet," Triton gushed. "He came in first. Then that other guy told me not to tell anyone he was under the bed, and that I should let Millie in. I didn't know what to do."

"Who is under the bed?" Seb asked his brother, holding his hand out toward Platonic in a silent gesture to ask him not to shoot anything. He waved Triton to open the door and escape, but his younger brother refused with a shake of his head.

"The funny African guy is under the bed," Triton answered.

"We don't call people funny," Seb lectured briefly.

"Who was in the closet?" Will's voice asked from under the bed. I knew it was him. I knew I would run into him tonight no matter how hard I tried to avoid him. He had already beaten me to the room.

"Nobody panic," I told them. "The guy in the closet

444

is Platonic."

"And Casper is going to stay underneath the bed," Platonic ordered. I didn't hear Will argue. "The three of you are not going to tell anyone what I look like," Platonic continued, looking at me, Seb, and Triton.

Platonic gave me a glare because I had just exposed him, but I didn't want Will coming out from under the bed ready for an attack. This wasn't exactly how I pictured everything going. I had anticipated being stopped before reaching the house, not while I was inside the house. Were my parents going to be the next to surprise me?

"Casper can be cruel, Millie," Platonic told me. "He gets people sent to jail for a really long time. It's pretty much a prison death sentence if you mess with him. You're never getting out. Did you upset Casper?"

"No," I answered, thinking about my uncle. I had seen him around in the games, but I hadn't spent any time trying to find him. Was he in prison for life now? Had Casper put him there? I grabbed onto Seb's arm which was still intent on holding me behind him. I needed the support.

"Casper follows this guy around," Platonic informed me about Seb. "That guy will never be free of Casper. You should know that before the kid tricks you into joining him in jail."

"He's not going to jail." I leaned into Seb, relieved to

understand why Platonic had stepped out of the closet. He thought that Seb was a sniper, and that he had lured me toward him, and that Casper was around to put Seb in jail. "Casper and Seb work together and Seb's never done anything illegal."

"You have," Platonic informed me.

I squirmed. I had no idea what he had me doing, really. I only guessed that I was helping him find people to sell to so he could spend more time actually playing the games and maxing out avatars. What had I gotten myself into? All I knew was that he'd seemed nice and that he'd offered me a way to get heiss, and he wasn't creepy. Seb reached behind him with his other arm so he was holding me to him in a backwards hug, protecting me from whatever tragedy I may have committed.

"You stole my credit card," Platonic said.

I gave out a sigh of relief. That, I knew about. I had done that on my own. I pulled his card out and tossed it to him. He had Triton pick it up for him, so that he didn't have to risk Will seeing him. Triton slowly inched over to complete the process while Seb glared.

"I'll pay you back for whatever honest amount Millie spent," Will promised from underneath the bed.

"You can't buy Millie from me," Platonic answered.

"Sure I can. You can leave Millie with me and never

look back."

From under the bed an envelope slid out with enough force to stop itself at Triton's feet. Triton didn't need to be told his assignment. He picked it up and handed it to Platonic, who opened the envelope and nodded.

"Okay. If this doesn't bounce, consider the heiss guzzler your own problem."

"It won't bounce," Will assured him.

"Do you want to stay here?" Platonic asked me. "You never mentioned having a love interest."

I fumbled with my words as my face went red. Everyone was looking at me, except Will, who couldn't. It wasn't like I had spent that much time with Seb to get to know him. Six months ago, I would have said gladly said I loved him, but it had been a long time since then. What if things had changed? Could I really call it love? Perhaps *interest* was the best word.

"Um... uh... yeah... maybe. I wanted to be near Sebastian," I answered, wondering how much money Will had tossed to Platonic. Whatever the sum was, it was enough to entice him to walk away. Where did Will get the money?

"Here's what you're going to do," Will stated to Platonic. "You're going to call Millie's parents and tell them where she is. We want you broadcasting that you found her and got the stubborn teen to go back home."

"She's not really a teenager," Platonic smirked at Will, "but alright."

He pulled out his phone and called my dad. I bonked my head into Seb, because I could hear a phone ringing through the door and down the hallway, and I was pretty sure I knew what that meant. My parents were indeed already here. Platonic heard the noise, too, but did what Will said. He gave off my location, along with the information that my parents were going to be hard pressed to move me since Visions had beaten them here.

Platonic gave me a short hug before he stepped out the window. I thanked him for his help, a little sad to see him go. He was strange, but we were friends. If he ever asked me for help, I wouldn't hesitate to help him. I wondered how much he would hesitate if I asked him for help again. From the other side of the open window, he answered my unspoken question.

"You know how to find me," he whispered before heading away and leaving me.

I watched him walk off as Will came out from under the bed, claiming that he'd known someone was in there with Triton the whole time, and that was why he had come in instead of heading me off. Seb apologized to Triton for getting him caught up in his messy problems. I sat on the bed, dreading talking with my parents. Will had told me that he could convince my parents to stop asking snipers and surfers to look for me. He said he would convince them to change their minds about heiss. I hoped he had a good plan, because there wasn't another person out there like Platonic that only worked for himself. It would be harder to hide with him again now that everyone knew where I was.

"You look better in the shorts," Seb told me, finally giving me the smile I had been waiting for. "But that shirt." He shook his head at it and tossed me one of his from the closet. "What did you do with my last shirt?" he asked me.

"I washed it," I answered, turning the corners of my mouth up to match his. He had such a beautiful smile. I had forgotten how amazing it was, but I hadn't forgotten the feel of it flashing my direction. I could stare at that a long time, just as I could stare at dream worlds.

I currently had Seb's shirt in a hotel room that wasn't too far from here. I had packed it with a few other items in a backpack when I'd run away from home. I could do without a lot of things, but Seb's shirt wasn't one of them. It reminded me of him too much. I exchanged my oversized shirt for Seb's new one with a smile.

"Millie," my mother's voice brought my attention to the bedroom door. Her blond hair was up, and she was comfortable enough in Seb's home to have taken her shoes off. I wondered what her impression of me was, since I was already wearing one of Seb's shirts exposing my team spirit colors.

"I don't regret any of it, Mom," I told her.

"Maybe not yet, but you've been with snipers. They're dangerous. Anything could have happened to you."

"I was with a surfer. It's different. You're the one who told the snipers to look for me." I was annoyed that after six months we still couldn't agree. Why couldn't I get my parents to realize that not every surfer was going to become a sniper?

My dad walked into the room next. He also had his shoes off. I wondered if it was a rule in the house, since my dad was usually tenser. To be on the safe side, I kicked my shoes off, too, and scooted them to the side. My father scanned over the shirt I was wearing, noticed the discarded disguise on the floor, and put an arm around my mother's waist.

"We're sorry, Millie. We should have listened to you the first time. These last few months have been really stressful. We just wanted to protect you from criminals," my dad reminded.

"Criminals are not the only ones who use heiss. They're actually the minority." I was just about to point out that Mom had been using heiss in order to roam my father's worlds, but she started talking instead.

"We know. We'll work together over the heiss

450

problem."

I rolled my eyes. Then I found myself sounding like Sebastian, and I knew exactly what he had been feeling and why his first reaction to me had been tears. It was never our written job to protect each other, but we'd become fierce advocates for each other's safety. I had missed him so much that I'd been willing to leave my parents for the vague hope that I'd find him again.

"It's not just the heiss, Mom. I could learn to live without it. It's the fact that I'd be leaving my friends unprotected. I have to know if certain people are alright, and the only way I can find them…" I trailed off, nearly in tears over my relief that Sebastian was looking so well.

"We would have helped you," my dad told me.

He looked at Sebastian, who nudged me and told me that Will had been following him the whole time, so I didn't need to worry. I looked over at Will and shook my head. I thought he had run away to hide from my uncle. How was I to know that he was really around Sebastian?

"We're going to do a lot of listening, I promise," my mom told me holding her arms out for a hug of truce. I glanced at Seb, Triton, and Will as my worry ebbed out of me. They were fine. Everyone was fine. I felt silly for taking so long waiting for Seb to use heiss again. I should have called Will. He would have told me if I had any cause to fret. If only I had found out that Will hadn't run!

"I'm sorry too!" I ran into my mother's arms, relieved to see her and embarrassed that Sebastian was watching. Like the last time we'd met up, my father created a group hug. We gushed over safe topics: how they were doing, and what they had eaten on the plane. I felt like I hadn't seen them in a million years. I was away on a secret spy mission and now just stepping back into reality. It was strange and comforting and at the same time. We could have continued talking, but I had spotted Seb's parents standing beside Nick and Leer. Seb's mother had red hair that matched the color of Triton's. His father was blond, tall, and lanky. I had never met them, and now I felt bad all over again.

"Sorry for invading your house," I mumbled. "I just…. Oh gosh! I wanted to see Sebastian."

"We heard that you'd be coming. It's alright. We always want to see Sebastian too," Seb's dad told me. I found myself liking him instantly.

My family group hug broke apart, and we all made our way out of Seb's bedroom and into the hallway.

"She's cute," Sebastian's dad whispered to him, making my face blush all over again. Leer decided to save me.

"Nick and I started a gaming partnership, but we've decided to merge with your father's company in order to retain the rights to our employees," Leer told me. That was all news to me. I didn't know that they were working on their own. I had been busy tracking surfers and handing things back to Tabitha. And now Nick and Leer were merging with my dad, and Will had told me that I would get to work with Sebastian. I could hardly believe it. A warmth crept over my heart, generating even stronger forgiveness toward my parents. They were going to let me work with Seb! I flashed him my excitement.

"Wait, so you really did start your own company?" Seb asked, looking at Nick. "I thought you'd still be working for Visions."

"I told you that we *branched* out," Nick replied.

"Is your company logo a tree?" I asked Nick.

"It's an acorn," Leer told me with a smile that I didn't believe.

"It's because you're all nuts." My dad's response made me *crack* a smile. I looked over at Seb, wondering if he was thinking of the same pun I was. I knew he wasn't when he spoke next thinking about food.

"Come on, Millie," Seb said, reaching out to take my hand. "I know that you eat trash when you feed yourself. I'm going to make you dinner."

"I had a bag of chips and a granola bar and pretzels," I told him, wondering what he had in mind. I'd known the idea of food would come up. I hadn't skimped on food because of it, though. I'd just wanted to reach Seb before Platonic found me. I guess I hadn't needed to try so hard. He had still beaten me into the house.

Leer pulled a face and mentioned putting me on a stricter diet. My mom started in with general questions about Platonic's treatment of me. I took Seb's hand and let everyone follow us into the kitchen while I answered my mom. Platonic was nice. No, I wouldn't tell her who he was, or how he made his money, or what we had been working on.

"Millie was categorizing snipers. She also identified gamers and other surfers who would want to buy things from Platonic." Will told her. "We're going to get her doing something better."

"Did you find them?" my dad asked.

"Yeah mostly," I answered, gripping Seb's hand that he tried to pull away to open the fridge. "You only have one hand," I told him as I pulled open the fridge for him. "Think you can handle that challenge?"

"Never letting go of you? Yup." Seb turned to me, grinning. I felt the rest of the room melt away as his green eyes met my brown ones. I was pretty sure I could handle that challenge too. "Top shelf. Can you grab a carton of eggs without dropping that, Miss Veronica?"

I reached inside to accomplish the task while trying

not to feel too giddy about holding Seb's hand in front of Nick and Leer. They weren't doing anything about it. I got my grip and took out the eggs, looking at Sebastian for the next task. He pulled me toward the other side of the kitchen to grab a pan.

"Are you referencing my game?" my dad asked.

"Millie makes a really good Veronica." Seb winked at me, and I wondered if he was thinking about our first kiss inside the tent. I bit my lower lip to keep from giggling.

"Were you the Flying Falcon?" my mom asked Seb, hitching up an eyebrow as if she hadn't realized it was him that killed their game yet. The blackout had cost my parents several thousand dollars as everyone was kicked out.

"I love that guy. Best game ever," Seb answered. "I'm not trying to suck up to you, but your graphics are great. If working with you includes testing games like that, I'll be there forever."

"The Falcon, huh?" my dad asked, eyeing us as Seb put a pan on the stove and I cracked an egg one handed. My fingers got messy, and I wiped them off on the front of Seb's shirt that I was wearing. He added a squirt of mustard to the eggs and wiped the mess off on my sleeve.

"Mustard?" I asked him shoving him for rubbing his hand on my arm.

"What was that? I mustard heard you wrong." He

455

laughed at his own joke and looked away before my teasing glare could make him blush.

"Let's scoot out of the kitchen," Seb's dad suggested. I gave the man a fond smile. Maybe if they really did leave the kitchen, I would ask Sebastian how finding his Dad went. Seb glanced at everyone with a similar wish. I could tell that he had questions of his own.

"Yeah, I guess," my mom agreed. "But, Millie, you're not staying here all night."

"Want my hotel key?" I asked her.

"Have you had any trouble waking up after getting to sleep?" my mom asked me.

I gripped Seb's hand harder. I still hated sleeping. I could get myself to sleep, but yes, waking up was hard. I had caved and was letting Platonic remove my baby book every morning. It was embarrassing that I still needed it. I had tried armbands, but they weren't effective enough. I didn't get any sleep with them, and I hadn't found anything else that worked but the rustling of crinkling plastic layers. My parents had trained that into me from infanthood. It was hard to get away from that.

"Maybe," I answered. Seb gripped my hand back and looked at me kindly, not caring that I slept like a baby with a baby book. How did he sleep?

"You have until ten," my dad told me as he stepped

out of the kitchen. I eyed the clock, noting the number of hours I was given to be with Seb, and smiled. Beside me Sebastian grinned at the same thing.

"How about midnight?" Seb whispered to me when everyone conveniently left us alone. "I might need a few dreams of you. I'll take you dancing."

"I know just the place." I smiled back at him. Dreaming wasn't so bad when Seb was there. Living was easier when Seb was there too. I was so glad that we saved each other.

"Hey," I said with only a brief glance at the kitchen opening. "I've had time to think about your proposal."

"The, uh, work proposal?" Seb asked, not making eye contact as he loosened the edges of the egg with a spatula and I held the pan steady. He was biting his lower lip while his eyes held a mixture of seriousness and teasing at the same time. I could hear our parents casually talking about something else from the other room, but I could feel someone's eyes on us. I glanced toward the kitchen opening briefly and spotted Leer who had strategically placed himself against a wall where he could see us. I was trying to ignore the bubbly feeling that was creeping up my insides. It was like the reverse effect of soda.

"There it is. That's the smile that broke into my heart," Seb told me.

"I think we should date first," I answered before asking what we were doing with the egg and learning that we were making me an egg sandwich. I located the bread which Seb insisted that we toast.

"I think we should date every day," Seb told me, "except for holidays and days where Triton has dance class. He wants me to teach him how to drive. Do you drive?"

"I think I drive you crazy," I told him, trying once again not to read too much into Seb's staying together proposal.

He chuckled and dropped my hand so he could get a plate and finish constructing my egg sandwich. When he turned back around, he was chewing and my sandwich had a hole in the middle with curved edges. I didn't want to start applying symbolism to that. It was a circle. Was he thinking this was a ring?

"A donut!" I said, instead of jumping in with my first conclusion.

"This might be the only kind you get with Leer watching your diet," Seb told me. He watched me eat it before making me a second one this time without the hole.

"I'm pretty sure I've exposed myself," Seb said, setting the sandwich plate on the table near the wall so that we could avoid Leer's gaze. I moved over to a chair that Seb pulled out for me. Right before I sat down in it, he moved into it himself. If I sat down now, I'd be sitting on him. I laughed at him and grabbed a new chair. "So, it would be nice to know what you're thinking."

"I was trying not to apply any symbolism to that ring," I answered.

"Am I allowed to apply symbolism, then?" Sebastian asked me, leaning in and placing a hand on my knee. If it wasn't for everyone being in the other room, I was pretty sure that I would have said yes.

"In our dreams, Sebastian," I answered.

"It's uncanny how dreams can turn into reality," Seb told me. Then he changed the subject.

Chapter 44

Sebastian

I let Millie and her parents drive away at ten o'clock. Nick and Leer were growing impatient. They kept looking at me and Will, expecting us to do something. Triton was picking up on the hesitancy.

"Guys, I've got this," I told all my bosses and my personal sniper. "I know this town inside and out."

I had spent my evening thinking over everything I knew about Millie's uncle. When he was sniping, he moved right beside his targets getting dangerously close to them before he ever did anything. He was often standing right beside them without them realizing it. He had taken the train with me every day after work. He had followed my stops for days, plotting over the best place to attack me. I could probably guess his moves tonight. By pretending this was a game, I could outsmart him.

461

He had not attacked any of us when we were all together. There was at least one person he was trying to impress in the group of us, and I didn't think it was me. Whether it was Millie or Juliet that he most cared for was to be determined, but I felt that the two of them were safer if they stayed together. That included keeping Jessie Ankerton with them too.

I went into my room and grabbed all black clothes, like the Flying Falcon. My mom moved to the door to block me off, as if she guessed what I might be going out to do. For that reason, I didn't tell her what I most wanted to say. My words of affection didn't make it to her ears.

"The clothes are cozy." I smiled and laughed as if she had the wrong idea of things. "Just seeing these guys to their hotel. I might watch TV a bit."

My parents didn't give me a curfew. My father strategically stood next to Triton, either making sure that my brother wouldn't charge out into the night after me or protecting him from the danger I presented. Why had I stayed with them? I should have split from my family when I first realized what a disaster I was. I wondered if my father had bought a gun and hid it in our house after I'd told him what I had turned into while he was gone.

I didn't see my work buddies to their hotel. They followed me around instead. My possible locations for finding Dante included the hotel room right next to Millie's, the stop light before they reached the hotel, the hotel lobby, and the parking spot beside the Ankertons' parked car. Dante was on the park bench across from the hotel. Currently he was sporting his own disguise of baggy clothes and hat with a ratty backpack. He looked like a hobo, but I knew it was him because that would be the best location to spy on the Ankerton's right in the open.

I took up the surveillance beside a parked car sitting down on the ground where I could see Dante while concealing myself. Will slid into place right beside me. We had Nick and Leer one call away from the police. I pointed out the hobo, telling Will that I was certain it was Dante. Then we waited.

Dante sat up, and with the extra padding around his middle and thighs he'd done a much better job with his disguise than Millie's. He took a swig of something that was wrapped inside a brown paper bag, and then laid back down. A few minutes later I heard Jessie's voice. He walked out of the hotel with another man beside him both dressed like they might be going out for a run. I looked at Will to find out who the other guy might be.

"Platonic?" Will guessed.

I shook my head no and hid my smile at how Will was trying to get information out of me. But then I frowned, because Will told me he had no idea who the other guy was. If this whole night was a game, I would expect that the real

Platonic would be close. Millie was helping him identify clients. Maybe *he* knew who the guy beside Jessie was. [1]

"Falcon." Will nudged me as I looked back at Dante. He was still lying down, but his posture was slightly different. He was holding a gun and pointing it toward Jessie. Was this the accident that he had been planning? I swallowed, putting my hand on Will's arm as he pulled out his weapon. There was something off here. Dante had not shot Jessie earlier when he'd had the chance. If he did so now, his involvement would be guessed by Millie and Juliet, and he would lose the very thing he was after. So, Dante would not want Jessie dead. Did he kill people? What was he after?

I flashed over the hospital note again in my head. I hadn't remembered dying. Wouldn't I have felt something else if I had died? What if I *hadn't* died and the sniper note was because Dante had told the hospital to write it? Therefore, I had been alive the whole time. Dante would not come to kill me unless I exposed him, which I wasn't going to do. Jessie had disowned him, but I didn't think Jessie had ever tried to expose the man for anything either. So why would Dante apply different reasoning to Jessie than me and want Jessie dead? The gun in Dante's hand had to be for something else.

I yanked out my phone and called Platonic. I had gotten his number off Jessie before he left for the evening.

"Half off Kingdom of the Monsters avatars," Platonic started to tell me.

"Who is the guy standing next to Jessie?" I asked, cutting off his selling tactics. "You're seeing this, right? If we were playing a game, I'd expect you to be around here someplace. Where are you?"

"Ahead of you," Platonic laughed. "And next to Jessie would be his current bodyguard."

"You can't be ordering more snacks," I heard Millie's voice whisper and then cut off. Platonic was already upstairs with Millie, probably trying to convince Millie that she was better off working with him now that Will wasn't around her.

"Where did Jessie go?" I asked him to judge where Platonic was standing.

"To get a soda?" Platonic answered. "Where is he?"

I grabbed Will's arm and aimed it away from Dante and toward Jessie. Will looked at me like I was crazy.

"Ask Millie which sniper has been trying to kill her dad."

"It's for you," Platonic said and passed her the phone.

"Which sniper has been after your dad?" I asked Millie. "Think really hard, Millie, because you might only have a few seconds."

"Uh…" I heard Millie stammer. "Not my uncle."

"I agree with you. Who? And what does he look like?"

"I…"

Will looked at me, understanding my actions. I didn't think that Dante was aiming at Jessie. He was aiming at the guy beside him. Did he think that the person beside him was the sniper after Jessie?

"He? Oh my gosh! It's Tabitha!" Millie shouted. "I got it, Seb! It's been Tabitha the whole time. She drove my parents out of the country!"

I scooted out away from the car, looking around for anyone who might resemble a Tabitha. I had never seen Tabitha, but Will knew exactly what she looked like. He jerked backward at the announcement, flattening himself against the car.

"Are you sure?" he whispered.

"Yes! I heard her threaten Leer to keep me alive. She wanted me close to her so she could lure my dad in. She had to be the one passing off the probe to Walter to complicate my dad's games with the Vikings and lure him out. It wasn't my uncle. Tabitha never went to check on my parent's house, because she never got on her plane. She stayed in the city waiting, and when I got fired, I spotted her looking for

466

me. She wanted me to lure in my parents, but when they came they were surrounded by Dante and Will. She was only hired at Visions three years ago, and before that she was working independently as a sniper. Tabitha stalks all my dad's games all the time and gets away with it because of Visions. Plus, she keeps 'losing' certain items that should get destroyed. I've returned a horseshoe to her three times already. She was trying to blame Rory for it all, but she's been going after my dad the whole time!"

I could add to that. Will had told me that Tabitha had gone ballistic when Millie had gotten fired and left Visions. So if this was a game, I would expect Tabitha to know that Will was here along with Nick and Leer. She would have followed them, because they would be able to reach Millie, and Millie was able to lure out her dad. And her dad was currently standing unprotected with the person that everyone thought wanted him dead aiming a gun in his direction. It was the perfect opportunity for a shot. I hung up the phone, returning it to where it just came from.

"Everyone stop Tabitha!" I shouted causing Jessie to flinch and duck down.

The man beside him ducked down, too, pulling Jessie away from the building toward cover since he had no idea where Tabitha was. I didn't either, but I was guessing that my voice would be recognized by all the other people here. And since Jessie hired the Veterans, I assumed his body guard came from that group. The Veterans would have figured me out.

I rolled between a new set of cars not a moment too soon. The reason why Will had jolted back was because Tabitha was right next to us. Her arm appeared over the top of the car we were hunkered behind holding a gun. Was she planning on taking us out along with Jessie and blaming the whole thing on Dante? Had she been here the whole time? Her shot missed my head and embedded itself into a car. I missed the rest since I was dodging between vehicles, trying to get myself clear. I stopped moving when Dante's voice screamed the all clear. Along with his shout, the sounds of police sirens could be heard rushing toward us as fast as they could come. I ran back to make sure that everyone was alright. I found Will and Dante standing together next to a woman who had purple hair. She was knocked unconscious.

"By all means, take the credit," William told Dante. "I'm just here protecting these citizens I was walking past."

I moved off as the police started showing up to get the news on the recent shooting. I found Jessie with his guard still hunkered down behind a car. I announced myself before getting too close.

"Millie says your sniper has been Tabitha this whole time," I told Jessie. "It's not been Dante."

"I guessed that when the shots started ringing out. We dated a long time ago before I dated Juliet. Tabitha was always interested in my work. I thought it was a romantic interest. We broke up over an argument when she asked me to delete a character from my game. She thought that it had been created after her, and that I was exposing who she was. I told her it was clearly coincidental. She didn't want to listen. After we broke up, I didn't keep track of her. In fact, I'd almost forgotten about that. Lots of people think that avatars are mirrored after them when they relate to the character's story. I guess she's been trying to break my games ever since."

My phone buzzed in my pocket and I pulled it back out, recognizing Platonic's number. Was it Millie? Nope, it was Juliet frantically asking me if she needed to worry about the sound of those police cars and the gun shots.

"We took care of it, Mrs. Ankerton," I told her. "Will and Dante just took down your sniper."

"You should get out of there," Platonic said. "Room three twenty-six. You don't want to end up on a police report."

Right. I didn't want my name getting added to a police report. Then my mother really would know what I had been doing tonight. I looked at Jessie, who gave me a nod of his head and didn't move from behind the car. Was he going to sneak out of here too? The police cars were rolling in, but with Will and Dante standing over the fallen body they became the beacons in the headlights.

469

"Hey, since I just helped save your life, can I date your daughter?" I asked Jessie.

"We'll see," Jessie answered.

I gave him a smile, unsure if that would turn into a yes. Jessie and Juliet had tracked me down looking for Millie and had found her because Will had dragged her over. They hadn't screamed at me for being her friend. Before Millie had shown up, they had asked me a lot of questions about my life goals and my friendship with Millie. They had wondered if Millie had ever come to see me since they were still looking for her. I was sure they could tell from my expressions that I'd wanted her to come find me. I dreamed of that all the time.

I slipped out of the area as fast as I could but didn't head into the hotel as Platonic suggested. The police could head there next. I ran home to the relief of my parents and younger brother, who were up watching TV waiting for me.

Chapter 45

Sebastian

I didn't care if Will was watching me. I suspected that he was, since I talked him into giving me heiss. I could picture Leer telling me that I needed to be hooked up first. I could picture Nick taking it away again. Will was easy. He gave me heiss along with tips to not get myself stuck behind invisible barriers. He talked to me about changing destinations and riding different waves. It was difficult to control exactly where I ended up right now, but Will had faith in me that I would figure it out quickly.

I wanted to rest myself on my bed while trying to find Millie, but Will advised against it for the same reasons that I shouldn't really fall asleep on my work table. I didn't want to confuse my muscle memory. So I laid on the floor of my room while Triton started asking Will a lot of questions that Will answered vaguely. Triton hadn't questioned anything when Will had come in my bedroom window

471

rather late.

"Am I employed yet?" I asked before the needle pricked my skin.

"Almost," Will answered. "Nick was fired. Leer turned him in for his illegal practices of using Visions employees to run his games. Then Leer felt bad about it and quit. One would think that they'd planned it." Will gave off a fake cough. "They don't work for Visions anymore, but the company still sees me as an employee. Nick and Leer want me to quit. Visions was thinking about getting Millie back, since she can't seem to leave them alone. She invades often and helps out. She likes to maintain an expansive presence rather similar to Platonic, casting her net wide so if anyone tangles the strings she has lots of other rope to work with. You'll have to be patient, Seb. You've been gone a while. People look for her a lot. You might not get a chance to see her on the first night."

I nodded and put the needle to my arm as I closed my eyes. My mind turned black and fuzzy again as I told myself to look for more heiss. Will hadn't given me very much. I wasn't sure how long I would be able to stay, especially since I wasn't starving for the stuff. I found myself back in the corridor leading to a host of games, only this time I wasn't stuck behind a counter pushing a button to send people skiing. Millie claimed earlier that she had the perfect place for us to meet, but that was all we had said on the subject. We had talked about a lot of other things after that. I looked around for Will expecting him to be close. What I saw was an argument.

"Woah, wait a minute, you seriously don't think I'm your missing daughter do you?" A girl who was being a four-foot-tall animated movie character asked. She had pink hair.

"Will you just go to bed?" asked another animated character with toothbrush pajamas.

"I'm not your runaway kid, woman, and if I was I wouldn't come home."

"I thought I asked you to stop upsetting my avatars," a much taller girl with red pigtails stepped over to them. Was it Millie? Was the first girl Millie? Will was right. I had been out of the loop for a while.

"Ten coins that pink-haired girl is the runaway," a guy in a superhero outfit told me, stepping over to my side. Was this Will? I didn't quite think so, but who was it? Millie's dad? I had heard the voice before... Wait. Obviously, this was Platonic. I didn't answer him, and the superhero moved over to the argument, pushing his face between everyone.

"Did you know that she is home? Happened just today," superhero claimed. "You guys aren't making anyone believe you. You're horrible at pretending to be that kid."

"I got Nixen to believe me earlier," the pink-haired person claimed.

"You got Nixen to laugh at you," the girl with red pigtails said.

I looked around again, shaking my head. I was rather lost. The only thing I could tell was that there were four other players standing around chatting, trying to confuse each other. Platonic waved bye to them and headed back to me. Who did he think I was?

"I guess you won," he told me, handing me ten coins. I held out my hand for them even if I hadn't placed the bet. I had white gloves on. A glance at the rest of me revealed I was a magician. Sweet.

"Okay so did he really pay you?" a woman selling cotton candy asked, stepping up beside us. I held out the coins, and she smiled, taking two and handing me cotton candy.

"Not you, by the way," she said to me. "I was asking the superhero, Captain Marvelous. Did under-the-bed man pay you or give you a threat in that envelope?"

Millie! Wow. I was being a little slow on the uptake tonight. I knew her voice. She just surprised me with how effortlessly she blended in with everything.

"He's trying to buy me out."

"Are you taking it?" Millie asked.

Platonic bobbed his head toward me, trying to figure me out. Millie smiled, and even if it wasn't her face, I could see her in there.

"Boyfriend. Pajama girl is Nixa. Braids is Tod. Pink-haired kid is hot dog lover. Will is selling turkey."

Boyfriend? I would take that title. I looked around, trying to spot who was selling turkey. The only thing I could see was a game to hunt for wild turkeys. Millie walked off, and I almost followed her, but Platonic shook his head at me. I found out why a few minutes later when a girl selling peanuts stepped up to us next.

"So are you taking it?" the new Millie asked, holding out a bag of peanuts to Platonic.

"Not a chance. It was nice getting my snacks brought to me," he told her.

"Sorry for taking your money," she told him, and I smiled at her for apologizing for stealing Platonic's credit card.

"I have an idea. I'll take the bribe," Platonic told her taking the bag of peanuts she held out. "Then I'll give it you. I want you back already. I'll give you a million dollars if you come work for me again. Why did you leave?"

"I've got to sell these peanuts," Millie answered. "But maybe a few side missions wouldn't hurt." She walked off again.

The arguing group of snipers split apart, and I guessed they moved into other characters by the way a few people laughed at each other suddenly from different lines to games.

"She's usually pretty active right now. They're looking for her still," Platonic told me. "You're better off going into a random game and having her find you."

He was probably right. I looked around one more time for Millie without coming to any conclusion about who she was. I scanned the games for what I could get into with the coins in my hand. I was just about to try out one where I would turn into an ant and build an ant farm, when a rabbit jumped out of a bag at my side, perked its ears up at me, and started to run away. The gesture reminded me of Millie turning into a teddy bear. I ran after the rabbit, plunking my coins down to enter a mansion.

As soon as I was in the new game I lost the bunny. I wasn't a magician anymore. I was a tourist and words were flashing on the screen, telling me my options. I ignored them, choosing instead to walk toward the back of the mansion where I could see a small group of musicians setting up. They started playing a few songs. After the second one I was glancing around, wondering if Millie would ever show up.

"Are you supposed to be sleeping?" the chimes player asked me out of the blue.

476

"Not me," I answered, hearing my voice come out sounding like a digital recording of someone else. My words didn't mesh together. Each word was clipped.

"Not me either," the chimes player told me. She held her hand out to me and I took it, already questioning the interaction. Maybe it was easier to meet Millie in real life. Here I was going to second guess everything. "Sorry I'm late, Mr. Rhino. My pal wanted me to order him some late night snacks," Millie told me. Was she talking about Platonic?

"You think he'll take the money?" I asked back.

"Maybe. He'll think about it. He doesn't want to work with my dad. Going to ask me to dance?"

"Yes," I answered, more certain that I had Millie before me, even if this particular avatar was double my age. "But it will be hard when I can't feel my legs. This makes me question something."

"What's that?" Millie asked me, taking my hands and straining to match her feet with mine.

"Is any of this real? Does it count?" I asked her.

Millie laughed, and I wished it was really her face that I was seeing instead of this older woman.

"Only dreaming, Mr. Rhino," she told me with a sigh. I cocked my head to the side, completely understanding. It was much easier to date her in real life than in a dream world, and even though I had seen her today, it wasn't good enough. I wanted to see her again already.

"Your curfew was at ten," the drummer informed us. Millie flicked her eyes over at the drummer, and then hugged me.

"Both of us are real, and we're going to be amazing. See you tomorrow," Millie whispered into my ear. I felt like hugging her super tight, but she put her avatar back where it belonged, leaving me to look after one of her parents who bade me goodnight. I could hardly wait for my dreams to become reality. Whatever we did Millie was always going to be my favorite angel.

Chapter 46

Millie

He was still alive and breathing, even though he was half gone. The stubborn fool wasn't giving up for anything. It was one of his character flaws as well as one of his attributes. I wasn't supposed to surf, but I couldn't help myself. I sat my avatar down on the edge of the brimstone. I forced myself inside a gnarly three-foot-tall elderly gnome to find myself right beside the two-limbed human with the slingshot.

"How many times have you cheated?" Seb asked me, putting his one good hand on his hip as he realized it was me that was looking around. He only had his left leg and his right arm. He had lost his other appendages battling a pair of identical wizards. I smiled at him.

"Really, you can't leave me to do all the work," he complained.

"I love you," I told him while he shook his head.

"Don't do that. You know I don't like you telling me stuff like that in games. It is very disturbing. Sometimes — like right now — you look like a man. I don't need random men telling me that they love me."

I laughed at him, trying to decide if I should kill his avatar to make him quit or just tell him again. Leer and Will had already tried to get him to quit. He ignored the written messages from Leer, and the verbal reminder from Will. He wasn't on heiss. He was just stubbornly trying to beat the game while half of him hung apart.

"Maybe we could put a rhino into the level and it could impale you on its horn."

"You're trying to make this worse?" Seb asked me pointing at his limply hanging arm. "I'm going to beat this game. Disrupting the gnomes didn't cut it. I need to find something else."

He scanned the area, trying to come up with another scheme. He had come up with five brilliant, bizarre ideas already, but he still couldn't reach the scepter in the veranda. I was starting to think that the game was impossible to beat on purpose.

"Come on. You have driving lessons to get to. You're going to be late."

"What time is it?" Seb asked.

480

He looked into the air, trying to read the time on his screen, but nothing came up. That was because he was unconnected. The unpublished game would have been shut off by now, except that Seb wasn't exiting, and no one wanted to turn off the game and cause him unnecessary risk when his body became confused. He finally left. Take that. I could wake him up from anything.

Seb was lying on my table when I opened my eyes. We normally worked on Nick's games, but the one today was from my dad, and Seb was determined to rip through it.

"You don't need to try to beat everything all at once," I told him as he leaned beside me, pretending like I was the one not waking up on time. I could hear Leer and Nick reminiscing over Seb's brilliant antics, but we weren't looking at them.

"Yes I do. I need to break more rules," Seb told me, pushing up on his arm and pinning me beneath him. He lowered himself down to kiss me while Leer's monitor started beeping like crazy from both our hearts picking up. Was Seb really going to make out with me right here? I wasn't complaining, but we did have an audience. I felt Seb's lips brush mine while I inwardly squealed with joy.

"Sebastian Tinsley," my father's sharp voice had him springing across the room.

"I had to make sure she woke up," Seb insisted, fiddling with his shirt while he walked to the door without looking at me.

"She wakes up better than you," my dad insisted.

"See you tomorrow," Seb told him.

He left the room as I sat up, glad that Leer had turned off the beeping sound as fast as it had started. My father gave me one of his protective looks. I could only smile. Sebastian poured his heart into everything that mattered to him, and I was going to keep it. He was never getting it free.

I had tagged him for good.

And Action!

Have you ever wanted to be a hero beloved by another person? Now is your chance. Don't let the virtual bullies intimidate you. You've made it to the end of this book, so you must have found something about it that compelled you to finish ALL the pages. Whatever the reason, other readers would love to know your impressions while they are fresh in your mind. Leaving an honest **Spoiler Free** review on Amazon and/or Goodreads saves the life of this author and future readers. Thanks virtual hero!

To see more content of what the author is up to feel free to stop by the author website at www.amandaheit.com You can also check out Amanda's Amazon Author page at https://www.amazon.com/author/amanda.heit

True Life Savers

This book would not be as fantastic as it is without the help of some very special people. Thank you from the bottom of my heart to my beta readers: Amy Fowler, Adam Morse, and Stephanie Fredrickson. Double thanks to my readers and editors Josiah Davis and Jessica Heiner. You all helped so much to make this book shine! Your feedback and encouragement will be traveling with me in my dreams.